Praise for the Che

**THE BODY IN 1**

M000290216

"Cherry Tucker is a strong, sassy, Southern sleuth who keeps you on the edge of your seat. She's back in action in *The Body in the Landscape* with witty banter, Southern charm, plenty of suspects, and dead bodies—you will not be disappointed!"

– Tonya Kappes,
*USA Today* Bestselling Author

"Anyone who likes humorous mysteries will also enjoy local author Larissa Reinhart, who captures small town Georgia in the laugh-out-loud escapades of struggling artist Cherry Tucker."

– *Fayette Woman Magazine*

## DEATH IN PERSPECTIVE (#4)

"One fasten-your-seatbelt, pedal-to-the-metal mystery, and Cherry Tucker is the perfect sleuth to have behind the wheel. Smart, feisty, as tough as she is tender, Cherry's got justice in her crosshairs."

– Tina Whittle,
Author of the Tai Randolph Mysteries

"Artist and accidental detective Cherry Tucker goes back to high school and finds plenty of trouble and skeletons...Reinhart's charming, sweet-tea flavored series keeps getting better!"

– Gretchen Archer,
*USA Today* Bestselling Author of the Davis Way Crime Caper Series

## HIJACK IN ABSTRACT (#3)

"Bust out your gesso and get primed for humor, hijackings, and a handful of hunks!"

– Diane Vallere,
Author of the Style & Error and Madison Night Mysteries

"The fast-paced plot careens through small-town politics and deadly rivalries, with zany side trips through art-world shenanigans and romantic hijinx. Like front-porch lemonade, Reinhart's cast of characters offer a perfect balance of tart and sweet."

– Sophie Littlefield,
Bestselling Author of *A Bad Day for Sorry*


## STILL LIFE IN BRUNSWICK STEW (#2)

"Reinhart's country-fried mystery is as much fun as a ride on the tilt-a-whirl at a state fair. Her sleuth wields a paintbrush and unravels clues with equal skill and flair. Readers who like a little small-town charm with their mysteries will enjoy Reinhart's series."

– Denise Swanson,
*New York Times* Bestselling Author of the Scumble River Mysteries

"The hilariously droll Larissa Reinhart cooks up a quirky and entertaining page-turner! This charming mystery is delightfully Southern, surprisingly edgy, and deliciously unpredictable."

– Hank Phillippi Ryan,
Agatha Award-Winning Author of *Truth Be Told*


## PORTRAIT OF A DEAD GUY (#1)

"*Portrait of a Dead Guy* is an entertaining mystery full of quirky characters and solid plotting...Highly recommended for anyone who likes their mysteries strong and their mint juleps stronger!"

– Jennie Bentley,
*New York Times* Bestselling Author of *Flipped Out*

"Reinhart is a truly talented author and this book was one of the best cozy mysteries we reviewed this year."

– *Mystery Tribune*

"This is a winning series that continues to grow stronger and never fails to entertain with laughs, a little snark, and a ton of heart."

– *Kings River Life Magazine*

# A COMPOSITION IN MURDER

# A COMPOSITION IN MURDER

## A Cherry Tucker Mystery

## LARISSA REINHART

HENERY PRESS

A COMPOSITION IN MURDER
A Cherry Tucker Mystery
Part of the Henery Press Mystery Collection

First Edition
Trade paperback edition | November 2016

Henery Press
www.henerypress.com

Copyright © 2016 by Larissa Hoffman
Author photograph by Scott Asano

Trade Paperback ISBN-13: 978-1-63511-113-2
Digital epub ISBN-13: 978-1-63511-114-9
Kindle ISBN-13: 978-1-63511-115-6
Hardcover Paperback ISBN-13: 978-1-63511-116-3

Printed in the United States of America

*To Sonja and Bob, thanks for all your love and support*
*& all your stories about Etta and Sadie.*

# ACKNOWLEDGMENTS

Arbor Terrace Peachtree City, thank you so much for the tour and stories about your senior living residence. You have a beautiful facility and only the amenities influenced me. All the criminal ideas came from my head.

Kristine Zepf, thanks so much for your help with what drugs to use to kill off my elderly victims. Debbie Krenzer, congrats on winning the Minion drawing and I hope seeing your name as the director of Halo House puts a smile on your face. I'm sure you don't drink that much coffee. Pat Werths, Ruth Barrineau-Brooks, and Julie Hallberg, I appreciate your choices in ringtones. Thanks for the help! And thank you to all the Mystery Minions for your support and encouragement. Love y'all!

Thank you to the Henery Press editors, Kendel, Erin, Anna, and Rachel, and to Art for everything you do.

A huge thank you to my family. Gina, Bill, Hailey and Lily for letting me use your house as a post office and for all your support. Mom for being a second set of eyes. To the Funks, Reinharts, and Hoffmans for spreading the book love. And especially to Trey, Sophie, and Luci for bringing me such joy.

# ONE

In a small town, someone invariably has an eye on your back. Also your front, middle, and every other body part. You just don't always know whose eye is doing the watching. That sort of scrutiny should make you more careful. Emphasis on should. I'd never taken much to "should'ves," having been more of a "get 'er done" type of gal. Although now I was paying for it.

That piper called an hour before "Art with Miss Cherry"—a name that made me wonder if Miss Krenzer knew I was teaching senior citizens and not kindergartners. Krenzer caught me in front of Halo House's lobby fountain. Not that I was doing anything wrong. Lately, I'm often found sitting on the cushioned bench of that particular fountain with my friends. Chatting and sipping our drink of choice. Back when I attended SCAD, I did the same thing with my art school peeps on one of Savannah's many fountains. Except we weren't drinking weak coffee.

I'd rather not say what we were drinking, but it was Savannah after all.

From the reception desk, Miss Krenzer leaned forward, spied me, and waved me over. After a quick round of elbow nudges, winks, and "now you've done it" from the seniors, I strolled to the front desk.

"Cherry, I got a call from Belvia Brakeman. Do you know her?"

"She's not one of my students, but of course, I know who she is. I love Meemaw's Tea. Grandma Jo always made her own sweet tea, but I think buying a jug is handy. Particularly for those of us who tend to forget the stove's on while we're painting."

"We're very fortunate to have such an astute businesswoman as Mrs. Brakeman living at Halo House." Miss Krenzer's smile shrank. "However, Mrs. Brakeman needs something of a more personal nature. Her daughter, Della Brakeman, recently passed."

"Hit and run while jogging. Terrible, terrible way to go. I don't condone jogging—not partial to it—but I was truly sorry to hear jogging took her life. Sixty is way too young, and that's speaking as a twenty-six-year-old." I shook my head. "My intel says Della Brakeman even wore the appropriate reflector tape accessories as she ran down Highway 34."

"Intel?"

"My..." I considered an appropriate description for Luke. "My friend, Luke Harper, is a deputy working on the investigation. Not that he's told me anything I didn't read in the paper. My friends at Halo House have told me more. With Della Brakeman in charge of operations and soon to take over as CEO of Meemaw's Tea, it's made a splash in the local news. And my buddies sure love local news. Particularly the one that's on before *Jeopardy*."

Krenzer glanced at the fountain where my friends waited, craning their necks and trying to hear our conversation. They couldn't. Among their age bracket, hearing doesn't tend to be a strength.

However, gossip was. More like a superpower than strength.

"Mrs. Brakeman specifically said to send you and another staff member. Someone discreet. I'm entrusting Jose from maintenance. You're not who I'd choose for the job..." She shot another look at my cohorts. Krenzer knew their superpowers and considered me guilty through their association. Couldn't argue that logic, as I did enjoy their superpowers. "But it's Belvia Brakeman," she continued. "You don't question her."

"Job?" I toned down the excitement in my voice. "I'll keep my mouth shut. And I won't say a thing about jogging to Mrs. Brakeman. I only said it to you, because I thought you'd agree about the perils of jogging."

She cast a look at her midsection.

I scrambled to cover my gaffe. "I understand privacy and sensitivity. I may only be a part-time drawing teacher, but I have come to feel Halo House is more than a speed bump in my portrait painting career. Premiere independent living is something I've grown to admire and respect. Halo House has become my home away from home."

"You do spend a considerable amount of time here. I worried we'd become an escape from your personal problems. But I'm glad to hear you're supportive of our mission."

Unsure of Halo House's mission, I held up a paint-stained hand. "Don't say another word. Let me help you on your other mission. The one for Belvia Brakeman."

"It's simple. She's written a new will and needs two witnesses to watch her sign it. It's all perfectly legal. But you can see why it's a delicate situation."

"A will? Shouldn't she wait for her lawyer?"

"Belvia Brakeman is..." Krenzer cut her eyes toward my friends and lowered her voice. "At ninety, she's still a whip-smart and savvy CEO who happens to run a corporation from her apartment suite in my facility. She's also endowed us with special funds for programs such as yours. Let's just do what she wants."

"Good idea."

"Her daughter, Coralee, is with her now. She'll assist you. I need to stay at the desk."

"I didn't realize she had more than one child. That must be a comfort to Miss Belvia. Does Coralee work for the family company too?"

Krenzer's lips thinned. "No. Coralee just arrived this morning with her family. They live in the Midwest. You better get going."

"Yes, ma'am. You can count on me."

"Just sign and get out. It's important that Belvia not feel hassled."

"The last thing I'd ever want to do is hassle someone who's just lost a loved one. Especially a sweet little ninety-year-old blind woman."

"Belvia Brakeman may be ninety and blind, but never call her sweet or little. Particularly to her face."

This diplomacy thing would be trickier than I thought.

Because the residents glutted the already slow elevators, I took the grand, front staircase. Belvia Brakeman resided in a two-bedroom suite near the bank of elevators on the second floor. Because of her fame, I always glanced that way, hoping to get a peek at the Queen of Sweet Tea. Today a man in creased khakis and a Halo House polo stood beside the door. When he wasn't glancing at his watch, he glanced at a clipboard.

"Hey, Jose," I said. "Miss Krenzer sent me up."

He smiled. "Hey, Cherry. I got a leaky bathtub to get at. Let's hope this doesn't take too long."

"Kind of exciting, right?"

He rolled his eyes. "In my time here, I've done this plenty. Georgia law says just two witnesses make it legal. And folks here change their minds all the time over who gets the family china and whatnot."

"That's disturbing. And sad."

Jose shrugged. "For some, it's the only way to get family to visit. Threaten to cut them from a will and they come running. I feel sorry for the residents."

"I can't imagine not visiting Pearl and my Grandpa Ed. And there's nothing to leave in a will. Pearl's not even blood kin."

"Maybe when you're rich it's harder to get your kids to like you."

"You're probably right there." I thought of JB Branson, the town patriarch and step-daddy to my secret Deputy Sweetheart, Luke. If JB were my relation, it'd probably take a hell of a lot of money to make me want to visit him. Not a good feeling when you're figuring out a relationship with the stepson.

"Let's get this done."

We rang the bell. A young woman answered and was

shouldered aside by an older woman wearing a Peruvian alpaca motif sweater and flowing alpaca printed pants. Dangling chandelier earrings also sported alpacas. I glanced at my cropped sweater featuring 3-D pompon polka-dots and pompon-fringed corduroy shorts. Chewed my lip and wondered if alpacas were in my destiny.

"Mother said she called someone." She looked at Jose. "Do you speak English?"

"Usually," said Jose.

"You have to understand English for this."

"I'll do my best, ma'am."

"What about you?" She eyeballed me. "Who are you?"

"Cherry Tucker, the art foundations teacher. Are you Miss Coralee? Mrs. Brakeman's daughter? So sorry for your loss. Your sister—"

"Yes, thank you. We just need you to watch Mother sign the will, sign it yourselves, and then you're done. That's all we need to make this legal. As long as you're not named in the will?"

"I wouldn't know, ma'am," I said. "But considering I don't know Mrs. Brakeman, I sincerely doubt it."

Jose nodded.

"Good," said Coralee.

We entered the small foyer and into a living area, furnished with mahogany and cherry pieces. Classy and uncluttered, like an attorney's waiting room. Without the knickknacks and memorabilia usually seen in the residents' homes.

The young woman who had answered the door sat on a couch. She gave us an embarrassed smile. "Hello, I'm Coralee's daughter, Pris—"

"Introductions aren't needed. They're not staying," said Coralee, hustling us through a door off the living area.

An elderly woman dressed in a navy wool jacket and slacks sat in a leather desk chair, an iPad in her lap. A single folder lay on the desk, no other paper in sight. The cherry desk held a computer, phone, and other equipment. Each piece rested precisely within a taped square. With the regal set of her raised chin and eyes that gazed into the near distance, I put two and two together.

"Miss Belvia," I said. "I'm the art teacher at Halo House, Cherry Tucker. Nice to meet you."

"Yes. I've heard of you."

"As an artist?"

"Not as an artist, no." Her chin inched a notch higher and swiveled away from the direction of my voice.

There's where art gets you in a small town. "I wanted to express my sympathy. My Grandma Jo knew your daughter Della. They had Sunday school together on Wednesday nights once upon a time, I believe. I've also heard how well Della treated the tea makers. You know how word gets around. Miss Della was well respected. I'm sorry about her passing."

"Mrs. Brakeman. I'm Jose on the maintenance crew. Very sorry about your daughter."

"Jose." Belvia inclined her head.

Belvia Brakeman really lived up to her royal nickname.

"Let's get to signing." Coralee tapped the folder sitting on her mother's desk.

"Coralee, just a moment," said Belvia.

This Coralee seemed eager to get this will signed and for us to get out. If Coralee grew up and had family in small-town Georgia, she should know better than to rush her mother. I didn't like her skipping the niceties of mourning etiquette before her sister's coffin had closed. Which piqued my interest in Mrs. Brakeman's will. And her daughter's hurry to get it signed.

"Pardon me, Miss Belvia, but how do you know what's written in the will?" As Grandma Jo had been a *Matlock* fan, I'd picked up a thing or two from good ol' Matlock. I wouldn't allow a will scam by this alleged prodigal daughter. I didn't know Belvia Brakeman, but I knew she was worth millions.

"I don't want to get ugly," I continued, "but as a witness, I can't let you sign something you can't see. Shouldn't Miss Coralee read it aloud so we can make sure you know what's in it?"

Coralee flushed. "How dare—"

"It's fine." Belvia waved a hand at her iPad. "Coralee doesn't know what's in the will. I used dictation software and printed it out myself. I'd rather no one read it until it's legally necessary. Thank you for trying to protect my rights though."

"Sorry, ma'am," I said. "That's amazing you can do all this business with your eyesight problems."

"I record my conference calls for reference and have all my reports audio accessible. As long as housekeeping doesn't move things around, I'm able to keep to business as usual."

Coralee narrowed her eyes on Jose and me. "If housekeeping's a problem, Mother—"

"I have no complaints." Belvia waved a hand in Coralee's direction. "When my eyesight failed completely, I wanted my office moved home, but Della didn't feel it appropriate to hold meetings at the Tea Grove. Halo House was our compromise, so we moved my office and living quarters here."

"I'm here now, Mother," said Coralee. "I can take over for you."

"You misunderstand, Coralee. There is a certain convenience to living here." Miss Belvia turned toward me. "I've not involved myself in any Halo House activities, so I'd only recently heard you were working here, Cherry. Having you as a witness gave me an opportunity to bring you upstairs. And Jose, thank you for coming too."

"Glad to help, ma'am." Jose stopped mid-bow before correcting himself.

"As Coralee said, this won't take but a moment. I'm grateful for your help, but I have more business today." Belvia felt on the desk for the folder, flipped it open, and allowed Coralee to guide her hand to the signature line.

Jose and I followed with our witness signatures. I attempted a glance at the final paragraphs, but Coralee slammed the folder closed, slid it into an open wall safe, and banged the safe door shut.

"That's done," said Coralee. "You can go now."

Jose bolted, mumbling condolences along with leaky bathtub reports.

"Cherry," said Belvia. "I'll call on you later."

"If it's a funeral portrait, I can start to work right away if you've got a photo of Miss Della handy."

"Funeral portrait?" Coralee's lip curled. "I'm sure that's not necessary."

"Not for a painting." Belvia's sightless eyes shot a look of reproof at her daughter. "It concerns your other talents, Cherry. I'll explain then."

Before I could answer, Coralee had edged me into the living room and shut the office door. Pris looked up from her book. The battered paperback showed a half-dressed couple groping each other. *The Rake's Revenge.*

I liked Pris immediately.

"I'm sorry about your aunt's passing. I understand you didn't grow up here and might not know anyone," I said. "If you want company you can find me around. There's coffee in the deli or the Last Call."

"Last Call?" said Pris.

"The bar attached to the restaurant downstairs. It's open to the public." I cast a sideways glance at the office door. "How's your grandma doing? This must be hard on her."

"It's hard to say since I don't really know Grandmother. She's kind of reserved, but that's to be expected, isn't it?"

I nodded. I couldn't reveal to Coralee's daughter I had a *Matlock* feeling about her grandmother's will. But *Matlock* feelings weren't anything new in the Cherry Tucker handbook.

However, I set my feelings aside. Not my circus, not my monkeys. I had my own big top filled with the flying variety of primates and spent enough time trying to duck and cover from their mudslinging. With this new job at Halo House Uncle Will had gotten me, I'd promised to be on my best behavior.

Unfortunately, *Matlock* feelings tended to bring out my worst.

# TWO

As I couldn't convince Miss Krenzer to make me an artist in residence at Halo House, I pointed my old Datsun pickup toward town and my real residence. My deceased Great Gam's 1920s Georgia bungalow. At one time it had been my art studio, now defunct thanks to Shawna Branson. My personal Branson nemesis.

We'd hated each other since high school when she was homecoming princess and I was asked to design the junior float. Perhaps my seven-foot Halo High angel had detracted from the homecoming court. I'd originally draped a toga on that angel. Not my fault the football team decided to enhance his body parts. The angel appeared real happy to share that float with Shawna.

She never forgave me. Also didn't help that our families hadn't gotten along since Reconstruction. She punished me by using ugly words and false rumors to put me out of business.

Recently, my brother pulled Shawna in his car to find out if they were accidentally related by way of my mother and her daddy. She punished him with a kidnapping allegation.

And for that, I'll never forgive her.

I parked in the drive, cut past all the junk in my carport, and entered my kitchen. My roommate, Todd, was out. But someone else was in.

A tall lean man with eyes of a mysterious gray that could almost be duplicated with Winsor Violet and a touch of Phthalo Green. His dusky burnt umber curls had a glint of transparent red oxide apparent in my overhead fluorescent light.

And his hands? I couldn't see his hands because after pinning me against the Formica counter, they were currently working their way underneath my pompon sweater.

I also couldn't see his smile or his dimples. But I could feel them beneath my lips.

And they tasted pretty damn good. Sizzling heat with a side of sugar.

"How much time do you have before you leave for work?" I asked against his raspy cheek. Even Luke's five o'clock shadow tasted good. And looked sexy as hell against the definition of his cheekbones and hard-edged jaw. I loved his days off when he didn't have to be clean-shaven, starched, and polyestered Deputy Harper. He'd soon head home to shave and change into his superhero costume.

"Not near enough." He had moved past my neck and headed south fast. My sweater had disappeared. My corduroy shorts and ribbed tights would be next to go on Luke's list of unnecessary clothing items. However, it was winter, and even though I lived in Georgia, standing bare-assed in my kitchen did not seem the brightest of ideas.

Particularly when my roommate was due home any moment.

Particularly when my roommate was my sort-of ex-husband.

"Wait up." I caught Luke's face between my hands and drew it north. "I've told you this before, any number of people have been known to walk through my back door. At any time of day. Or night."

Luke leaned his body into mine. "That's why I installed the deadbolt." A dimple winked and his hands began a new journey.

"I can't lock Todd out of his own house."

The hands stopped roaming. "Sugar, this is not Todd's house. This is your family's house. Isn't it time for him to move along?"

"Let's not talk about that right now."

"Fine. I had other things on my mind than talking." His hands grasped my waist.

"Actually, I do want to talk. I'm having a *Matlock* moment."

His hands fell from my waist and he cocked his head. "Mayberry Matlock?"

"Matlock didn't live in Mayberry. Andy Griffith lived in Mayberry. Although he was a sheriff, so this might work for both shows."

Luke folded his arms. "What might work?"

"Today I had to witness Belvia Brakeman signing her new will. And you know what I think?"

"Hard telling."

"Something's up with that family. Her long-lost daughter showed up and seemed real pushy about making Miss Belvia sign the will. Doesn't that strike you as odd?"

"I'll tell you what's odd, you thinking about Belvia Brakeman while I'm kissing you." Luke placed his hands on either side of my legs and leaned forward until his forehead touched mine. "How'd you end up witnessing Belvia's will?"

"She asked for me. As the deputy in charge of Della Brakeman's hit and run, have you met her sister, Coralee?"

Luke pulled away. "Oh no. We aren't doing this. No ma'am. Della Brakeman's death is an active investigation."

"You suspect foul play. I can hear it in your voice."

"Didn't say that, although getting struck by an unidentified vehicle and left to die makes it a suspicious death. We generally don't throw around words like foul play."

"Matlock did." I kissed him, but before he could surge ahead, I broke contact to murmur against his lips, "So any suspects? Are you looking at Coralee Brakeman or whatever her married name is? When did she get to town? If she's the big inheritor of Meemaw's Tea fortune, that's an awful big motive."

"Cherrilyn Tucker." Tiny kisses spread across my cheek, trailing heat. "Are you interfering in an open investigation when I just told you it was none of your beeswax?"

"No, sir, Deputy Harper. But I did not get good vibes from Coralee and I'm worried about Miss Belvia."

"Let's work on another type of vibe." The kisses moved to my neck.

I shivered under the onslaught. "I'm also wondering why Miss

Belvia wants to see me again. It's sure not for a funeral portrait."

Luke pulled back to study me. "What did you say to her?"

"Nothing, other than I wanted to make sure no one had tampered with her will. She signed blind, you know."

"Lord Almighty. You know Mrs. Brakeman's a powerful woman? Meemaw's Tea is on one of those *Fortune* lists. Don't mess around with that family. Especially with this suspicious death hanging over their heads."

"I'm not. She requested to see me. Something about my other talents. Said she'd heard about me."

"Other talents? Like this one?" He whispered a suggestion in my ear.

I slid my hands from his chest to his shoulders. "Todd really will be home any minute."

"Then we have a minute. This is not a problem."

The door handle jiggled and a knocking commenced.

"Cherry?" Todd called through the kitchen door. "You in there?"

"Just a sec," I hollered, struggling with my sweater.

Luke lifted me off the counter but kept me trapped in his arms. "This is not how I want a relationship."

"I know."

"I want you all to myself for longer than ten minutes. Preferably with no mention of Todd McIntosh, hit-and-run deaths, or *Matlock*."

"I know."

"We need to take care of this mess with our families. I deal with messes at work, I want peace at home." Luke leaned into me. "As for home—"

He finished the sentence with another kiss. One hot and deep enough to scorch my tonsils. While Luke sauntered out the front door, I unlocked the kitchen deadbolt.

"What's with the lock?" Todd glanced around the kitchen.

The Viking doppelgänger still wore his brown cargo shorts delivery uniform. He also still wore the slot machine cherry tattoo on his right calf, marking his Cherry Tucker time. That was the problem with tattoos. The ink lasted much longer than some marriages.

"What were you doing? Sleeping?"

"Not really." I fought off the alizarin crimson invading my cheeks.

"Your sweater's on backward. I thought you had just gotten up."

Alizarin crimson flared into cadmium red. I escaped through the archway leading to my living room. Through the big picture window, I saw Luke ambling along the sidewalk. He had parked his big black jacked-up truck elsewhere, much to my relief. Hopefully, Todd hadn't spotted it.

"What's this?" Todd called.

I traipsed back to the kitchen and found my buff blond roommate waving a piece of paper. I gave it a second's thought, realized Luke had left it, and leaped for the paper.

Todd laughed and held it above his head. Why tall people think it's hilarious to see we vertically-challenged folk bounce around their legs like a terrier after a treed squirrel, I'll never understand.

I stopped bouncing and kicked his shin.

He handed me the paper.

"Thank you." I waved at the fridge. "There's cold chicken in there for dinner. And I picked up tea and beer. So nice to have a steady paycheck. You want to chow down in front of the TV?"

"Thanks, baby. Don't need dinner, but I appreciate the beer." He pecked my cheek and sauntered to the fridge while I checked out the note Luke had left. "You okay?" Todd hung on the open fridge door, concern brightening his cerulean blue eyes and worry lines fretting his normally unlined face.

"I'm okay." I folded the paper, shoved it in the back pocket of my shorts, and forced a smile. "It's nothing."

"I know you, Cherry, and you're not okay. What was on that paper?"

Todd needed to forget about that paper.

"Todd, how about instead of fridge beer I buy you a fresh pint at Red's? I want to talk to him about firing Casey."

He bounded toward me like a puppy hearing the word "walk." But upon reaching my side, he jammed his hands in the pockets of his shorts and began shuffling backward. "I almost forgot. I can't go to Red's."

"Why?"

Todd found interest in the overhead fluorescent light. I checked it for a dead bulb, but not seeing one, I returned my attention to Todd. "What are you doing tonight?"

"I...kind of...have a..." Todd's focus moved to the upper cabinet behind my head. "A date."

"Oh." I sucked in a breath.

As an eligible bachelor, Todd was a hot commodity in Halo. He hadn't been with anyone since our relationship had moved from friendship to marriage to annulled in a fit of Vegas craziness. That was just over a year ago.

But even with my feelings for Luke, Todd still held a special place in my heart. Probably why I couldn't ask him to move out of my house and why we were still best friends. I should have been prepared for this moment.

I wasn't prepared for this moment. But I could fake it.

"That's great," I said. "Who's the lucky girl?"

Todd took a visual inventory of our kitchen. Light fixture, cabinets, and now the floor.

"I am sincerely happy for you. I hope y'all have big fun. Where are you taking her?"

"Not Red's." His words tumbled over his tongue trying to spit them out.

"Okay, then. Glad I won't be cramping your style." I crossed my arms. "What are you not telling me, Todd? Can't be that you're dating my sister, because Casey's already married."

He gave a weak laugh.

"Good Lord. It's not Casey, is it? That girl has done some

things, but I would never have held her to this. God Almighty, Todd, are you that hard up?"

His eyeballs finally found mine. "I'm not hard up."

"Good to know. Who the hell are you not going to Red's with?"

Taking a deep breath, he delivered the name like it was a firing squad's last shot.

"Shawna Branson."

# THREE

The County Line Tap—owned by my friend Red and locally called Red's because it's a much nicer establishment than the old County Line Tap, making a differentiation necessary—was our local joint and only a few blocks from Great Gam's house. I left the Datsun at 211 Loblolly to hoof it to Red's. It was a chilly walk to the squat corrugated-metal building that appeared more roadhouse than it actually was. But I needed to ice off the fire in my gut.

Todd was family. More than family, because I liked him better than some of my family. Enough so that I married him for five minutes and lived with him now. He was my best friend. Also my incarcerated brother Cody's best friend. The person who stood between Cody and freedom was Shawna Branson. And here was Todd. Sleeping with the enemy.

I shook off that thought. I didn't want to go *there*.

Inside Red's, I stomped past the tables of families eating hushpuppies and burgers. At the old wooden bar, I plopped on a stool and held up a finger.

The finger caught in Red's peripheral vision. He turned from a chat with another customer and spotted the body joined to the finger. The smile stretching between freckles dimmed. He shot toward my end of the bar, a hand up in defense.

"I hope you're not here to make trouble, Cherry," he began. "I couldn't do anything about it. You know what was happening to my business. It wasn't personal—"

"I am not here to make trouble. I'm here to drown my sorrows like every other barfly." I snagged the rag from his hand, wiped my spot, and reached for a napkin. "I'm in desperate need of a beverage. Preferably a cold one that starts with a b and ends with an r."

"I'm talking about me dismissing Casey and you showing here to chew out my ass."

"To be honest, it was on my mind, but I've got bigger fish to fry now."

Red waved a hand around the bar. "This is the most customers I've had in three months. That included the holidays. Restaurants can't stay afloat in those circumstances. It was either Casey or everyone would be out of a job."

Nodding, I reached over the counter to fish a mug off the drying rack, and set it before Red.

"There's a shitload of Bransons in this town. Or those who work for Bransons. That's like ninety percent of my customer base. What was I going to do?"

I sighed, hoisted myself on the bar, and stuck my mug under the tapper.

"I can't support the staff and pay my bills with what you and Todd eat and drink."

Tipping the mug, I pushed the tap forward and waited for it to fill. I let the suds run over the side, shut the tapper, and leveled off. Scooting backward, I hoisted off the bar and reached for the beer.

Red wiped off my sudsy mess and set a new napkin before me. "I had anonymous calls, Cherry, telling me that although they loved eating here, my wait staff gave me a bad reputation. Or flat out, if I didn't fire Casey, they'd never come back."

At first, the beer cooled what burned in my chest. I drew in the nectar, refreshing the parched wasteland that had been my mouth, but the aridity bloomed into a verdant pasture of weeds. Sharp words. Nasty retorts. Ugly comebacks. I focused on coaxing the icy sweet amber into numbing my building anger instead of spawning a thicket of hate.

"One kind soul finally told me the Bransons had made it known that businesses who hired Ballard kin should be banned in light of what Cody did to Shawna."

"Allegedly did to Shawna," I reminded him.

"I was blackballed right alongside all y'all."

"Until now." I fished a five-dollar bill out of my pocket and set it on the bar next to my empty glass. "I guess I won't tar up your establishment with my presence. I'll be taking my company elsewhere."

Red's freckles disappeared as his skin deepened in color. "I didn't mean—"

"I know exactly what you meant, Red. Business before friendship."

"Cherry," he pleaded.

"I'm not in the mood, Red. One knife in the back was enough for tonight. Two knives make for a hard night's sleep."

I spun away and stomped through the crowded tables. The walk home was chilly but did little to cool off my anger. Instead, I had worked myself into a good lather. Todd's Civic had disappeared to wherever one took Shawna Branson on dates. My bungalow looked too small for the giant-sized feelings swelling within me. I needed company. Something to take my mind off the Benedict Arnolds in my life. I contemplated the few establishments where I could have a beer and gab in peace to blow off this steam. Other than Red's, most Halo enterprises were closed at night and on Sundays. They also didn't serve what wasn't allowed in the blue laws. There were plenty of places in Line Creek, but I didn't want to drive that far.

And then I remembered Halo House had a bar. The Last Call.

Where nobody remembered my name.

Perfect.


The Last Call looked like a typical hotel bar. Adjoined to Halo House's fine dining space, the bar and restaurant were open to the public, although neither were advertised in the local phone directory under "Eating Establishments." Halo House also had a twenty-hour deli (open three a.m. to eleven p.m.), a pool bar, and room service.

"I am telling you," I said, hopping onto a leather barstool, "Halo House is something else. Always someone to talk to. Lots going on. Buses that take you anywhere you want to go. I just love it to death."

"Don't say that five-letter word too loudly around here." The bartender, a retirement-aged woman with frosted tips in her burgundy hair, had a surprisingly edgy north-of-the-sweet-tea-line accent. She flashed a look around the walker and cane set, playing cards and chatting at the cocktail tables. "Or at least don't shout it." She extended her hand. "I'm Rosie. You look familiar. Whose granddaughter are you?"

"I'm Cherry." I shook her hand. "I'm Grandma Jo's girl, but she isn't here. Actually, she passed ten years ago. Cancer."

"So sorry. Had it myself and kicked its can in my fifties. I'm one of the lucky ones. What brings you to the Last Call?"

"Beer and company mostly. I teach art here."

"Right, you're the painting lady. Heard that's a popular class, although some are anxious to get to the good stuff."

"Good stuff?" I considered the fundamentals I had covered. "We've done linear, one-point and two-point perspective. We're working our way to line and plane variations using still life objects, but I thought they should master drapery to understand depth and shadow first. They're probably anxious to get to the still lifes. Drawing cones and cubes can get tedious."

"Sounds boring as hell, but I don't do art." Rosie pushed a beer toward me. "No, I'm talking about models."

"Models? This is a fundamentals class, not a life-drawing class."

"Sweetheart, these ain't the kind of folks who sign up for 'Learn to Draw Tippy the Turtle' in the back of a magazine. They like you well enough, but you've got to keep them interested."

"They're learning more than Tippy the Turtle in my class. But I will take your advice and push us faster into two-D representation."

"Better make it three-D if you know what's good for you. I saw the poster you made. It's bait and switch otherwise."

"An Ingres-styled odalisque is a classical subject. I thought the class name, 'Art with Miss Cherry,' needed clarification. I painted the odalisque to show my serious intentions for teaching all the fundamentals." Straightening my shoulders, I gave her a nod. "Miss Krenzer said Halo House never had such interest in a class before."

"That's because you've got a naked chick lying on pillows."

"Only semi-nude. Pretty normal for an odalisque." I forced a smile, using Grandma Jo's advice about politeness to strangers. "I appreciate your opinion, but I have a degree in painting. If you don't have the basics, you can't jump into life drawing. The human figure is challenging. It's not just rendering what you observe, it's also capturing emotion and personality."

"Degree-schmegee." Rosie rolled her eyes. "There's too much going on at Halo House. There's a hot yoga class starting. Those art students will drop you like a bad penny. They've got short attention spans when it comes to activities. Time's precious here."

My eyes widened. "I'll lose my job. I can't lose my job to something called hot yoga."

"Then you better get cracking." Rosie leaned an arm on the bar. "You must have a mostly female class. Don't bore them with a constant parade of boobs. They've all seen that before. However, the ladies are taking the class because the boobs will attract the men."

"But I was hired to teach art, not pornography." My chin rose with my dignity. "That is a distinction this town has difficulty understanding. And I feel it's my job to elucidate the people of Halo on the difference between fine art and tacky titillation."

"You're going to elucidate yourself out of a job," said Rosie. "Don't get all uppity with your art crap. I may be new to the area, but I'm a quick study. Just because these folks have money and a long history in the county don't mean they don't want tacky titillation. They've lived a long time and they're tired of minding their manners. They want a good time in their final years."

"Making quality art is a good time."

She poured a shot of bourbon in a wineglass and filled it with Diet Coke. "Let me show you something about quality in Halo House. People 'round here act snobbish at times, but money don't buy good taste. Nor does it buy good sense."

I leaned forward. I may draw the line between good and bad art, but I never drew a line when it came to hot gossip.

Rosie sipped on her cocktail and nodded toward a woman sitting in a corner by herself. She smiled and waved as people walked by. "That's Eleanor."

"She looks lonely." I turned on my stool. "I should sit with her a bit."

"She's not lonely, she's stoned out of her mind."

"The poor thing. Is it her medication?"

Rosie chuckled. "Eleanor calls it medication. When I was growing up, we called it reefer."

I swiveled back and almost knocked my beer over. "She's high?"

"Not only does she roll her own, she grows her own."

"What?"

"The community garden."

A waiter strolled through the bar from the restaurant and deposited a basket of chips and a side of guacamole in front of Eleanor. She high-fived the waiter and dug into the chips.

"I wasn't expecting that," I admitted. "Grandma Jo was a strict Southern Baptist. She wouldn't even try her sister's homemade muscadine wine. Grandpa Ed has been known to dip from time to time and will drink a beer at a ballgame, but that's as far as he got on the controlled substance list."

"Poor kid." Rosie snorted. "Do you think your generation was the first to shock their parents? Just because you're old doesn't mean you're as straight-laced as your Granny. Hell, there's plenty of baby boomers in Halo House. That should tell you something."

I wasn't sure what that was supposed to tell me, but I would give Rosie the benefit.

"What else is going on at Halo House?" I swung around on my stool to observe the crowd.

A couple had put money in a brightly lit jukebox and was dancing to Tom Jones. Next to the jukebox a line of women had formed, some pointing out songs to their friends, others tapping their toes while they waited.

"That's Two-Dollar Frank," said Rosie. "He's one of our bachelors."

"Two-Dollar Frank?"

"Two bucks a dance. For his mad money. And exercise to boot. He charges more for horizontal dancing, if you get my picture."

"Good Lord. Halo House *is* like a college dorm. Where's the keg hidden?"

Rosie smiled. "Now you're getting it."

"I get your point." I hopped from my stool. "Excuse me a minute. I need to use the ladies'."

I cut through the tables of card players and chatter. At Eleanor's, I slowed to give her a hello. She peered at me through her thick glasses and offered me a chip.

"Looking for anything else?" Eleanor winked. "You cool? We could party in my room if you're cool."

I'd gone to art school. I was not naive. But for Halo, this was a bit disconcerting.

Grabbing the wheelchair bar, I slipped around the corner and into a side hall toward the bathrooms. Near the end of the hall, a young man chatted with an elderly woman, one I recognized from class.

"Hey, Miss Hazel," I called out, then remembering to raise my voice, I called out again. Miss Hazel didn't always wear her hearing aid.

The young man extended a hand toward Miss Hazel. At my holler, he dropped his hand and shoved it in his pocket. With a scowl, he backed away from her and bumped through the men's room door. Miss Hazel turned slowly, panic striking her features.

I rushed forward and took her arm. "Miss Hazel, are you all right?"

"I'm fine." Her wispy voice drew in breaths between words. "Just fine, Cherry."

"You don't look fine. Can I help you to your room? You look like you could use a lie-down."

The hand patting my arm trembled. "No, hon. Leave me here. I'll catch my breath in a minute. You go on with wherever you were going."

"Just the ladies'. Are you sure, Miss Hazel? What if we walked into the Last Call and got you a seat?"

She took a deep, quivering breath. "No, baby. You get. I'm fine right here."

"Miss Hazel, who was the man talking to you? Your grandson? Has he upset you?"

She shook her head and gave me a push. "No, not my grandson. We were passing a few pleasantries. Don't worry about it. You get."

Reluctantly, I left her clinging to the wheelchair bar.

Pushing through the ladies' room door, I stopped, turned, and left it open a crack. No doubt about it, she looked frightened and eager for me to leave. I didn't trust the young man. He appeared a few years younger than me, around his early twenties. His ball cap had been pulled low and I couldn't see his face other than a scowl. His t-shirt had exposed several tattoos and one in particular caught my eye. A stylized revolver. On his neck.

I hoped it meant he was just a gun buff.

A moment later, the young man slipped from the bathroom and found Miss Hazel. I tensed, ready to spring if Hazel needed me.

"She gone?" he asked.

Hazel placed a hand on her chest and nodded.

"Give it to me now before someone else comes," he said.

She slowly pulled her purse off her shoulder and tried to grasp the zipper with her trembling fingers.

He snatched her purse, unzipped it, and snatched something from inside. "This'll do for now. Later, Miss Hazel."

He tossed her the purse and she pulled it to her chest. "When will you come again?"

"I'll let you know." He flashed a grin and touched the brim of his cap, exposing tattooed fingers. "Pleasure."

As the guy moseyed toward the ladies', I pulled the door back in place, then swung it wide. It slammed into his shoulder. I bounded from the bathroom.

"Sorry about that," I said. "Didn't see you. I'm Cherry. And you are?"

"None of your business." Glowering at me, he rubbed his shoulder blade. With one last sharp glance at Hazel, he strode down the hall.

I turned toward Hazel, but she had made it to the other end of the hall and turned a corner. I resisted going after her. I'd embarrassed her enough. Instead, I followed him. At the entrance to the bar, I waited.

He continued toward the lobby, strolling past the big fountain. I waited for a beat, then hurried to peer around the fountain. He had disappeared. I circled the fountain, then approached the front desk.

Miss Krenzer looked up from her book. "What are you doing here this time of night?"

"Thought I'd rustle up some company at the Last Call. I saw a man pass through here. Kind of wiry looking, twenty or so. Tatted up with a beard and hat, like every other guy that age. Who was he?"

"I didn't see anyone." Miss Krenzer glared at me over her readers. "If you want a date, try another bar. It's not professional."

"Lord, no, I don't want to date him. I'm worried he's bothering Miss Hazel."

"Why?"

"I saw them standing together in the hallway and she gave him her purse. He took something from it. Hazel looked scared."

"Did you ask her about it?"

"She said she was fine and wanted me to leave her alone."

"Did he steal her purse? I'll call security."

"He didn't actually steal it. She was getting something for him and he got grabby when she took too long."

Miss Krenzer tapped her book with a finger. "Miss Hazel has her wits about her. If she said she was fine and wanted you to leave, she probably meant it. Some of our residents have issues with giving away their things and money to strangers, but not Miss Hazel."

"You should call security anyway."

"I'll send someone to Miss Hazel's room to check on her." She looked from me to the door.

I followed her look to the door, then swiveled to glance up the grand staircase. "I wonder where he went."

"Goodnight, Cherry."

I'd check on Hazel myself. Tomorrow after class. If the young guy was harassing her, I had to help. Grandma Jo had taught me to always take care of my elders.

# FOUR

The next morning, as I was put off breakfast by thoughts of Todd with Shawna, I decided to avoid Todd, skip my microwavable Jimmy Dean, and grab something at Halo House. Todd wasn't always the sharpest wrench in the toolbox, but he made up for it with steadfast loyalty, easy companionship, and overall good looks. I figured Shawna had an ulterior, nefarious motive for dating him.

I'd made a promise to Uncle Will to "cool it on the hijinks and whatnot" until Cody's trial. The slip of paper I'd kept from Todd was exactly that. Ammunition against the Bransons, particularly Shawna. By finding this information, Luke betrayed his mother's-by-marriage people. For me. To help clear up the god-awful mess that put my brother Cody in jail, helped my sister into unemployment, and made me lose my Halo art base.

However, as much as I wanted to get Shawna to drop the charges against Cody, I didn't know if I had it in me to blackmail her. Or to shame her family. Not to mention the repercussions that would ensue, like the exhuming of our Tucker family skeletons. Namely my mother.

In the Halo House parking lot, I hopped from the Datsun and strolled into the marble lobby with a box of Dixie Delites under my arm. At eight in the morning, the place was already hopping. Today I had Hazel to check on and a class to teach, but also felt anxious to find out what Belvia Brakeman wanted with me. The box of chocolates was my excuse to drop by.

At the front desk, Krenzer waved me over. "Belvia Brakeman wants to see you."

No excuse needed.

I grinned. "I'm free. I'll see her in a minute."

"Considering you teach one class a day and it's not for," she checked the schedule, "another five hours, I'd agree you're free."

I shrugged. "I miss college."

"You can learn a lot from your elders." Krenzer smiled. "That's all right then. Just don't wear anyone out."

I decided not to elucidate her on the difference between missing college and missing learning and headed toward the stairway. A small crowd hung around the fountain, holding coffee mugs and chatting.

"Morning, Fred. Miss Ada," I called. "And Miss Hazel."

Miss Hazel looked away, but Fred waved.

I scooted to the fountain, unsure of the best way to broach Hazel's situation with Young Grabby Hands. Particularly when she hung with the two biggest gossips in Halo House. Fred liked to chew the fat as much as my Grandpa Ed, and Ada had the lowdown on nearly everyone. I'd known Fred all my life, but had met Ada and Hazel through my art class. Just like in school, a common interest had joined us together.

Unfortunately, the common interest was our interest in everyone else.

"Charlene, you're late," barked Ada. She eyed the box under my arm. "Who's that for?"

"It's Cherry. And actually, I'm early." Ada seemed sharp in most areas but my name. Considering she was seventy-eight, I forgave her. "The chocolates are for Belvia Brakeman. My Grandma Jo said to always bring an edible to the grieving. If they don't feel like eating, their kin surely will. Lucky I did because Miss Belvia wants to see me."

"If you bought that at the Piggly Wiggly, it's not good enough for Battle-axe," scoffed Ada. "Might as well hand it over to someone who will appreciate store chocolate."

I smiled and tightened my grip on the Dixie Delites. "Battle-axe?"

"In school, they used to call her Battle-axe Belvia Brakeman. Not my class. My oldest sister's. I'm younger. And better looking." Ada opened her mouth and pointed. "Still have my own teeth too."

I turned toward Hazel, who stared into her coffee. Normally, she'd have a comeback for Ada's sass. "What's going on today?"

"We're interested in seeing who shows to visit the CEO," said Fred. "You heard Coralee, the younger sister, is here? She hasn't been back in more than thirty years. She ran off to California—"

"Iowa," said Ada. "Joined a commune or some such nonsense. And Battle-axe said, 'Don't bother coming back until you get your head screwed on straight.' So Coralee didn't."

"I guess they came back for the funeral?" I asked.

"Coralee didn't show for her father's funeral but did for her sister. Shows you who wears the pants in this family," said Fred. Then added, "The Brakeman women," in case we couldn't guess.

Ada glowered at Fred, but couldn't find fault in his statement. "I bet Coralee thought this was her chance to play prodigal daughter. Maybe nose her way into the family business."

"You think?" My mind took a *Matlock* wander.

"Anyway, we're hoping to see a skirmish."

"That's horrible." I gave Ada my best "grow-up" eyebrow raise, usually saved for my own siblings.

"Get off your high horse, Charlene," said Ada. "Back in the day, Coralee and Ron, Della's husband, never got along. And Coralee's husband, Wally, is about as opposite from the Brakemans as you can get. It'll be plenty entertaining."

"Poor Miss Belvia."

Ada snorted. "Battle-axe did nothing to stop it back then. She all but encouraged the rivalry between the two sisters. Thought it'd make them stronger so they'd have an edge in the business world."

"Times were different for women in the workplace then. Have you seen *Mad Men*? Now that Joan Holloway..." Fred whistled. "Never saw anyone like her in my office, I can tell you that."

Ada smacked his arm. "Are you still binge watching that Netflix stuff? I told you to cut down on the idiot box."

"It's an award-winning show, Ada." Fred rubbed his arm. "Take it easy. You know I bruise easily."

I eyed Hazel, still ignoring us. "You okay, Miss Hazel? You seemed shook up last night."

Ada and Fred stopped their tussle to check out the flush creeping through Hazel's powdered cheeks.

She shot me a hard look. "Everything's just fine."

"What happened?" asked Ada. "Did you have a spell or something?"

"No, I did not have a spell." Hazel rose from the bench. "If you'll excuse me, I've got things to attend to in my rooms."

I watched her leave, then spotted Ada and Fred's questioning gaze.

"Should we be keeping an eye on Hazel?" asked Ada. "She might not admit to feeling puny, but someone should know if she's sick."

I chewed on my lip, thinking about Hazel and Young Grabby Hands with the pistol tattoo. "Does she have a grandson who visits much?"

"I'm not sure," said Fred. "Hazel doesn't get many visitors."

"Poor Hazel," I said. "I wonder if she's lonely and this guy is taking advantage of her."

"What guy?" Ada's eyes gleamed.

I considered Hazel's privacy amid these nosy Nellies, but my concern for Hazel overrode that propriety. "Last night, I saw a young man with a gun tattoo messing with Hazel. He took something from her, but she claimed it wasn't a big deal."

"Hazel's savvy," said Ada. "Likely it wasn't a big deal."

"Do you have something against tattoos?" Fred rolled his sleeve and flashed the U.S.N. eagle on his bicep.

"It's not the tattoos, it was the attitude accompanying them that bugged me." I fixed my fists on my hips. "It looked like the guy was pressuring Hazel to give him something."

"Forced her? Like a mugging?" said Fred, cracking his knuckles.

"No, she took too long getting something out of her purse, so he grabbed it."

Ada rolled her eyes. "Hazel has arthritis."

"She looked scared. Where's your concern for Hazel?"

"Hazel's a big girl."

"No, Ada, she's not. Hazel's actually tiny." I eyed the troublemakers. "If y'all would keep an eye on Hazel, that'd be helpful. Let me know if you see anything amiss."

"We'll watch out for her," said Fred. "Don't you worry, Cherry."

"I'd appreciate it." I turned toward the grand stairway. I needed to see Belvia before the visitation visitors consumed her time.

"That Charlene," said Ada. "Thinks we can't take care of ourselves. Hazel knows what she's doing."

"I heard that," I said. "I'm still standing right here."

"Fred can't hear if I whisper," said Ada. "And I can't help it if you're rude enough to listen in."

"Look out for Hazel." I waved the Dixie Delite box. "Humor me."

Ada rolled her eyes. "Don't worry about us humoring you, Charlene. You see enough of that in your art class."

# Five

At Mrs. Brakeman's door, I buzzed, pleased I'd spent the five bucks to get the chocolate. Then swooped the box behind my back when Coralee answered. Her eyes had zipped past me to the Dixie Delites like a hawk sighting a baby bunny.

I was just mean enough to want to get credit from the Queen of Halo House. Particularly knowing I had been summoned.

"What do you want?" Coralee centered herself in the doorway.

"Nice to see you. Once again, sorry for your loss."

Coralee's eyes did not waver from the chocolate. It seemed my sentiments couldn't compete with Dixie Delites. She pointed at my box. "If you're dropping that off, I'll see Mother gets it. She's busy."

"Actually, Miss Belvia asked for me. Left a message at the desk."

"If she's expecting you, I guess I'll let you in." Coralee swung open the door. "There are a lot of people who want to talk to my mother. Trooping in since daybreak. Mother is up early and they all know it."

No Pris on the couch reading today. Nor anyone else. I guess the visitors had already untrooped.

I followed Coralee through the small living room toward Belvia's office.

"I can take the candy for you." Her hand darted toward the box.

"Is Miss Belvia diabetic?" At her head shake, I smiled. "If Miss Belvia's been up for hours, she might want a little sugar."

Rolling her eyes, Coralee rapped on the office door, then opened it. A droning electronic voice shut off.

"It's that girl..." She looked at me. "Who are you again?"

"Come in, Cherry," called Belvia Brakeman.

I stepped around Coralee and into the office.

"Coralee, make yourself scarce. I want to talk in private." Miss Belvia's imperious voice rose from the desk. Turned toward the computer, the tall-backed leather office throne effectively hid her.

Just like the Wizard of Oz, I thought.

"I'll wait in the living room," said Coralee. "And Mother, she brought candy. I'll take the box for you?"

I tightened my grip on the Dixie Delites.

"I'd like you to leave the apartment," said Belvia from behind the chair. "Give us some privacy."

"Really, Mother." Coralee's lips pulled tight. Glancing at me, she slid them into a smile so artificial it gave me the willies. "I can stay in the apartment without interrupting your meeting. Where else would I go?"

"That will be all, Coralee."

"I guess I could check on the room for the viewing."

"Good idea." Miss Belvia waited until we heard the front door shut. "Sit down, Cherry."

"Can I put the chocolates somewhere for you?"

"Not now." Belvia swiveled to face me. "I called you in because of your behavior yesterday. It affirmed something I've heard about you."

Having heard this conversation starter previously in my life, I squirmed and resisted the urge to chew my bottom lip. "Ma'am, I'm sorry for whatever I did."

"I don't normally have strangers suspecting I may be cheated by fraud."

"I get suspicious about a lot of things, and I promised my Uncle Will to curb that habit. I'm trying. It does get me involved in business that is not my concern. Sometimes with a certain criminal element. Although those involvements, I think, have been good for the community, by helping folks and such. But particular parts of the community tend to—"

"Your concern for my welfare is appreciated, Cherry. But I'm not worried about what the community believes. I respect people who say what they think. Particularly when the thinking is strategic."

I straightened. "Thank you."

"Why did you think my will might be fraudulent?"

Considering her current high approval of my intelligence, I forewent any mention of *Matlock*. "Mostly because of your sight. And your age. Also with a company like Meemaw's Tea, you're worth a penny or two. Forgive me for saying so, ma'am."

Her chin lifted a notch. "Of course. And this Uncle Will. That's Sheriff Will Thompson, isn't he?"

"He is. At least for now." I sighed, thinking of Uncle Will's recent stress. "The election's coming and he's running against an outsider. It's been a while since he's run against anyone." I didn't mention Della's hit and run didn't help. Or that the outsider was backed with Branson bucks.

She brushed past the politics. "So you have some knowledge of law-enforcement procedures. The police are investigating Della's death."

"Yes, ma'am. An accidental death is normally manslaughter. But for a hit and run, that's first-degree homicide. You bet Sheriff Will's investigating."

"And if it was deliberate? Della's death?"

"Hit her on purpose?" I wouldn't admit my thoughts had gone there for a minute. "You think Della was murdered?"

"The police are still calling it a suspicious death, but they think there's more to it. I believe they are investigating Ron Newson, Della's husband. He has an alibi though."

"I'm sorry to hear that. Must be awful, having just lost his wife." No wonder Luke wouldn't tell me anything. "But what can I do for you?"

"I know the police will need sufficient evidence before they can make an arrest. If the perpetrator is associated with Meemaw's Tea, they may have the resources to make an arrest difficult."

"By resources, you mean expensive lawyers."

She smiled in acknowledgment. "My intention was to pass the CEO chairmanship to Della this month when I officially retire. I want to keep Meemaw's Tea a family-run company. For some, Della's death is a game-changer, as harsh as that sounds."

"You think someone in your company murdered Della? To advance their career? Can't you do a mental-health screening? Weed out the psychopaths?"

"Do you know anything about multimillion-dollar companies with private shareholders?" She eyed me, despite the blindness. "They're not run by the weak or by fools. My board members can be ruthless. I hire my administrators for that quality. You may joke about psychopaths, but by definition, they can be found in the business world. Egocentric, amoral mercenaries. Not necessarily violent, but still obsessed with their own agendas. Usually, that's money and power. Meemaw's Tea is worth a lot of money and the CEO is a position of power."

Almost made me glad to be poor and powerless. But now scared to drink bottled tea.

"I sense your discomfort. I'm not a psychopath and neither are Meemaw's Tea employees." She stroked her neck and pulled at her pearls. "This is not someone outwardly insane. Just protecting their interests."

"Protecting their stakes with murder?" I didn't know much about business, but Belvia sounded too eager to find Della's slayer in her company. At ninety and facing a crisis in her life's work, maybe her daughter's death was too much of a shock. "Can't you fire the board?"

"They are shareholders themselves. Since the Sarbanes-Oxley Act, anything to do with company governance has become complicated, particularly for the CEO and chairman." She grimaced. "I relented to shareholder demands for an independent board of directors, but I've been fighting with them ever since. We all want profit, but I intended to keep this company in the family and closely held."

"I don't understand—"

"Cherry, with your background, your relationship with the police, and your work at Halo House, you can be useful to me. I want you to find out the culprit before their name hits the news, particularly if they are related to Meemaw's Tea. You're an outsider with my company, but an insider here at Halo House. A fresh set of eyes on my people and you can visit me without notice. I'm under quite a bit of scrutiny now."

"This is a criminal matter, ma'am. I can't interfere in an investigation. Not only would my Uncle Will tan my hide, he'd have me arrested."

"I'm not speaking of interference. A separate investigation. I know you've done this before."

"My previous experience was helping friends when they had nowhere else to turn." I didn't like the thought of someone like Belvia Brakeman assuming I'd do a job. Particularly a job where my qualifications were vague at best. The friends I'd helped were the downtrodden, not the trodders. That's what bugged me about the upper crust of small towns. Assuming the rest of us would willingly lick their boots because we hadn't reached their apex of success.

I didn't lick boots. I wore them.

"You see me as rich and powerful, but I'm still ninety and blind, Miss Tucker. And vulnerable. Remember those feelings you had yesterday when you suspected tampering with my will?"

Dangit. She had me there.

"As founder, chief shareholder, and CEO, I can appoint the new head of Meemaw's Tea, but I won't until this business with Della's murder has been solved. I want to put preventative measures in place before the arrest happens. To protect the company. With the changeover to Della and finding a new COO, the shareholders were anxious. Now the shareholders are panicking. If her death has to do with Meemaw's, I need to keep this out of the media and resolve the issue quietly."

"What do you mean by 'preventative measures?'"

"If the perpetrator works for me, I'd pressure them to confess." Belvia rapped her iPad cover. "A financial carrot or stick to get them to comply with the law. After all, you'll know who did it, even if the police don't have evidence to make the arrest. A confession would help the sheriff."

"Sounds like vigilante justice to me."

"I need to know for the sake of the new company president." She bowed her head, rubbing her temples. Dropping her hand, she stared in my direction. "Yesterday, I named my replacement in the will and trust by making them majority shareholder. Not even my lawyer knows who it is. I'm not revealing my choice until the issue of Della's death is resolved. But in case anything should happen to me, I wanted a safeguard. I'm old."

"You have that little faith in the sheriff's department?"

"If someone did kill Della to advance their own agenda, it puts me in danger too."

I hadn't thought about that. Mainly because the whole idea sounded far-fetched and crazier than a peach-orchard pig. But if Della had been murdered, I couldn't allow an elderly blind woman to go unprotected. One who was asking for my help.

"I don't know if I could match wits with a diabolical businessman."

"Never doubt yourself, Cherry. As a woman, plenty doubted I could create a company like Meemaw's Tea. We brew 300,000 gallons of tea a day and ship the jugs to every state as well as internationally. It's my legacy we're talking about. I wanted to hand it over to Della and now she's perished. Possibly due to some snake in the grass."

"I hate snakes," I muttered, thinking of the proverbial snakebites I'd suffered.

She smiled in victory. I'd forgotten her sharp hearing. Belvia Brakeman hid her age and disability through the strength of her charisma, once again reminding me of the Wizard. But I wasn't as easily duped as Dorothy.

"I don't think I'm qualified." I rose from my chair. "You should leave this to the sheriff's department. They'll give you fair warning before making an arrest."

"You have a brother in jail, don't you? Cody Tucker. Charged with a forced abduction of a Shawna Branson? She wasn't hurt and there's no evidence he had a weapon. She made the emergency call from her phone while sitting in the front seat of his car. When the police made the arrest, he didn't resist. She hadn't been restrained in any way. Why was his bail set so high with such flimsy evidence and when your family is closely associated with the sheriff?"

Belvia knew about my personal Wicked Witch. I sank back into the chair. The Wizardess wanted me to get the damn broom.

# SIX

Belvia Brakeman wasn't just the Wizard. She was also the Godfather. Her high-handedness rankled me, using my brother to lure me into striding the gray line between truth and obstruction.

But it was an offer I couldn't refuse.

Her proposal was connected to county politics and legal representation that'd get my brother's charges reexamined and likely dropped. It might exonerate my family name. And ease the pressure off my relationship with Luke Harper.

Not that our families wouldn't continue hating each other. That bull had left the pasture years ago.

The offer would also toss a bucket of water over my Wicked Witch. Or at least knock a chip off Shawna Branson's shoulder. Petty, I know. But at least I wouldn't have to resort to blackmailing Shawna myself.

Money and power were a mighty thing. Heady to think at the snap of Belvia Brakeman's fingers many of my problems would just go away.

Dropping the box of Dixie Delites on a side table in her living room, I took in the spare furnishings that reminded me of a doctor's reception area and realized that was the intended purpose. She didn't just live in this apartment, it was the nerve center for Meemaw's Tea. Since I'd been at Halo House, I'd witnessed business types visiting the Brakeman suite. All sorts of people came and went from her apartment. If someone wanted to murder Belvia, it'd sure be easy.

Hopefully that was paranoia talking.

I drove to Line Creek, where I had a standing appointment at Forks County Corrections. My resentment ebbed as giddiness bubbled inside me. Thanks to Belvia Brakeman, it was possible my brother Cody wouldn't have to stare at the same cement block walls much longer. Not that I felt confident in my ability to help her. But the mere chance buoyed my hope and made me feel better than I had in months.

In the visitor's room, I slid onto an orange stool to wait. A door opened, but instead of a deputy escorting Cody, the sheriff strode through and stopped before my table. Uncle Will had played defensive tackle for the Bulldogs thirty years ago. He'd maintained the bulk and while some of the bulk had slid south, his nickname, The Intimidator, still rang true.

Today, however, his countenance showed more fatigue than intimidation.

"What's going on?" I said, half rising from my stool.

"There was an altercation." Uncle Will held up his hands. "Cody wasn't involved, but they had to lock down the cells in his area."

I placed a hand on my chest to prevent my heart from dislodging. "Is he okay?"

"He's fine. Wasn't anywhere near the fight. Wanted me to tell you myself."

"Uncle Will..." I bit my lip to prevent tears from escaping.

He lowered himself on a stool and gathered my hands in his. "Your brother's okay. He's in minimum security. This isn't Sing Sing. It's the county jail, but we do get some idiots who cause trouble from time to time. You know this."

"I know," I mumbled. A few tears escaped and I swiped at them with the back of my hand. "I hate this."

"Cody did something stupid and he's paying the price. He accepts that."

"He doesn't deserve to spend the rest of his life in prison for it though." I lowered my voice. "Forcing Shawna Branson into his car to do a DNA kit was wrong. Charging him with a felony kidnapping is reprehensible on her part. He could get twenty to life."

"The charge had more to do with Shawna's attorney than her, hon. Don't lay it all on her."

"Shawna could tell her attorney it's ridiculous. And we all know who really hired the attorney. JB Branson. The man who wants to unseat you as sheriff for his own candidate." I studied his serious warm sepia gaze. Thought about relating Belvia Brakeman's words back to him. But I didn't want Uncle Will to know I'd involved myself with one crazy family to solve the craziness in my own. "This is political, isn't it?"

"When you're sheriff, everything is political. It doesn't help having Cody in my own jail during an election year. Between his trial and the election, your family will be dragged through the mud. It's easy to want to blame others, Cherry, but sometimes you just have to haul on your boots and try to not get stuck in the mud. Remember your name's been in the paper as much as Cody's."

"I hear you." I shuffled my boots. A backfire on this decision to help Miss Belvia could incinerate Uncle Will's reputation as well as mine. But exonerating my brother would be worth the risk.

His deep voice gentled. "I'll arrange for Cody to call you later. We'll get through this, baby girl."

"I'll do my best to help Cody." I gave him a teary smile. "And you too."


That evening on the phone, I listened to Cody's brief account of the altercation and sensed his underlying fear. As much as I hated giving him false hope, the boy needed some good news to brighten his gloomy outlook.

"Listen, Cody," I said. "I don't want to rile you up, but someone in town offered to help us. Maybe get you a new lawyer. Also, they might speak to the Bransons and clear up the mess. As a mediator."

"Who's that?" His voice rose.

"Just a friend. They want me to take care of something first. And in exchange, they're willing to help us."

"Really? Lord, Cherry, I needed to hear this. I didn't want to tell you, but I've been feeling pretty bleak about this trial. That arraignment didn't go too well for me."

"I know, honey."

"And a new lawyer. You think they'd do better than the one I got now?"

"Any lawyer's better than the one you got now. But listen, Cody, there's no guarantee, so don't start packing your orange jumpsuits yet."

"I know. But, Sister, I..." He choked back a sob. "You don't know what this means to me."

"I know, hon. Hang in there. I'll do my best to get you out. I have to do something for this friend before she'll grant our wish."

"This friend's an angel of mercy. I've been praying," he whispered. "This is like a miracle."

Dorothy's friends had thought the Wizard miraculous too. Whereas I knew the miracle was small town power. Money instead of smoke and mirrors. But money was a hell of a lot more effective.

I had a hit-and-run driver to catch and I didn't feel good about it at all.

# seven

Over my morning coffee, I eyed the blond Viking sitting across from me. Like most mornings, he sat before a mixing bowl filled with cereal. A mug of sugar and cream with enough coffee to create a very pale ochre. The local paper opened to the Halo High School sports page. And headphones turned to eleven.

Most mornings I drank my coffee, immersed in my own musings, and accessorized my fashion choices with a glue gun, paint brush, or Bedazzler. Today I studied my roommate, trying to fathom a reason for his betrayal.

I rapped on the table.

Todd glanced up, then pulled off his headphones. "Hey, baby."

I tried to relax my face, but couldn't pull it off. Instead of "How was your date?" I blurted, "What's the big idea of taking Shawna Branson out?"

"It's like this," said Todd.

I waited for a whole half-second for his explanation. "Like what?"

Todd sighed. "I thought I could learn something about Cody's case if I dated her."

I felt the tension in my neck release. "And?"

"Didn't work."

"Of course it didn't work," I said. "Of all the harebrained schemes. Shawna knows where your loyalties lie. She may be a lot of things, but she's not stupid. For mercy's sake, she reminds me of the failure of our thirty-two-hour marriage every chance she gets."

"Yes," he said. "She did bring that up."

I snorted. "I can't believe she went out with you at all. What happened? Did your date take you to the drive-in, where his ex got on the PA and announced you as trashy with the morals of an alley cat?"

"What?" Todd shook his head. "No."

"Good, because I'd hate for you to endure that humiliation. Shawna Branson's done that before, so I wouldn't put it past her. Of course, it did make me popular with a certain segment of the male high school population that night. Until they found out I wasn't really alley cat material."

"The drive-in isn't open in the winter."

I patted his hand. "That's okay, honey. What happened?"

"I took her bowling."

"Shawna went bowling?"

"She's good. Would have cracked 100 if she hadn't broken a nail."

"Bet she howled about that."

Todd shook his head. "Not too much."

I couldn't imagine Shawna not making a stink over her broken nail. "So I guess she wanted to dish on me. What'd she say?"

"Not too much. Just that she'd been sorry to hear our relationship didn't work. Then she said, 'But not that sorry.'"

"Aha." I removed my finger from its heavenward point. "She was rubbing our noses in it. I guess she got tired of trash-talking my family and is now going after you."

"I don't think that's how she meant it," said Todd. "Because after she said 'not that sorry,' she kissed me."

My neck prickled. "And what'd you do?"

"Kissed her back."

"How'd you do that?"

Todd flashed me a sharp look. "It's been a while, but I haven't forgotten how to kiss a gal, Cherry."

"I meant how could you do that?" I clutched my stomach. "Todd, you'll give her the wrong idea. Not that I'd give Shawna Branson the time of day, but it's wrong to lead her on like this."

He shrugged. "She's good at kissing."

"That's beside the point." I studied his face. "Wait, you didn't enjoy it. Did you?"

Todd's eyes cut away. "Only a little?"

"It's like I don't know you right now."

"That's funny," he said, jetting to the door. "Shawna said something real similar."


The thought of Todd and Shawna sharing spit had put me off thinking about Belvia's case. I hadn't done any research yet, but Della's viewing had been scheduled for later that day. I figured Belvia would stay busy with visitors and I'd catch her in a day or two.

I donned my visitation dress and puttered to Halo House. Belvia had said her retired assistant would give me a list of names—Meemaw's Tea suspects—to help me in my "thinking." Then asked me to check out the list and report back to her on my "thoughts."

Much like the Wizard, Belvia didn't let people idly "think" about what she wanted them to do.

Molly Kern also lived in Halo House. Belvia said she'd arranged for her former assistant to live down the hall, because of their "dear friendship" and because she could still rely on her, even though Molly had retired. Belvia had talked a lot about Molly—more than anyone else—giving me a rundown of their history. They'd worked together for around fifty years. Belvia had trusted Molly as much as Della. I wondered if Molly liked her "retired" living arrangement, spending the rest of her life still at her boss's beck and call. But for a kick-butt suite at prestigious Halo House, maybe it was worth it.

I sped through the lobby, waving hello to my friends at the fountain, and darted up the grand staircase to the second floor. I passed Belvia's apartment, where a small crowd had convened. At suite 210, a woman peeked out. Her smooth bobbed hair swung beside ears where delicate pearls rested in the fold. More pearls gathered around at the neck of her black suit. Just like Belvia's.

I smoothed my Prussian blue visitation dress. I'd stitched two-dimensional wings on the back. Lace with added seed pearls. I felt it soothing for the bereaved to see this reminder of the hereafter. Using lace and pearls was my nod toward convention.

"Are you Cherry?" she said. "I'm Molly Kern."

"Heard you were Mrs. Brakeman's assistant for fifty years," I said. "That's some dedication. She must have been a great boss."

Like a good personal assistant, Molly demurely smiled with her mouth shut. She ushered me inside. Compared to Belvia's austere waiting room, every flat surface in Molly's crowded space had been covered with memorabilia. Small glass and crystal animals. Hummel figurines. And a curio cabinet of Precious Moment statues.

Molly handed me an envelope and waved me to sit next to her on a chintz sofa. "Belvia said you wanted a list of board members and executives. Are you helping her with something? I know she could use a new assistant."

I slid backward on the overstuffed chintz couch and propped myself forward with a tasseled pillow. "I'd be a terrible assistant. I'm just checking into some things for her."

Molly sighed. "She could use a new assistant now that Belvia's overseeing operations since Della's COO position stands empty."

"At ninety? Why doesn't she get somebody at the company to help her? Didn't Della hire someone to take over her job, knowing she'd soon be CEO?"

"I try to stay out of office politics. But if you need anything, Della had an office manager, Donna Sharp. I refer most business calls to Donna." Molly's pale cheeks quivered. "I still get calls and not just from Belvia. Hard to let me go after fifty years, I suppose."

I felt sorry for Molly. When Grandma Jo finally quit her position on the church council, the church folks acted like she never left, constantly asking for help. It frustrated me. They wore her out, yet she wouldn't refuse anyone. Even after we found out about the cancer.

Molly looked just as tired. Belvia had also asked me to "keep an eye on Molly while you're getting this business sorted out." Now I realized why. Belvia didn't want Meemaw's Tea folks bothering Molly. Even if Belvia seemed to feel a right to call on her.

Ninety and blind, nevertheless that chafed me.

I tapped the envelope against my palm, wondering if I could rely on this Donna to help me instead of Molly. "Would Belvia find Donna trustworthy?"

"I suppose so. Donna told me she's expecting a promotion."

"Because of Della's death?"

"I wouldn't put it that bluntly."

"Sorry, my Grandma Jo used to say I'd not just tell how the cow ate the cabbage, I'd paint you a picture as well."

"What exactly are you doing for Belvia?"

"It has to do with Della's death. To be honest, I'm worried about working for Miss Belvia. She's pretty insistent, isn't she?"

"Belvia Brakeman doesn't take no for an answer. But whatever she promised to pay you, she's good for it. She took care of my retirement situation. Didn't even sign a contract, she just made it happen." Molly clasped her hands together and beamed. "Belvia always gets her way."


In the hallway, I scanned the list. Apparently, Belvia didn't trust anybody, including her own lawyer. Too bad Miss Belvia hadn't involved herself in Halo House friendships. Thinking about corporate takeovers during her daughter's unexpected death surely wasn't good for a ninety-year-old woman. It wouldn't be good for anyone.

Thinking about Halo House friendships, I followed my gut instincts up a floor and to another hall, toward Miss Hazel's apartment. I rang her buzzer, knowing this time of day she liked to watch "that cute little Kelly" privately, without Ada's peanut-gallery comments.

"She's not home."

I spun around, my hand on my chest. "Rosie. Didn't hear you." The bartender I'd met at the Last Call stood behind me. Sweatbands circled her wrists and forehead. Burgundy pin curls swirled around the sweatband, matching the raspberry whirls in her shiny leotard. "I'm headed to that new yoga class. Don't know where Hazel is, but haven't seen her since early this morning."

"I wanted to check on her."

Behind Rosie, a figure slunk around the corner from the stairway. He paused, spotted us, then turned back to the stairs. I recognized the hat, but it was the swagger that caught my attention.

"Hold that thought, Rosie. Gotta go." I hurried down the hall, grabbed the handrail for support, and swung around the corner.

Below me, the hat bobbed in view, then disappeared at the turn toward the landing.

"Hey," I called, stumbling on the low deep risers. Safe for shufflers and cane walkers, but dangerous for a foot chase.

At the landing between the two floors, three women stood chatting. "You'll fall running down the stairs like that," said one senior. "Slow down."

"Did you see the young guy?" I said. "Where he went?"

"Who?" said her friend.

"Sorry, I'm trying to catch someone." I edged past them and tripped on the first step.

"Slow down," they called after me.

Six more steps and I reached the next landing. Grabbed the handrail and swung to the second-floor hall. No Young Grabby Hands. My eyes fixed on Miss Belvia's open door. A group of suits stood inside, chatting.

I could sense her, sitting on the throne/desk chair in the inner office sanctum, waiting for news on her daughter's killer.

Ignoring that thought, I shot down the stairs, halted on the remaining landing, and gazed at the lobby below. Fred and Ada sat at the fountain. At reception, Krenzer chatted with a guest. The activity doors were closed. Another group of seniors filed out the glass front door toward a waiting bus.

I raced down the grand staircase and halted before Ada and Fred. "You see a young guy in a hat come through here?"

"You'll break a hip taking the stairs like that, Chelsea." Ada cocked her head. "What's going on?"

I glanced around. "If he came down here, you must have seen him. Where'd he go?"

"Lose a date?" Fred winked. "Didn't see any young man come down the stairs. Grab a coffee and sit a spell. Visitation's this afternoon. Folks starting to pour in already though."

My hands rested on my hips, but my neck prickled with anxiety. "How does he disappear like that?"

# EIGHT

"When you invited me for a late breakfast, I thought we'd go to the Waffle Hut." Luke cast a glance around Halo House's lobby and shoved his hands in the pockets of his jeans. "You can leave campus, can't you?"

Having failed in my mission to find Young Grabby Hands and force him into a stalking confession, I called Luke and told him about Hazel. I also invited him to breakfast to begin feelers on my next mission. I hoped to convince (or connive) my deputy into sharing some background information on Della's accident.

Besides, I was hungry.

"As much as I love to be scattered, smothered, and covered, you can get good eats here too. This is neutral territory. Last time we ate out, the waitress refused to serve me."

"You threatened to draw her a picture in maple syrup. On her clean table."

"After she made that remark about you 'taking out the trash for dinner.' What'd you expect me to do?"

"Let me handle it."

"I don't need you fighting my battles, Luke Harper."

"Don't I know it." His gray eyes flashed.

I placed a hand on his arm and guided him to the fountain. "Let me introduce you to some of my friends."

"This is the Ada and Fred you've been hanging out with?" Luke whispered as we approached the pair arguing about the most recent *Castle* rerun. "I thought they'd be younger."

Fred shook his hand. "What are your intentions with Cherry?"

"Breakfast?"

"Lord, that was ages ago. Cheryl was going to sit with us and watch the Brakeman crowds. They're showing up early for the viewing," said Ada. "There may be a fight. Or at least a scuffle. We have front-row seats."

"I see." Luke folded his arms across his chest and cast me a long look. "I'm getting a better understanding about your choice in friends."

I scowled at Ada. "There's not going to be a fight. You're making trouble."

"Something'll happen. Folks have been trickling in all morning, leaving messages for Battle-axe at the desk. Very few she grants a hearing, but they hang around anyway. By the visitation, this place will be packed to the gills. Krenzer probably didn't consider that when she let the Queen Tea Bee hold a viewing here."

Luke snagged my elbow. "We're getting breakfast and you're telling me all about what you and your buddies are doing stalking the Brakeman funeral guests."

"Let her go," said Fred, holding up a shaky fist. "Unless you'd like a bite of my knuckle sandwich."

Luke dropped his hand from my elbow. "I'm law enforcement."

"Means you can keep your record clean." Fred pulled back his fist, then grasped the wrist to keep it upright. "I'll do the time if it means protecting this young lady. I served in Korea, son."

"He's fine, Fred." I placed my hand on his arm and guided his fist to his side. "Luke's one of the deputies investigating Della Brakeman's death. Fred was best friends with Grandpa Ed's brother, my Great Uncle Stan. Fred gets a little overprotective."

"Good idea bringing this cutie along for a gab, Cheryl." Ada clapped her hands. "He'll have insights on the visitors we don't know. I'll save your place while you get us more coffee."

"Have you gotten any leads on who might have hit Della?" I asked.

"Nothing worth reporting." He rocked back on his heels.

"Come on," said Ada. "You gonna deny an old woman? I live for the 411. And my clock's ticking."

"You're a feisty one." Two dimples gleamed in Luke's cheeks. "Okay, I'll give you a small scoop. But you can't tell this to anyone."

"Who are we going to tell?" asked Ada.

Probably the entire staff, residents, and guests of Halo House. But I kept my mouth shut. If it took a seventy-eight-year-old woman to get a tidbit from Deputy Tight Lips, I'd take it.

"We've figured out the tires by the marks. Luckily, the soft shoulder gave us some imprints. Found yaw marks on the road too. They gave us an idea of the types of vehicles that would use those particular tires."

"And?" said Fred. "What kind?"

"Nothing special."

"Do you know who the vehicle belongs to?" said Ada.

"Not like we've got cameras on a county road. I'm checking through the DMV plate registration for similar makes. It'll take a while."

"Could you tell if the hit and run was accidental or deliberate?" I asked.

"Happened at dusk. All sorts of things to consider."

"Dang." Ada rested her chin in her hand. "I'd like that sucker caught by the funeral. It'd sure make Battle-axe rest easier."

"I thought you didn't like Miss Belvia," I said.

Ada shrugged. "She's got a lot on her plate. Of her own making, but still."

Maybe her full plate had brought on Belvia's suspicions and crazy plan for me to play detective. "Is Miss Belvia the paranoid type?"

Ada rolled her eyes. "If you're paranoid, you'd worry about what other people think. So, no."

"Doesn't that happen when some people age?"

"Sure, in dementia or Alzheimer's. Or with certain medication. But that's not the case with Battle-axe. If her enemies got a whiff of brain deterioration, they'd have forced her to step down a long time ago. She's got her wits together, I'll give her that."

I frowned. "So if it seemed she was paranoid, they'd remove her as CEO? How can they do that? Meemaw's Tea is her company."

"A company that big couldn't survive if it was run by someone who couldn't play hardball anymore," said Luke. "The shareholders would sell. Or threaten to sell. She's had Della to back her though. She made Della work her way up to COO, but Della's been in charge of operations for almost twenty years."

"Did Della play hardball like her mother?"

"Yes, indeedy," said Ada. "Della's a chip off the old Battle-axe block."

"Luke, did you know Della and Belvia were already fighting with the Meemaw's Tea board over leadership issues? Some were threatening to call a shareholders' vote for a takeover or merger if she didn't go public." Belvia had explained as much to me. "They think taking Meemaw's from a private family-owned company to a public corporation would be more profitable to the shareholders. And themselves. Even though Meemaw's Tea has been plenty successful."

"Maybe they were tired of Belvia and Della keeping most of that success," said Ada. "And money."

The lines around Luke's eyes tightened. "What's your point?"

"Seems to me, if there's a rival company who wanted to buy out the shareholders at a big price, the shareholders would make a whole lot of money. Except Belvia and Della are still the majority shareholders and no one can take over management without a majority vote or shares. It'd be easier to get the sale to go through if the Brakemans were out of the picture," I said.

"You think someone took out Della?" said Ada. "Hoo boy. Belvia'd be on a war path if she knew what you were thinking."

I chewed a nail. Yesterday I'd thought Belvia's surviving daughter had messed with the will. Today I'd moved on to corporate takeovers. Matlock would tell me I was in over my head.

Luke scowled. "Who said anything about murder? We're looking at a suspicious death. Now, if you excuse me, I'm strolling out to the visitor's parking lot to peruse vehicle tires. Next time we'll do breakfast with actual food."

"Don't you want to stay for the visitation?"

"Can't. I'll pay my respects later."

"That tire thing was barely anything. Y'all will release that to the paper."

"And like I said the other night, I don't talk about active investigations." He kissed me on the nose. "You're cute when you're mad."

"If you knew what's good for you, those words should never be thought, let alone uttered, in my presence."

"Oh, I know. Makes you madder." He winked. "And cuter."

With a flash of dimples, he strolled to the parking lot.

"Cheryl, your boyfriend is a hottie," said Ada. "When you're done, send him to my place. I could listen to police stories and look at that eye candy all day, that's for sure."

"Ada, really." Fred rolled his eyes.

"What?" Ada poked him. "Jealous?"

"Don't worry, Fred." I folded my arms. "Ada would soon learn Luke's about more trouble than he's worth."

"Too much man to handle?" Ada polished her fist on her polyester blouse. "I can take him."

"Nah," I said. "It's his family. They're the bunion on my family's heel. Always have been. We've always been rural route to their in-town address. Grandpa Ed said the Bransons walk like they've got a stick up their behinds and a crick in their necks from looking down their noses at us. But I'm hoping to fix that with my new job."

With a wave of Belvia's wand, the Bransons would look at the Tuckers differently. I smiled. But for that, I needed to find Della's killer. My smile faded. I hadn't done diddly in that respect.

"That boy's a Branson?" Ada fanned herself. "I'd never seen a Branson look that good."

"Step-Branson, actually. He takes after his real daddy."

"Ballards hold grudges worse'n anybody in the county though," said Fred.

"We call it remembering facts, not holding grudges." My finger rocketed skyward. "Did you forget John Branson Senior vetoed my Uncle Bug's nomination for town council? He hated the Ballards so much, John Senior went through the petition until he found Dan Cleermont had signed his nickname instead of his real name. Got Uncle Bug knocked right off the ballot. That's the kind of stuff they do."

"John Senior's been dead at least twenty years. So's your Uncle Bug." Fred laughed. "No, you don't hold grudges at all."

"Calm down, Cheryl," said Ada. "So your honey's a Branson. You'd only have to put up with them for holidays, birthdays, and every other Sunday."

"Luke doesn't like the Bransons. There's the kicker. JB's his stepdad. They've never gotten along."

Ada sucked in her breath. "JB? He's worse'n John Senior. I can't imagine any kid calling him grandpap, let alone one of yours. Better hope that Luke's worth it."

That thought had not crossed my mind. But now it was out there, flashing red neon inside my skull. JB could be my future child's Papaw.

The Bransons' only grandchildren would be Luke's. JB's only son had passed a year ago.

No wonder my family felt hostile towards Luke.

"Cherry don't look so good," said Fred.

Ada cackled. "That poor Luke. I just ensured a white wedding, if they ever get that far."

# NINE

I needed air. Although there were plenty of oxygen tanks around Halo House, I went for fresh. And because I needed something residing in my brain besides Branson babies, I decided Della's murder would do the trick. I had a couple hours before the viewing and figured I'd get the ball rolling. Not knowing much about company politics, I began within my comfort zone. The scene of the crime.

The stretch of road where Della had been hit wasn't far from Halo House. Meemaw's Tea Factory had been built southeast of Halo on a thirty-acre spread, partially hidden in a small valley surrounded by pine-covered hills. The county highway had been recently paved, unlike the bumpy county road where Grandpa Ed's farm resided. Someone had erected a small white cross to mark the scene of the accident, and a bouquet of flowers had been laid next to it.

I parked my truck on the opposite side of the road and cut across the highway to stand by the cross. A chain-link fence ran the perimeter of Meemaw's property. With the narrow shoulder and the fence, Della wouldn't have had much of a chance to get out of the way.

"Why were you jogging here?" I muttered. "This may not be the city, but there's still enough traffic to make it dangerous."

Keeping my ears open to said traffic and my eyes open for scuff marks or tire tread, I sauntered along the shoulder. Reaching

Meemaw's Tea gates, I turned around and headed past the white cross. I had almost given up when I found a trampled area—likely made by deputy feet—and what might have been tread impressions.

The marks meant nothing to me, but I supposed Luke and his coworkers had lifted the area with Traxtone or another casting substance. However, if the white cross was a fairly accurate indication of where Della had been hit, it would seem the vehicle had driven onto the shoulder.

If Della had jogged out the gates and turned right onto the highway, she would have been running with the direction of traffic. More likely, she was at the end of her jog, headed back to the factory, and facing oncoming traffic. I didn't know Della, but I figured she was smart enough to watch for approaching cars in this way. Most joggers did.

The skid marks Luke had mentioned were located in the middle of the road. On the opposite side was another trampled area, but this time, I guessed it had been created by a vehicle making a wide turn. Like they had been facing Della and swerved from one shoulder to the other.

After hitting her head on? I spun toward the white cross, then looked over my shoulder toward the tire marks.

Or coming out of the factory, the vehicle had passed Della and made a wide turn to go back toward her. Thereby crossing the road to hit her from behind. Going southeast. At dusk, the accident couldn't be blamed on the sun.

Unless the driver had been out of their mind drunk, this first-degree homicide was murder.

No wonder Luke was keeping his mouth shut. This wasn't just criminal homicide; the evidence implied a malicious intent.


Near the scene of the accident, Meemaw's Tea gates stood open. I scuttled back to my truck and drove through the gates, but found the parking lot mostly empty and the front doors locked. A sign had been taped to the glass door announcing Della's visitation and date of the funeral. Inside a giant floral wreath on a stand had been set up near the empty reception area.

Trudging to my truck, I glanced over Belvia's list of company people. Thank the Almighty the list didn't include every person who worked at this huge factory. Mainly the board members, the company lawyer, and Della's assistant. A wave of anxiety crashed into me every time I looked at the sheet. Their positions were mostly initials. Initialed job titles didn't happen much in my world. Initialed names, all the time. But jobs tended to end in man. Policeman. Postman. Fireman.

I guessed the more money you made, the longer your job title.

Before I stepped into my truck, a golf cart whirred toward me and a security guard waved a hello.

"We're not open today," he called. "Shut down in honor of Miss Della. Most everyone's gone except for a few employees watching the tea kettles."

"It's nice to see some things are still more important than business," I said. "I was surprised so many people were gone."

"Did you know Miss Della?"

"Miss Belvia," I fudged. "She wanted me to check on a few things."

"Who did you want to see? Someone in the office? Donna Sharp's still here. She might help you."

"Isn't she Della's assistant? I figured she'd be at Halo House with everyone else."

"Been here all morning." The guard shrugged. "Always something to do, isn't there? Especially if you work for the Brakemans. You want me to get her on the horn?"

I waited while he radioed into the building, wondering why Donna Sharp hadn't left for the viewing. Hopefully she'd see me anyway. Della's assistant would have insights into the board mess and might point me toward someone who had wanted to rid Meemaw's Tea of the Brakemans. Likely, Luke had already talked to Donna, but he'd keep that information to himself. I hoped she'd reveal to me what she might keep from the police.

I still couldn't attune myself to the idea that a business person would turn to murder to resolve a company dispute. I always thought white-collar greed stuck to lying, cheating, and stealing.

"Looks like Donna left," said the guard.

"Guess I'll catch her at the visitation. Thanks."

He folded his arms on the golf cart steering wheel and shook his head. "You'll have to see her when she gets back."

"Gets back? From what?"

"Don't know. Amy in dispatch said Donna had to go out of town."

"Out of town?" I gave my brain a mental shake. "Donna Sharp's not going to her boss's viewing or funeral?"

"Dunno." He gave the brim of his hat an unneeded adjustment. "Any case, she's not here. Guess you'll be heading out?"

"Guess so." I clambered into my old yellow Datsun under the guard's watchful eye and then aimed the rusty pickup back toward Halo House.

By the time I returned, hired deputies had appeared to conduct traffic in and out of Halo House's parking area. The lobby had filled with a thick parade of Forks County citizens eager to pay their respects to the Meemaw's Tea family.

At one, Ada, Fred, and I scooted toward the banquet room where the viewing was held. A long line had wrapped through the halls, waiting for the banquet room doors to open. Unlike the three of us, most of the residents had queued early.

By one forty-five, the line hadn't moved.

"I'm gonna find out what's going on," said Ada. "Hold my place."

"Don't bother the family," said Fred.

"Fred, you worry too much. The banquet doors are still closed. Maybe someone doesn't know how to open them."

"You don't think they would ask the staff for help?"

"We're not all as brilliant as you, Fred."

"See what you can find out," I urged. "Hurry, though. I've got a bad feeling."

With a triumphant look, Ada marched up the hall. Five minutes later she returned.

"Belvia's not down yet," she said. "They're waiting on her call."

"Isn't someone with her?" The hair on the back of my neck rose.

Ada shook her head. "She wanted to be alone. She'll call Coralee when she's ready."

"Coralee's waiting inside?"

Ada nodded. "With the rest of the family and the head honchos from Meemaw's Tea."

"What about Miss Molly? She's not with Belvia?"

"I don't know Molly, so I didn't ask. But they said Battle-axe wanted time to herself."

"How long has she been alone?"

Ada shrugged. "When Battle-axe tells everyone to get out, you get out and wait for her call. We'll all be standing in this hallway until the cows come home if she decides she doesn't want to start."

"Hold my spot."

"Where are you going?" asked Fred.

"I'm popping up to Miss Belvia's."

"What don't you understand about her 'wanting to be alone'?" said Ada.

"If she kicks me out, she kicks me out," I said. "But I have a horrible feeling I've failed her." Before I even started.

Ada rolled her eyes with a wave of her hand. "According to Belvia, everybody's failed her at some point."

"Not like this."

# TEN

I found the door to Belvia's apartment unlocked and called out. When no one answered, I entered, leaving the door open behind me. I sped across the Spartan living room to the office. Cracking the door, I peeked inside, calling again. No Belvia. But her safe stood open.

My heart lunged up my throat.

Stacks of manila envelopes and jewelry-sized boxes filled the cavity. I couldn't tell if she'd been robbed. It didn't look like it, but Belvia was particular—I couldn't imagine her leaving a safe open.

Questions about the safe could wait. I needed to find Belvia.

Backing into the living room, I took the next ten steps in two flying leaps toward the back hall. A doorway opened onto a small closeted dressing area with two doors on either end. Hollering her name, I pushed open the door to my right and checked the neat, sparse bedroom, then reversed to the separate bathroom. The door stood slightly ajar but blocked. Pressing my face to the crack, I peered through and saw Belvia's black suited legs cock-eyed and sprawled on the floor.

"Hang on, Mrs. Brakeman," I called. "I'm getting help."

I ran into the bedroom. Found a phone on the bedside table. I pressed the first of the preprogrammed buttons. Della's voice asked to leave a message. I tried the second button. After three unanswered rings, I broke the connection. Hitting the third button, I was put on automatic hold at a law office.

"You've got to be kidding me," I shouted. "Why don't you have Halo House staff in your top three, Belvia?"

I dialed the sheriff's office. "Tamara, it's Cherry. I'm at Halo House. Room 200. I think a resident is dead or dying in her bathroom."

"Why in the hay are you calling me?" said Tamara. "They've got staff there. It'll be faster."

"I don't remember their number. And I'm panicking."

"Calm down. If the victim's not wearing their pendant, there should be an emergency pull in the bathroom."

"Can't get in the bathroom. Her body is blocking the door. Just call them."

"Already on it," said Tamara. "And sending an ambulance. Stay on the line, baby."

"I won't hang up, but I'm not staying on the line. This phone has a cord. A cord, for pity's sake."

I dropped the receiver onto the bed, sped back into the dressing area, and pressed my face against the crack in the bathroom door. "Miss Belvia," I shouted. "I've got people coming. Stay with me."

Two minutes later, two orderlies and a nurse appeared.

"Mrs. Brakeman's in there." I pointed. "But she's fallen and blocking the door."

One orderly ran from the room and reappeared with a toolkit and more people. Five minutes later, the door to the bathroom leaned against the wall and Belvia was surrounded by caregivers.

"What's going on in here?" Coralee strode into the small hallway, followed by Molly. Seeing the hubbub, Coralee hurried to the bathroom door.

Molly stopped in the hall entrance, wringing her hands.

I abandoned my position in the bedroom doorway to place an arm around Molly and led her into the bedroom. Sinking onto the edge of the bed, we watched the scene through the open doorway. A nurse shooed Coralee from the bathroom then received a scathing indictment on Coralee's rights "to see her mother."

"I understand," said the nurse. "But we need the space to work. We're doing everything we can."

"She's supposed to be downstairs at my sister's visitation. What happened?"

"I can't say right now. As soon as we can, we'll let you know."

"Can you save her?"

"Ma'am, why don't you have a seat? Give us a minute, please."

"Oh my God." Coralee turned from the bathroom, her hands covering her mouth. Seeing me, she dropped her hands. "What are you doing in here?"

"I'm sorry, Coralee. Why don't you sit down?" I stood and waved at the spot next to Molly. "I came when I heard your momma hadn't made it to the viewing."

"Mother said she'd call us. She wasn't feeling well." Coralee cast a glance at Molly, then tottered to the bed to sit next to her. "I did what she wanted. You don't question Mother."

Molly looked at me. "Belvia paged me a few minutes ago. I came up as fast as I could."

I thought about the numbers I had dialed. "That was me. I pushed her speed dial numbers, trying to reach the front desk. You didn't answer immediately so I pushed the next button. After getting her lawyer, I gave up and called the sheriff."

"The sheriff? Why did you even come here?" Coralee's eyes darted from me to the scene in the bathroom.

I glanced over my shoulder and saw a nurse shake her head.

My thoughts flew to my brother in Forks County Corrections, waiting on my miracle. The Wizardess hadn't yet granted my wish. Guilt clenched my gut. This wasn't about me. Poor Belvia had been taken before she'd gotten justice for her daughter. And maybe not by a natural death, as she feared.

"Your mother told me—" I stopped before I said, "she believed she could be murdered."

Coralee cocked her head.

"To check on her." I finished lamely, then swallowed my tears. "And I let her down. Will you excuse me?"

I left Coralee and Molly to comfort each other. Staying with the grievers would have fallen under Grandma Jo's "necessary duties." But I needed to take care of Miss Belvia's last requests, which meant another quick call to the sheriff's department. Someone needed to examine her office before five million more people trooped through her door. Miss Belvia had relied on my suspicious hunches and I needed to go with my gut on this one. For her sake.

With my phone pressed to my ear and my voice tuned to hush, I pushed open the office door and peered inside.

"Explain this to me," said Luke on the other end of the line. "I'm off duty. I should be sleeping. Why do you want me to look at Belvia Brakeman's apartment? Sounds like the staff is taking care of it."

"I don't like the timing. We were waiting for her to come down for Della's viewing."

"Sugar, she's ninety."

"Her safe was open, although it doesn't look like anything's missing. But her door was unlocked. It felt suspicious."

"It doesn't sound like a robbery. You think everything's suspicious."

"I know. Belvia really liked that." I sniffled. "Anyway, you're one of the officers investigating Della's hit and run. It should be you. Make sure everything's okay."

He let out a long sigh. "Actually, I'm not home, but nearby. I can be there in a few. Don't touch anything. If I'm coming, it'll be official."

The crash cart holding Belvia made its way through the living room and out the door. Molly hurried after the nurses, but Coralee didn't appear.

"What do I do if someone wants in her apartment?" I said. "Coralee is already here. More are sure to follow."

"Keep them out." He hung up.

"And how will I do that?" I muttered.

This was what I got for unraveling my scruples for Belvia.

Embroiled in another death. It didn't seem to matter what I did. Lately, it felt like God had sent me a personal pestilence of dead bodies.

I must be praying wrong.

As the staff exited Belvia's rooms, gawkers peered inside. The front door banged open and an older man walked in. Following him, another middle-aged man and Coralee's daughter, Pris. Her long-haired bearded companion wore wire-rimmed glasses, baggy pants, and a striped cardigan. Coralee's husband, Wally, I assumed. Behind them, I heard the murmurings of a growing crowd. Distant sirens blared outside.

I strode to the door to head them off. "I'm sorry, but y'all need to wait outside."

"Who are you?" The older man was dressed in a dark suit. His glasses looked designer, his receding hair styled. The suit flashy. He couldn't be from Halo. Or trying too hard if he was.

Atlanta, I thought. With the size of Belvia's company, Atlanta was a possibility.

"Cherry Tucker, sir. I'm the art teacher here. Police are on their way and they want the premises sealed until they arrive."

"Why are the police coming?" asked Wally. "I thought Belvia had a heart attack."

"Company policy."

"No, it's not," said the man, who apparently didn't need an introduction of his own. "Where's Coralee?"

"I'll get her if you step into the hall." My hands flapped toward the door. "Maybe y'all could go to Molly's apartment."

"Who?" said Wally.

"Miss Belvia's old assistant. Old as in retired. Although she is a senior." I cut off my babble to eyeball the stranger. "And you are?"

"Ron Newson. Della Brakeman's husband." His eyes narrowed behind the dark frames. "The goddamned bereaved."

"I'm sorry, Mr. Newson. But I just got off the phone with a sheriff's deputy. They do want this apartment sealed off for now. I'll find a place for you and your family to sit privately."

Ron Newson scanned the open office door behind me, then the living room. Before I could stop him, he tromped past me to the bedroom hall. Wally scurried behind him.

"Excuse me," I called, not entirely sure how to politely accost the bereaved for not following orders.

Pris shuffled a step toward them, then glanced at me. "I'll try to get them out."

"Thanks." I locked the apartment door and closed the office, then hurried after them. Their words reached me before I entered the suite's closeted area. Concerned with their tone and the use of my name, I backed around the corner to listen.

"...Cherry Tucker. Did she call the cops?" said Coralee. "I know my rights. It's suspicious, her being here."

"She's just doing her job," said Pris.

"She's the activities girl. Give me a break. It's not her job to worm her way into my mother's trust."

"You don't know that."

"I know you don't call the cops when someone has a heart attack. Particularly someone as old as Mother."

"Coralee's right," said Wally. "We don't do what the pigs say just because they want to look around. They could plant stuff, you know. We should be watching them, not the other way around."

"Dad—"

"And anyway," said Coralee, "who exactly is this Cherry Tucker? Ever since we got here, she's been hanging around Mother. Just like that Molly person. They're looking for handouts. If their names appear in that will, I'll sue."

"Molly worked for Grandmother."

"So what's she still doing here?"

"Let's talk about this somewhere else." Pris's voice skittered across the icy tension. "The police will be here any minute."

"This is my mother's apartment. I'm her daughter. I'm not leaving."

"I'm sure it'll only take a few minutes and then we can come back."

"It only takes a few seconds for the pigs to plant stuff," said Wally. "We can't let them in here."

"Maybe Mother paid off the cops," said Coralee. "It wouldn't surprise me if she asked them to take away evidence before the family can look at her papers."

"What are you talking about?" said Pris. "That's crazy."

"You think she and Della made that much money from sweet tea? I'm sure there's payoffs or something she wanted buried. Or money hidden in offshore accounts she doesn't want us to have. How would I know? Not like she ever told me anything."

"Mom, you didn't talk to her for thirty years."

I totally misjudged the paranoid in the family. The award went to Coralee. Or maybe Wally.

One voice hadn't offered an opinion. Which is what I got for listening at doors instead of doing my job. Sucking in my breath, I plowed through the hall and into the bedroom.

Coralee's head jerked. "Why are you still here? What in the hell is going on? You keep showing up and yet I'm not wanted? I'm her damn daughter. Who in the hell are you?"

Sprawled on the bed next to Coralee, Wally studied me. "It's okay, babe."

"It's not okay. Mother told me to—" Coralee's eyes narrowed. "I want to know what you and Mother were talking about yesterday."

"Not now," I said. "Where did Mr. Newson go?"

"He's in the bathroom," said Pris.

"Dammit." I amended my curse with an apology and sped to the bathroom.

The bathroom door had been taken off its hinges and leaned inside the doorway. Behind the door, Ron stood in front of the sink, staring at something in his hand. The medicine cabinet stood open.

"Did you open that?" I said, pointing to the cabinet. "What do you have? Did you find it in here?"

He placed a bottle in the cabinet and turned to face me. "What's it to you?"

"Sir, please don't touch anything. If you took something, put it back exactly where you found it. The police will—"

"You still haven't explained why the police want to check the apartment of a ninety-year-old woman who's had a heart attack. Do they not have anything better to do? Because they still haven't found the asshole who hit my wife."

"I am real sorry, sir, but due to the circumstances of your wife's death, the police want to examine—" I was reaching and he knew it.

Ron took three steps forward and shoved a finger into my chest. "You're lying and I'll have you fired. You've got no authority over me and you sure as hell know it. I'm not doing a damn thing you say. If the police have a problem with that, they can throw my ass out."

"Point taken," said a cool voice behind me. "And if you don't remove your hand from that woman, I will do exactly that."

# ELEVEN

I spun around and Ron's finger flew from my chest.

Luke stood next to the bathroom door, his hands resting on his hips. Behind his shoulder, Miss Krenzer craned her neck. Luke didn't glance at me, but Krenzer raised her eyebrows, giving the definitive "what do you think you're doing" look.

"Deputy Harper," I said. "This is Ron Newson. Miss Belvia's son-in-law."

"We're acquainted."

Ron folded his arms and resumed his hostile staring, but now toward Luke instead of me.

"Okay then." I slipped around Luke to stand next to Krenzer.

She grabbed my arm and backed us into the hallway. "What's going on? Why did you call the police?"

I attempted a "let's not talk while we're surrounded by the crazed family of a possible murder victim" look.

Her eyebrows drew inward and she opened her mouth to speak.

"I'll explain later," I whispered.

Ron Newson shoved past Luke. "What do the police have to do with my mother-in-law? She had a heart attack. Hell, I have people downstairs waiting to express their sympathy on the death of my wife. Why don't you catch the drunk who hit her instead of bothering us?"

"Pigs," shouted Wally, walking from the bedroom. "F. U. We know our rights."

"Dad." Pris's face reddened. She grabbed his arm, pulling him into the hall. "Come on."

With all the hostility and bodies, the hall felt tighter than an old pickle barrel. Closed-lipped and unmoving, Luke eyed everyone from his bathroom sentry. I took a cue from him to keep my mouth shut.

"I'm sorry about Mrs. Brakeman." Krenzer pasted on a face that put my best customer service smile to shame. "Why don't we get a cup of coffee in my office? I'm sure Deputy Harper will only be a minute. Everyone's understandably upset. People here for the viewing and now this? Such a shock. Let's go downstairs."

"I need a scotch, not a coffee," said Ron.

She patted his shoulder and gently pushed him toward the door. "That can be arranged."

Pris pulled on her father's sleeve, then took her mother's hand. "Come on. There's nothing you can do for Grandmother now. Go with Uncle Ron. I'll speak to the funeral staff if you'd like."

"Goddammit." Ron glanced over his shoulder at Pris. "Don't talk to any of the Meemaw's people. They can't know what's happened yet. This'll kick up a mile-wide shit storm."

Pris nodded. "Of course. I'll tell the funeral director we've been delayed and we'll make an announcement in a short while."

Krenzer waited for the four to move out the front door, then shot a look at me. "We're having a chat later," she whispered. "I need to get all these people out of my building first."

"Yes, ma'am." My fingers twitched my dress. "How's it looking down there with the viewing?"

"Bedlam. I shouldn't have agreed to have the visitation here. I knew it would be packed." She shook her head. "Of all the days for poor Belvia to pass, but that's how it goes, you know?"

I didn't think that's how it went, at least in Belvia's case. But I kept my mouth shut.

After the front door shut, I turned to Luke. "Sorry I couldn't get them out. Ron had taken something from the medicine cabinet. Did you see it?"

"Didn't see anything but his finger aimed at your chest," he growled.

We reentered the bathroom. Luke strode to the medicine cabinet and pulled a notebook from his pocket.

"I don't know if the cabinet door was open earlier," I said. "Belvia was blocking the door so I couldn't get in here. Once they got the door off the hinges, the staff took over the area. I didn't see a thing. Could have been opened by Belvia, the staff, or Ron Newson."

"It sounds like she had a heart attack," said Luke. "She probably opened it, looking for medicine, and then collapsed. Why are you worried about tampering?"

"With Della's death, Belvia was facing a lot of company problems. Problems I don't understand, but she made it sound like buzzards circling for a kill. There's also a huge inheritance at stake. Just seemed curious that Belvia'd have a heart attack in the wake of all that's going on."

"She's elderly, Cherry. And like you said, under a lot of stress. It could have brought on the heart attack."

Guilt stabbed me. I'd barely started the job and she'd already died on my watch. "What about the safe?" I blurted. "Because of her eyesight, Belvia puts everything away carefully."

"If she took ill in her office, she could have left the safe open, hon." Luke took a deep breath. "But let's check this place out. I'll do a walk-through with my camera, then ask the sheriff if he wants me to take evidence."

"Thank you. Our relationship was cut short, but I felt like Belvia understood me in a way other people don't." Whether I wanted to take the job or not, she'd asked for my help because she trusted my creative thinking and skeptical nature.

"I know not everyone gets you. I'm glad she did. I'm sorry she died, sugar." Luke gathered me into his arms, then kissed the top of my head. "Put your mind to rest now."

But I couldn't put my mind to rest. Not when Belvia's death lay on my conscience. I realized I'd already ditched my earlier misgivings. Belvia knew someone had murdered Della. Possibly herself too. And Belvia believed I could figure this out. The sheriff's office was limited by the law in their hunt. If correct in her hunch that the perp's wealth and power would stymie the investigation, Belvia did need someone free of red tape to sniff around Meemaw's Tea suspects. I planned to extend my hunt to the family too.

I'd complete my assignment for Belvia by finding Della's killer, even knowing there'd be no payoff. I'd failed Cody and failed Belvia, but I knew she'd still be counting on me to get her justice. Even from beyond the grave.

I waited in the living room while Luke stalked through the apartment, shooting the various rooms from different angles with his digital camera.

Returning from the bathroom, he slipped the camera into his deputy bag, rested his hands on his hips, and studied me without seeing.

I knew that thoughtful gaze. "What did you find?"

"There wasn't anything missing from the medicine cabinet. That was easy. Everything marked off and labeled. Don't know why the door was open, but she could have been reaching to take something when she fell. No heart medicine in there. General pain medication. Lidocaine patches, that sort of thing."

"Okay. But you saw something."

"Damn." Luke ran a hand through his curls and yanked on a tuft. The lock remained standing as his hand dropped back to his hip. "There's one folder in the safe that's empty. Unmarked."

I took one step toward the office before I lost two steps. Glancing at the hand on my elbow, I cocked my head and gave Luke a "what the hey" look.

"Hands off the office, sugar."

"I know."

"Then where are you headed?"

"Hon, I respect your position of authority. But I know that you know that Della wasn't hit by a drunk driver or someone blinded by the sun. She was murdered. And I'm worried her mother was too, even if it does look like a heart attack."

His jaw tightened. "I'm not saying anything about Della Brakeman-Newson's death. The sheriff doesn't want anything in the press. This is a high-profile case with persons of interest who will not take the limelight lightly."

Dammit, Belvia was right. It only strengthened my conviction to do the right thing by her.

"In other words," I smiled to soften my words, "you don't want anyone to lawyer up before you have solid evidence to bring them in. You're pretending a drunk driver could have hit Della Brakeman-Newson. Until you have strong evidence to prove otherwise."

"Pretending? We haven't said one word about a drunk driver, that's a rumor. We haven't said diddly squat except we're investigating a hit and run, which is true." He scowled. "We're getting ahead of ourselves with Belvia Brakeman. I can take evidence. Check for prints on the safe. But if the coroner says it's natural causes, it doesn't matter. Unless other hard evidence comes to light."

"Like you arrest whoever ran over Della and they admit to inducing Belvia's heart attack?" I smiled at his frown. "Deputy Harper, you know there are things I can check into that you can't. You've got your protocol as an officer of the law. I've got my protocol as the friend to a victim."

"What protocol are you talking about?"

"Remember Miss Belvia had me witness her will? She was vetting me for a particular task."

"What task?"

I didn't think he'd take kindly to "beat the sheriff's office in their investigation of a homicide." I took a moment to gather a better turn of phrase.

"Miss Belvia wanted me to interview certain Meemaw's Tea

personnel who've been causing her trouble. Get my take on them. She trusted my instincts for judging people."

"She certainly doesn't need that information now."

"I feel I should do it anyway, to pass on to the new leadership. And if anything pertaining to her or Della's demise comes to light—perhaps the slip of a wagging tongue?—I'll deliver that information to you."

"As long as you don't get in our way, I won't stop you. I'll warn you though. These 'interviews' will tick folks off. And I've found most of them tick off easy. The higher-ups particularly. Are you getting paid for this?"

I shook my head. "It was a private deal between me and Miss Belvia. Too bad, because her offer was something that could've benefited more than just me. To be honest, originally I was humoring her. I wanted the payoff but didn't take the task seriously. And I feel horrible about it."

He considered me for a moment. The stormy gray in his eyes lightened. "I'm glad you called me, sugar. I was nearby, saw the ambulance, and headed over anyway. But your call meant you thought of me and the law first."

His hand traveled from my elbow to squeeze my hand. A dimple deepened one cheek. I stepped toward him and angled my face up.

A gray-eyed baby with similar dimples popped into my head. Followed by the image of JB and Luke's mother cooing over the adorable bundle of joy.

Weird. I pulled my eyes off Luke's dimple, my fire suddenly cooled.

"You okay? You don't look so good all of a sudden." He grabbed my shoulder to steady me. "Is it the shock of finding Belvia?"

"I'm fine." I took a calming breath and blinked away the baby. "What about the safe?"

"Same deal as the medicine cabinet. I can check each of those envelopes to see if their insides are missing too. They're labeled.

However, if anyone took an envelope or anything else from the safe, I'll have no way of telling unless the safe has a contents list somewhere. And the empty folder? No idea if that's anything."

We edged into the office. Luke shuffled through the safe's envelopes and boxes, looking for missing contents. He dropped the empty folder on her desk.

"I don't know, Cherry." Luke ran a hand over his head, sending more curls askew. "My initial feeling is Belvia had just opened the safe when she took sick."

"There's a problem with that assessment."

"What's that?"

"This looks like the folder Belvia used for her new will. I saw Coralee place the folder in the safe. And we have no idea what was in the will I witnessed because Belvia made sure no one read it. Did you find a will in there?"

"I did not." Luke raked another fist through his hair. "Dammit."

# TWELVE

After a night spent painting away my anxiety, I woke with a completed sweet tea still life and a stronger grip on my resolve. Belvia would expect results, not moping. I had no real plan, other than making my way through her list of company suspects, but hoped I'd be struck by some investigative thunderbolt.

Or at least my suspicious intuition would kick in and point me toward a more effective method. Meanwhile, I had a class to teach. And students who excelled in hearsay. I was counting on them to help me with my list of family suspects.

At Halo House, still life drawing did not meet the interests of my students. Most had abandoned their drawing to sit in clusters and chat about Belvia's sudden departure in the wake of her daughter's viewing. I gave up on getting them to sketch fruit and settled in with my homies to sort out the shocking events.

"So sad about Belvia," said Fred. "Never thought she'd go like that. She was a tough old bird."

"Old birds gotta die sometime." Ada bent over her drawing. Her hand shook as she drew a lemon, then scribbled it out.

I leaned over Ada to hug her, but she shoved me away. "Get off, Chloe. I don't need your hugs. It's not like Battle-axe was inhuman."

"No, but you've known her most of your life."

"And I've hated her most of my life."

I pursed my lips. Ada's concentration on sketching lemons hadn't fooled me. She rarely participated in our art fundamentals class. At least not when it came to drawing. I would leave her be, but I could feel Ada's pain.

Hazel tossed her pencil and pushed her paper away. "Enough of this. What was that sheriff's deputy doing with you yesterday?"

"Nothing much." I picked up Hazel's abandoned pencil and set to shading her lopsided circle into an apple. Luke had sworn me to secrecy. The lightspeed of gossip at Halo House meant I needed to keep my mouth shut about Belvia's starring role in a suspicious death.

Unfortunately, keeping my mouth shut was harder than turning lopsided circles into apples.

"The deputy's her boyfriend," said Fred.

"Not officially. Our families don't approve, remember?"

"She doesn't want his kin fouling her genetic line," said Ada. "His step-daddy is a Grade-A sumbitch."

"But what's he doing here?" continued Hazel. "The other deputies stayed in the parking lot, directing traffic. I saw that one upstairs with you."

"Am I not allowed to bring boys upstairs?" I joked. "Were you spying on us?"

"More like you were spying on me." Hazel's mouth pulled tight. "Stop nosing into my affairs."

"Chloe ain't nosing into your business," said Ada. "Cool it, Hazel."

"You cool it, Ada." Hazel slid her chair back, eased to standing, and shuffled to the door.

"Wow," said Fred. "I've never seen Hazel leave in such a huff. She couldn't get away from you fast enough."

"Hazel's defensive," I said. "Somethings going on with her. Did y'all notice anything strange about her behavior lately? You think she's on new meds?"

"No." Ada shot the words out quicker than her usual rapid-fire twang. "So why was Deputy Harper in Belvia's apartment yesterday?"

I put Ada's hasty segue into my "check into this later" account and used a segue of my own. "Tell me more about Della's husband Ron and that side of the family. I've not been too impressed with Coralee or her husband, although I will say her daughter, Pris, is nice."

Ada took my bait with relish. "Ron hasn't worked in years. Unless you count 'managing their finances.' Della was focused solely on the company, so he plays, if you catch my drift."

"I get it." I examined the bruised banana and moldy apple I had drawn and sketched an inchworm creeping toward the fruit. "Why work when you don't have to? And why stay loyal to your wife if she doesn't pay attention?"

"I wish I were a kept man," said Fred. "That sounds pretty good."

The remark got him a few offers from widows within earshot.

He waved them away. "What Ron should have been managing was his son. Parker's a mess. Burned through his trust and likely will do the same with the inheritance from his poor momma."

"I guess he'll get more at Belvia's passing?" I mentally added Parker and Ron to my list.

"Probably," said Ada. "Although you never know with Belvia."

"Parker does visit Belvia a bit," said Fred.

"He's hoping it will pay off."

"You're so cynical, Ada."

"And you're naive, Fred."

Before their bickering grew into a full-blown feud, I interrupted. "Any news yet on how they'll do Della and Belvia's funerals? Will they wait on Della's now the viewing's canceled?"

"Cooper's doing Della's, of course," said Fred. "I suspect they'll use the same for Belvia."

"You think the ones who are left will spring for a separate event knowing Belvia's already paid for Della's?" said Ada. "It'll be a double funeral."

"A double funeral." I shook my head. "What is this world coming to?"

"That's life in the fast lane for Halo," said Fred.

"You know who'll have the details about the funeral?" I said. "Molly. I wonder how she's doing. This must be a horrible shock for her."

"Who's Molly?" said Ada.

"Belvia's retired assistant. Don't you know her? She moved to Halo House soon after Belvia. Belvia paid for Molly to move in next door in case she needed help."

"Figures Battle-axe wouldn't let her go. She kept her minions close and everyone else at arm's length."

Ada's bitter tone made me wonder if she had once been in Belvia's inner circle. "Minions over family?"

"Except Della, but Della had been cast from Belvia's mold."

"Coralee too," said Fred. "Except Coralee did the unthinkable and left."

"Kicked out," said Ada.

"Left, then kicked out," said Fred. "For a hippie commune."

"Don't think it was hippies."

"Either way." I held up my hands. "Della's out of the picture and now Coralee's back."

"Looks like Belvia's out of the picture too." Ada sighed.

"That's what worries me."

I found Molly in her apartment. She had cast off her suit and pearls for a magenta sweat suit dotted with crystals and sequins. I had to catch myself before my eyes watered and embarrassed her. She led me inside her figurine-crammed living room.

"I'm sorry for your loss," I told her. "I can't imagine what you must be feeling. You've known Belvia for so long."

"Thank you. At our age, it's to be expected, but still hard to let people go." She motioned for me to sit. "Did they find out what happened to her?"

"It sounded like a heart attack."

"Poor Belvia." Molly shook her head. "She never did slow down. And it's starting up again. Coralee keeps calling me, wanting me to set up a new meeting with the board members so she can make an announcement. And help with Belvia's funeral. Della's assistant isn't around."

"Coralee wants to call a board meeting already? And wants you to plan the funeral?"

Her eyes filled with tears. "Belvia needed me to check in on her. That was okay. I didn't even mind helping Belvia with Della's funeral plans, but this is too much." Her hand fluttered. "I'm sorry. It's been a long week."

No wonder Belvia wanted me to keep an eye on Molly. It sounded like she suffered from "can't say no" syndrome and Coralee was taking advantage.

I took Molly's hand and squeezed. "You leave Coralee to me. Turn off your phone for a while. Is there anyone to check on you?"

"There's just me. Sister and I never married. She had her career too, until she took sick and passed. We enjoyed living together. I was grateful Belvia bought this apartment so I wouldn't have to be alone. She promised to keep it in her will. I suppose I'll find out later if I get to stay..." Molly passed a hand over her teary eyes. "You must think I'm terribly selfish, worrying about my apartment when my friend just died. I've been in a state."

"No, ma'am. I'd be anxious too. But I'm sure Miss Belvia's word is good."

"That's true." Her smile wobbled. "Belvia always followed through."

"She'd promised me something too, if I completed a task for her. Said she'd ensure it somehow. I was thinking in a will..." Embarrassed, I waved away the thought. "Never mind. Now it's my turn to feel selfish."

"What did you mean, dear?" Molly's brows drew inward.

"You've got enough to worry yourself. I'm being silly." I reached for her hand again and patted. "I'll check on you. You've got friends here."

"Thank you."

I glanced at a framed picture on the side table while Molly

reached for a tissue to blot her eyes and nose. The sepia-toned photograph of two little girls in sailor dresses and bows had been tinted to add pink to their bows, cheeks, and lips. "That's adorable. Is that your sister? Y'all almost look like twins."

"We're eighteen months apart." Molly picked up the frame and handed it to me. "Sister had darker hair, but people often got us confused."

"My sister, Casey, and I are eighteen months apart too. We don't look anything alike, but they still get us mixed up." I handed her back the frame. "What was your sister's name?"

She took a deep breath and sighed. "Maggie."

A knot formed in my throat. Belvia had mentioned that poor Molly had lost her sister about six months earlier. Now her mentor too. "I hope you can make friends here, Molly. Halo House has a lot going on. Why don't you join my art class?"

"Not now. But thank you, dear. When everything settles. I'm not ready."

"I understand." I pushed off the couch, then held up a hand to keep her from standing. "I'll show myself out. Just rest. This has been a rough week. You deserve a break."

"Thank you, Cherry."

"And don't worry about Coralee. I'll take care of everything."

My previous business experience was a failed art studio, specializing in portraits. And classical-styled pieces no one wanted to buy. Mostly because they were nudes and the studio was located in Halo, Georgia, where art is often bought in Piggly Wiggly parking lots or at craft fairs. Despite three thousand years of art history, the showing of skin in a painting—men or women's—sent most of Halo into an apoplectic tongue-wagging frenzy. As opposed to a buying frenzy, which would have kept my art studio afloat.

Although the classic nude did seem popular with my Halo House students. Apparently, for the wrong reasons.

Anyway, I didn't know shinola about the corporate world and

needed an education in business ASAP. Particularly to unravel the mysterious initials accompanying everyone's names. Halo House had a library. Not a public library, but one of those rooms with a fireplace, comfortable chairs, and card tables. Like something you'd see on one of those PBS miniseries where rich people read books. The rich people at Halo House read books, but mostly they used the library for dominoes and bridge.

However, the library also had five rarely used computers. The residents had abandoned desktops for the newfangled tablet PCs. Harder to type on, but someone from the local electronic shop, Gizmo's, had taught a class on how to use voice commands. Now everyone walked around with iPads, shouting at Siri to open *CSI* on Netflix.

I still had a flip phone and an old Apple iMac. And no internet because of the aforementioned failed art studio.

One table had been pulled near the library door, partially blocking the entrance. The woman sitting behind it had thick glasses, hair styled like Einstein's, and wielded a rubber stamper.

"Do you have a library card?" she said.

"No, ma'am. I'm just using a computer for a minute." I flashed my volunteer badge. I could see the empty computer carrels beyond the wall of shelves holding large-print titles and the take-and-share paperbacks.

"You can't check out a book without a library card."

"Yes, ma'am."

"And please whisper."

The only other people in the library were this woman and a foursome playing canasta. And the canasta group wasn't whispering.

"Yes, ma'am."

Appeased, she scooted the table to the left.

Google found me the Meemaw's Tea webpage. The company founder was Belvia Brakeman. Her daughter, Della Brakeman-Newson, was in charge of operations, giving her the title COO. Aside from the initials, I made a mental note to file that under "things I already knew." The website touted the wonders of Meemaw's Tea and Meemaw's Tea family values. I mentally filed those under "things that don't help me none."

The professional photo of the Meemaw's Tea board accompanied photos of the big tea players accepting awards and doing charity work. I checked Belvia's list of possible tea-haters against the company photo. As an assistant, Donna Sharp did not get website exposure. Nor did Molly Kern. However, the board members on Belvia's list had a lot of coverage on the Meemaw's Tea website. Company glamor shots and photos of them in Santa hats passing out gifts and bottles of sweet tea to underprivileged children.

I hoped they included toothbrushes in their stockings.

Two of the board members—Lisa Russell, Director of Human Resources, and David Wells, Director of Accounting—had even more coverage in the financial news outside the company website. Both Lisa and David were emphatic about Meemaw's Tea leadership changes. With a few potshots directed at each other. And most of the comments made public after Belvia's retirement announcement in a recent *Wall Street Journal* article.

I filed those items under "very interesting" and "you should talk to Lisa Russell and David Wells."

Next, I googled Donna Sharp. Facebook said Donna was going on vacation. I wanted to congratulate Donna on letting local burglars know her house would be empty for a week. And at the same time ask her why she was going on vacation instead of to her boss's funeral.

Did Della's death warrant R&R? I would think Meemaw's Tea would depend on Donna at a time like this.

Google gave me Donna's address. I hoped to catch her before she left for her beach house. I didn't like the thought of possibly losing my best source of info on Della.

Nor did I like the thought of Della's assistant absconding after Della's murder. And Belvia's.

# THIRTEEN

I found Donna Sharp's vacation plans odd in light of what had happened. It was one thing to tell the office she had to catch a flight. But then to make a public announcement on Facebook after her boss had died in a tragic accident? Stupid and callous.

I wouldn't think stupid and callous would make it into the Brakeman inner circle. Something was up with this woman.

Someone else thought the same. As I pulled onto Donna Sharp's quiet street, I noted a familiar black 4x4. An off-duty someone else. Or someone doing plainclothes detective work.

That thought sent a delicious shiver through me.

I parked beside Luke and he rolled down his window to greet me. The setting winter sun reflected in his aviator sunglasses. The rosy, amber hues produced a pretty complement to his dark curls. But the cop shades also kept me from ascertaining the degree of his surprise at seeing me in Donna's neighborhood. I figured it somewhere between what-the-hell and I-should-have-known-she'd-show-up-here.

"What are you doing?" His voice registered in a cool cop pitch. He wasn't giving anything away, although I detected a slight uptick in the corners of his mouth.

"Seeing if Donna's around. Coralee's trying to get Molly to come out of retirement. I want to help Molly. I figured Donna might know what to do."

True according to my previous conversation with Molly, by the way. Or at least true enough to cover my butt from interfering in an "active investigation."

"Donna Sharp's supposed to be on vacation."

"Then why are you here?" I winked. "I now have a hunch she's hiding out at home."

"A hunch, huh?" Luke pursed his lips, then flashed me a smile. "Tell you what, knock on her door and ask for a cup of sugar. Tell me what happens."

I pulled in a breath. "Really?"

"Sure, nothing against the law with asking for a cup of sugar. I want to know who's in the house with her and I've got to report in soon. She probably won't answer." He lowered his sunglasses to appropriately eyeball me with his flinty grays. "If Donna does answer, don't go to any extremes. Don't barrel through the door. See if she'll invite you in. Just talk to her about the Molly predicament and let your gaze wander. Watch how Donna acts and look around for evidence of anyone else there."

"Like who?"

"A Brakeman in-law."

"I betcha I know which one." I sucked in my lips, thinking of flashy Ron Newson. "That sumbitch. His wife's body isn't even laid to rest."

"Sugar?"

"Yeah?"

"When you knock on her door, don't rub your hands together and cackle. That look in your eye makes me nervous."

I saluted Luke and puttered to the end of the cul-de-sac. Donna lived in a small community on the outskirts of the county seat, Line Creek. Access to the interstate meant most homeowners worked in Atlanta. These neighborhoods made me sad. No children playing outside. The lawns looked professionally groomed. Neighbors who probably weren't even friends on Facebook.

In that case, they wouldn't know Donna had allegedly gone on vacation. Her staycation would be the perfect place to hide. From whom? And why? Molly said Donna expected a big promotion. Or was that canceled when Della didn't make it to CEO?

I parked in Donna's empty drive and strode up the sidewalk to her front door, pulling my fleece hoodie tight. By all accounts, she didn't look home. I knocked and to my surprise, the young woman answered. In sweats. With her dark hair pulled into a sloppy ponytail. I expected something more appropriate from the "I'm doing my dead boss's husband" line of apparel.

Which would be, I don't know, satin or silk? Something trimmed in feathers?

"Yes?" Donna's brown eyes were puffy and, like her nose, red.

I adjusted my attitude toward Donna. Bless her heart, she wasn't very good at hiding out. If that's what she was doing.

"Hey, Donna. Sorry to interrupt you. I'm Cherry Tucker, a friend of Molly Kern's. I guess you heard about Belvia."

Donna jerked a quick nod and pressed her trembling lips together.

"Molly's having trouble with the Brakeman family asking her to do business-related work. She's grieving herself. I'd like to help her out and thought you might know what to do. Can I come in?"

"Um." Donna glanced behind her.

I followed her gaze but couldn't see past the small foyer.

"I'm trying to stay out of things right now."

"I totally understand." Which I didn't. "Everyone thinks you're on vacation." Which she wasn't. "You need time to yourself." During a crisis at work.

Her hunched shoulders drooped and her breathy voice became whispery. "I couldn't face everyone. They won't leave me alone."

"Who won't leave you alone?"

Again, Donna glanced over her shoulder.

I craned my neck to see around her and she body-blocked me.

Her voice grew louder. "Thanks for dropping by, Cherry. I appreciate your sympathy. That's very neighborly, but I am leaving on vacation in a few minutes."

"For real?"

She nodded like a jackhammer had switched on in her neck. "Yes. For two weeks. Tell Molly, HR will get a temp to help out in the meantime. If the temp's good, they'll hire them permanently."

"Molly said you were getting a promotion. Were you going to follow Della when she took over as CEO or something else?"

"I was. But with Della's accident, we didn't think...I mean, I didn't think it appropriate to stay on."

"I'd think they'd need your help in this time of transition. Who would know better how the company works than the assistant to the Chief of Operations?"

Donna's face flushed to match her nose and puffy eyes. "I dropped off my resignation letter at the office today."

"Is that why 'they' won't leave you alone? Because they need your help and you won't give it?" I dropped my voice to a whisper. "Or are 'they' bothering you because you know what happened to Della?"

"No." Her hands flew to her mouth, covering her cry.

Behind the wall, a distinct cough sounded.

Donna glanced over her shoulder, then grabbed the doorknob. "So I have to go. On my vacation. Tell Molly I said good luck."

I shoved my boot in the jamb. "Donna, if you're not around to help, you know folks will call Molly to ask her how this and that works. The same thing happened to my Grandma Jo. Molly is in her eighties. It's not fair to have all this dumped in her lap. She's genuinely grieving Belvia."

"I'm genuinely grieving too." Fat tears rolled down Donna's cheeks. "I can't help Molly. I'm sorry." She shoved the door against my foot.

I slipped out my boot and stepped off the small porch. The door slammed shut. To my left, trimmed hollies burgeoning with bright berries surrounded a bay window. With a quick glance around, I edged toward the window. A sliver of interior light poured through a crack in the heavy curtains. I sidled between the prickly hollies and peeked through the slit in the drapes. Even with her back to the window, Donna's folded arms, bent head, and hunched shoulders proved her grief was no act.

Wearing another slick suit, Ron Newson approached Donna. He placed a hand on her shoulder and appeared to speak. Donna trembled. Gathering her into his arms, Ron pressed her head against his shoulder and rubbed her back. He continued his murmurings but had cast his eyes to the ceiling.

His gaze dropped and fell on the crack in the curtain.

I froze.

Ron's eyes narrowed and trapped me in his hardened gaze.

Donna's head lifted, and he pulled his attention from the window to her.

I backed out of the hollies and ran to my truck.


Luke followed me from Donna's subdivision to a nearby barbecue joint, The Speedy Pig. He grabbed sandwiches and Cokes while I settled into his Raptor 4x4. While I split up the BBQ booty, he slipped an arm over the seat back and waited, knowing I'd put food before factualizing.

"You were right." I unwrapped a sandwich and took a deep bite of pulled pork. My words were muffled by porky goodness. "Ron's with Donna. They looked chummy. She'd been crying."

Luke caught a tendril of my hair and wound it around his finger. "What'd you tell her?"

"The truth. That she needed to help Molly. Which Donna refused to do."

"Why's that, do you think?" A soft smile played on his lips as he studied me.

"Because Ron was there, listening. Donna said people wouldn't leave her alone and assumed I knew who she was talking about. She wouldn't clarify. And she skipped the visitation to turn in her resignation."

"Interesting." Luke let me finish off my last bite of pulled pork but caught my fingers before I had a chance to lick them clean. "Promise me something."

"What?" I curled my sticky fingers around his. "Don't say drop this business about Belvia Brakeman. I've got to see it through. I promise I won't step on your toes. I'll tell you everything I learn."

"That's not what I meant." He shook his head. "It's about the information I left you the other day."

Billy Branson's arrest and parole records and current address. Luke's secret investigation to get Shawna off our backs. Shawna, like the rest of Halo, thought her daddy had run away with my mother. Luke had found proof that Billy had landed in prison instead. Whether it had anything to do with Christy Tucker or to where she had disappeared was still a mystery. Ten months later, she sent us baby Cody. Leaving him with unanswered questions, namely his paternal parentage.

Unfortunately, Cody decided forcing Shawna to do a DNA test would give him the answers he wanted.

"Talk to Shawna about her father. Soon," said Luke. "It might change her mind about her kidnapping allegations since it clears Billy Branson's involvement with your mother. As law enforcement, let alone Cody's arresting officer, I can't reveal I got you this information from the DMV and warrant databases. That would complicate your brother's case worse than it already is. I'm sorry, sugar, but you have to do this without me."

Dammit. If I'd kept Belvia from dying, or at least solved Della's murder first, this wouldn't be an issue.

Shame flooded me. But I didn't want to talk to Shawna about anything, let alone be the bearer of bad daddy news.

"About that. There's been a development that makes this a bit trickier."

He dropped the curl to slide his hand to the nape of my neck. "What development?"

My gaze flew to the window. "It's Todd."

"What about McIntosh?"

The air grew noticeably colder. Despite the heat blasting from the Raptor's vents.

"Todd went on a date with Shawna."

I looked over just as the expression on Luke's face crossed from wet hen to crowing rooster. I couldn't tell if he was choking or trying not to laugh.

A moment later a long breath wheezed from his nose. "Shawna's going out with Todd? What is she thinking?"

"What is *she* thinking? What's Todd thinking?" I jerked away from Luke's hand. "Todd's going bowling with the enemy. Shawna's up to something and poor Todd got sucked in by her—" I gestured with my hand.

"Her what?"

I gestured again. With more swoops.

A bubble of laughter erupted.

I punched him.

"Lord Almighty," he said. "I'd pay good money to see those two on a date."

"It's not funny. Think about what this'll do to Cody. He's sitting in jail while his best friend is consorting with the very woman who put him in there. Todd's lost his mind and I've got to help him get it back."

"Hold on one minute. Todd's a big boy and if he wants to date Shawna, you've got to let him. This may be good for us. If Shawna's getting—Ow." He rubbed his arm where I slugged him. "What I meant to say is if Shawna's happy, she'll be more receptive to speaking with you. And drop the charges against Cody."

"I don't know how she'll take the news that her daddy's been in the state pen. Twenty years for criminal trespass and home invasion burglary? And now Billy Branson's out and lives a county over? She'll think I'm blackmailing her."

"If you put it that way, yes. We need to work on your social skills. Why don't you say," he cleared his throat, "'Shawna, this whole mess with the charges of Cody kidnapping you has been one big misunderstanding, and I wanted to get to the root cause so we can end it.'"

"I do not sound like that."

Ignoring me, he continued in the falsetto drawl, "'Cody wanted to know if y'all were a DNA match, but only because he found those photos of our mother with your daddy. He's never known who fathered him. But I found out where Billy Branson's been and why he hasn't contacted you. Let's put the past behind us. You don't want a twenty-one-year-old to spend his life in jail because he's just looking for his parents, do you?'"

I folded my arms. "Shawna will never believe I'm sincere."

"You could try." Luke caught my hand and kissed my knuckle. "For us."

"It won't work." Luke was a fixer. He couldn't help himself. But finding Shawna's father wasn't a magic bullet.

"Lay out the truth to her. If she doesn't change her mind, at least it'll be out in the open. Neither of you can move forward with your lives without knowing what happened to your parents. I know Billy Branson isn't your mother, but now you know she hasn't been with him for the last twenty years. That's something." He placed my hand on his shoulder and drew me closer. "Whatever happens, we'll get through this."

"I hope so."

"I know so. Cherry, I—" His gray eyes darkened from gentle rain to summer storm. Pulling me closer, he bent his head. Soft lips slid over mine, tasting like barbecue with his special kick of heat. Strong yet gentle hands tangled in my hair and skated down my back.

I tightened my grip on his shoulders before sliding my hands into his luscious curls. "Luke."

"I know."

We couldn't voice the words. Yet. We both hated the vulnerability. For different reasons. Our future was uncertain. But everything felt right in the world when he wrapped his arms around me. Here, walls between us fell and a new one emerged, surrounding and protecting us. Our own domain. We'd made progress. Getting my brother out of jail would help.

Our domain had an incredible furnace. I unzipped my coat.

Luke sighed and deepened the kiss.

I closed my eyes.

The gray-eyed baby appeared. Wearing a Georgia Bulldog onesie. And this time, he had a twin whose fair hair and cornflower blues matched mine. They giggled and cooed in JB and Wanda's arms. And in my mind's darkest place, I watched them take those babies away.

And never felt more vulnerable.

I jerked, ramming my forehead into Luke's nose, and slid off his lap. Scrambling for an excuse that didn't include baby hallucinations, I said, "I expect you've got to get to the sheriff's office and clock in."

Luke rubbed his nose. The summer storm had quieted and winter clouds had crept in. "Something wrong?"

"Oh, no." I swung open the passenger door and leaped from his truck. "Just don't want to make you late. Thank you for the sandwich and good luck with the investigation. See you later."

I swung the door shut, clambered into my Datsun, and cranked the motor.

It wasn't until I was halfway home I realized I forgot to tell Luke that Ron Newson had seen me spying through Donna's window.

# FOURTEEN

The next morning, Hazel didn't show for my drawing class. Neither did two of the four men who had signed up. Made apparent by the remaining women who pointed out that fact to me as I explained the day's lesson.

Surrounded by the remaining women, Fred cheerfully picked up his charcoal pencil and focused on "planar analysis and line variation using drapery." The class grumbled but arranged their cloth and began sorting shadow from light on the heavy paper I had passed out.

Except for Ada.

"This is not good, Chandra," said Ada. "You lose the men and you'll lose the gals too."

"Ada, honey, I'm Cherry. Remember?"

Ada rolled her eyes. "I thought you wanted us to bring in material for modeling. Why don't you use this stuff for togas instead? You'll get the men back." She hung the blanket over her shoulder and minced across the floor like she worked a runway.

"Y'all aren't ready for the human form. I promised I'd take this job seriously. We'll do gesture drawing soon though. I promise."

"Ada, sit down," said Fred. "All that moving around is changing my light."

"Give me a break. Your light is the overhead fluorescents." She held the blanket before her face and peeped around it. "Draw me, Fred."

"You'll break my paper."

I fought off a shudder. Ada's drapery peek reminded me of Ron Newson spotting me the night before. "That gives me an idea. Come with me, Ada." I pulled her into the back of the room. The students abandoned their drawing to watch us. I motioned for them to follow. "Ollie, you and Martha hold up these blankets like so. And Ada, stand back there."

Ollie and Martha held their cloth above their heads. A small gap appeared between the hanging blankets. I stood before the crack and peered through.

"Ada, can you see me?"

Ada waved. "This beats drawing. What are we playing at, Chandra?"

"I want to know if I could be spotted peeking through a window." As I said the words, I realized my mistake.

The class hooted. Martha dropped her blanket. Ollie turned bright red.

"It's not what you think." I held up my hands.

Ada glanced from Ollie to me. "Even it were true, you wouldn't be the first, Chandra."

Ollie beat a fast exit and a groan emerged from the females.

Ada smirked. "I think Ollie left to sign up for hot yoga."

"Why?"

"He claims delirium from medication, but Ollie's been known to peek at unsuspecting dressers in the women's locker room."

I slapped a hand against my face. "Y'all don't live in a retirement home. Halo House's more like an ongoing Roman bacchanalia."

"Then let us draw that and be done with it. Ancient Rome is classical, ain't it?"

I stopped my eyes from rolling to watch my students and their blankets leave.

Ada waited until only Fred remained, shading in drapery folds by his lonesome. "Chandra, what was that thing with the blankets really about?"

I hesitated, knowing Ada's gossip superpowers, but she

seemed serious. Unusually so. "I went to see Della Brakeman's assistant last night. She was upset, but someone was with her. I took a peek to see who it was and that someone might have seen me through the living room curtains."

"And that someone was Della's husband?"

Fred looked up from his drawing. "You're pretty sharp, Ada."

"Ron might not have seen you if it was dark outside. Or at least, he might not be able to identify you. You're lucky they didn't call the police though."

"There was a deputy in the neighborhood. He actually sent me to check on Donna."

"Is that your Romeo?" She winked. "What's he think about having a Peeping Tom for a girl?"

"I'm not a Peeping Tom. But he doesn't know about Ron seeing me either."

"I'd be careful," said Fred. "Ron's got money and clout. If he thinks you know about his affair, he may try something. Plus, he's waiting on Belvia's will. She could be vengeful. I wouldn't doubt she'd have some clause in there about fidelity for her daughters' spouses."

Belvia was vengeful enough to hire a suspicious-minded artist to find her daughter's killer. I nodded in agreement. "Do you think Ron is dangerous?"

"Even a lapdog will snap if you try to take away its bone, hon." Ada patted my back. "You watch yourself. And not just with Ron. Anyone with a stake in Belvia's empire will be doing whatever they can to protect their claim."

"I made a promise to Belvia to help her with something."

"Anyone with any sense would stay away from the Brakemans." Ada shrugged. "But go on, do-gooder. It's your funeral."


My suspect list wasn't getting any shorter. In fact, by adding the Brakemans, it had grown in length. I itched to whittle down the list.

The Meemaw's Tea bigwigs would've returned to work by now. I pointed the Datsun in that direction and hoped at least one would show obvious signs of homicidal mania.

Just to make things easier. For Belvia's sake.

In Meemaw's Tea factory lobby, I examined the double funeral wreaths and the updated announcement written by Meemaw's public relations department.

Two horrific murders that had decimated Meemaw's Tea leadership in just under two weeks. That was my spin, anyway. The PR department's announcement described the tragedy as "sudden deaths of our beloved founders."

"When are the funerals?" I asked the receptionist.

The older woman shook her head. "We don't know yet. It's so tragic."

"I heard Donna Sharp quit. Did they find her a replacement yet? I'm a friend of Molly Kern. She's concerned."

"I'm not sure about Donna, but how is Molly?" asked the receptionist. "I haven't seen her in ages, not since she had to retire. She was in recently, but I missed her."

"She's taking Belvia's death pretty hard."

"Of course, they were close. Molly was the only person who Belvia trusted as much as Della. I think Molly's retirement is what determined Belvia's decision to finally step down. Poor Molly, her sister's passing took the wind out of her sails. I don't think Belvia wanted to work without Molly."

"Molly worked into her eighties. Isn't that almost twenty years past normal retirement? And Belvia was ninety."

"But she didn't act ninety. They loved Meemaw's Tea. Both rarely missed a day of work even with Molly's heart problems and Belvia's glaucoma. It was their life." She sighed. "I'm sure Della would've done the same. Probably why she exercised so much. To stay healthy."

Hard to argue that point. It almost seemed Meemaw's folks were expected to work until death. Literally. I asked to see Lisa Russell. Maybe her outspokenness about "seeking new leadership for the next generation at Meemaw's" wasn't unreasonable. Maybe she felt folks should retire by seventy-five or so.

"If you don't mind my asking, did Della often jog during working hours?" I said after the receptionist finished her call to Lisa Russell's office.

The receptionist didn't seem surprised at the question. I supposed when someone's struck while jogging, the topic came up. "Sure. We have a gym here at the company, but Della didn't like to use it."

"Why's that?"

She blushed and fidgeted with her rings. "Della and Belvia liked to keep themselves separated from everyone else."

"Della would rather run along a highway than work out with y'all?"

"I think she liked to jog to clear her head." The receptionist flashed me a bashful smile. "But that's why Molly and Donna were invaluable to them. They were the human link between the Brakemans and the company. Molly was really missed when she retired."

Human link. I wasn't mistaken in feeling Belvia had given off regal vibes. Maybe she and Della had given one too many "let them eat cake" remarks for their employees' liking.

# FIFTeeN

Lisa Russell, Human Resources Director, had human resources of her own. An assistant who seemed terrified of her, shooting down my hope that Lisa Russell would be the reasonable Meemaw's Tea personnel who could explain her public backstabbing of Belvia as a misunderstanding and misrepresentation by the press. There seemed to be a plethora of people with motives for ousting the Brakemans from their empire.

That was the problem with empires.

"Are you sure you made an appointment?" The young woman's hand trembled above the phone. Possibly because she forgot to breathe while she spoke. "Ms. Russell's very busy and I don't see your name on her list and I can't let you in if you don't have an appointment."

"Tell her I'm Miss Belvia's new assistant."

The girl gaped. "But ma'am. Mrs. Brakeman? You know? Passed?"

"I'm a predeceased hire. But still recent."

I saved her the trouble of calling and rapped on Lisa Russell's door. The office phone buzzed. The girl babbled. Lisa Russell let me in. With a healthy dose of suspicion.

Seemed Belvia hired more besides me based on that personality trait.

Lisa Russell also looked as competent as Belvia Brakeman. Of course, she was younger, but she had the power suit, intelligent countenance, and brisk no-nonsense attitude that spelled Brakeman material.

Just like the attitude Molly had before Belvia's death, I thought. Poor Molly.

"How are you possibly a new hire for Belvia?" Lisa demanded. "I run HR and all hires go through me."

Lisa Russell liked to cut to the chase. I did too. But I couldn't let Lisa Russell know she'd made Belvia's list of possible murder suspects.

"I had a personal relationship with her, ma'am. I admit I fudged the explanation to your assistant, but she seemed in need of a simpler answer than I was prepared to give."

"What exactly are you doing for Belvia?"

"I'm protecting her interests."

Lisa blew an irritated sigh out of her nose. "And what do you want from me?"

"For Belvia, I'm also protecting Molly Kern's interests. She's having some issues with Coralee Brakeman wanting to put her back on the job. Molly's distraught with these deaths. She's in no position to return to work."

"Of course not. Molly must be in her eighties."

Thank the stars I wasn't the only one who thought passing the three-quarters-of-a-century mark should get you out of hard labor.

"But," Lisa continued, "I have to be careful about age-related suits. Her age is not a factor in whether she can do the job."

"Jiminy Christmas, aren't there any elderly labor laws? Or do we only protect children from overwork?"

Lisa's forehead crinkled. "Is that a joke? Because legal issues are no laughing matter."

"If only they were." I sighed. "Molly doesn't want to work. I asked Donna Sharp to see if she could help out."

"Donna no longer works here."

"That's what Donna told me too." I gave Lisa a chance to fill in any details, then gave up waiting. "She said y'all would get a temp?"

"That's standard practice."

"So what can I do about Coralee Brakeman bugging Molly? Is there a phone number and name I can give Coralee?"

"Coralee is not an employee of Meemaw's Tea. She may own some stock, but she isn't on the board. There's no reason to give Coralee any information."

"She's trying to get Molly to put together a board meeting or something."

"Preposterous."

"Maybe so, but it's still happening. And I've got to do something to make her leave Molly alone."

"Restraining order?"

Now she can make a joke. Some comedian. But only at Coralee's expense. Did I detect some anti-Brakeman hostility? "I take it Coralee isn't welcome to step into her sister's shoes?"

"Is that what Coralee told you she was doing?" Lisa's voice sharpened.

"Coralee hasn't told me anything. But here she is. Prodigal daughter and whatnot."

"Prodigal, my ass. Pardon me." Lisa's fair features reddened. "But that's all I need. Another Brakeman trying to interfere with our growth."

"Didn't Della and Belvia want growth?"

"Of course, they wanted revenue growth. But they wanted change through internal, not external, growth."

"External like going public? I saw your interview in the *Investor's Business Daily*." Where she had publicly criticized the founder and president.

"Changing from a private company to a public corporation is an example of external growth. So is a merger." Her chin rose. "And bringing in fresh talent. Family companies can be successful, but they can also stagnate without new people."

"I guess you can implement your ideas now." I studied her reaction. "Unless Coralee gets involved."

She glanced away.

"What happened on the day Della died?"

"Nothing." Her eyes snapped back to me. "I already talked to the police. What's going on here?"

"Just curious. Such a tragic accident. Maybe Della was distracted by something at work and didn't see the car." I forced a carefree tone and smiled. "Can I tell Molly Donna will be replaced soon?"

"I already said that," she snapped. "Did Coralee send you?"

"And I already said I'm not involved with Coralee. I'm helping Belvia by helping Molly."

"I don't know why Molly would be worried about Donna. Molly hasn't worked since her sister died. That was like six months ago. Although I never did understand why Belvia kept her on so long. But then I never understood why Belvia herself didn't retire. Now look at her."

"Yep, now she's dead."

"That's rude." Lisa flicked her eyes toward the door. "Get out. I'm busy. I don't know why you're bothering me with Molly's problems. She doesn't work here."

I left with a wave for her beleaguered assistant. I hadn't learned much except Lisa Russell's convictions remained consistent with her interview in the financial papers. However, I was still surprised. I assumed the person in charge of people would be more of a people person.

In the corporate world of sweet tea, I felt out of my depth. A family-values company built on antagonism and backstabbing. If Belvia's heart attack was truly a heart attack, it was no wonder she had one. Despite her age.

Kind of soured the sweet tea, in my view.


I found my way to the Director of Accounting's office. Here I expected a cold, calculating (literally, he was in accounting after all) financial despot. Instead, David Wells had an office full of fully clothed teddy bears. He also liked to wink and chuckle. I watched out for elbow nudging and found my way to a chair before his desk.

Bears in various states of historical dress peered at me from the wooden bookshelves and filing cabinets. Which, I'll admit, made me nervous. I've never been partial to dressed animals. It's unnatural. They're already wearing fur.

"A friend of Belvia's is a friend indeed." David leaned back in his leather office chair and rocked as he talked. "I'm sorry for your loss. She was a great woman."

"That she was. And I'm sorry for you and the company too. I've got no stake in Meemaw's Tea—not even a single share—but before she died, Belvia charged me with a task to complete at the time of her demise. Checking on the management. To see how y'all are doing for a report for the new CEO. Of course, we don't know who that'll be yet..."

"You're visiting all the management?"

"Yep, I just came from Human Resources."

David stiffened and the rocking halted. "You talked to Lisa?"

"Yes." I watched him glance at one of the bears, then return to rocking his chair. I could still feel his tension but had the feeling I could work this conversation in my favor. He wanted to play ball, either to make himself look good for the report or, knowing Lisa, to make a better impression than she had. "When Belvia insisted I do this job, she had just lost Della. Of course we had no idea Belvia would also pass away so soon."

"It's a great shock. Belvia and Della. At one time. I don't know how we'll recover."

"Is the company in trouble?"

"Not yet. But I've been comparing valuation ratios and looking at the internal rate of return." David tilted forward and placed his hands on his desk. "There's been some decline since Belvia's retirement announcement. With Della's accident, even more fluctuation. And finally with Belvia's death, I've seen a sharp downward spike. It's not good. We'll need strong leadership to recover. But I know what to do."

He glanced at a bear wearing a suit, glasses, and a tie. "Isn't that right, Milton?"

"That's...too bad." I had no idea what he was saying. Milton the bear didn't help me either. But unlike Lisa, David wasn't revealing any antipathy toward the Brakemans. "What do you think will help?"

"Short term, to stay the course Belvia had mapped out. To soothe our investors, suppliers, and purchasers. What we don't want is sweeping change." He looked at Milton for reassurance.

"And long term?"

"I would propose leadership from within. But leadership in tune with the original culture of Meemaw's." David winked. "We don't want to become the next Snapple. Snapple is already Snapple."

"I see." Which I didn't, but I also didn't talk to stuffed bears. "Do you and Lisa Russell differ in opinion on what will happen to the company?"

David's chuckle sounded forced and it didn't result in a wink. "You could say that."

"And what about Coralee Brakeman? Now that she's back, maybe she wants to get involved in her family's company."

"I didn't even realize she was interested in the company. She's been gone so long..." He turned from Milton toward a bear in a white wig and long coat. "Adam would say she should be given a chance. Exercise benevolence toward Coralee. She is, after all, a Brakeman."

"And do you agree...with Adam there?" I pointed toward the bear in the old-timey wig.

"I'd like to talk to Coralee first. After all, you have to consider the shareholders." David turned from Adam to me. "She may also align herself with non-Brakeman values. Who knows?"

"What if she aligns herself with Lisa Russell?"

All good humor and love of bears fled from David's features. "Human Resources may block me from serving the Brakeman vision for Meemaw's Tea because of petty differences. But if Lisa Russell tries to exercise her influence to undermine the Meemaw's Tea foundation?" He glanced at another bear, this one wearing an old-fashioned scholar's robe and curly hair. "I don't know what I'll do, Malthus."

I shivered. David spent too much time alone crunching numbers with his bears. Maybe he missed the "human link" to the Brakemans. "It sounds like you were aligned with Belvia and Della's ideas. In the news, you said you had strong feelings about leadership changes at Meemaw's Tea. Did Belvia and Della support your ideas?"

He seemed surprised at the question. "Of course. I'm sure they did. I was against Lisa Russell's push to bring in outsiders."

"Do you think they wanted to promote you to COO? Before Della died, I mean. She'd planned on becoming CEO and her old position would need to be filled. Although I guess it still does."

"I hadn't heard officially, but—" He winked. "I think I was the best candidate. And I'm prepared to take on CEO now too."

"You don't know for sure how they felt about you?"

"They knew I supported their vision." He pulled at his neck collar. "They weren't the best at communicating their feelings. But not to their discredit."

"Some of the board members were often visiting Belvia at Halo House to vocalize their ideas. You weren't one of them?"

"I visited, but not to push ideas. It wasn't necessary. I didn't earn my promotions or get on the board by being pushy."

Pushiness seemed to be a Brakeman prerequisite. And they admired strength. David Wells wanted to climb the corporate ladder by being nice? It didn't make sense. "How did Lisa become director and on the board if she was in blatant opposition to Belvia's authority?"

His nose wrinkled. "Lisa's the type who could get away with criticizing authority at Meemaw's."

"What type is that?"

"She's a woman, isn't she?"

And on that note, I thought I'd best leave. Before I did something to one of his bears.

Between the Brakeman family values and the Brakeman hiring principles, Belvia and Della might have created an anti-Brakeman Frankenstein. Weak men and bullish women abounded. Finding someone who benefited from their deaths was too easy. Lisa wanted to make money off the company by selling it.

David thought he deserved to take the reins through his commitment to the Brakeman cornerstone. Had he heard otherwise? Neither had been thrilled that Coralee Brakeman was interested in dipping her toes in the sweet tea pond. After such a long hiatus, they didn't consider her a viable Brakeman.

And were those motives enough for murder? That was tricky. I wondered what ripples I had caused by chunking that stone in their pond.

# SIXTEEN

After meeting the other Meemaw's Tea staff on Belvia's list, I learned they neither cowed to Lisa Russell nor the Brakeman women but seemed appropriately committed to their jobs and families. In other words, none of them set off my suspicion meter. However, I didn't cross off Lisa Russell or weird David Wells like I did the others. I also kept Donna Sharp, the unhappy homewrecker.

Despite Belvia's beliefs about a snake in her company grass, in my opinion, the most obvious motives for murder lay within the Brakemans themselves. Particularly those who thought the new will might mess with their inheritance.

Not knowing who stood to gain or lose by terms of the new or the old will made me anxious to meet the lawyer, Harry Hunt. He was also on my list but did not return my calls. Seemed like a good reason to shift focus to the Brakemans for now. As much as they made my lip curl.

Cooper Funeral Home might bury a few birds in one shot. Coop knew everything about everyone. It was his job. Particularly when he was hosting that family's funeral. I'd help Molly, learn more about the Brakemans, and have an excuse to do something with Todd. Todd loved getting mixed up in business that wasn't ours and didn't bother with the law-and-order side like Luke did. He would visit Cooper's with me, particularly if he knew it was a Brakeman fact-finding mission disguised as funeral assistance.

I drove the old Datsun home, thinking of Todd and the adventures we'd been through. Not including our failed Vegas wedding. I needed to find someone for Todd. Someone who had a bloodline who didn't run from vile and scheming.

Which meant not Shawna Branson. To be fair, I should also find someone for Shawna. Someone who lived in real far away country. Like Japan.

At 211 Loblolly, I parked next to Todd's Civic in the drive, skirted the junk in my carport, and banged open the kitchen door.

"I'm home," I announced. "And I've got plans for us. You'll never guess where we're going—"

My words dropped from my lips and fell at the feet of the vile and scheming person whom I had spent my drive wishing away from my best friend.

"Do you always overstate the obvious?" Shawna's overplucked brow rose a fraction as she turned in her chair.

My chair. My kitchen chair. Her zebra-printed butt was planted on my flippin' kitchen chair.

Dear Lord, I thought, if I hitched my wagon to Luke's, our children would be step-related to this woman. We'd have Thanksgiving, Christmas, and Easter with Shawna.

Every year.

Every holiday I'd be staring at Shawna's animal-printed tushie. Blood pounded in my ears and my stomach rolled.

"We could hear you banging through the drive before you slammed in here," she continued. "Folks three streets over know you're home."

I peeled my stare off her zebra derierre to meet her blue-green eyes. A color I liked to call Jezebel Jade. "Yes, I'm home. In my house. My Great Gam's bungalow by way of my Grandpa Ed." I unclenched my fists and placed them on hips lacking the soft man-bewitching roundness that graced my kitchen chair. "And since this is my home, Shawna, I am wondering what in the hell you are doing in it."

"Ask Toddsers. I thought it was his house too." Tossing her thick auburn hair over her shoulder, she turned to face the Man Who'd Betrayed Me.

At least Todd had the decency to blush and avoid my fiery look.

"Toddsers," I drawled. "May I speak to you in *my* living room?"

I dropped my drawing satchel on the counter and stalked into the living room. Once my professional studio before the hyena wearing zebra ran my business into the ground in order to push forward her own.

Shawna doesn't even paint. She colors over photos.

Todd slunk in behind me. "I know you must be a little surprised."

"Surprised?" I laid a hand on my chest. "Don't you mean shocked? Flabbergasted? Galled? Kicked in the flippin' gut? What in the hell is going on, Todd? I was about to invite you to Cooper's Funeral Home, but now I don't know what to think."

"As fun as visiting funeral homes can be, I can't go." Todd scratched his head. Troubled lines skated his normally smooth worry-free forehead. "You see, I kind of have another date."

"Another date? You just had one. How many dates do you need?"

"I can't say." His fingers abandoned the brain massage to tap a pattern against his cargo shorts. A pattern that might have been an SOS signal. "Shawna showed up here a little while ago and asked me out."

I blew out a sigh. "That's different. You weren't expecting her. Let her down easy. I don't want her throwing anything. It's not like I have the money to replace furniture or appliances."

"The thing is, I already told her yes. Meaning, I'd go out tonight."

I dropped my voice to a fierce whisper. "You may think cuddling up to convince Shawna to drop the charges is a good idea, but I'm telling you, Todd, you're trying to cuddle a honey badger. Those critters look cute, but they are mean as hell and just as deadly."

"Honey badger?"

"Confusing, I know, since she generally wears leopard print." I folded my arms across my chest. "Tell her something came up. I need to speak to Cooper about Belvia and Della Brakeman's funeral. He might know some details about the family's plans. And other stuff."

"What other stuff?" Todd's SOS pattern sounded more like artillery fire.

"Stuff like who might have murdered them. Now you can see what I'm working on."

"Murdered?" screeched the voice behind me.

The hairs on the back of my neck rose at Shawna's cackle.

Dagnabbit. My oversized mouth and my oversized ego had kicked my undersized butt.

"Belvia and Della Brakeman weren't murdered. Della was killed by a drunk driver and Belvia had a heart attack." Shawna strode into the living room and slid an arm around Todd's waist. "That's called bad timing, not murder."

I flinched, then curled my lip. "Mind your own beeswax, Shawna. This is between me and Todd. Until the autopsy proved her death was natural, I'm not convinced."

Todd glanced between us, then stared at the ceiling. Likely hoping the hand of God would rip off the roof and snatch him on the spot rather than get between two back-arching, claw-baring, hissing women.

Men.

"You're the one not minding your own business, Cherry," said Shawna. "My family associates with the Brakemans, of course, so I know all about Belvia's unfortunate passing. Why are you stirring up trouble where there isn't any? Does Sheriff Thompson know you're trying to play detective again? All you'll do is help him out of his job. November's coming awful quick this year and there'll be questions about his niece involving herself in another crime."

"I'm not 'involved in a crime,' Shawna. I'm assisting the sheriff's office with crime detection." I raised my chin a notch. "And I also know the Brakemans. Knew Belvia, that is. She asked for my help specifically because of my superior sleuthing skills. Or skills in suspicious thinking. I suspected her will might be fraudulent, which it wasn't, but it impressed her nonetheless."

Shawna brayed laughter and squeezed Todd into her side. "I guess you're right about Cherry being crazy. I didn't know you meant literally though."

"I didn't mean—"

My well-honed stink eye cut Todd off. If that idiot wanted to pretend to date Shawna for my benefit, he could at least refrain from talking ugly about me. No need to take the pretense that far. I turned my stink eye toward Shawna. "Who did Belvia Brakeman ask for help? Not a Branson, but me, Cherry Tucker."

"You think whatever you want, honey." Shawna snorted then sauntered from the living room, pulling Todd with her. "Come on, Todd. I want to catch a late lunch at Little Verona's and we need to pick you out something other than cargo shorts. Speaking of help, I'd love to take you shopping for new clothes. Cargo shorts are so done. We'll go after our early dinner."

"Your cargo shorts are fine, Todd. Pockets are handy," I hollered, for a reason unbeknownst to me. Seething, I spun on my boot heels and slammed out of the house.

By the time I had parked in Cooper's lot, anger had drug its sharp teeth from my neck, replaced by the sting of remorse.

Not only had I spilled Belvia's secret to a bigger gossip than Ada, I had also given the Branson family more ammunition to shoot my Uncle Will right out of his sheriff's seat. Something else I might have saved by protecting Belvia from murder.

I thunked my head on the steering wheel, wishing I could bang out the stupidity. I didn't know which made me more idiotic, my pride or my jealousy. Both left me with no choice but to prove Belvia Brakeman had been murdered.

Either that or eat a hell of a lot of crow between now and November.

\*   \*   \*

Cooper Funeral Home, a renovated Victorian on Halo's northeast side, had fascinated me from a young age. Not because I was interested in death and gore, but because the quiet reverence often abounded with the lively irreverence of friendship squabbles, family jealousies, and curiosity seekers. Southerners, such as those found in Halo, could do overwrought emotion like no other. If you wanted a good show, you either found it in a revival tent or Cooper's.

I'd say a bar, but the town is dry. You have to cross the tracks to Red's to get the alcohol-infused version of overwrought emotion. Halo does that well too.

Because of Della Brakeman's importance, I had figured a grander funeral parlor in Line Creek or Atlanta would be used. Meemaw's Tea factory employed folks from all over Forks County, but the business suits were as likely from Atlanta as they were from Line Creek. As a child raised in Halo, Belvia must have felt loyal to Coop. The Coopers had buried all sorts of Brakemans over the years. Cooper Funeral Home had kept a revolving brood running the family business since time immemorial.

Like the Brakemans, but longer and without any murders.

I found Cooper in his office. Unfortunately, a big bear of a man filled one of Coop's guest chairs. He raised a paw in greeting, then leaned back with a growl and assessed me under lowered brows. When not in his office, on call, or shooting the breeze with my Grandpa Ed, Sheriff Will Thompson could often be found in that chair. He had gained the habit from his days as county coroner. And, like me, Uncle Will was also drawn to the morbid entertainment of Cooper's.

"Hey there, Cherry," said Coop. "What can I do you for?"

"I'm curious too," said Uncle Will. "Your family is healthy and accounted for. What brings you to Cooper's? I hope not scrounging for information on the Brakemans."

Dangit. Uncle Will knew me too well.

"I got to know Belvia at Halo House. As you know, Uncle Will, I'm the one who found her." I offered Coop my best customer service smile, knowing it would be wasted on Uncle Will. "I'm wondering about the arrangements. How the family's faring and so on. I'm helping out a friend of the family, actually. Someone Miss Belvia asked me to check on."

"You were hoping Coop would know gossip," said Uncle Will.

Cooper's wild eyebrows knotted. "I'm sure Cherry's looking to be helpful."

"Cherry's always looking to be helpful, Coop. It's the best and worst of her personality." Uncle Will leaned forward in his chair. "Tell me about this sudden friendship with Belvia Brakeman, who I know you had not met previous to this week. Deputy Harper said you convinced him to mark her death as suspicious even though it looks natural. That takes some good convincing."

"Deputy Harper found evidence that supported my theory, didn't he?"

"Your theory was based on an empty unmarked file folder."

"That held a new will."

"In your estimation."

"Belvia's lawyer didn't have a copy?" asked Coop.

Uncle Will shook his head. "Got kind of indignant about it, actually."

Lawyers. My hackles rose along with my blood pressure. "Coralee can attest to that new will just as well as Jose and me, who officially witnessed it. Not that Coralee knew what her mother had written in it. Miss Belvia told me she wanted to keep a lid on the contents. With Della's sudden death, Miss Belvia updated it to put someone else in control of Meemaw's Tea in the case of her untimely passing."

"Ninety is hardly untimely."

I raised an eyebrow. "Are you looking at the lawyer? Sounds like Miss Belvia didn't trust him."

"You and the CEO of Meemaw's Tea got mighty tight in two days, did you?" Uncle Will ignored my aside and leaned back in his chair. "Deputy Harper's checking her computer files for a copy of the alleged missing will. Someone could've taken advantage of her heart attack's timing and stolen it. Theft and burglary with possible intent to commit fraud, says Harper. Hard to prove though, if the witnesses didn't see what they signed."

Damnation.

"You still haven't answered my question," said Uncle Will. "Why were you suddenly chummy with Belvia Brakeman?"

"I didn't know it, but when she asked me to witness her will, Miss Belvia was screening me for a job. She had done some research on me."

"What job?"

"A consultant-type deal," I said, test-driving my newly acquired corporate speak. Better for the sheriff to believe my services were business and not murder-inquiry related. "An external probe into staff relations. Uncovering corruption in the upper ranks."

"She wanted you to investigate her employees while we're doing our own investigation into her daughter's accident?" He pursed his lips. "Last time I checked, you were an artist, not an 'external probe.'"

"Miss Belvia wanted my help. A ninety-year-old blind woman. She liked my naturally suspicious mind. What could I do?"

"Belvia Brakeman might've been ninety and blind, but she was ferocious as a hungry grizzly in the spring." Uncle Will crossed his arms. "Don't pretend differently."

"What did you find out?" asked Coop.

"Not a damn thing. Didn't even start." My eyes felt hot and I blinked to clear the haze. "Was more caught up in what she could do for me than what I could do for her. Little did I know, not a day later, they'd take her away on a crash cart. I wished I could've told her something."

Or somehow prevented her murder, but Uncle Will wouldn't take kindly to that remark either.

"I doubt she went to her grave worrying about you slacking on the job," said Uncle Will. "She had a good long life. Get back to your art teaching. Your external probing may get in the way of my official inquiry."

"I feel I should finish the job. It might be of help to others."

"You're helping others at Halo House. Helps me out too, you know. Just telling Coop my election troubles are already heating up and it's still eight months away." He ambled toward the door with a goodbye to Coop and a backward glance at me. "I won't remind you of your promise to keep a low profile, for me and for your brother."

"You just did." I raised my brows.

"Glad you caught that, then."

I waited until Uncle Will sauntered down the hall and turned to Coop. "So are you really doing both Brakeman funerals?"

He nodded. "It'll be a zoo. I'll have to hire extra attendants and the sheriff's office to conduct traffic."

"I guess they can't wait long, what with Della's situation."

He caught my drift. "Soon as the morgue releases Miss Belvia. Coroner's got the poor woman now. Sheriff Will did ask for the full workup. Then I'll get her."

"How was the family? In case I need to send over a casserole."

"I didn't think casseroles were your forte, hon."

"I'll get Casey or Pearl to make it." I waved my hand, hurrying him around the mundanity of casserole fixing. "Coralee Brakeman's trying to foist the new funeral arrangements on Miss Belvia's retired assistant. The poor woman's eighty-two, if she's a day. I feel it's my duty to get involved with this family. Miss Belvia asked me to look after Molly."

Cooper leaned back in his chair and massaged his chin. You'd never hear his opinion on those who crossed his threshold, but Cooper had his tells. Coralee had made an impression on Coop, likely not different than mine.

After much chin massaging, he found his words. "But what can you do? Sounds like Sheriff Will wants you to leave the Brakemans be."

"This has nothing to do with his investigation. Let me run

interference with the funeral plans so Coralee stops bothering Molly. Where's Coralee staying? With her brother-in-law?"

"I believe Mr. Newson and Miss Coralee don't see eye to eye on many things. I doubt he'd invite her to stay in his house." Coop's long fingers skimmed the air before landing on his chin. "Although Coralee's family's staying in Belvia's late home, the Tea Grove. Della's house is on the same property."

"Just dandy. I can visit everyone in one shot." I rose from my chair and headed to the door. "Thank you, Coop. You need anything, give me a holler."

"That's just fine, Cherry. But watch yourself, hon."

"Why would you say that?"

He sighed and stroked his chin. "I don't know Coralee and her people well enough. She's been gone too long."

"Yes, I know." Coop's inability to get to the point drove me nuts, but I didn't want to rush him. If he was going to dish, it was worth waiting.

"But Ron Newson and his son..." Coop sighed again and massaged his neck with his palm. "They've not had to live like other folks. Richer than Croesus, you know? Della and Belvia weren't bad women. They were generous with their families. But they also punished as harshly as they rewarded. Very exacting in their expectations, yet without giving direction to meet those expectations. It gets confusing, living like that."

Talk about confusing. "What are you trying to say, Coop?"

"You ever met an animal that'd been abused as much as it was rewarded?"

"Like a pit bull rescued from one of them fight clubs?"

Coop nodded. "That's what I'm talking about with Belvia's family. Be careful."

# seventeen

Despite Coop's warning, particularly after Ada and Fred's own words of caution, I felt no real worry in calling on Belvia's kin. My cover would be to help with the funeral, at least to get Coralee from bothering Molly. Why would you bite the hand offering to feed you? But to guarantee my hand didn't get bit upon arrival at the Tea Grove, I'd come with actual food. Grandma Jo often lectured it was only proper to bring victuals to the mourners.

I'd wave a casserole like a white flag before crazy Coralee and ruthless Ron.

And because I wasn't much of a casserole maker, I decided to check on Grandpa Ed and his lady friend, Pearl. Pearl was an extraordinary victual maker. The farm lay west of town, the opposite direction of Halo House and Meemaw's Tea.

The farm lane was a treacherous rutted affair. Hell on my old Datsun's shocks as well as on my jaw, which remained clenched from the jarring and tension due to a pack of obnoxious goats allowed to roam wild in the farmyard.

Grandpa Ed's monstrous billy, Tater, loved to play chicken with my truck. But the game had new stakes. Tater now had his own herd to torment me. The spawn of Tater and Pearl's prize Saanen, Snickerdoodle. Snickeraters and Taterdoodles. Itty bitties born of forbidden love. Forbidden by Pearl, who felt her sable too good for the mongrel billy.

I gripped the Datsun's wheel and slid forward on the bench

seat, peering through the bug-spotted windshield. The goats had chewed most of the decorative foliage planted by my late Grandma Jo. Two massive trees blocked the view to the farmhouse, a rambling brick ranch with a semi-rotted screened porch. Generally, the kids preferred to ambush me from behind those trees. The bitties darted from hither and yon, shooting towards my truck with a terrifying speed and accuracy that would catch me unawares. So teeny I often felt them before I saw them. The Datsun's body was covered with tiny hoof dings.

Like a swarm, they attacked in tandem. Like a pestilence, they descended from all sides.

This time, I caught a dark streak in my drivers' side mirror. I tapped the brakes at the split in the lane and checked the other mirror. Ahead, I saw a larger body of white emerge from behind the great oak.

"Shit." I trounced the brakes, hit a bigger rut, and near about bit my tongue in two.

Checking the sides again, I scanned for tiny creatures. They remained invisible in the dry dead landscape. But I didn't trust my eyes. I could feel them close, watching and waiting. I flicked my gaze forward, locking eyes with the majestic buck. He tossed his head and pawed the earth, eager to take the Datsun head on.

Tater wasn't stupid, just ornery.

But somewhere out there, the kids also waited. And their momma, Snickerdoodle, who scared the bejeezus out of me. And a terrible mother. Who let their kids play in traffic?

Letting out my breath, I eased the truck forward.

The old goat limped from the tree to block the lane. He dipped his head to level my grill with his great horns.

I glanced in the mirrors and swallowed hard.

A few yards behind my tailgate, the sable trotted. Her belly still distended, udders hanging low, she looked uncomfortable yet determined. And full of post-pregnancy hormones, making her extra fierce. Like it was my fault her mate had taught their offspring to play with moving vehicles.

I sped up, then glanced forward. Her goat paramour charged toward me.

"Dammit." I swerved. Bumped off the track and bit my tongue again. Accelerating through the dead grass, my eyes flicked from windshield to rearview.

Behind me, Snickerdoodle picked up speed.

Tater changed course to angle toward me.

The back of my neck grew warm and tingly. Two sickening thumps jarred the truck, echoed in the rusty metal panels of my side doors.

I braked, hit a mangled azalea, and jerked to a stop. Cracking the door, I peered out and saw one dancing kid, a fawn with white spots. He hopped in a circle, kicking his rear legs in glee. I slammed the door, slid across the seat to check the other side, and felt the crunch of horn on metal.

I rolled down my passenger window. "Tater, you idjit goat, stop beating up my grill."

The second kid, white with one brown spot, leaped toward the Datsun.

"No," I cried. "Get away from my truck."

Two loud thunks sounded from the bed followed by a trapping of tiny feet. I spun in my seat. Snickerdoodle had hefted her heavy belly over the tailgate with ease. The tiny white goat dancing in the bed was joined a moment later by her brother. Snickerdoodle charged toward my rear window.

I had about three seconds before they'd be on the roof. Theoretically, I could drive to the house with the goats in the bed, keeping them off balance until I stopped. But I couldn't move. Tater slammed into my grill like an offensive lineman pushing a sled on roster-cut day. The kids hopped on the roof, carving designs in the rust with their sharp baby hooves. Snickerdoodle's launch from the bed rocked the truck. Little goats slid down the windshield and she dented my hood with her heavy landing.

If I weren't such a good granddaughter, I'd give up on the farm altogether. But I needed casseroles and information as much as I needed to see how the old man and his lady were doing. I looped plastic grocery bags over my shoulders, hopped out, and ran to the house.

Behind me, the herd abandoned the truck for the chase.

I made it into the kitchen with the groceries, but without the back hemline of my winter hoodie. That resided in Snickerdoodle's mouth.

At the kitchen door's bang, Pearl swept in from the living room. She wore a flannel shirt that hid her goat tattoo, the tail flapping against her jeans. Running a hand over her hair's short iron-gray spikes, she heaved a long breath. "Oh, it's just you."

"Nice to see you too, Pearl." I dropped the groceries on the counter. "I could use some help. I need to bring food to a family who's lost two. You make the best corn casserole."

"Of course." She strode toward my grocery bags to assess my shopping. "Good, you brought chicken. That'll make it a main dish. Cornbread mix? Always make cornbread from scratch. I swear, Cherry, you ought to know the fixings by now. You eat enough of it."

I knew when to keep my mouth shut and let her continue her food ramble, substituting my poor ingredients for her better. While she chopped chicken, sautéed, and mixed, I snagged a glass of tea from the pitcher in the fridge. The tea had the perfect blend of sweet to bitter. Didn't make your teeth itch and didn't taste like a bush. Refreshing enough to make me breathe an "ah" after a gulp.

"Did you buy this tea or make it?" I asked.

She gave me a look to say I was about the stupidest person on the planet. "Why would I buy tea?"

"Some people do. Belvia Brakeman made a fortune on it."

She snorted. "Good for Belvia Brakeman."

"Do you know the Brakemans?"

"Don't know Belvia, but I knew Della. Went to high school together. Is that who this casserole is for?" She eyed me. "Those folks don't need casseroles, Cherry. They got their own chef to cook for them."

"Maybe they don't need the casserole, but they need the love behind it."

"The love I'm imparting into this cornbread or the love you've imparted into asking me to make it for you?" She raised a brow.

"The Brakemans lost Belvia yesterday too. A mother and daughter within almost a week. That's pretty hard, ain't it?"

"I suppose." Her eyes drifted to the cornbread mixture. "Della's accident was shocking. She must have been running with music blaring in those ear thingies."

"Did you know her husband? Ron Newson?"

Pearl wrinkled her nose. "Not really. He's not from around here. Think she picked him up while in college up north. I saw him at town doings from time to time though. Don't think he liked living in Halo, even if it was in a big house with enough land that he didn't have to see the neighbors. From what he said, sounded like he spent more time in Atlanta than Halo. Man didn't work. What kind of man doesn't work?"

I shrugged. The men I knew who didn't work were looking for work. "Did you meet their son? Parker."

"Nah. I've heard about him though." She tapped a spoon against the bowl and shook her head. "He went to that private school over on the other side of the county until he was kicked out. Then he got sent off to different day schools around Atlanta."

"He's grown up now. Sort of."

She stirred chicken into the batter. "Della waited until she was in her forties to have a child but then never talked about her son. I always thought that was strange. Only ever talked about the tea company."

"I heard Della was really into her career." When Pearl nodded, I continued the spate of chitchat. "You think Della had any enemies? Like through the business?"

"Enemies? Who has enemies?" Pearl dumped half a bowl of batter into a disposable aluminum pan. She spread the mixture as she talked. "If anybody has enemies in that family, it'd be her husband. Men who don't work get into trouble. Especially if they're going to Atlanta all the time."

"That's an interesting point. You think he could've got into trouble enough to have his wife killed?"

"What do I know about that sort of trouble?" Her words sounded too sharp for the wobble in her voice. "I got trouble of my own to bother with anyone else's. Here." She shoved the trays in my direction.

"Thanks." I watched her pack away the ingredients, then toss the measuring cups and spoons into the dirty bowl. "Who were you expecting today?"

"What do you mean?" The dirty bowl clattered into the sink. The frying pan followed, banging against the metal bowl.

"You said, 'Oh, it's just you,' when I came in. Which generally means you thought I'd be someone else."

She flung the whisk in after the pan and picked up the long knife. I flinched, but her shoulders slumped and the metal knife found a gentler path to the sink. "My Ed. I mean your Grandpa Ed."

"He does live here."

She bowed her head over the sink.

"Doesn't he?" I eyed her. "What's going on?"

"He went to visit your brother in Line Creek today."

"The county jail, you mean."

She tightened her lips. "Yes. They're talking to a new lawyer."

"New lawyer?" Did Belvia come through for me before she died? Hope soared and I chuckled to cover my excitement. "That attorney assigned to Cody is about as new as you can get. I think Tater's older than that guy. I didn't think we could afford a real lawyer. Did someone volunteer to help us?"

"Lawyers only volunteer if there's something in it for them, child." Pearl smacked the faucet handle, drowned a dishrag, then cut it off. "No, y'all can't afford a real lawyer. Even if Cody wins his case, it'll still cost an extra arm and leg. But Ed's hiring someone new anyway."

Hope crashed, scorching a landing strip from my chest to belly. I wrapped my arms around my midriff and fought to concentrate on Pearl's struggle. "How can Grandpa afford it?"

"You said it yourself. That court-appointed idiot has done nothing for Cody. Wanted him to plea down. I told Ed something's got to be done and now he's doing it."

I thought about Belvia's analysis. "The evidence against Cody doesn't hold water. Something else is going on."

"Tell that to Cody's lawyer. He wants to enter a guilty plea and hope for the best. Y'all have been sticking your head in the sand while your brother faces kidnapping charges. He'll get life. What sort of attorney admits defeat without trying?"

"One that doesn't want to face Bransons in court."

"Exactly. That kid lawyer's smart enough to know to hang a shingle in Forks County, he's got to work with Bransons."

My eyes smarted and I gnawed on my thumbnail to distract my tear ducts.

"Ed visited the bank after the lawyer." Pearl swiped the counter with the dishrag, keeping her eyes away from mine. "He'll have to start selling off the farm. Probably start with the back acreage. But there's no road out there except through the front lane. I tried to tell him no one's gonna buy this land without access. The house and barns'll all be part and parcel."

"He can't do that. Ballards have always owned this land."

"What else can he do? The bank's not going to let him mortgage the farm. It's a losing proposition for them. You think any of your kin would buy it?"

"No one's got that kind of money. Damn banks. And damn lawyers." I blinked back another tear and allowed anger to ferment in its place. Anger grew better ideas than sorrow. "What about my house? That makes more sense. It's in town. It won't get much since the house is old and I haven't had the money to renovate, but the land will be worth something."

"Your Grandpa won't kick you out. He can't chuck out one kid to save the other."

"That's ridiculous. Cody's my brother. I'd rather go homeless than y'all lose the farm."

Pearl's head drooped. Leaving the rag on the counter, she faced me. Her eyes gleamed with unshed tears. "I knew you would offer. I told Ed, but he wouldn't let me mention it. He's out at the co-op now, trying to scare up interest in the acreage. But what about your roommate?"

"I'm not too happy with Todd at the moment. Do you know who he's seeing?"

The scent of scandal lured her away from her distress. "Todd's seeing somebody? I always thought he was sweet on you. Seemed like he was waiting on you to get over that Branson boy business."

I forced my eyes not to roll. "Luke Harper's not really a Branson. And certainly not a boy."

She snorted. "When you get to be my age, he is. And your Grandpa Ed says if his momma is married to a Branson, Luke Harper's a Branson."

"Luke doesn't like the Bransons any more than we do."

"No boy will turn his back on his momma. And if he would, would you want someone like that?"

I chewed my lip. She had a point. If I stayed with Luke, I'd either end up with Branson babies or a man who'd break the fifth commandment for me. And then resent it, because the boy did love his momma. Wanda Branson had her faults, namely falling in love with someone like JB, but her intentions paved a path as good and sweet as any road to hell. Luke would never abandon his mother.

If I stayed with Luke, I'd be a Branson. A traitor to my family. And hating his.

Dammit, love was hard. Made hunting a murderer feel easy.

# Eighteen

The Datsun and I traveled east of town. Wealthy Halo families, like the Branson clan, generally preferred the new gated community on the north side with the golf course and private club. But the Tea Grove had been carved from old farmland. Timber separated the property from its neighbors. In Halo, new money liked old land. My friend, Max Avtaikin, also lived on this side of town. Another Halo inhabitant who preferred the respectability of a faux-antebellum estate without involving himself in the mire of town politics.

Like Max, the Brakemans had a grand wrought-iron gated drive, but this drive split midway to circle before both homes. Matching brick three-storied houses with wrought-iron railing porches and balconies overlooked the front gardens. Almost more fortress than house with the wings and side additions. I parked at the split, unsure who lived where. Even the flower boxes looked alike.

What happened if you had a few too many? Did they ever get the houses confused? Wander into the wrong bedroom?

I wondered how Coralee felt about this blatant evidence of the strong mother-daughter bond between Belvia and Della. Was it a slap in the face after all those years away? Or did this weird intimacy drive her off?

With Della gone, maybe Coralee had thought she could slip into that spot. Switch the alpaca sweaters for pantsuits. Make a grab for the tea throne.

I hopped from the truck, grabbed the casseroles, and took the path to the right. Mounting the porch steps, I looked for clues to the residents and came up empty. Pressing the bell, I prepared myself for anyone, but not the person who answered.

The kid with the gun tat.

My face heated. With everything that had happened with Miss Belvia, I hadn't followed up with Hazel. But if Grabby Hands was a Brakeman, what was he doing hassling Hazel?

He narrowed his eyes, scanning me head to toe, then sneered at the plastic-wrapped parcels in my arms. "We're not buying and you're trespassing. Sign on the gate says no sales calls."

"I'm not selling anything. I'm bringing y'all a casserole. Are you Parker Brakeman-Newson?"

He jerked his head. A head connected to a neck covered in more tattoos than just the stylized revolver. Among others, I noted a decorative seven, three Rs, and a pyramid of three dots. The Sweet Tea Prince thought he was a gangbanger.

"Why're you bringing me a casserole?" he said.

It was like he didn't live in the same country as me, let alone the same town. I shoved a pan into his arms. "To express my condolences about your momma and grandma. That's what we do. Bring food."

"You want a receipt or something?"

"A receipt?" I shook my head in wonderment. "I told you, it's a gift."

"Happy funeral?" He rolled his eyes, backing into the room with the casserole. "Listen, man, thanks or whatever."

The door swung. I shoved my foot over the threshold to prevent it from shutting. "It's a common practice around here, bringing food to those in need."

"Have you looked around? Do you know who we are? We don't need your food. I can see your truck, you could use handouts from us."

I sucked in my breath. "I'll let that slide as you just lost your momma. You must be having a hard time."

"Yeah, right." He scanned me again. "I know you from somewhere."

"We had a slight exchange at Halo House. You were stealing from an old woman's purse. Ring a bell?"

"I wasn't stealing. She had something that was mine and I was getting it for her. Being helpful." He flashed his teeth, more snarl than smile.

"Why would Hazel have something of yours? Just what were you doing?"

"You don't need to know my business." He kicked the door and it banged against my boot. "Get the hell off my property or I'm getting my piece."

"Piece?" I said. "Are you referring to a firearm? We're having a conversation about you and my friend, Hazel. Why are you bringing up weapons?"

"What's going on out there?" called a male voice.

"Nothing," hollered Parker, then muttered, "You and me are done."

"We'll see about that." I pushed the door wide to walk into the foyer. "I'm bringing y'all a casserole, Mr. Newson."

Ron Newson strolled through an open doorway. His business suit had been traded for a polo. "Parker, what's the issue?"

"No issue, sir." Parker glared at me, then turned toward his father. "Someone from town brought us food."

"Food?" Ron looked at me. "We didn't order food."

"It's a local custom. We bring food to those in distress." Where was I, on Mars? "It's a gesture of good will. And I don't need a receipt."

"Then why all the shouting?"

"Your boy has..." I cut a look toward Parker. He'd be even less likely to explain his confrontation with Hazel before his father. "Parker and I had a misunderstanding."

"About the food," said Parker.

Ron waved at the pan. "Take it away. We don't want it."

Parker shoved the pan at me. I grabbed it, balancing a pan on each arm. They were starting to ache under the strain. Cornbread casserole was not a light dish in more ways than one.

Ron turned to leave.

Young Grabby Hands had caught me off guard. I'd forgotten my prepared questions and found myself floundering. "Mr. Newson. Remember me? I found Mrs. Brakeman. Later, I found you in her bathroom. You took something from her medicine cabinet."

He whirled around. "What?"

"You're the one who found Grandmother?" said Parker.

"I knew you looked familiar." Ron Newson strode across the marble foyer and stopped before me. "You called the police."

"She did what?" Parker inhaled spit and coughed.

I hid my smile. I'd sort out Parker soon enough. He couldn't bother my friends, particularly if they were elderly, and get away with it. Even if Hazel didn't want my help.

"Yep, I called the sheriff. He's a good family friend. I figured better safe than sorry when it comes to the death of someone like Mrs. Brakeman." I studied Ron. "So why look in the medicine cabinet? What was in the bottle you were holding?"

"It was nothing important." He spoke slowly, then flashed a look at Parker. "I don't know why I picked up that bottle of pills. I wasn't thinking."

"Had y'all been to Miss Belvia's earlier?"

"Of course. We checked in with Belvia when we arrived for the visitation."

"Anybody use the bathroom?" I tossed a hypothetical, wondering if he'd catch it. "If someone accidentally left their medication in Belvia's bathroom, she might have taken it by mistake. Causing her heart attack. Maybe you picked up that bottle because it looked out of place?"

Folding his arms, Parker cut his gaze between me and his father.

"What is this?" Ron took another step toward me, forcing me to back onto the threshold. "Are you dropping off food or did you come to question us? You lied about the necessity of bringing in the police. You're lying again. Who are you?"

"I work at Halo House. I'm an artist and a friend to those who live there."

"Belvia Brakeman didn't have friends. Who are you working for?" He paced forward. "Coralee? A competitor? Or someone else?"

"I can't be concerned out of kindness for Belvia?"

Ron stepped closer and grabbed the door, hovering over me. His eyes glittered. "No, kindness has nothing to do with it. I suggest you keep your curiosity to yourself. You know what they say about curiosity."

"You mean about the cat?" I found myself on the porch.

"Exactly." The door banged shut.


I still had two casseroles. I followed the path to the matching house. This time, I marched up the steps with less swagger, rattled by my confrontation with Ron Newson. Originally, I'd hoped to get an unprepared answer about his rifling through the medicine cabinet. In his police testimony, he'd give Luke a more thoughtful answer. One created by an attorney. But finding Parker as Hazel's hassler had discombobulated me.

Young Parker wasn't to be trusted. Now I knew why he hadn't understood my casserole. His father must have been raised in some sad place where neighbors didn't share food. And his mother must have been too busy with the sweet tea dynasty to teach Parker proper etiquette. Or to not shake down seniors.

If only the public knew the traditional tea they were drinking came from a family of no tradition.

I used my elbow to ring the bell at Belvia's house and noticed the one major difference between the two homes. A wheelchair ramp had been built on one end of Belvia's porch. It made my heart knot for Belvia, even with the irritation I felt due to the mess she'd made of her family.

Coralee answered the door. She all but threw her hands in the air at my appearance.

I'd made an impression.

"You again?" she said.

I shoved a casserole toward her. "Hey, Coralee, this is for your family. To eat. It's to show my sympathy over the death of your mother and sister. And I don't need a receipt."

"I know what a casserole's for. Do you think I'm an idiot?"

"No, ma'am. It's just that...never mind. Anyway, I'm also here to offer you help. I know you asked Molly to lend a hand, but she's retired and elderly, so why not take me on? Since I'm not retired and young?"

She pushed away the pan and grabbed the door. "No way. I don't want your help or your casserole."

Again, I resorted to shoving a boot into the jamb and letting the door slam into my foot. Looked like a stop for ice at the SipNZip would be next on my itinerary.

"I sincerely want to help you. Miss Molly's not up to the task."

She gave a snort insinuating Molly's slacker mentality.

"Coralee, the woman is eighty-two."

"You're trying to nose into my mother's affairs. What are you looking for? I'm not paying you and I'm not giving you a job at the company."

"I don't want to work for Meemaw's Tea. Your momma asked me to look out for Molly. Whatever you need, consider me instead. Miss Belvia thought me reliable."

"Why would my mother—a corporate executive—ask you—a hick artist—for help?"

I squished my lips to the side, debating a qualified answer that didn't include sass-back to the bereaved. "I'm friendly?"

Coralee rested her hands on her hips. "My mother never once cared about anyone being friendly."

"You got me there." I shuffled the heavy casseroles. Kindness also hadn't worked with Ron. Brakeman family values didn't cover many virtues. "In all honesty, Miss Belvia liked the way I suspected you of messing with her will. Kind of crazy to trust someone who's suspicious, but that's the way it was."

Coralee opened her mouth, then closed it.

I waited for her scathing retort but it never came.

"Fine," she said. "I'll see you in the morning. Eight o'clock sharp in Mother's office."

The door slammed. I still held two casseroles, feeling like a Girl Scout who couldn't give away her cookies.

Looked like I had another job that had nothing to do with art and everything to do with getting myself into the Brakemans' business. Uncle Will was going to kill me.

I trudged toward the split where the Datsun waited, dripping oil and rust on their perfect drive. Winter dusk had turned to full darkness, shrouding the surrounding landscape. Decorative spotlights lit the houses, but on the drive I could barely see my truck, let alone my own feet. Laden with congealing concrete-like casseroles, there was no rooting through my bag for a phone or tiny flashlight to light my path.

My boots clopped along the blacktop and the faint scent of chili and corn wafted from the heavy casseroles. My stomach rumbled its displeasure. Luckily, no one was around to hear what sounded like a bowling alley on tournament day.

After the day I had, cornbread casserole sounded pretty damn good.

"I guess I'm free to partake of these, since nobody wanted them," I said to my stomach, then immediately felt guilty. Should I be eating rejected funeral casseroles? What would Grandma Jo think? "I should bring one to Molly. But the second is fair game."

My stomach gave its assent.

Footsteps broke the interlude of my gut chat. Hurried patter unlike the clunking I was making. I stopped to glance behind me. In the foreground of the lit houses, a figure darted across the drive into a stand of trees. The hunched shape flitted in a jagged pattern, making it impossible to tell from which house they had come. Or if they had come from a house at all.

Goosebumps flushed my already chilled skin. "Hey," I called, then clamped my lips shut. The stalker could be a Brakeman or an interloper sneaking around the Tea Grove.

And in either case, wouldn't Belvia have wanted to know who prowled her property?

Because I sure as hell did.

I tightened my grip on the pans, scooted off the drive toward the tiptoer, and ran into a hedge of waist-high azaleas. Raising the pans to my shoulders, I tried to step over the azalea. One boot crashed through the hip-high shrub. My left leg stuck mid-swing, sprawled over the bush. I jerked my right foot and felt the thicket of branches catching my boot. I wiggled my hips, trying to get the left leg over, but the azalea spread deeper than I realized.

"Dammit."

A rustling sounded in the grove. Furtive rustling as opposed to small critter rustling.

Quieting my squirm, I lowered the pans to rest near my outstretched leg. I leaned forward and squinted at the grove. Past the azaleas, taller bushes made a ring around a grouping of trees. By their spreading branches, I judged the trees as those ornamental cherries that looked pretty in the spring, although that was neither here nor there. It wasn't spring and I couldn't see worth a dang. However, someone skulked around the plantings. The crunch of dry leaves and shuffling of pine straw told me the skulker moved lightly and slowly.

I squinted at the shadowy tree forms. Spotted movement behind a trunk. The skulker wore dark colors and had something pulled over their head, likely a hood. I felt exposed, straddling a bush with nothing to cover my blondeness or winter paleness in my apple-green fleece coat with the hand-stitched poppies.

Why had I chosen metallic thread for the poppies? Why hadn't I tanned at the Get A Glo this winter?

Because I hadn't known I'd be stuck in a bush holding cornbread casserole while hiding from a tree stalker.

Like a worm on a hook, I floundered over the azalea. The

interlocking branches held my boot. My other leg still hung over the bush, unable to give me leverage. With aching hands, I gripped the pans and rocked. Which did nothing except scrape the insides of my thighs with azalea branches.

Those marks would take some explaining.

Giving up, I called out to the tree stalker. "Hey there. I'm kind of stuck. Can you give a hand?"

The quiet gave way to more rustling.

"I know you're in there."

The rustling died. The stalker had disappeared. But footsteps pattered on blacktop. They had snuck from the trees to the driveway.

I twisted to see behind me and a flashlight blinded me. Squinting, I teetered on one leg. "Hello?"

The flashlight beamed on my face.

"What are you doing?"

The footsteps changed from patter to hammer and the flashlight beam widened.

I twisted forward, pulled at my boot, then looked over my shoulder. I still couldn't see, but could tell the Tree Stalker ran toward me.

"Stop," I yelled. Gripping a casserole, I heaved it around my body. The aluminum brick slammed into the drive and splattered with a similar thud and splat of an airborne pumpkin.

The flashlight's beam swerved to follow the pan's arc, then hit my eyes again.

I grabbed the other pan and held it before my face, blocking the light. The awkward twist of my waist put a kink in my lower back. My arms shook with tension.

Why didn't they say anything? That spooked me more than the skittering about.

A hand shot out beneath the flashlight beam.

I threw the pan at the stalker.

They swept away the casserole. Cornbread flew into the azaleas.

My body pivoted. The hand slammed into my back and thrust me forward. I nosedived over the bush, but my boot didn't give way. I hung upside down, one leg still stuck in the bush. My body crushed the dangling free leg. My bag flipped over my back and thunked me in the head.

My attacker ran from the scene. A few minutes later, an engine sputtered.

"Wait," I screamed. "That's my truck."

The Datsun peeled out of the Brakeman drive. As best it could. The Datsun hadn't burned rubber since 1989. Still, my little yellow truck was gone.

The Tree Stalker had stolen my truck. And I now hung upside down over an azalea. The smell of cornbread casserole permeated the air. Not caring I'd nosedived and caught on a bush, my stomach howled. I yanked on the messenger bag tangled around my shoulders, spilling the contents. Feeling around the ground, I found my phone, flipped it open, and pushed a number.

"I need to report a robbery."

"Cherry?" Luke's voice sharpened. "Where are you? At home? Did someone break in?"

"No, my truck was stolen."

"Are you sure? Why would anyone steal that truck?"

"Good question. But I need you to hurry. I'm getting light-headed from hanging upside down. With that and all the casserole everywhere, I might be sick."

"Come again? Where are you?"

I sighed. "The Tea Grove. The Brakeman estate. I know what you're going to say and I don't want to hear it right now. Just please come get me before one of the Brakemans finds me upside down in their bushes. It won't be pretty."

# NINETEEN

Luke found me digging for the boot I had lost wriggling from the bush. With his Maglite, he helped me retrieve the boot and the contents from my dumped bag. The casseroles I left for raccoon or coyote but swore Luke to secrecy about their demise.

If Pearl ever found out I'd fought off an attack with her casseroles, I'd never be fed again.

After a round of "what happened" and "you did what" and "what in the hell were you thinking," Luke gripped my shoulders and gave me his stern cop face. "Don't think for one minute I believe you were just bringing sympathy casseroles to the Brakemans. Why were you really here? What's going on?"

"It's a two-parter. First, I don't want Coralee bugging Molly. I came to offer her my services instead."

"Uh-huh." He conveyed a lot of doubt with his agreement.

"Second, after seeing him with Donna Sharp, I wanted to know why Ron Brakeman-Newson was holding that medicine bottle. Donna was on Belvia's inquiry list, you see, and by association, I'm following up with Ron. I thought I might catch him unaware."

"You want to run that by me again? What does Ron Brakeman-Newson's possible evidence tampering have to do with his side-of-fries job performance? If you really are vetting Mrs. Brakeman's senior management team, which is as unlikely as bringing sympathy casseroles out of sympathy."

"Don't get caught up in the details." I fluttered my lashes, which he ignored. "Back to Ron. He probably had answers prepared when you questioned him, right?"

"Who I question in an active investigation is not your concern. Do I need to tattoo that on your forehead in order to get it planted in your brain?"

"I don't think tattoos work by osmosis." I gave him my customer service smile. Likely a wasted effort. "Ron didn't give me a clear answer about the medicine. Once he realized what I was doing, he got huffy with me. Almost threateningly huffy."

"Threateningly huffy?"

"In a vague sort of way. Parker also got huffy, but in a nervous, fearful way. Probably because I caught him stealing from Hazel."

"What? Who?" Luke's hands fell off my shoulders to grip his belt. "The Hazel from Halo House you mentioned earlier? Parker Brakeman is the kid who accosted a senior?"

"I wouldn't say accosted. But it's him all right. Speaking of tattoos, it's a great way to identify a perp."

Luke pivoted toward the houses. "What did he steal?"

"I have no idea. And Hazel will deny it. Won't press charges, I bet, although I don't know why."

Luke's jaw tightened.

"You hate it when you can't defend a victim, don't you?"

He nodded.

"Could we play bad cop, good cop with Parker? Just this once? Maybe he'll break."

He swung a smirk toward me, then pulled me in for a hug. "I wish I could, sugar."

I relaxed against him and closed my eyes. A golden-haired baby with gray eyes and dimples materialized.

The twins had merged. Probably thanks to Pearl's "that boy's a Branson" rhetoric.

Dagnabbit. These imaginary babies were forcing me to look at the future. Particularly the next twenty years' worth of holidays. Unless Luke and I moved to one of those far off countries, like Japan.

I shoved him away. "Thanks for the hug, but I don't want to mess your uniform. It'll be hard to explain casserole stains."

"What gives with you? You're blowing hot and cold worse than a window unit on the fritz."

I faked a laugh and gave him a semi-playful shove. "Oh, stop. You know how much I love you."

As his eyebrows arched, I fought off an external wince accompanying my internal cringe.

Of all the stupid, stupid comebacks. Here I was, kicking his imaginary babies out of my head, so why would I go there? Talk about sending mixed signals.

Lord, how embarrassing.

I spun toward his car. "Guess we should get going. Let's file that motor vehicle theft report while the details are fresh. I knew I shouldn't have left my keys in the truck."

"Hang on now." A hand landed on my shoulder.

I turned but kept my focus on his neck. I didn't want to see any emotion—negative or positive—crossing that ruggedly handsome face. Thankfully it was dark, which would hide the crimson staining my own cheeks.

The hand slid to my upper arm and squeezed. "Cherry?"

Chewing my lip, I waited.

"You want to talk to Ron Newson again?"

My eyes rose to meet his. The dark made it hard to see, but I could feel them smiling.


A butler answered Ron Newson's door. I guessed he was a butler because of his age and politeness and because he wasn't a Brakeman. However, I'd never met a butler. He didn't wear one of those tuxedo-type deals or even a suit, but he did have a nice cardigan. I kept my mouth shut and let Luke do the talking. Luke wore his Forks County deputy uniform, which I felt trumped the cardigan.

"Mr. Newson isn't available," said the quasi-butler.

"There's been a vehicle theft in his drive," said Luke. "If Mr. Newson doesn't speak to me now, he needs to speak at the sheriff's office. I'll follow him in my vehicle."

"Mr. Newson shares a drive with Mrs. Brakeman," said the Quasi-Butler. "Perhaps you should speak to someone in the next house. I believe Coralee Brakeman's family is at home."

"I'd rather talk to Mr. Newson." Luke rocked on his heels and gave Quasi his cop smile. "As you know, Coralee's a guest in that house."

"I'll take your card for Mr. Newson." Quasi was not backing down.

"And you are?"

"I'm also a guest." He began closing the door.

"Just a minute," I said. "What about Parker? Ron and Parker were just here. I spoke to them myself. Unless they're the ones who stole my truck."

"Of course they didn't steal your truck," said Quasi.

"I wouldn't dismiss a victim, sir," said Luke. "The perp shoved her into a bush and fled with her truck. Assault and theft. Considering the timing, that would make Ron and Parker both suspects. I strongly suggest they speak to me now."

"One moment." The door shut, leaving us on the porch.

"Dangit. I forgot to stick my boot in the jamb," I said. "You reckon they're still at home?"

"Because of Belvia, they might be tired of dealing with reporters and asked someone to answer for them. Or they didn't want to deal with any more sympathy casseroles."

"Or they spied your blueberries flashing all over the drive and are hiding."

"That too."

"Or one of them pushed me into a bush and stole my truck."

"I'm still trying to figure out why someone would do that."

"Me too." I crossed my arms and set my foot to tapping.

Luke looped an arm around my shoulder and pulled me into his side. "About what you said earlier—"

The door opened, Luke dropped his arm, and I released the breath I held.

"I'm afraid Mr. Newson and Mr. Brakeman will have to speak to you at the station tomorrow," said Quasi. "It's late and they are already in bed."

"My ass," I said. "Parker's too young. No way he's in bed. It's not that late."

Quasi's eyebrows climbed a few centimeters.

Luke handed him a business card. "Make sure they show up tomorrow morning. And I'll take your name too. For my report."

"Very well." Quasi slipped Luke's card into his shirt pocket and handed Luke one of his own. With a quick goodnight, he shut the door.

I peered at the card in Luke's hand and gasped. "Harry Hunt. That's Belvia's attorney. Not a butler. He wouldn't return my calls."

"He's been avoiding me too. I've been dealing with his associate on the missing will. Harry Hunt wasn't Della Brakeman-Newson's attorney. I wonder what he's doing at her house." Luke tapped the card against his chest before sliding it into his polyester shirt pocket. "This is getting interesting. You want to add assault to the vehicle theft report? I've a feeling we'll find your truck nearby. Maybe no malice was intended, but I'd love to get one of these Meemaw folks on a bunch of charges. It smells to high heaven of fish."

I clapped my hands and danced on the porch. "Let's go fishing."

We found the Datsun abandoned on the road. Easy enough for someone from the Brakeman estate to have abandoned it and return home undetected through a span of trees. At the Forks County Sheriff's Department, Luke and I filled out paperwork for assault and vehicle theft. Something I normally wouldn't consider, but Luke needed the paperwork to bring in Ron and Parker. While he typed, I pondered the point of the shove and steal.

"The perp didn't want me to see them," I told Luke. "Maybe it wasn't Ron or Parker, but someone else sneaking around the estate."

"It would've been easier for them to sneak away than push you and take your truck. They brought notice to themselves this way." He shook his head. "Probably it was Parker, ticked off that you were snooping. Seems like something a kid would do. Knock someone down and take a joyride. Don't worry, I'll get a confession out of him on this and whatever he stole from Hazel."

"That makes sense. If Ron wanted to do me harm, he'd flatten me like he did his wife." I bit my lip. "Whoops. Freudian slip. Ron Newson's personality hasn't improved since our first interaction."

"You think Ron Newson killed his wife?"

"He and Coralee have million-dollar motives. Isn't the spouse usually the most likely? And he's inheriting a sweeter deal what with Belvia's death on top of Della's. He's likely the largest stockholder now too. Unless that missing will changed things."

"Ron Newson had an alibi for Della's accident."

"Dangit. That's right." I drummed my fingers on his desk. An alibi for Della's hit and run, but not necessarily for Belvia. The entire family had been at Halo House that morning. "Have you gotten the cause of death for Belvia Brakeman yet?"

Eyes on his keyboard, Luke shook his head. "The coroner still has her. Maybe tomorrow."

"I need some good news. Tell me y'all have a strong suspect in Della's hit and run despite Ron's alibi. Even if you don't have the evidence to back it up."

He flicked me a sad look. "Wish I could, sugar. My strongest lead is the tire marks and I've got no witnesses. To be honest, I'm frustrated with the sweet tea people. They've been no help. And of course, the family has circled their wagons."

"Rich folks are good at covering their tracks, aren't they?"

"I don't know about that. But they're smart enough to not speak to me without a lawyer present. Which means I get nothing useful in an interview."

Exactly as Miss Belvia assumed they'd do. I understood her frustration. Frustration that led her to choose me for her witch hunt. "What about Coralee? Where was she when Della was killed? Coralee or Wally could've pushed me too."

"Cherrilyn Tucker, stop bullshitting me about researching staff issues for Mrs. Brakeman." Luke scowled. "Watch your back with the Brakemans. You already landed in the shrubbery tonight."

"You think Coralee pushed me?"

"Nope, I still think it was the kid." Luke reclined in his desk chair and folded his hands on top of his head. "I want to know what he was doing with this Hazel. And why she doesn't want to talk about it."

"Me too. I've got Ada and Fred watching her."

"I guess that's all right." He scooted his chair to face me. "You keep out of it though. If she complains about you harassing her, that'll eventually get to Sheriff Thompson."

"I hope we can get Parker. You think y'all do a lineup of hoodies? I've always wanted to pick a suspect from a lineup."

"As dark as it was, I don't think it would stand in court. You want to prosecute if it was him?"

"I don't know. Depends on what he's doing with Hazel."

"Just in case she doesn't want to file?"

I nodded.

"Good. I wouldn't press charges for getting knocked into a bush either. But Parker doesn't need to know that." Luke leaned forward to plant a small kiss on my lips.

Small but potent.

I drew back and pretended to fix my cuff. Finding casserole smeared in the seam helped to keep my eyes off Luke's.

"You want to talk about what else's going on with you? Nobody's around."

Tell him I had temporary baby schizophrenia? I shook my head.

"Sug, have you considered Cody's attorney could use Billy Branson as a witness for the defense? It could help his case. The shock of learning he might be Shawna's half-brother placed Cody under duress. The lawyer can show circumstances led Cody into thinking Billy's his father."

I sighed. Luke returned to this topic more than Myrtle Jones' stories about her 1958 trip to Paris. And Myrtle Jones had dementia. "Besides telling Shawna, you also want me to give Cody's lawyer the information you found about her daddy?"

He nodded. "I heard Cody's getting a new attorney."

"The court-appointed one wanted Cody to plea out." I closed my eyes. Belvia had understood the implications of Cody's arrest better than I did.

Luke squeezed my knee.

I opened my eyes. "Some think this trial has more to do with making your boss look bad than with Shawna's vanity."

Luke lifted his hand from my knee to run it through his curls. "Politics can get ugly."

"You heard anything about that?"

"Certainly not from the sheriff." His half-smile didn't hide the stress in his eyes. "And when I'm around the house, folks tend to keep their political opinions to themselves."

"By folks, you mean Bransons. They think you're a traitor, huh?"

"They're aware I'm seeing you if that's what you mean. We didn't try hard enough to hide it."

"Kind of hard when JB's got the whole town spying on us."

"JB's got bigger fish to fry than worry about who I'm dating."

"Yeah, the fish being my Uncle Will. JB wants his out-of-towner in the sheriff's seat next fall. Considering my brother's arrest has been made into Halo's crime of the century, I'd say JB's candidate would love to point out Sheriff Thompson's relationship to the incarcerated in his campaign stumping. Besides that, Cody's arraignment was a joke. Everyone knows JB had Judge Ackerman in his pocket. JB's godfather to Ackerman's grandson. They play golf together every Thursday, for pity's sake."

"I know, sugar. One of the reasons I grew up hating this town was the strength of the old boy network." Luke strummed his fingers on my knee. "All the more reason to take that information about Billy Branson to Shawna. She can't guarantee who will reside over the actual trial. In light of that evidence, Shawna may decide the case can't stand and withdraw her charges. She must know it'll boil down to a he said-she said sort of battle between the attorneys. And if y'all have a good one now—"

"In light of that evidence, Shawna'll go ballistic." I covered my face with my hands. Luke was too forgiving of his step-cousin. And too focused on using the Branson family secret as a Hail Mary pass to solve our problems. "I'm going to lose my house and my brother." And you. But I kept that haunting thought to myself.

"Your house?"

"It was the house or the farm." I sniffed back a tear. "If Shawna doesn't drop the charges, it's the only way we can afford the new lawyer."

"Darlin', I'm sorry." Leaning forward, he took my hands in his and pressed them to his lips. "Then don't tell the lawyer, if you think it won't help. That may be better anyway. If JB heard his brother could be a witness for the defense, he'd find your mother to use as a witness for the prosecution. They'd want her to discredit Billy and throw y'all off."

It was a good thing I hadn't eaten any of that casserole because that idea almost made me lose the little I had in my stomach.

Once again, I selfishly wished Belvia hadn't passed and had saved me from dealing with this ordeal. I also wished she hadn't mentioned it. That Pandora's box of hope had opened, then slammed shut.

My brother's future was at stake. I was losing my house. My family would never forgive Luke, despite his feelings about his stepfather. Even Todd had foolishly wrapped himself in Shawna for our cause, and God bless him, wasn't savvy enough to resist her charms. The Bransons would also make sure Uncle Will would lose his position as sheriff, because of a dumb blunder by my idiot brother.

Everyone and everything I held dear seemed to be slipping away.

But who was I fooling? Belvia would only have granted my wish if I could find her daughter's killer. I wasn't a detective, just a creative thinker. All I'd done was add more suspects with motives to her list and pissed off some powerful people with my lack of nuance.

"I don't know why I'm doing this, Luke," I said miserably.

"Because it's the right thing to do. Your judgment's sometimes misguided and your quest for justice stronger than your common sense, but you always try to do the right thing. That's one of the things I love about you, sugar."

We locked eyes for a long moment, both of us silent. His wistful smile made my stomach knot.

*I love about you.* We kept skirting the issue of us, and he used Shawna to avoid speaking of the future. Maybe he was also worried about Sunday dinners at the farm, where the pecan pie would be served with a side of hostility.

If I feared having Branson babies, did he fear kids with Tucker genes? What did we have to offer besides child abandonment, unemployment, and jail sentences? Good with our hands and raising goats?

Not that I'd claim the latter.

It wasn't until the drive home I reanalyzed his words and realized his "doing right" speech had pertained to Shawna. Whereas I'd been thinking of doing right by Belvia's last request.

Our crossed wires could be another sign. We may be able to start our engines, but we had no map to show us how to get anywhere.

# TWENTY

The next morning, I nuked a sausage biscuit and eyed Todd from across my coffee mug. He appeared more dazed and confused than normal, which could mean a lot of things or a whole lot of nothing, as it was Todd we were talking about. We both needed an early start. I was meeting Coralee to help with her funeral preparations and whatever else she deemed necessary. Todd was driving his truck on the day route. Where he possibly snuck in stops for sugar with Shawna.

That thought turned my sausage biscuit to dust and my coffee to vinegar. Even if he faked their relationship, it still felt too real.

I felt pinched between a hopeless relationship with Luke and a doomed friendship with Todd. Someone needed to pay and that someone was the woman with whom Todd currently attended. The man needed to cogitate on this fact whilst toting those brown boxes.

And I admit, I wanted him to hurt like I was hurting. I had gotten that low.

"I guess you haven't seen Cody lately," I said. "Grandpa's fixing to get him a new lawyer. The old one wants him to plead guilty."

Todd dropped his spoon into his cereal bowl and looked up from the box of Honey-Os he'd been reading.

"Although I shouldn't tell you this as you're dating the enemy now. Did you plan on telling Cody who you're seeing?" I took satisfaction from his stricken look and rubbed a few angry tears from my eyes. "By the way, I'm losing this house paying for Cody's lawyer. You better start looking for a new place."

"Baby." Todd pushed from the table. "When did this happen?" I held up a hand to keep him from hugging distance. "Don't you 'baby' me. Save that for Shawna."

"Cherry, it's not like you think."

"Tell me how it's not, Todd. You kissed her and you liked it. She's been in my house with you doing God knows what." I waggled a finger. "And keep whatever that is between you and God because I do *not* want to know. Actually, keep it out of my house."

"We're not doing anything—"

"Told you I didn't want to hear it." I swiped another tear. "Although I guess I'm losing the house anyway."

"Shawna's not all that bad. Never thought I'd say that," he amended quickly. "But I've seen a whole new side of her. Not that I've traded loyalty or anything. I'm still hoping our dating will help y'all out. But she's been more interesting than I thought. I should tell her you're losing the—"

"If you tell her one gol'darn thing that has anything to do with Cody, I will never forgive you." I stomped to the door.

"Wait a minute."

"Never is a helluva long time, Todd. Think on that," I hollered and slammed the door.

I took my bad mood to Halo House. Ada and Fred had possession of the fountain seats and assessed my demeanor before I opened my mouth.

"Who tee-teed in your grits, Christine?" said Ada. "You look like hell."

"It's Cherry. I had a rough night and a rougher morning." I glanced up the grand stairway. "And I need to see Coralee first thing, which is a heavy cross to bear this early."

Fred handed me his cup of coffee. "Here, I haven't had a sip. You need it more."

I fell on them both, relishing their hugs. If only I could move into Halo House. Friendships here were easier, the breakfasts tastier, and the coffee free-flowing. Luke could even have conjugal visits.

I'd heard that was popular at Halo House too.

"What's the matter?" said Fred. "Man troubles?"

"I've got man troubles, roommate troubles, and family troubles. But I'm also worried about Hazel. Did you know the young guy stealing from her was Parker Brakeman-Newson? Della's son?"

"Dadgum," said Fred. "I knew that kid was trouble."

"Are you sure he was stealing from Hazel?" said Ada.

"He took something from her purse. Saw it with my own eyes. Ada, why do you keep backing off this issue? You're acting as cagey as Hazel."

She blinked at me through her glasses and shrugged.

"The innocent old woman act won't work with me. What do you know about Parker and Hazel?"

"Nothing." She folded her arms. "Except you keep hounding Hazel and I don't like anybody hounding nobody."

Fred glanced from Ada to me. "I'll talk to Ada, hon. You better get if you're meeting Coralee. She's already here."

Ada glared at Fred. "I don't need a talking-to from you or Christine."

"You need something, Ada. Honesty for a starter. Parker's no good. At his house last night, someone accosted me and stole my truck. Probably Parker." I held up my hands, calming their anxious questions. "I'm fine, truck was nearby. Was bringing them a casserole. But someone doesn't like me asking questions."

"Asking questions about what?" Ada stuck her tiny fists on her bony hips. "You need a dose of honesty too, girl. Fess up. Why are you really helping Coralee?"

"To get her off Molly's back."

"Who's Molly?" asked Fred.

"Belvia's old assistant, remember? She lives here. Y'all need to form a welcome committee or something. I think Belvia was her only friend." I took Fred's coffee and started toward the staircase. "See y'all in class later. We're working on perspective again today."

"With models?" Fred said hopefully.

"With a ruler."

"Not if you want to keep your students," muttered Ada.


Pris answered Belvia's door. She wore a sloppy ponytail and circles beneath her eyes. "My mom said you might come. But I can make up an excuse if you want to back out now. I wouldn't blame you at all."

"That bad?" I waved off her worry and stepped inside the door. The room had changed from reception area to dining room. The table from the kitchen had been dragged into the middle and all available seats made a wide ring around it. "Interesting look. Y'all planning on a big family meal? I'd think the Tea Grove would give you more room."

Pris shook her head. "It's for a meeting. Mom wanted it here instead of the factory. And she didn't want anyone 'nosing around' Grandmother's house."

I raised my brows at the last remark but held my tongue. Coralee might be cataloging the family china. "How are you doing with your grandmother's passing? I guess you didn't know her too well, but it must still be rough."

Her eyes moistened, but her voice remained steady. "It's weird, mourning someone I didn't know but should've. I feel like I lost out."

"Understandable."

"When we arrived on the fourth, Belvia and I had a good talk. She said she'd been checking on me since I was born, even when my mom wouldn't talk to her. She was proud of my MBA and the work I've done with my own startup." Pris sniffed. "Strange too. Knowing someone was watching me all those years."

"That's nice though." I thought of my own mother, who hadn't done the same. It wasn't like Grandpa Ed and Grandma Jo had blocked communication, they simply couldn't find her. "At least you had that conversation. I'm glad for you. It's good you took the time off from work to see Belvia too. I bet that gave her some peace in her final days."

"Makes me angry at my mother, actually." Pris darted a vicious look at the office door, then swung an embarrassed gaze to me. "Sorry, I don't know why I'm telling you this. I haven't had anybody to talk to since I came here."

"No family of your own?"

She shook her head. "Never worked out. And I've been busy working."

The office door opened, revealing stacks of folders and the blipping computer. Coralee stepped out. As I had predicted, she had traded the alpacas for a business suit. Wally peered over her shoulder. He had kept his hipster hippy apparel.

I, too, had traded my visitation clothes for something more business-y. Harlequin tights and a matching orchid and magenta sweater dress with crocheted paintbrushes tacked in a diamond shape across my chest. I figured if I were working for free, I might as well advertise my skilled paid services as an artist.

Pris stepped sideways. "Cherry's here. I'm headed out."

"If you take the car, pick up Wally's prescriptions." Coralee turned to me. "I need you to make coffee."

"Yes, ma'am," I said. "For the three of us? How many cups do y'all want?"

"For the entire Meemaw's Tea board, which doesn't include you. Find donuts or something too." She eyed my dress, then noticed my befuddled look. "What is it?"

"I thought I was helping you with funeral plans."

"The funeral's fixed. My mother left instructions with Cooper and we're combining it with Della's. I thought you said you wanted to help?"

"I do." Witnessing a board meeting could put my suspicion meter to good use. Better to see the interactions between members now that I'd met everyone individually. "Where's the coffee pot?"

"In the kitchen, of course. If there're not enough cups, call the office." She tossed me a look that spoke of my innate idiocy. "Hurry it up. They'll be here any minute."

"Yes, ma'am."

"And get Molly in here to take minutes. She said she wasn't feeling up to it, but it'll do her good. Get her mind off mother's passing."

"I'll take the minutes."

"Do you know how to take minutes? This is important. Everything has to be recorded."

I crossed my fingers behind my back. "No problem. I'll check with Molly to see if she's got a form or something."

"You're certain you can handle this?" Coralee flicked lint from her suit sleeve. "This is an important meeting. I'm announcing my role as head of Meemaw's Tea."

"I can handle it."

She pivoted to reenter the office.

"You're an artist." Pris cocked her head. "Do you know how to take board minutes? I'd help, but I actually have plans."

"I'm a quick learner."

"You're protecting Molly."

"Yep."

But I was also protecting Miss Belvia's interests by investigating Coralee's very big motive for murder. Pris had said they'd arrived on the fourth. Two days before her aunt Della was killed. Now I knew Coralee also had opportunity, I felt even sorrier for Pris.

Her mother could actually be worse than mine.

# TWENTY-ONE

Call me skeptical, but if everyone thought Coralee had appeared just to attend Della's funeral, why had Coralee dragged her family to Halo when Della wasn't yet dead?

Did Luke and the sheriff know Coralee had motive and opportunity to mow down her sister? They must know. That was basic investigation work. I was the one who hadn't bothered to ask Coralee and her family for alibis. Once again proving Belvia should've asked someone more qualified.

I found the coffee, started a pot to brew, and left Belvia's apartment. I needed to talk to Molly, but I slipped into a corner and dialed Deputy Harper.

"Done with my shift and just getting to bed," he answered. "Want to join me?"

Luckily, the folks roaming the halls couldn't hear or see well. Otherwise, they might have caught my gasp and the Rose Madder flooding my cheeks.

"Not appropriate?" He laughed.

"I'm at Halo House."

"You can't tell me that the single seniors don't get it on."

"There's more bed-hopping here than in the dorms at Southern. However, I can't condone dirty talk in the halls."

"What are you now, the Halo House RA?"

"An interesting item came up. Coralee's holding a board meeting this morning at Halo House to announce her self-promotion to CEO of Meemaw's Tea."

"Not surprising, although in poor taste, as they hadn't buried her mother or sister."

"Have y'all found the will yet?"

"The alleged missing will is part of an active investigation."

"I take that as a no. According to Coralee's daughter, Pris, they arrived on the fourth. Did you know about that?" I waited for a moment in radio silence. "I can hear your wheels turning, but your jaw needs oil. Care to comment, Deputy Harper?"

"No comment."

"No comment as in you didn't know?"

"No comment as in you're close to interfering in an active investigation. I can't let anything leak or it could be used against us."

The dial tone told me I wouldn't get to know Coralee's tire report.

My brain percolated faster than Halo House's Mr. Coffee machines. And I felt just as wired. Molly answered the door in a fuzzy pink robe. Surprised she wasn't yet dressed, I feared the accumulated stress had taken its toll. I wanted to hug her, but she hung back.

"What can I do for you, Cherry?"

"I heard Coralee wants you to take minutes at a meeting today." I patted her hand. "But don't worry. I offered to do it for you. Is there a form you use or do you write down what everyone says? I thought you could help me."

"I could give you an example. Let me see if I can find one in the files."

Following her inside, I waited in the living area and she continued into the back hall. The sad-eyed porcelain children smiled at me. I wondered if the Precious Moments artist ever had to teach drawing to elderly sex maniacs.

I turned my mind from the business of art and picked up the framed photo of the sisters. The pair were similar in appearance, but what about in personality? Della and Coralee also looked similar, but one had gone into business and the other had run away.

Could one sister replace another like Coralee hoped? That could be the reason she didn't return to Iowa with her inheritance and leave the Meemaw's Tea people to sort things out for themselves. Besides family dynamics, the money and the power made for a powerful siren call. Her mother and sister had been powerful enough to frighten grown men like David Wells.

Molly's footsteps plodded in the hall. I returned the picture frame and pivoted to meet her.

"Here." She handed me a sheaf of papers. "I printed off a meeting. It should give you a template."

I glanced at the top sheet and noted the date. "Was this your last meeting?"

"It was the last before—" She gazed at the photo I had set down. "I retired."

"I know that's when you lost your sister." I nodded toward the picture. "I'm sorry to bring up those memories. Thanks for this."

"Thank you for helping." She shoved her hands into the pockets of her robe. "I guess you better get back to Coralee before she comes looking for you."

I walked to Belvia's apartment, reading through the report. The format was easy enough. Della was among those who had attended, naturally. Curiously, Belvia had been absent. I skimmed the Chief Executive's report (read by Molly), the boring Finance Committee's record, and slowed at the Board Development Committee's minutes.

Lisa Russell had stated that "upon the retirement of Belvia Brakeman, if Della's named CEO, a COO from outside the company should be hired."

Della had disagreed with hiring from outside because she felt there were "good candidates from within." David Wells agreed with Della and offered to throw his hat in the ring for COO.

Aha, I thought. Lisa Russell is consistent in her assertiveness, but the bear lover is not as wishy-washy as he pretends.

Lisa Russell had continued, "Upon Belvia's retirement, the timing would also be good to take Meemaw's Tea public." She'd also cited a study on the price of share values with forecasts for future prices based on an initial public offering.

My eyes bounced on the number, wondering how many shares everyone already had. If Lisa Russell's estimation was close, these people could buy their own tea companies.

Della had disputed the numbers though. "A rival company would more easily manage a buy-out if we went public. Belvia and I won't sell. When she retires, Belvia intends to keep her shares, except for those given to me by right as CEO. My mother always intended to keep Meemaw's Tea a Brakeman family company, not a public corporation."

A motion to form a selection committee for a new COO was seconded and passed.

Despite Della's protests, a motion to form a research committee for converting Meemaw's Tea status from private to public was seconded and passed.

From what Belvia had intimated, I could read between the lines of the report and imagined the heated debate that had taken place. The board members must have waited until Belvia was absent to discuss these sensitive topics. Della had fought them, but the hawks had already begun circling.


Belvia's apartment looked like an ad for Men's Warehouse, except the room teemed with suited women. Besides Wally, who did not wear a suit, Harry Hunt—the lawyer, not butler—and David Wells comprised the few men. David Wells wore the dagger stare honed on Lisa Russell as his fashion statement.

I don't think Lisa Russell noticed.

"Where have you been?" Coralee hissed. "Wally had to get the donuts."

"Free help is hard to find," I reminded her. "I was at Molly's, learning how to take minutes."

She eyed the paper in my hand and snatched it.

Bereaved or not bereaved, I'd have snatched that report back. But I had promised Uncle Will no public displays of anything that would draw negative attention to myself—and therefore him—and this room abounded in important members of Forks County.

Meaning voters.

Coralee glanced at the report and blanched. "Why would Molly give you this? These minutes are highly confidential."

Several heads turned our way. Lisa Russell raised an inquisitive eyebrow.

Coralee lowered her voice. "Did you read this?"

I shrugged. Like I cared what happened in a corporate board meeting. Although I did, because it might point to Della and Belvia's murder.

Or suspicious deaths, if you're more technically minded.

"Molly thought I could use it as a template," I said.

Coralee rammed the report inside a leather folder. "Of all the stupid...Just sit in the corner and take notes."

I ambled to the couch, grabbed a sketchbook and pencil from my messenger bag, and settled in to watch the show. If Coralee was so gol'darn worried about what I read in those minutes, why ask me to take notes at another "highly confidential" meeting?

Made me wonder if Coralee had the intelligence to murder her sister and mother. She certainly had the gumption. And the audacity.

Also the insensitivity.

I'd have to ask Luke if those traits made for a good killer or just made me want Coralee to be the perp since I didn't like her.

That would be disappointing.

Reaching for a donut, I elbowed my messenger bag and knocked it over. Pencils, brushes, and other items fell on the floor and rolled beneath the couch. I dropped to my knees, slid my hand beneath the couch, and felt for my supplies. My finger grazed something small and smooth next to the fat sofa foot. It stuck. I bumped the leg, then dragged the object toward me. I thought a wayward eraser had gotten stuck beneath the leg, but I pulled out a partially flattened capsule. Half cobalt green and half cream. Someone's medicine? Belvia was careful. And the apartment looked spotless.

I shoved the pill into my bag and pushed up on the couch, swiping my hand beneath the foot. This time, I rescued a green half-shell of the pill. Also flattened.

"What are you doing?" Coralee's voice blared over my shoulder.

I glanced up, my fingers closing over the half pill. "I knocked over my bag. Everything spilled under the couch."

"Leave it." Coralee bent over. "I'll have a cleaning service in here later. They can set aside your things."

Poking my hand into my bag, I dropped the half-capsule to the bottom. "Gotta wash my hands."

In the bathroom, I locked the door, turned on the water, and opened the medicine cabinet. With everything marked for Belvia's blindness, it only took a few seconds to open the few medicine bottles for a pill comparison. I crouched underneath the sink, searching the shelves. Eye drops, lidocaine patches, osteoporosis tablets, Metamucil, aspirin, and other over-the-counter painkillers.

No green and ecru capsules.

Someone had been medicating in Belvia's living room. In his evidence search, Luke hadn't found any pills. Although they had been partially stuck beneath the sofa leg. This was no carry-in-your-purse-in-case-you-get-the-sniffles-or-a-headache pill. A half-capsule meant they either cut the medicine or dissolved it into something else.

For themselves? Or for Belvia?

A knock sounded on the bathroom door. I shut the cabinets and cut off the water, then turned the latch.

Wally stood in the doorway. "They're ready to start."

"Alrighty."

"Good thing they got the bathroom door back on, right?"

"Yep." I studied him for a minute. Had Wally been medicating in Belvia's living room? His eyes looked cloudy. Coralee had asked Pris to get his prescription.

"Find anything interesting under the couch? Loose change? Gold coins? An earring?"

"I didn't find any earrings." I slipped around him and returned to the sofa. Someone had set my bag on top. I glanced inside and saw my sketch detritus had been tossed inside. Before I could fish for the capsules, Coralee caught my eye. I pulled my hand from my bag and placed it in my lap. Coralee had sent Wally to retrieve me. If she had seen the pills in my bag, I wouldn't draw attention to them. I'd turn them over to the sheriff before I showed them to Coralee, victim's daughter or not.

My resolve had returned. My gut felt Belvia had been correct. Someone had wanted her dead.

I couldn't wait to find out if those green and cream pills had caused her heart attack.

# TWENTY-TWO

From the couch's corner, I doodled board members' faces while Coralee called the meeting to order.

"Coralee," said Harry Hunt. "I realize you're representing the Brakemans, but you still need to follow procedure."

"I invited all of you and I'm running this meeting," said Coralee. "We can do this officially after the funeral. It's a tragedy what's happened to my sister and my mother. But before you start talking amongst yourselves about who will take over this company, you should know it's me. Meemaw's Tea is a family company and it's staying in the family."

The room's atmosphere darkened as the emotional temperature dropped. A squall of righteous indignation roiled from the suits.

There was that motive again, staring us all in the face. I took notes. For Coralee, but also for myself and the Forks County Sheriff's Department.

"But Coralee, we haven't even done the reading of the will." Harry's voice remained gentle but firm. "Your mother's wishes..."

A heavy knock on the front door resulted in a group flinch.

Wally opened the door and was pushed aside by Ron and Parker.

"What's going on in here?" Ron Brakeman-Newson unbuttoned his dark wool coat, revealing another smart suit. "Why wasn't I informed there'd be a board meeting?" He pointed Parker to the couch.

Parker took a step, then spotted me. Scowling, he plopped on the far edge.

I scooted over to needle him. Two more people with motives and opportunity, if the pills I found were used to poison Belvia. The medicine could belong to anyone in this room. The sweet tea folks had been floating in and out of Halo House since Della's accident. Before Della had died, they'd attended Meemaw's Tea meetings and clandestine parleys with Belvia in her apartment. Not that I suspected any as pill poppers, but if the woman who lived here believed she might be murdered, dosing her coffee with a controlled substance would be one way to do it.

"Ron, you've never taken an interest in the company before," Coralee said. "Why would I assume you'd start now? Why don't you just continue living off my sister's money and head back to the golf course?"

"Y'all settle down." Harry made calming motions with his hands, but Coralee and Ron were too busy shooting death laser glares at one another to notice. "It's not appropriate to air your family squabbles—"

"You're one to talk, Coralee," said Ron. "Where've you been all these years? You didn't make it to your father's funeral. I might be golfing, but at least I don't pretend reconciliations after the *Wall Street Journal* hints Belvia's stepping down."

I noted that little fact in my sketchbook, making sure to capture the look on Coralee's face in a quick sketch. Now I knew why Coralee appeared just before Della's death. Belvia must have known it too. So why did she fear a snake in the grass in her company and not her family? Or did she not see a difference between the two?

The board members followed the accusations with the decorum of a Wimbledon tournament.

"It's true, I saw that article. It reminded me time is precious." Coralee's hard features softened. "So I came back to make amends."

Ron rolled his eyes.

"I think we should adjourn," said Harry. "You've both suffered tragic losses. Emotions are high. It's better to discuss business with a clear mind."

"It's obvious what's going on," said Ron. "Coralee's making a power grab. I'm here to make sure Parker's not left out in the cold. It's a family company and by rights, he needs to be involved."

"Parker?" Coralee snorted. "What does he know about running the company?"

"We could say the same for you." Ron narrowed his eyes. "I can coach him. And he regularly visited his grandmother, unlike the other side of the family. Belvia's been talking to him about Meemaw's Tea since he was knee high."

I glanced at Parker. He stared at the floor, chewing a thumbnail. I wondered if he'd adopted that habit during the Meemaw lessons. Would Ron coach Parker or use him like a ventriloquist's dummy?

"Here's what's clear." Lisa Russell looked over her red bifocals and rapped a pen against a notebook. "Neither of you understand what you'll do to and for the company. That's what we've been trying to tell Belvia. It's time to take Meemaw's Tea public. You have the ability to make that happen, assuming you'll both be majority shareholders."

Pushing her readers on top of her blonde bob, she pulled a sheet of paper from her folder and waved it. "My committee's putting together a list of possible CEO and COO candidates. It started as a family business, but it doesn't have to remain one."

"That's not Meemaw's Tea values," said David Wells.

"Don't get marketing confused with operations, David." She turned to Ron and Coralee. "You can be involved in board meetings, but stay out of the day-to-day operations. I'm done with a puppet board. Meemaw's Tea needs real leadership."

"And your name's on the top of the CEO list, isn't it, Lisa? You aren't searching outside the company like you claim," said David Wells. "Why was your committee looking for a CEO when we all knew Della would assume that position?"

I sketched Lisa Russell and noted David Wells' accusation.

"I've been advocating for a board director's position separate from the CEO for a long time," said Lisa. "It would have circumvented all this current hoopla."

"Enough," said Harry. "It's indecent to speak of these things now. Belvia's shares will land in the hands of who she wanted running her company. In her previous will, it was Della. There's been mention of a new will, but the details are inconclusive. I won't discuss it. It will be cleared up soon though."

Coralee quickly hid the smile skating across her face. Ron shot Parker a look that told him CEOs don't chew their nails in public.

The complication of a missing will made these two goobers look even more suspicious.

I must have sighed out loud because it caught Ron's attention. "What's she doing here?" He pointed at me. "There shouldn't be anyone in this room but board members and family."

"She's working for me," said Coralee.

"I knew it." Ron narrowed his eyes.

I delivered my best customer service smile to the crowd craning their necks at the interloper. "Actually, I'm working for Belvia."

"What do you mean?" Harry's lips firmed. "Belvia didn't inform me of this. What are you doing for her?"

"That I can't say. But you could call it last requests."

"Just what we need, another person trying to grab the company purse." Lisa Russell stood. "I'm checking into you, young lady. You haven't impressed me a whit. Harry, when is this reading of the will?"

Harry cleared his throat. "The police have intervened. Understandable, with Della's accident and Belvia's sudden demise. We have to wait until they give us permission to analyze how Belvia wanted Della's inheritance bequeathed."

Nice feint by the lawyer. No mention of suspicious deaths or will theft.

"I want to be informed," said Lisa. "If Belvia's wishes are questionable, I'll contest it."

"You can't do that," said Coralee.

"Belvia would not want her company to suffer," said Harry Hunt. "We all know that much."

The group nodded their heads, but no one looked relieved. Coffee cups were shoved to the middle of the table. The assembly edged out and wasted no time in leaving.

Tossing my sketchpad on the couch, I stood. "Can I speak to you, Mr. Hunt?"

"Harry, I want to talk to you first. Privately." Coralee opened the office door. "Cherry, you stay right there. I'll get to you in a moment."

Harry glanced from me to Coralee, then walked into the office.

Dangit, foiled by Coralee. I blew out a sigh and eyed the untouched plate of donuts.

As I reached for one, Ron grabbed my elbow. "What are you doing for Coralee?"

I yanked my arm from his grip. "Taking meeting notes. And I'm not working for Coralee."

"You've been spying on my son and now you're involved in company business. I don't like it."

"And I don't like your son stealing from elderly women's handbags." I glared at Ron, then turned my anger on Parker. "Don't think I won't press charges for knocking me down and stealing my truck."

Parker jumped off the couch, pinning me between him and his father. "I told you to stay out of my business."

"Not here," Ron barked at Parker. "You watch yourself, young lady. You have no idea what's at stake."

"I know that if you lay your hands on me again, I'm taking it to the police. You and your son are creating a nice rap sheet."

Ron leaned into my ear. "I'd advise you to think twice about that. I can't always control my son, but I can buy him an excellent defense. I take it you and your brother know about such things. I've looked into you, Miss Tucker."

My face heated. Before I could open my mouth, Ron shoved

around me, knocking me into the table. Parker kicked my bag where it lay next to the couch. The contents scattered. Again.

"Hey," I cried.

The office door opened. Harry peered out. "What's going on?"

"Just speaking with Miss Tucker." Ron smiled. "I'm trying to understand why she thinks she should involve herself in our affairs. You'll have better luck than me, Harry. I'm sure there's some legal arm twisting you can do. You're good at that."

He followed his son out the door, slamming it on his way out.

"Ron's going to be a problem," said Coralee.

I wasn't sure if Coralee spoke to me, the lawyer, or herself.

Harry flicked her a quick glance, then turned his attention to me. "Miss Tucker, we need to talk. Let's find a quiet place."

"I agree." I bent to scoop the contents back into my bag, reaching beneath the couch to grab my phone. While I was there, I groped for more pills. Feeling none, I wondered if Coralee had cleared them out while I was in the bathroom. I looked up and found her standing over me again.

"Why do you keep poking around that couch? I need you this afternoon."

"Yes, ma'am." I kept the edge out of my voice.

"We're going to the tea factory. I want you to take notes." She picked up my sketchbook. "And real notes. What are these? Cartoons?" She flipped a page. "Are those devil horns on my head?"

I snatched the sketchbook back. "I'll transcribe these into words for you. Later."

Harry and I chose the Last Call, figuring it quiet this early in the morning. We figured wrong. Rosie worked the bar again. The stools had been filled with a khakis-and-polo crew, sipping Bloody Marys. A golf tournament blared on the overhead TV.

"Hey, Cherry," called Rosie. "It's five o'clock somewhere. Come over and join us. Reruns of Pebble Beach are on the tube and I've warmed up the blender."

Never had I met such an early drinking crew since my college tailgating days with Luke. "We'll take some coffee and a table, thanks."

Harry and I tucked in next to the jukebox.

"Who are you representing, Mrs. Brakeman or her children?" I said. "Why were you at Ron Brakeman-Newson's house last night?"

"I was Belvia's personal attorney. I now deal with her estate," said Harry. "But I can't discuss any of it with you."

"I witnessed the new will. Me and Jose, who works maintenance. Also, Miss Krenzer knew she was signing a new will because Krenzer sent us to do the job. Coralee watched us and her daughter Pris knew about it too."

"Did you have a question or are you relating some sort of deposition?"

"My point, Mr. Hunt, is that five people knew Mrs. Brakeman signed a new will. Can't you hold off the reading until it's found?"

Harry folded his hands around his coffee mug and studied the swirl of cream slowly dissipating into the raw umber liquid. After an excruciating minute, he said, "What if it's not found?"

"Is there a reason to think it might not be found?"

"Isn't the fact that it's missing reason enough?"

"But it's not—"

"I hope, Miss Tucker, you're not about to utter the word 'fair.'" A smirk winked then disappeared. "Fairness has nothing to do with the law."

"I was going to say conclusive. I know the Sheriff's looking at her computer records."

"He needs a warrant for that."

"Are you saying you're not letting him look at her computer files?"

"I'm saying he needs a warrant. There are confidential business records in her files."

My frustration index rose with my indignation. "What do you think, that the sheriff's department would leak the secret sweet tea recipe?"

He sipped his coffee.

I sat on my hands to keep from tearing my hair out. "Listen, Mr. Hunt, you're protecting Miss Belvia and I admire that. I'm trying to do the same. It seems a lot of people say they have her interests in mind, but none of us are sharing information."

"So share. What do you know?" He kept his features mild and his voice even, but the words worried me. They implied there was something to know that I shouldn't. "What are you doing for Belvia?"

That was the piece of information I couldn't share. He could tip off the killer unintentionally or deliberately. With all this money at stake, there were other interests to be served. Interests that would pay off later. If anyone could see an endgame, it'd be a lawyer.

Probably why Miss Belvia didn't trust him.

"Mrs. Brakeman was fixing to commission a series of portraits for Meemaw's Tea," I lied. "For her retirement. A gallery of the company presidents. Herself and Della. We were discussing Della's replacement. Because I study the personality of the sitter before painting, she wanted my opinion on various candidates."

He cocked his head.

"I can be judgmental. And not in a good way. I'm not proud of it. But Mrs. Brakeman saw it more of an asset than a flaw."

Harry nodded.

Who knew admitting my failings would be my best cover? "She'd ask me to size everyone up and report back. I plan to finish the assignment, even with her death. Maybe because of her death."

"And what will you do with this report once you're done?"

"Give it to her successor, I suppose."

"Even if your opinion of her replacement is negative? What if her shares go to someone you find disreputable? Perhaps you'd do better giving it to me. Or dropping it all together."

"I'd rather wait and see what happens."

"The investigation is still ongoing. You're familiar with one of the deputies, I believe? The one who was at the house last night."

"Deputy Luke Harper."

"And you have strong ties with the sheriff."

Was there anyone in this town who didn't know my business? "You could say that."

"We can trade information. I'd like to know what's going on in the investigation. I can provide you information about anyone you like."

This time, I took the deep-thoughts moment with my coffee cup. I couldn't attempt mental chess with a lawyer. Harry Hunt played closer to the vest than Todd at Am-Pro Poker night. Why did Harry want information on the investigation? For the same reason Belvia did, to keep it out of the press? Or to prevent the police from catching the perp? What if he was the perp?

That thought chilled my coffee.

"I'd like information on yourself. Do you represent her personally and professionally? Do you have a stake in Meemaw's Tea too?"

"Is that pertinent? Do you think I want to become CEO?"

"I—" I'd been caught in my own web.

Harry stood and collected his briefcase. "Thank you, Miss Tucker. You've been very helpful."

"Wait. Didn't you want to exchange information?"

His smile did not match the cold set to his eyes. "You told me everything I needed to know."

# TWENTY-THREE

I grabbed our empty coffee cups and walked them to the bar, reviewing my conversation with Harry Hunt. He knew I wasn't vetting candidates for Meemaw's Tea. But did he know I was vetting suspects?

This was why my family didn't like lawyers. Sneaky sumbitches.

Rosie placed the cups beneath the bar, then rested her arm on top. "You look down in the dumps, honey. Sure you don't want something to put a pep in your step?"

"That's real sweet, but it's early." I used to take my worries to my favorite bartender, but now Red had fallen to the dark side like almost everyone in this town. Including Todd. I heaved a sigh and slid onto a stool. "Rosie, I've got troubles with a capital T."

She grabbed a fresh cup of coffee and slid it before me. "Man trouble? Job trouble? Or is it varicose veins? They can hit early."

I flicked a worried glance at my orchid and magenta harlequin tights. "More like trouble knowing who to trust."

"Sounds like man trouble to me."

"I trust the man. I don't trust his family." I shook my head. "But actually, that's not what I was talking about."

"But that was first on your mind." Rosie patted my hand. "Sorry, honey. Think real hard about how much you love this guy though. You marry him and you marry the family. I speak from experience."

I buried my head in my hands. "Not what I wanted to hear."

"Of course not. You're in love and you want the fairy tale. Don't you know Prince Charming came with a mother-in-law? Now, what's the story on the other people you can't trust?"

I couldn't speak of Belvia's possible murder with Rosie, but she could help me with Hazel. Dropping my hands, I stole a glance around the room, then lowered my voice. "I heard Parker Brakeman-Newson hangs out here. Belvia's grandson."

Rosie's drawn-on eyebrows shot to her hairline. "That's not who you're dating, is it?"

"Lord, no." I curled my lip. "I need some intel on Parker."

"Intel?" Rosie flashed a quick look around the bar. "I'll see what I can do. Check back tomorrow."

The house phone rang in the midst of my thank you. Rosie held up a finger and trotted to the back wall to answer. I fished a few dollars from my bag, laid them on the bar, and hopped from my seat. Before I reached the door, Rosie hollered my name.

She had a hand over the receiver and pointed at the phone. "It's the front desk. Miss Krenzer says there's a phone call for you. If you want, the hall phone'll be quieter." She pointed at the Bloody Mary crowd golf-clapping a tee off.

Thanking her, I left to use the hall phone. In a small recess near the bathrooms, Halo House residents could rest on a comfortable chair next to a sturdy yet delicate-looking table to call their friends. In case you felt like catching a drink at the Last Call and wanted to see who could join you. Or to ask a pal to bring extra Pepcid for Taco Tuesday in the deli.

Another wonderful Halo House amenity.

I picked up the phone and dialed the front desk, wondering who was trying to track me down but didn't have my cell number. Probably one of my Halo House buds.

"Just to remind you," said Miss Krenzer. "This phone is not meant for personal use."

"Yes, ma'am." Only my RA back in Savannah was stricter than Krenzer. "Who's calling?"

"I assume one of your students. Let me connect you."

I hoped it wasn't a student calling to critique my teaching. They needed shading techniques before tackling the human form. The cow skull still life was next in line.

The line beeped.

"Mornin'. Cherry Tucker speaking."

A long pause made me wonder if the student on the other line had forgotten why they'd called. Unfortunately, that'd happened before.

No heavy breathing. They hadn't fallen asleep.

"Hello—"

"Stay out of our business."

I jerked and almost dropped the receiver. The voice sounded like Darth Vader had gone deep-sea diving. "Who is this?"

Another second delay and the deep gurgly voice continued, "You are in over your head. Get out before it's too late."

"Ada, did you get a new app? I've heard this one. Try the ghost voice. It's real fun. Beverly Ameson's got it set on her phone."

"This is your last warning."

I rolled my eyes. "You can do better, Ada. I know you're ticked at me, but keep up the pranks and you're getting a goat in your bedroom."

Darth Vader switched to Helium voice. "This is not a joke. Next time you're getting more than a shove. And your friend—Ada?—might too."


I walked from the hall in a daze. This person—Parker Brakeman-Newson topped my list—had not just threatened me, but Ada. I was used to threats. But Ada wasn't involved in Belvia's death. I hoped the caller had only used Ada's name because I had referred to her.

Which meant I'd put my friend in jeopardy.

It was time for a chat with Mr. Parker Brakeman-Newson. He had too many names and too much thuggish swagger for my liking. By Halo's standards, adult males who relied on Daddy to get them out of trouble invited open season on ass-whooping. Parker could hide behind Ron's lawyer, but not without a fight. He'd already cost me two fine casseroles. If it was Parker who'd threatened us. I felt sure as rain it was.

At the main desk, I asked Krenzer again who called.

"I was too busy to take a memo and they were hard to understand," said Krenzer. "I thought it might be Earl Junior or Sissy Mason because they use their tablets to communicate. Such a help for stroke victims. I figured if we couldn't find you, I'd take a message."

"Could you tell where they called from?"

"An outside line."

It was impossible to know if the caller was in Halo House or not. Probably a smartphone, judging by the app they used. I needed to find Parker. I also needed to drop off possible evidence with the sheriff. I took a spin toward the door.

Krenzer called me over. "Where are you going?"

"Out. Dangit. Do I have class?" I glanced around for a clock. Halo House was worse than Vegas when it came to clocks. I might need to start wearing a watch like everyone else. Usually, I relied on my friends getting me to class on time. "Am I late?"

"No. Come into the office for a minute. We need to chat."

I turned the corner from the front-desk window and slipped through the Dutch door kept locked from residents who liked to rifle through mailboxes.

"Why did you call the police when you found Mrs. Brakeman?" said Krenzer. "You should have gone through me. It caused a big kerfuffle. There's talk that the police will show up if you pass away in your apartment."

"I'm sorry. Is it making folks nervous? The deputy was a friend. I thought bringing him in would keep his investigation low-key, yet still official."

"Didn't work. And not nervous. Excited." She jammed a pod into her coffee maker and smacked a button. Empty pods threatened to escape the trashcan beneath the counter.

"Excited?"

"The 911 dispatcher's been busy today." Krenzer faced me, her nostrils quivering as the scent of freshly brewed beans filled the office. "Janet Presley called the sheriff when Ray Howard didn't come down for breakfast at his usual time. Ray had stayed in his apartment. With a female companion. The police and I found him in a compromising situation. Ray was not happy. Neither was Janet when she found out about Ray's lady friend."

"Oh boy."

"You cannot bring in the police without going through me." She whipped the coffee mug to her lips and took a deep breath. "We need to make it clear that Belvia's death was an unusual situation."

"Tell them there was a robbery."

"That's a horrible idea. I'm not going to frighten our residents."

"I guess you shouldn't tell them she was murdered either." I slapped a hand over my mouth, then cursed my brain for forgetting to hit the mute button.

"Murdered?" Krenzer choked on her coffee. "Belvia Brakeman had a heart attack."

"Yes, ma'am. That's what they say," I said, following Harry Hunt's neither-confirm-nor-deny speak.

Krenzer set down her mug. "Is that why the police wanted to look at her medication history?"

"Do you have her medical records?" I toned down the hopefulness in my voice.

"We keep records to know what drugs are in-house. For safety. And if someone needs assistance in an emergency, we can give the list to the EMTs and hospital."

"Sounds like the medical examiner found something in her system. Did the police say what drug they were looking for?"

"Digoxin. Like Lanoxin or Cardoxin. Many residents take those for heart symptoms. But not Belvia. She was healthy besides the glaucoma. Except for hip issues. She didn't get much exercise because of her eyesight and focus on work."

And she was ninety, I thought. But Krenzer was right. Belvia appeared more likely to kick butt than kick the bucket.

Krenzer placed a hand on her chest. "The police must be mistaken. Belvia took glaucoma medication and sometimes used pain patches. I don't see how she could have gotten heart medications."

"Tell me about this glaucoma medicine. Was it eye drops? Pills?"

"Drops. Alphagan, if I remember correctly. It decreases pressure and fluid in the eyes. There may be some heart side effects. But it's not like she could have overdosed on eye drops. She'd been using them for a long time."

My mind raced. Could someone have put the medication from the capsules in Belvia's eye medication? Would the powder inside the pills dissolve in eye drops? Had I found the key to her heart attack?

My fingers itched to pull a capsule out, but I didn't want to wave a possible murder weapon in Krenzer's face.

"Did she take any pills?" I forced my voice toward conversational. "Maybe she got the wrong medicine."

"I guess it's possible, but how could she have gotten heart medication? You've seen her place. Everything was organized to aid her disability. If she had switched her pills it would have been OTC pain meds or vitamins."

But I had looked in all her vials. Belvia didn't take green and cream capsules. Krenzer was right. There were barely any pills to take.

"Belvia was wearing a pain patch when she had her heart attack." Krenzer's gaze drifted over my shoulder. "She was facing her daughter's funeral. She might've asked someone for something stronger and they gave her the wrong stuff."

"That's what I'm thinking too." Switched the pain meds with capsules. But not in an accidental I-can't-tell-my-digoxin-from-my-oxycontin. And that made more sense than putting the powder in her eye drops.

Krenzer placed a hand over her mouth. "How awful. What a terrible accident."

"You should tell the residents that's what the police are checking. It might be a good warning about sharing medications." I placed a hand on the Dutch door lever. "Wait, doesn't her retired assistant, Molly Kern, have heart problems? I thought Belvia had told me that. Does she keep medicine at her place? Maybe Miss Belvia accidentally took hers. Those two are still very tight."

"Just a moment." Krenzer turned to her computer. "No, I don't see heart issues listed."

"Her sister died. She could've been the one with heart problems. Maybe I misunderstood."

"Certainly. But there's heart medication in just about every suite here. So many were visiting Mrs. Brakeman. It could've been anyone." Krenzer checked her wristwatch. "Class starts soon."

Dagnabit. So much for my errands. I'd have to run the pills to the sheriff's office and hunt for Parker later.

"And Cherry." Her voice had returned to its normal no-nonsense clip. "Use chain of command in emergencies. Call me before you call the police."

"Yes, ma'am." I opened the door and slid through.

"One more thing: your student numbers are dropping. You need to make the class more interesting or you'll lose the spot. Hot yoga has become popular. We're opening another class."

"When?"

"This week." Krenzer raised a brow. "It's not enough to make friends here. If you want to teach, you've got to keep students. As much as I believe in art therapy, we need to make the seniors happy."

If only Krenzer knew the kind of therapy those degenerates really wanted.

# TWENTY-FOUR

Krenzer was correct. Half of my class had disappeared. To hot yoga or to the bar to watch Pebble Beach. The half remaining outwardly groaned at my cow skull. One woman, Tootie Woodward, broke a perfectly good piece of charcoal in half. Tossing her apron on the ground, she stormed off, muttering, "Not wasting the rest of my good days on bovine nonsense."

Luckily, Ada and Fred encouraged the remaining crew to stay with promises of models "after we get the hang of this sketching business."

When I replied with "I promised no such thing," I received a "You better rethink that one, missy."

Hazel was a no-show again.

As I pointed out techniques for contouring and encouraged bolder expression, my mind raced from Hazel's absence to Parker to the pills to my expected afternoon excursion at Meemaw's Tea factory with Coralee.

I raced from Halo House parking lot—a Datsun euphemism for puttering at the highest speed possible without causing smoke—and hightailed toward the small city of Line Creek, Forks County Seat and home to Forks County Sheriff.

Normally, I would stop at the Lickety Pig to soften Uncle Will with barbecue. But no time today. I caught Uncle Will in the parking lot and thanked the lucky stars I didn't have to run the usual gauntlet to talk to the sheriff.

"Well, now." He thumped the top of his Crown Vic. "To what do I owe this pleasure?"

I held out the palm containing the green and cream pill and its half sidekick.

"I'm not that worried about the election."

"What do you mean?"

"The Prozac." He grinned but his eyes didn't contain any mirth. "What're you up to, girl?"

My excitement dimmed. Dammit, not heart meds. "I found these in Belvia Brakeman's apartment. Under her couch. I thought it might—"

"Get in the car."

"I don't have time."

"I think you do." He walked around the brown and cream sedan to open my door. "We're taking a trip to visit your brother."

"What? Why? Uncle Will, I've got stuff going on today. He's not expecting me." I caught his glower and got in the car. The heavy door slammed shut behind me and I shuddered.

Despite his size and girth, he slipped into the driver's seat with an easy familiarity. A half-minute later we pulled into the parking lot of Forks County Jail. Handily located across the street from the Sheriff's Office. We checked through the back entrance. Uncle Will's hand steered my shoulder as he guided me through doors and halls and into the visitor's room. We took seats on the orange stools and waited.

"What am I really doing here? What lesson should I be learning?" I searched the concrete block walls for a clock.

"Getting your priorities screwed on straight." Uncle Will glowered at me. "You find more fascination in other families' problems than your own. What were you doing hunting for pills under Belvia Brakeman's couch?"

"I honestly was not looking for anything but the contents of my bag, which had spilled. They were an accidental find and I had hoped something you could use in your investigation. The pills were half-wedged beneath the leg. Easy to miss."

"And you were in Belvia's apartment because..."

"Coralee asked me to help." I gave him my biggest customer

service smile. With eyelash fluttering for extra oomph. "You know how Jesus asks us to watch out for widows and orphans."

"Visiting prisoners is on that list too. Particularly when one's your own brother."

"Listen, Uncle Will, I know there's heart medicine in Belvia's toxicology report. I didn't know those pills were Prozac." I peeked at him from under my lashes. "Prozac can't be disguised for digoxin, can it?"

"No. Belvia Brakeman didn't have a Prozac prescription. The woman was too proud and too busy to be depressed. Where did you hear about her toxicology report?"

"Halo House. And I was wondering about the tire tracks. Did you compare them to Coralee's? Did you know her family was already in Halo when Della died?"

"Do you mean my team wouldn't think to check on the immediate family related to the victims in two suspicious death investigations?" The chocolate-brown eyes slitted. "I take it I'm not getting your vote in the next election?"

"Of course you are." A rush of heat slapped my cheeks. "I didn't mean anything. I've been privy to the Brakeman inner circle. And thought—"

"The Bransons are looking for more ammunition to use against your family. And you're involving yourself with the Brakemans? You can't get more visible in this county unless it was the Bransons themselves." He pointed at his head. "Do you see the steam emitting from my ears?"

"Sorry, sir." I dropped my chin, then looked up as a deputy escorted Cody through a door. Orange was not a good color on a Tucker. We were much too fair. However, Cody's beard had been trimmed and he'd put on a couple pounds.

He grinned at my wave. "Hey, sister."

Uncle Will permitted us a brief hug, then motioned Cody into his seat. "I understand we're getting you a new lawyer."

"Yes, sir. That's what Grandpa said. Cherry had something to do with this, didn't you?" Cody grinned at me.

I shook my head, trying to keep the disappointment out of my eyes. "That's all Grandpa."

"How's Todd? Haven't seen him this week, and he usually stops by."

My cheeks heated. "He's good. Don't worry about it. Been busy. Barely seen him myself."

"I sure hoped he'd stop by. He was going to give me some pointers. I've been playing poker with the guys." Cody glanced at Uncle Will. "For candy bars. We take those chocolate bars and divide the blocks."

"I'll be sure to remind him." My smile was as weak as my will. "And bring y'all chocolate next time I come."

What was clear—and blatantly obvious in Uncle Will's approach—was I needed to get a grip on more pressing matters. Getting Cody out of jail should come first. Now that I couldn't count on Belvia Brakeman's assistance, I had to put away my pride and follow Luke's advice. He was right, we had no better plan. I'd tell Shawna about her father. Hope she took it as good will and not blackmail. But also hoped it made her realize Cody had no malicious intent toward her. He'd just been a kid wanting to know who his real father was and had gone about it badly.

I couldn't bring myself to tell Cody his "angel of mercy" had died before she'd helped us.

Our fifteen minutes passed. Uncle Will nodded at the waiting deputy. Cody and I exchanged another hug. He clung to my neck, reminding me of how he used to curl in my lap as a little guy, miserably missing the momma he never knew. "Love you, Cherry," he whispered. "Thanks for getting me that new lawyer. That was your plan, right? Your miracle?"

"Love you too." Drawing back, I looked into the eyes that matched mine, despite the color difference. "I'm doing whatever I can to get you out of here."

"I know you will." His lips hinted at a curve before drooping. Ducking his head, he shuffled to his warden and disappeared through the door that barred the inmates from the outside world.

Uncle Will's hand dropped to my shoulder.

I let him guide me back, barely aware of my surroundings for the tears.

In my truck, I rang up Coralee. After leaving a message on her voicemail, I called Pris with the number she'd left me. Pris was at Meemaw's Tea factory but hadn't seen her mother yet.

"I'm in Aunt Della's office, trying to sort out a mess. Lisa Russell asked me to come in and look at a software problem they were having. She knew it was in my wheelhouse and I'm killing time." Pris sucked in her breath. "Sorry, that was a bad choice of words considering I meant waiting for the funerals."

"If you see your momma, tell her I'm not coming. I've got my own family business to tend." I exhaled, my stomach cramping at the thought of my impending confrontation with Shawna. I'd rather confront Parker about his prank call threatening Ada.

"Mom's still at Grandmother's apartment." Her voice dropped. "It was nice of you to offer to help her. I know you were just protecting Molly. You'll be happy to know I've met the replacement for Della's assistant."

"That's a relief. I'll tell Molly myself. I don't think she's handling Belvia's death well."

"I'm sure my mother hasn't helped. To be honest, I was reluctant to make this trip with her and Dad. But I wanted to meet Belvia and hoped it meant my mother had changed her ways."

"What ways?"

"She's got some issues." The answer was vague despite the bite in her tone. "And Wally has codependency down to a science. He self-medicates, if you haven't noticed."

"I'm sorry."

She huffed out a long sigh. "Don't be. They've made their own mess. I've resigned myself to taking care of them. Work helps with that. I wish I had reached out to Belvia instead of believing what Mother had always said about her. And now it's too late."

"You can't help that, Pris."

"Thanks, but I've made some unwise choices myself. Now I've got to deal with the consequences."

I winced at the harshness in her tone, which sounded more derisive than bitter. After offering her a few more consoling remarks, I hung up.

Her last statement confused me, but I let it go, realizing I'd driven halfway to Halo House instead of toward Shawna Branson's. Rather than turn around, I decided to visit Molly and give her Pris's news about the new assistant. While I was at it, I could do a quick Parker sweep.

Even my subconscious excelled at procrastinating.

Back at Halo House, a crossing flurry of afternoon activities caught me in the lobby. I spotted Hazel sneaking off to Rosie's hot yoga class. A swarm of DAR ladies scooted—half of them literally—toward the library for their monthly High Tea, held at two o'clock. Waiting until four ruined dinners.

Nobody had seen Molly, which told me she grieved alone. I snagged Ada in an attempt to force new friendships on Molly. Together we elevatored to the second floor to give Molly the news that Coralee wouldn't bother her anymore.

We waited outside her apartment door.

"Candy, this is taking forever. I was planning on checking out the hot yoga," said Ada. "We could leave a note on her whiteboard."

"It's Cherry. Molly lost her best friend. Be more sympathetic."

"Not like that never happens here." She snorted. "Why don't you sign her up for an activity? It's more natural than your attempt to shove people at her. Maybe this Molly wants to be alone."

"I already asked her to join my art class."

"Refused, huh? She's a smart one, then." Ada grinned at my glare. "What are you trying to do? Put all your little projects in that class?"

"My Halo House friends are not projects, Ada."

"Tell that to Hazel." Ada folded her arms. "Looks like Molly's not home. Or she doesn't want to talk to us."

"Coralee's still in Belvia's suite." I spun in that direction. "I hope she didn't drag Molly into that apartment to make Molly help with her something."

We hurried down the hall to Belvia's apartment. Ada rapped a withered knuckle and the door swung open.

"Weird. Someone must be home though." I poked my head through the wide door and called out for Coralee. The lamps had been turned off in the living room, but light spilled from the office door. "If Coralee's making Molly work, I'm having a fit."

"Can we go in?" asked Ada. "I've never been invited to Her Highness's house."

"Just a minute. They could be in the office. I'll check." I left Ada in the doorway and scooted past the boardroom/kitchen table, calling for Coralee and Molly as I went. From behind the office door, a tinny voice spoke without inflections or rests. The spew of words almost sounded like gibberish.

"Coralee? Is Molly with you?" I rapped, but the electronic voice continued its monologue without a break.

A frisson of electricity shot through me and the hair on the back of my neck stood on end. "Hello?"

Pushing the door open, I stepped inside. The big office chair faced the computer. A scrolling marquee of numbers lit the top of the monitor, while the electronic voice read from a window opened below. A blue cursor lit words as the narrator repeated each in its rapid monotone. A metallic smell assailed my nose, giving more life to the robot voice.

My eyes darted from the computer to the chair. Suit-jacketed arms hung on either side of the chair's armrests. Pants-suited legs sprawled beneath the desk, hanging from the chair like she had given up on sitting and had slid into an awkward napping position.

"Coralee?" I placed a hand on the chair back and yanked it off. The leather felt sticky. My stomach took a noxious roll. I peeked around the edge of the chair.

Coralee lay slumped, propped by her hanging arms, her head lolling to one side. Dried blood had spattered her shirt, the chair, and the desk.

I took a shuddering breath, tasted the sharp metallic scent, and cut off the breath. My hand dangled away from me, as far from the rest of my body as I could get. My chest squeezed, wishing for the breath I was not taking. I let it out, then bit my tongue not to scream.

With a quick pivot, I shot out of the office and slammed into Ada. I made a grab for her elbow, pulled back my dirty hand, and pointed at the door. "Get out. Get back in the hall."

"What're you doing?" said Ada. "I'm not high and mighty enough to get a peek at Belvia's living room? What's in that office? A throne?"

"No." I flapped my hands. "Go. Downstairs. Go to your yoga class. The bar. Just go."

"Why?" Ada craned her neck. "What's the big deal? Coralee and Molly having a meeting?"

I shook my head.

"What in the hell is wrong with you, Cherry Tucker? Did you see Belvia's ghost or something?"

My head swiveled to and fro, agitating like a too wet dog, but I couldn't stop the shaking. It started with my head, worked its way down my neck, and into my hands. "Go." My voice sounded as rusty and tinny as the computer's.

"How much coffee did y'all have today?" Ada shoved past me.

Too busy convulsing, I couldn't stop her.

The office door swung open. "Holy shit. Is that a pencil stuck in Coralee's neck?"

It wasn't just a pencil. It was one of my drawing pencils. The one I had used to take notes during her board meeting. Easily recognized by my dental prints.

My teeth marks. On my pencil. Which someone had used to kill Coralee Brakeman.

# TWENTY-FIVE

While Forks County's finest scoured Belvia's apartment, Deputy Wellington sat with Ada and me in Ada's apartment. A victim blanket had been draped around my shoulders, which had helped quiet the shakes. A paper bag had been rubber banded around my wrist, but I'd finally got to wash it off after Evidence finished with me.

"That's the most disgusting thing I've ever seen in my life," said Ada. "And I'm seventy-eight."

"I told you to get out," I said. "I told you not to go in there."

The deputy's eyebrows twitched. "And why's that?"

"Because I didn't think a seventy-eight-year-old should see a dead body."

"Good Lord, do you know how many funerals I've been to?" said Ada.

"How many of those funerals had a body with a pencil stuck in the neck? Huh, Ada?" I rubbed my temple. "Sorry. I'm just a little upset right now."

"It's shock," said the deputy.

"Don't think so. She's overprotective and it makes her huffy," said Ada. "If anyone's likely to have seen bodies impaled by pencils, it's this one."

"True," said the deputy.

"You know her?"

"Everyone at Forks County Sheriff knows Cherry." Wellington

smirked, then turned his attention to his ear piece. "Sheriff Thompson's on his way."

"Great." I hunched inside the blanket and fought off a shiver.

"Got a record, does she?" Ada's lips quirked. "Where's her cop boy toy? Why isn't Deputy Heartbreak here?"

"He's off the clock," I said irritably.

"Maybe you should call him."

"Maybe you should cut it out, Ada."

We looked up as the door opened. Uncle Will and Fred strode inside. I pulled the blanket tighter around my shoulders.

Fred hurried to Ada. "Are you okay?" He dropped on the couch next to her and wrapped an arm around her.

She shoved him off. "I'm fine. I'm not the one with a pencil stuck in her neck."

Uncle Will glanced at the deputy. "You got this, Wellington?"

He nodded. "Got statements from both. Her hand's been wiped. Got her fingernails too."

"Let's take a walk." Uncle Will crooked his finger.

Leaving the blanket with Fred and Ada, I shuffled to Uncle Will. He squeezed my neck, led me out of Ada's apartment, then crooked an arm around my shoulder, pulling me into his massive frame. "You okay, girl?"

I nodded. "That was my pencil."

"Cheer up," he said. "I don't think that's what killed her."

I forgot about my sour stomach. "What killed her?"

"Not sure yet, but the arterial spray wasn't enough for me to believe she bled to death."

"Wasn't enough?" I grimaced. "It was enough for me."

"Plus, there's no evidence of her fighting back. If someone's going to stab you in the neck, wouldn't you have put up a struggle?"

"Hell, yes." I hugged the man. "Thank you."

"I knew how you'd feel. Guilty as all get out about that pencil. I recognized it right off. No eraser and you always nibble the end. I used to fear you'd get lead poisoning." He wrapped his powerful arms around me, dropped a kiss on the top of my head, then pulled me off his body. "Now we're going to talk about the reason you were in Belvia Brakeman's apartment. Barely an hour after we had a talk about you not getting involved with the Brakemans."

"First, did y'all check on Molly?"

He nodded. "Molly's fine."

"Thank the merciful heavens. I kept asking Wellington to let me see her and he kept telling me to sit tight."

"Good for him for following orders. Those were my exact words." He guided me into the elevator.

"I was looking for Molly, not a Brakeman. Pris said her mother was still at Belvia's. I thought Coralee might've bugged Molly into helping again and she might need a rescue. When Ada and I knocked, I could tell something was wrong. I sure didn't mean for Ada to get involved."

"I'm sure you didn't." His tone was drier than a week old biscuit.

"Anyway," I said hurriedly, "I guess whoever did this found my pencil lying around?"

"If you were going to hope for such a thing, I'd say I hope so."

"Why?"

"Because Ron Newson's pitching a fit about you being at the scene of two deaths."

I opened my mouth, then bit my tongue to stop the words I didn't want to use in front of Uncle Will. "It does look bad, doesn't it?"

"Oh, yes."

"You're sure now Belvia's been murdered?"

"Looking pretty good for that. That's three Brakemans in about two weeks. And Belvia full of digoxin with no heart problems? Don't know how that happened yet, but we'll get to the bottom of it. Plus there's Della's hit and run." He rubbed his chin. "All we've got left of the Brakemans are grandkids and sons-in-law."

"And company suits."

The elevator dinged and we wormed our way through the

gawkers. Deputies held the crowd back. Uncle Will stepped through their ring. I followed, scanning the crowd. Peering over an outstretched deputy's arm, Hazel stood on her toes, balancing her weight on a tripod cane. Her eyes searched Belvia's doorway, making me wonder if she looked for Parker.

I tugged on Uncle Will's sleeve. "Are Ron Newson and his son in there?"

"No. Someone told Ron before we could get to him. Coralee's family was at the plant, but I had them brought to the Tea Grove. I'll head out there later." He glanced at me. "I want you to walk me through what you saw."

We entered the living room. The couch had been pulled out. Evidently, my Prozac find had prompted a more thorough search. On the boardroom/kitchen table, a small plastic number marked a Derwent 2B sketching pencil and a tube of Burt's Bees.

"So that's where my lip balm went?" I said. "Front right sofa leg is where I found the pills. My stuff rolled under the couch this morning. I didn't stop in the living room when I found Coralee. The lights were off. I heard the computer talking and saw the lamp on in the office."

We moved toward the office. The door stood open. A deputy stepped aside, and I pointed at the computer screen.

"It was reading something aloud. Miss Belvia had dictation software. I noticed the computer first. I guess because it was talking. The chair back blocked my view, but I saw Coralee's arms and legs then grabbed the chair." My lip curled at the thought. "Coralee was all slumped like she'd slid halfway down. With that pencil sticking out of her neck. My pencil..."

Uncle Will patted my back. "You saw the pencil and then?"

I cleared my throat. "Remembered Ada was with me. She was in the living room." I rubbed my temple. "I stood there like a damn idiot and let her look in the office."

"How long was Ada in the office?"

I blinked to clear my mind of the pencil. "I don't know, half a minute at the most? Not long."

"Didn't see if she touched anything?" He acknowledged my head shake with a grunt. "Do you think Ada would've taken anything from the office? Maybe not meaning to?"

"No. Why would you think that?"

He pointed at the desk. It took me a moment to register what he meant, then the empty rectangle amid the speckled blood splatter stood out.

"No way." I moved closer, no longer disgusted by the gruesome scene. "What was that?"

"I believe it was a box." He pointed beneath the desk. "Look in the trash can."

I moved to the other side of the chair and peered in.

"Chocolate wrappers." I sucked in a breath. "You said the pencil didn't kill her. But Coralee was eating my Dixie Delites. Dammit, if someone's trying to frame me with my pencil, then why are they hiding my box of chocolates?"


My witness statement over, I found a quiet corner to leave a sympathetic message for Pris, then headed for Halo House's exit. Either myself or that apartment was jinxed. Belvia Brakeman's suite was a revolving door for bodies. I didn't know whether to be sad or horrified. Knowing Ron had an alibi for Della's death, Coralee had been my prime suspect. And she had left this world with my pencil buried in her neck.

What did that mean? Did the pencil stabber know it was my pencil or had it been a random pointy object grab? And if it was my Dixie Delites she'd been eating, why did the killer take the box?

I had not acted quickly enough for Belvia and now had failed her surviving daughter. Even if I didn't like Coralee—or thought she had murdered her mother—I should have done better. What did I know other than everybody and nobody had a motive? My tire tread was wearing thin from all the spinning. I'd focused on my brother and abandoned the Brakemans. Or I'd focused on the Brakemans and neglected my brother.

Uncle Will would question the family and the rest of the Meemaw's Tea personnel. But I also knew all would lawyer up. If the sheriff couldn't find a smoking gun, how could I?

I snuck past the front desk before Krenzer lodged a caffeine-fueled complaint about my latest police involvement. Before I made it to the door, Rosie stopped me. Actually, her shiny crimson leotard caught my eye. Mainly because the black tights and purple leg warmers drew attention to the leotard's high cut. Who would want to exercise in a thong? For that matter, who would want to walk around in public in a thong?

"Going to a dance class, Rosie?"

"Hot yoga. I'm telling you, it brings in more men than the cooking classes." Rosie smoothed her Lycra.

I shook off the mental image of Halo House men watching Rosie hot yoga-ing in her thong-o-tard. "Point taken. Gotta go, Rosie."

"Wait, I've been looking for you. Remember how you asked me about Parker Brakeman-Newson?"

"Yes, ma'am."

She slipped me a piece of paper. "This may help."

I thanked her, hurried out the door, and checked the paper in my truck. I recognized the address as a Halo county road. It looked like I'd be meeting someone named Palmetto at six o'clock. Finally, a break. Even if it wouldn't help the Brakemans or my brother, at least I'd find out why Parker was harassing Hazel. With Coralee's murder, I'd almost put his prank call out of my mind. I couldn't let him get away with threatening Ada.

I hoped Palmetto was named for the tree and not the bug. Knowing Parker, Palmetto was likely a cockroach.

# TWENTY-SIX

Back at my soon-to-be-not home, I found Todd moping before the TV. He had draped himself over the couch to watch a poker tournament. My mood darkened. Todd was the monkey wrench in my already overcomplicated life works. A showdown felt inevitable.

"I saw Cody today," I said. "He asked about you."

Todd's slump grew slumpier.

"I guess I'll call the real estate agent about selling this place. You know, to pay for my brother's lawyer."

He didn't budge from the couch, but a hint of consternation flickered on that poker face.

Martyrdom did not suit me. Neither did passive aggression. I'd rather go for the jugular and be done with it.

"Todd, I can't stand this. Because of Shawna, I'm losing my brother, my career, and now my home. I'd hate to lose you too, but if you stick with Shawna, I can't see us resuming the friendship we had before."

"I don't want the friendship we had before."

It took me a minute to pick my jaw off the floor. It'd take longer to pull the knife out of my back. "I guess you told me. When are you moving out?"

He straightened from his slump and smacked the remote to cut the TV. "I miss having a girl. Shawna's filling that gap. I'll admit, I didn't think I'd like her this much."

"Like her this much?" I gasped. "So get another girl. Why does it have to be Shawna?"

"Because you ruined me for everybody else. Most girls around here won't touch me because they're scared of you. Except for Shawna. And most girls aren't as exciting as you. Except for Shawna. She likes to scheme as much as you do."

"I'm not a schemer." My chin rose. "I'm a planner."

"You're jealous."

"Am not." My bottom lip pushed out. "I'd be happy if you were with anyone else but Shawna."

"I don't think so. You won't admit it to yourself because you like to be right. You and me?" Todd drew to standing. "We had something special. All those crazy capers. It was fun."

"We can still have fun, Todd. Just as long as it doesn't involve a Branson."

His cerulean blues narrowed until they glinted cobalt. "There's the problem. You can involve yourself with a Branson, but I can't."

"You chose the wrong kind of Branson. Besides, Luke's a step-Branson, not a real one." The gray- and blue-eyed babies danced in my head. Who was I kidding? Luke was still a Branson. "Okay, it's not fair. You're right."

"Me and Shawna, it's complicated. I don't know if it'll work. But you've been breaking my heart ever since you annulled our marriage and started seeing Luke Harper. I want you. Shawna'll have to do. Who else is there in Halo?"

It made me queasy to think Shawna could be my substitute. How could he think we were similar? "Was this even about Cody? Have you been dating my nemesis to teach me some sort of lesson?"

His jaw tightened. The words ground from between clenched teeth. "I loved you, Cherry. Still love you."

Finally the words I'd both dreaded and wanted to hear. From the wrong man. My heartbreak flared into anger. "Then you shouldn't have screwed up our one-day marriage. For an ace card player, you have piss-poor timing. Need I remind you that *you* spent *our* wedding night in a Vegas jail? Because you couldn't resist 'just one more' poker game."

"I knew I could win," he cried. "And I did."

"And you got the crap beat out of you, were arrested, and all the money you won went toward bailing you out."

"And paying for you to fly home by yourself. I let you go then but ever since, I was biding my time, waiting for your temper to cool. Then Harper showed. And you've been dancing to his tune ever since."

I didn't know what grated me more, that he'd played me like one of his poker opponents—bluffing the seriousness of his feelings until he had a better hand—or that he thought I could be played by Luke Harper. "I can't help it if Luke and I have a history."

"I've known you longer."

Heat spiraled up my neck and into my cheeks. "I'm caught in Brakeman drama and this soap opera is throwing me off my game. I've got more important things to do than listen to this."

"I'm not the one throwing you off and you know it."

We glowered at each other from across the room. My chest hurt and my hips ached where my fingers had dug into my sides to keep them from shaking.

Dammit if Todd wasn't right though. I was jealous. This wasn't just about Shawna. I wanted to keep Todd but without the romance. I was the worst possible friend.

My pride told me to walk. My heart told me to stay.

I ducked my head and spoke to the stained pine flooring. "After college, I never got over Luke. I should have told you when we were dating—probably shouldn't have dated you in the first place—but I didn't want to lose you and I didn't know Luke'd come back to Halo. I don't know what'll happen between me and him, but I'm sorry I've been hiding it from you."

Todd grunted, but unfolded his arms from his chest and shoved them into the pockets of his cargo shorts. "I don't like it. I don't like him. But I'm glad you finally admitted it."

"Can we still be friends?" I bit hard on my lip to keep my eyes from tearing. "Please?"

"I've been going back and forth on that for a long time. I want more..." He shrugged. "But I don't want to lose you either. We've been friends too long."

I dropped my hands from my hips and flexed my fingers. "But what about Shawna? What's Cody going to think?"

"I know you, Cherry. You've got something." Todd's segue surprised me. "What was on that paper you tried to hide from me the other day?"

"Dangit." I banged the hardwood with my boot heel. "I never could keep anything from you. You're too good at playing it cool. I'm never sure what's going on in your head."

"I'm not selling you out." He crossed the room, stopping before me. "I want to help Cody too. And not just because he's my best friend. Y'all are my family."

"You feel guilty about seeing Shawna."

"It didn't go the way I planned."

"What does?" My bitterness fled. I loved him too. Despite the misbalance in our feelings, we'd been together too long to stay angry. "What I have, it's sensitive. You can't tell Shawna."

"Why haven't you used it yet?"

"Believe it or not Todd, I don't hate Shawna enough to hurt her."

"Must be bad."

"It's big. And holding on to it feels as bad as not telling." I took a deep breath. "I know where her father is. And where he's been. She'll blame my mother and transfer that blame to me and Cody."

Todd's eyes widened. He massaged his jaw, then dropped his hand. "I can tell it's been hurting you to hold on to it. I'm sorry I've been making it worse."

"I've been doing the same to you."

He reached for me. I stepped into his arms, letting my head fall against his chest. One of his big hands patted my back, then slid to cup my head. I wrapped my arms around his waist, comforted by the steady thumping beneath his pecs. We hugged until awkwardness made us untangle our arms.

Stepping back, I looked up and studied the serious expression staring back at me. I wasn't ready to deal with serious expressions, particularly Todd's. I sought another distraction. "You want to talk to a dude named Palmetto with me?"

He grinned. "Of course."

"I need to catch you up on everything going on at Halo House. I found another murder victim today."

"I missed this." His lack of surprise reminded me of how much we'd been through.

"Me too."

Todd's forehead tightened.

I took a step back, worried we were headed toward another deep moment. "Everything okay, hon?"

"Is Palmetto named for the tree or the bug?"

The address Rosie had given me took us to a farm lane Todd and I recognized from our former Halo High days. Just past the crossroads of two highways, the lane led to an abandoned barn on the edge of a field used for grazing cattle. Having been graffitied by every high school class for the last thirty years, the paint kept the abandoned corn crib from rotting out altogether.

The spot was a popular destination for country kids. Set far enough from the road no one could see you drinking or smoking or getting frisky. Set far enough from the farm no one cared as long as you didn't upset the cattle.

"How old is this Palmetto?" asked Todd after I'd explained the Brakeman murders, Parker's stalking of Hazel, and the threats toward me and Ada.

I shrugged. "I don't know for sure if he's a person. But he's supposedly got intel on Parker Brakeman-Newson. If they're about the same age, I'd say early twenties."

"I never liked it when graduates showed and tried to hang with us when we were in high school."

"You didn't complain when they brought beer. Palmetto must have something that'd make high schoolers tolerate him."

We knew not to drive up the lane, but to park behind the line of cars and walk. The chilly temperature made me dig my gloved hands into my pea-green peacoat's pockets and I felt glad I had worn something warmer than my ripped fleece hoodie. Our boots scuffed the dirt road spotlighted by Todd's phone-turned-flashlight. Down the lane, we could hear music and the familiar strains of teenage laughter and excited talking. Flickering light and the scent of woodsmoke drew us forward, but as we grew closer the scent of something more pungent also hung in the air.

"We should've brought beer," said Todd.

"That's all I need, to get busted for giving alcohol to minors."

"I meant for us."

"Let's get a drink after this." I smiled. "I know a great bar where you can meet my new friends."

He wrapped an arm around my shoulder. "I'm glad I came."

We trudged forward, ignoring the car to our left. Low giggles followed a blistering joint trail, passed amongst the little lawbreakers.

I was glad I had brought Todd and not Luke, who would've felt compelled to ditch my Palmetto intel for a pot-and-underage-drinking bust.

At the corn crib, we moved between the small huddles, asking for Palmetto. A young punk with his pants belted low and enough piercings to set off a metal detector pointed us toward the opposite side of the building. Long weeds slapped our legs. The stench of pot grew stronger. The ground was littered with other paraphernalia. Evidence of a harder form of recreation I didn't know existed among Halo's youth.

"I've a feeling where this intel is headed," I said.

"Things have changed from our time. I saw kids drinking wine and it wasn't Boone's Farm. It even had a cork."

"Kids grow up fast these days. And they start early. I had to sneak out after curfew to do this stuff. Don't their parents care they're not home at dinner time?"

On the far side of the corn crib, we found a tall lanky young man with a crewcut and a face fit for a Clearasil commercial. Spotting us, he pinched the burnt end of his joint and slipped it into his pants pocket.

"Palmetto?" Still didn't know if it meant tree or bug. He was tall and thin, like the palm.

He squinted in the dark. "Who's asking?"

"Cherry Tucker. Rosie sent me."

"Right." His gander took long enough to curl my lip and for Todd to tighten a hand on my shoulder. "You don't look very old. What are you, a nurse?"

"I'm an artist." I hid my confusion. "Do you know Parker?"

He fingered his lip, still giving me the eyeball. "Look, why did Rosie send you? Are you selling or buying?"

I didn't want to give away my ignorance, but it sure was hard to play smart when I felt this dumb. "What's Parker doing? Selling or buying?"

He stood there, still playing with his lip, studying me.

"I know Hazel too," I hedged. "I'm looking to help her out. If I knew what Parker wanted with her, maybe we could make a deal?"

"Now I know who you are." He grabbed the backpack at his feet and slung it over a shoulder. "I didn't recognize you at first."

"What do you mean?"

He stepped toward me, flashed a look at Todd, and backed off. "Parker's going to be pissed at Rosie. You should've minded your own business."

"Hey, wait," I called, but Palmetto had skittered into the neighboring field. His long legs flew over a fence and he disappeared from view.

"Bug, not tree," I said. "And I hate palmetto bugs."

"Hard to catch," said Todd.

"They're a damn nuisance. And they give me the creeps."


We scanned the fields for more cockroaches, but like his namesake, Palmetto had swiftly disappeared. My concern remained with

Parker and what he was doing with the Halo House ladies. Palmetto was the key. I had a strong hunch it wasn't Parker who had pushed me into the bushes and stolen my truck. It had been Palmetto. Seemed like something a nasty bug would do. Probably didn't want me to see him flitting away from the Tea Grove.

Todd and I retraced our hike around the corn crib. We stepped around one couple groping on a blanket and avoided another nestled on a rusting plow, sharing a cigarette. They gave us the teenage version of the stink eye.

"These kids must know Parker," I said to Todd. "If not personally, by reputation. Do you think they'll talk to us?"

"Can't hurt to try." Todd shrugged. "But better be careful. No one likes a narc."

"Is that how we look? Like narcs?" I shook my head. "It wasn't so long ago that I was rolling around on a blanket beneath the eaves of the corn crib."

"Don't feel bad. You're not that old. You still have it in you."

"Are you kidding me? The ground is cold and hard as a brick. My corn crib snogging days are long gone." I pointed toward a group of youngsters huddled around trash burning in a metal can. "Let's talk to that crew. At least it'll be warm."

We approached the small bonfire and wormed our way between teens.

"Hey there." I held my hands before the flames. "That's better."

The disenchanted youth cut me glances filled with disdain. Almost as good as Ada's.

"Is Parker showing tonight?" I asked. "I've got something for him. From Halo House."

A girl in a knit beanie glanced at the guy standing next to her. His thick glasses, long curly hair, and beard screamed hipster wannabe. His letter jacket screamed, "I'm still in high school." Neither spoke.

"Palmetto said he might be around," I suggested. "And I need to talk to Parker."

"I don't know." The girl bumped her elbow against hipster letter jacket and they walked off.

We were left with one guy. Sullenness marked his features. Sullenness and a neck tattoo. He shoved his hands in his coat pockets and kept his eyes on a piece of burning cardboard. "What do you want with Parker?"

"Mostly I need to talk to him. Do you know anything about Halo House?"

"It's an old folks' home."

"Actually, it's a premier senior-living residence."

His glare made Todd poke me.

I gave the angry youth my best customer service smile. "Tomato-tomahto. Do you know what Parker's doing there?"

The guy pulled a phone from his pocket, thumbed the screen, and stalked away.

Behind us, a voice murmured, "She wants to know about Parker."

I whirled around. The beanie girl spoke to another guy. Spotting me, the girl ran toward the lane of cars. The new guy—with a jacket of denim rather than letter—motioned toward me and trudged toward the corn crib.

"Todd, follow the kid with the phone. He might be texting Palmetto or Parker. I'm going in there." I pointed at the corn crib.

"That shed's rotting out," said Todd. "Be careful."

"You be careful too. That guy looks like he's in Halo High's young thugs club."

"I doubt he's in a club, Cherry. I don't even think he's in high school."

I glanced over my shoulder. The denim jacket guy had slipped into the corn crib. "Gotta go. Catch you in a minute."

Inside the corn crib, my nose wrinkled at the musty smell of wood rot and mildew. I had forgotten how narrow the corn crib was, even with the old bins and floor ripped out. Above us the slatted walls widened and stars winked through a hole in the roof. I could hear the rustling of birds roosting in the eaves.

I hoped they were birds. Just like I hoped the scrabbling sounds closer to my feet were mice.

Through the gapped wall slats, I could see the shadowy movement of teens milling around outside the crib. Their presence bolstered my courage. Denim Jacket didn't sport the neck tattoo and hostile attitude of our bonfire friend. I approached him more readily.

"Hey," I said. "You must know I'm looking for Parker."

"I don't know anything, girl." "Girl" finished on a high-pitched giggle.

I had traded hostile for high. I sighed. But high would be more likely to talk than hostile. "What's your name?"

"Jordan." He giggled. "I already know yours."

"Jordan, do you know Parker?"

"Sure, everyone knows Parker." Jordan circled the narrow space, trailing his hand along the walls.

I pivoted to track him. "What's Parker doing at Halo House? There are elderly ladies involved. Grandmothers. They could get hurt."

"You've got it all wrong." Jordan roamed to the crib's far end and leaned against the wall. "He's helping them out."

I followed, stopping next to him. Centering his dilated eyes in my direct gaze, I placed a hand on his sleeve to hold him in place and leaned against the wall with him. "Tell me how he's helping. Because I ain't seeing it."

"You don't need to see nothing." Jordan shoved an elbow against the wall.

My back hit open air. I glimpsed the wall swing out behind me. Arms shot through the opening. The middle section was nothing but a flap of plywood. Jordan shook off my hand and shoved me against the hole. Behind me, hands came up and over my shoulders, pinning my arms above my head. I squirmed and kicked. Another set of arms reached inside to hold my torso. I opened my mouth to scream and Jordan slapped a rank-smelling hand across my mouth.

He leaned in and fixed his other hand on my throat. His rotted smile stunk worse than his hand.

The kid was on meth.

I was in trouble.

Two more guys entered the crib, followed by Palmetto. Jordan firmed his hand against my mouth and cranked his head to watch Palmetto over his shoulder.

Freed from his foul breath, I took a quick inhale of hand stench.

"You still here asking questions?" Palmetto slunk across the narrow space and pulled something from his pocket. "Not so smart, are you?"

I couldn't see around Jordan. But whatever Palmetto had in his hand probably wasn't helpful to my plight.

Noticing my struggle to see, Palmetto raised his hand and flicked open a knife. My eyes must have widened because he laughed.

"If you ever ask about Parker and the Halo House bitches again, I'm cutting you. Not just you, but I'll get those women too. There's more where they came from."

I struggled but the arms behind me held tight to my torso and shoulders. Without thinking, I jerked a leg up. Palmetto retreated before my knee connected with his crotch.

"You're messing with my bankroll, woman. And you're messing with my boy, Parker. Should have done more than just shove you in the bushes that night."

To my relief, he shoved the knife into his pocket and continued backing away. Before darting out the door, he tossed Jordan a hard look.

"Gank her. Make her bleed."

# TWENTY-SEVEN

Fear never caused me to freeze. It worked as a catalyst. Adrenaline pumped to race through my system and enhance all my senses. My brain fired neurons like a submachine gun. All my thoughts honed toward survival. I wasn't powerful, but I reacted quickly. Plus Uncle Will had forced self-defense lessons on us. I'd probably make a great soldier. If I could stand taking orders and wearing those drab uniforms.

Which I could not.

My eyes narrowed on Jordan. I pitied this waste of youth. He was going to fail in his mission to cut me because I would not let Palmetto and that poor little rich boy, Parker Brakeman-Newson, hurt the women of Halo House. It riled me to extremes they would utter that threat. I did not yet know why they held such antipathy toward the elderly, but I would find out and stop them.

As soon as I stopped stinky Jordan and his cohorts from ganking me.

Taking a deep breath of Jordan hand stank, I bit down. Hard enough to draw blood.

I prayed I wouldn't get rabies. Or something worse.

Jordan yowled and jerked his hand away. His other hand slid from my throat to hold the bite. Surprised, the bodies behind me shifted. Their clutch loosened. I jumped, pulled my knees up, and caught my feet on the lip of the opening. Shoving my weight backward, I heaved through the window. My butt crashed into a body. He toppled back, slamming into his friend. We tumbled like dominos. Jordan lunged to catch me and fell half out the window.

I stared at Jordan dangling above me and shoved both elbows into the soft tissue below. Someone grunted and my ground moved. Screaming for Todd, I kicked and elbowed my way to semi-standing. Kicked again and fled.

Bedlam had broken in the lane. Kids ran helter-skelter. Blankets billowed behind them. Bottles and cans rolled, clanking against their boots.

No wonder no one had paid attention to my attack.

"Todd," I called. "Where are you?"

I ran toward his Civic. Whirling around in the lane, I searched for him while keeping my eye out for Palmetto and friends. Motors roared. I sidestepped a Blazer backing around me. Across the road, an F-150 slammed into a wire fence. The wire caught against its grill and the truck's tires spun. Rebar posts groaned and bent, pulling from the hard-packed earth. Freed from its wire holster, a picket sailed through the air.

"Idiot," I screamed and hollered at the nearby teens to move from the flying fence.

The F-150 shot forward, pulling the fence with it and churned the field beneath its tires.

A hand grabbed my elbow.

"You're not ganking me." I shot my arm out and pivoted, angling my freed elbow toward my attacker's neck.

"Cherry." Todd's hand flew to protect his face.

I dropped my elbow and lunged at Todd. Leaping high, I grabbed him by the shoulders in a quick hug. "I'm glad to see you. Palmetto tried to have me knifed."

He gave a weak laugh, but his eyebrows creased. "That wasn't very smart of him, was it?"

I pulled on Todd's coat. "Come on. We've got to get out of here. This sort of retreat means one thing."

"I told everyone at the bonfire I called the police. Then I called the police."

"Thought so."

In the distance, sirens wailed.

In the Civic, Todd threw an arm over the back of my seat, checking for wayward drunk kids as he reversed into the lane.

"Head toward the corn crib," I said. "If you keep following that path, you'll get to the farmhouse. We're better off leaving that way because the deputies will block the county highway to trap these kids."

"You don't want the police to know you were here?"

I shook my head. "I don't want to waste time talking to the deputies. I need to question Hazel and Rosie and find out what the hell is going on."

"Who's Rosie?"

"A Halo House resident and bartender at the Last Call. I'm worried, Todd." I'd told him about my weird phone call. "It had to have been Parker who made that call. He threatened Ada and now they're threatening Rosie and Hazel. I don't get it though. If it were Eleanor in the Last Call, I'd understand, except she grows her own. But Rosie and Hazel? They're not potheads."

Ignoring the ramble, Todd directed a question to the heart of the matter, as only Todd could do. "Could these women be dealers?"

"In Halo House? Who'd buy their product? Everyone is on some kind of drug, but it's all prescriptions." I shook my head. "I don't see it. Rosie warned me Halo House wasn't full of angels, but drugs and murder? It's not like Halo House is the projects. It's a luxury independent living facility."

"You think the Brakeman family are drug dealers? Smuggle stuff in their sweet tea shipments? Killed by a rival dealer?"

"Todd, this isn't Columbia. Two middle-aged sisters and their elderly mother died. Businesswomen, but still."

"They could smuggle it with the sweet tea. Who would look in sweet tea?"

"Smuggle what? Corn syrup?"

Our tiff was interrupted by a siren. Blue lights flashed in the distance.

"Dammit," I said. "Get me out of here. I can't get caught at the corn crib. Uncle Will will tan my hide."

Todd turned off his lights, cranked the wheel, and we bumped up the rutted lane toward the farm house. I turned in my seat to watch for blueberries. Two Forks County sheriff vehicles turned onto the lane. Todd stopped before the farm entrance. I leaped from the car and ran to unlatch the gate. The Civic crept through, I hopped in, and Todd rolled into the drive. He parked in the farm driveway behind a Lariat big enough to hide his hatchback. Luckily, in order to be left alone at the corn crib, the kids knew well enough to stay away from the farm.

I hoped the deputies hadn't seen our illegal entering.

"Cherry," said Todd. "I'm worried about this Palmetto guy. Having you knifed is serious. We should go back and tell the officers what happened."

"Here's the thing. If we're busting Parker, we need to get him on more than hearsay. Parker wasn't here tonight. His daddy told me Parker's got an expensive attorney on call. I've a feeling that lawyer is Harry Hunt. In that case, Harry might also be covering his own ass for a big payout. I need Palmetto to get to Parker. But I need to find out what they're doing at Halo House first."

"What if Hazel and Rosie are doing something illegal?"

"I don't think they murdered the Brakemen women if that's what you mean. They're too nice."

"Murderers are never nice?"

I ignored Todd's obvious confusion about sweet old ladies versus lady killers. "I do think Hazel and Rosie are in trouble. But if they knew Parker was a dangerous criminal not worth protecting, I'm sure they'd understand and turn him in. That'd be evidence. Not hearsay."

"I don't know about this, Cherry. I think you're deluding yourself about these women."

"Todd, we're talking about grandmothers."

"You've met my grandma. She's sweet, but she also ran a bust-out joint in her kitchen."

"That's different. I love Mimi McIntosh." I thought about her homey kitchen where she served illegal poker with homemade hooch and cookies. "I guess she might have had something to do with you becoming a gambling addict though."

"My point being, Cherry, just because Hazel and Rosie are old doesn't mean they're turning in this Parker. They could be up to their sweet little noses in drugs and murder."

"Hell, Todd, you'd think we were talking about Lizzie Borden and Bonnie Parker, not two retirees who love hot yoga and disco dancing."

"Even criminals have to retire. And from what I've heard, you need a criminal's paycheck to live at Halo House."

"I guess you have a point. Let's hope they want to bust Parker and Palmetto as much as I do. If they don't, I fear those boys are going after my girls."


After checking in at the front desk, we headed to the Last Call to look for Rosie. I knew Hazel wouldn't answer my ring. The adjoining restaurant was already closed, but the bar was hopping. Eleanor sat at her usual corner table, eating nachos. Two-Dollar Frank grabbed his next partner for a Sinatra stroll.

An elderly female bartender manned the bar, but she wasn't Rosie. Pins covered her crocheted vest. The largest read, "When You're Out of Schlitz, You're Out of Beer."

At least I was dealing with a professional. "We're looking for Rosie. She's not working tonight?"

Schlitz shook her head while she agitated a martini shaker. "I can call her apartment if you want."

"Please." I pushed a dollar toward her. "For your trouble."

She winked, snatched the dollar, and shoved it into her Playtex.

"I don't know what you see in this place," said Todd. "It gives me the creeps."

"Stop being ageist." I sighed. "But in light of what just happened, I guess I know what you mean. The Halo House vices used to seem harmless and cute."

"I guess a narcotics drug ring can never seem cute."

"We don't know it's a drug ring for sure." I thought about Palmetto and his nasty friends. "Yet."

The bartender returned. "Rosie asked if she could meet you in the activity room."

We thanked her and left the bar. Walking towards the foyer, I studied the residents I passed, looking for clues of a drug ring, but my brain would only register sweet grandparent-y types. I still couldn't believe Hazel would involve herself with thugs like Parker and Palmetto.

At the activity room, I rattled the locked knob. "Why'd Rosie want to meet me here? Why not her apartment?"

"Psst."

I whirled around.

A shrunken man dressed in various shades of brown and green stepped from behind the fountain. If we'd landed in a Tolkien novel, he might have been a hobbit. He motioned with his hand.

I looked at Todd and he shrugged. We scooted toward the fountain and followed the tiny man to the hall off the bar. The same corridor where I had found Parker stealing from Hazel and had received my disturbing phone call. I shivered.

The little man stopped near the men's restroom. "You looking for Rosie?"

"Yes, sir."

"Library. Sit in the leather chairs by the fireplace." He touched the side of his nose and slipped into the bathroom.

"I feel like I'm in the *Twilight Zone*," said Todd. "This has been the most bizarre night ever."

"*The Sting II* must be on Netflix again." I shook my head. "I don't like it. All this subterfuge means they're up to something."

"Who?"

"My students. They've aced shenanigans and are now majoring in criminal capers."

The crazy-haired librarian manned the library door once again. When we attempted to go around her, she rammed her card table into our knees and shook her date stamper at us.

"Ma'am, I'm meeting somebody," I said. "By the fireplace."

"You can't take a book without a card."

"Yes, ma'am. I know."

"Your books are due in two weeks. Return them late and there will be a nickel fine."

"Yes, ma'am."

We edged around her table and scooted toward the leather chairs facing the fireplace.

"Nothing scarier than a retired librarian," said Todd.

"You should meet the retired teachers. That'd be Rosie and Hazel." I glanced around the room. "Speaking of, I don't see Rosie."

"This place is making me jumpy. Where are your friends?"

"Ada and Fred? Probably asleep."

My adrenaline rush from the corn crib and Halo House antics had fizzled. Weariness dropped its heavy mantle around my shoulders. The aches and bruises from falling out of a plywood window—even a low window with the cushioning of two young thugs to break my tumble—had taken their toll. A person named Palmetto had demanded my evisceration. These women were dealing with sadistic goons.

I rubbed my hip. The generously padded leather chairs beckoned. The comforting scent of pine and Bengay mingled with the sounds of the crackling fire. It was hard to believe a drug ring could occur in such a snuggly atmosphere.

I fought the urge to rest before the fire. The chairs looked like heaven and a nap sounded all too fine. "I don't see Rosie." Surliness crept into my tone. "This is ridiculous. I'm going to her apartment."

"Stay where you are." A stage whisper rasped from behind the closest bookcase.

I walked behind the bookcase. "Ada, what's going on?"

"Rosie wants to give you the slip. She didn't know you were trying to bust Hazel by asking about Parker."

I willed my blood pressure to drop. Didn't work. "Where's Rosie now?"

"She and Hazel are on the road." Ada smirked. "Like *Thelma and Louise*."

"You know Thelma and Louise died in the end, right? Drove their car off a cliff?"

"Okay, maybe not like *Thelma and Louise*. But they're laying low until you chill out."

"Ada, I'm not trying to get them in trouble. I want to help them. Parker's no good. The women in his family are getting killed off, for heaven's sake."

She pursed her lips and removed her small fists from her bony hips. "I know it. I told them to cheese it, but they don't want to listen. They're in too deep."

"In too deep of what?"

Todd appeared behind the couch. "Is this Rosie?"

"It's Ada. Rosie flew the coop. With Hazel."

Ada shuffled sideways and I grabbed her sleeve. "Where do you think you're going? You're telling me what Hazel and Rosie are doing with Parker."

She gave me a long look, then opened her mouth and screamed.

# TWENTY-EIGHT

I would like to say this was my first time in the can, but it wasn't. There was that scared straight lesson after I'd been caught drinking on Merriweather Lane with half of the junior class. Of course, I was the only one in the junior class who spent the night in the drunk tank. Then there was that night I'd spent in Line Creek Police Department's holding cell. That was for obstruction, but the charges were dropped.

This was the first time I'd been charged with something by a private citizen. As the accused who had done nothing wrong, it ticked me off. Royally.

At least Todd was allowed in my interview room to give witness testimony. Testimony he'd given to Deputy Luke Harper, who was on call. Unfortunately. And testimony more helpful for the one bringing charges against me. Unfortunately.

Unfortunate just might be my middle name.

They had called Luke from a bust of young people partaking in illegal activities on a private property near a certain corn crib off a well-known county road.

I kept my mouth shut. If you thought my suspicion meter ran high, you'd never met Deputy Heartbreak.

"You have to get me out of here, Luke." My voice sounded sharp. I wasn't ready for begging. My anger was too real.

He grinned. "I asked if I could get a copy of your mugshot. For my wallet."

"Very funny. There was no mugshot."

I folded my arms over my pea-green pea coat.

"Harassing sweet little old ladies." Luke shook his head. "You're gonna lose your job, sugar."

"I'm not harassing anyone. And Ada's not sweet. Everyone knows that." I snorted. "For weeks she can't remember my name. But she certainly knew it well enough to file that complaint."

"That Ada is a feisty one," said Todd. "She reminds me of you."

"I thought so too." Luke slid his cool gray gaze to Todd. "By the way, how's Shawna?"

Todd's face reddened. "Fine, I guess."

"We're making a nice mess of things for Cody, aren't we?" The corner of Luke's lip lifted.

"The mess was already there," said Todd. "I caught the tail end of it. Besides, in court, they aren't going to care who Shawna's dating. But they will care who the arresting officer's been seeing on the sly."

"Hey." I snapped my fingers. "We've got elderly women who've run off."

"I'd think you'd be more concerned with your own mess," said Luke.

"Those ladies are my mess. They're my students." I didn't feel it necessary to mention Hazel had dropped my class and Rosie disdained it. Small details when contending with an elderly drug ring. "Ada's wily. She screamed and pretended to faint to get out of my questioning. We'll have words tomorrow and get to the bottom of this. I'll let you know what I learn."

"Not unless Ada drops the restraining order. No more Halo House for you."

"You've got to be kidding me. How am I going to find out what Parker's doing if I can't go to Halo House?"

"Don't you mean 'How am I going to teach my class if I can't go to Halo House?'" Luke leaned into me. "You don't need to find out what Parker's doing. That's my job."

"He's not telling you anything and you know it. He'll lawyer up faster than you can say 'rich daddy's boy.'"

Luke turned to Todd. "Why do you encourage her in these schemes?"

"It's easier to step aside then get steamrolled. More fun too."

I ignored them. "Ada's my friend. She's not keeping the restraining order. Fred won't let her."

"I met Ada and Fred," said Luke. "Ada's not going to listen to Fred. Ada's going to do whatever it takes to get you off Hazel and Rosie's backs."

"Luke, this is serious. There's a drug ring involving Parker Brakeman-Newson at Halo House. If I can't talk to Ada, then you need to arrest her."

"On what charge?"

"Aiding and abetting." I tapped my chin. "And obstruction. Yes, obstruction. She has information about a criminal activity. I know she does."

"So you think it's unfair of your friend to file a restraining order against you, but you're coming up with charges willy-nilly for a senior citizen?"

"It's for her own good."

"She'd say the same about you." Luke's smirk turned serious. "Listen, this is not just about Ada. The sheriff's worried about you."

"What're you talking about?" I hadn't told Uncle Will or Luke about Palmetto. I feared he'd add "fleeing the scene of a crime" to my charges.

"The sheriff's thinking of holding you as a suspect in the murder of Coralee Brakeman."

"What for? You know I had nothing to do with her death."

"Sure, but the rest of the county doesn't. Ron Newson, for example, who's been giving us hell about your interference. That lawyer, Harry Hunt, is another example. Let's see, I could name a few more—"

"I've done nothing wrong." I flashed him my fiercest look. "I've done my best to not interfere with your investigation. Only asking a few questions here and there. Just keeping my ears and eyes open. And it's gotten me nowhere. I don't know any more than y'all."

"Considering we're the authorities, I'd hope not."

"I thought I'd never live to see this day. If Uncle Will calls me a suspect, he's trumping up charges to placate voters."

"This is not about his reputation. He'd do it to protect you while we continue the investigation. He seems to think your friendship with Belvia Brakeman might put you in harm's way."

I waved off the complaint. It was my interest in Parker Brakeman-Newson that put me in harm's way. Of course, I wasn't airing that to Deputy Heartbreak.

"You were first on the scene for two murders."

"Can I help it if I keep ending up in the wrong place at the wrong time? There's no evidence to hold me."

"Oh, but there is. Remember that pencil planted in Coralee's neck? And the chocolates she ate that were a gift from you? All of Belvia's Lidocaine patches were soaked in digoxin. Someone had also injected the chocolates with digoxin. We found traces of it on the wrappers. Unfortunately for Coralee, they didn't mix with the amount of Prozac in her system. Wasn't it Prozac you found while you were doing what? Snooping in a private board meeting?"

"Digoxin? In her pain patches and the chocolates? The Prozac I found was Coralee's..." I straightened on the uncomfortable plastic chair. "Sounds like premeditated murder to me. I brought those chocolates over the day before Belvia died. You think Coralee's death was just accidental?"

"My thoughts on Coralee Brakeman's death are not the point." Luke's cool gray gaze narrowed into icy points of hardened lead. "The point is, it was your chocolates and your pencil. If I didn't know you, I'd put you on a list of potential suspects myself."

"Dammit, you know this isn't fair."

Luke's anger dissipated and he squeezed my knee. "Lucky for you, we do know you and your inclination to involve yourself with victims. Sheriff Thompson's not locking you up."

"Good." I brightened.

"For now."

\* \* \*

Todd and I set off in his Civic under the deeply disapproving gaze of Deputy Luke Harper. Under no circumstances was I to look for Rosie and Hazel, nor was I to contact Ada. I was also to leave Parker Brakeman-Newson alone. And for good measure, any other Brakeman.

But he didn't say anything about Palmetto. And I really wanted to squash that bug.

"You're not afraid of Palmetto?" asked Todd.

He knew threat of imprisonment would not quell my vindictive nature. Not just my name and reputation were on the line. Nor my job. Part-time as it was. Parker and Palmetto had threatened my friends. Who happened to be little old ladies.

Little old ladies who might have criminal tendencies and a ruthless streak when it came to protecting their interests. But that's probably why we were friends.

"I met Palmetto without knowing who he was," I said. "I'm going in prepared this time."

"Prepared how?" Todd's fingers tapped a rapid staccato. "Like going home to get your shotgun prepared? Or having police on standby prepared?"

"I can't have the police on standby, Todd. You heard what Luke said. Uncle Will would sooner lock me up on false charges than let me stand-off with Palmetto."

"So you're getting your gun?" His quick staccato rhythm disintegrated into haphazard thrumming.

"Don't be ridiculous."

He let out a long breath.

"If I had my gun, I'd want to shoot that sumbitch. Getting my gun would be premeditated murder. If I do something to Palmetto, I'd rather it be self-defense."

I glanced at Todd's whitened features and laughed.

"I'm joking," I said. "We're keeping this meeting public and civil. Palmetto's just a wannabe thug. I've dealt with wannabe thugs

before. If he wanted to gank me, he would have done it himself
right there on the spot. That's what a real thug would do. Very
unprofessional to give me all that time to escape."

"You're not making me feel any better."

Besides the corn crib, Todd and I created a list of Forks County
active hot spots for wayward youth. There weren't many at nine
o'clock on a Wednesday night. The Tastee Treat. The paintball
grounds. The bleachers behind Halo High School. And a cruising
spot in Line Creek, a short length of asphalt between the
Cinemaplex and Walmart that included a strip mall holding a
Krystal's and a questionable liquor store.

We tried the Tastee Treat first because I was hungry and could
go for a chili dog. Halo High had a stronger lock on the athletic
fields than I remembered from my misspent adolescence. However,
the paintball place, Splats, was busy. Wednesday night was their
BOGO coupon night. They had to compete with the midweek
church school crowd.

The parking lot was filled with battered trucks, hatchbacks,
and dirt bikes. All heathens, evidently. Looked like a young adult
jackpot to me.

We approached the tin shed admission booth. A young guy in
a Coors Racing Team cap took tickets.

"You want to be on the same team or opposing sides?" he
asked.

"We're looking for someone. A dude named Palmetto," I said.
"Tall and gangly like the tree. Personality like the bug."

"Don't know him. But you're welcome to look for him on the
fields."

"Great." I turned toward the gate.

"Got to buy a pass. You got your own gun and ammo?"

I shook my head.

"Then you're gonna need that too. Plus you have to rent a team
vest."

I looked at Todd. "This is some kind of racket."

But Todd had that boyish gleam to his eye. Like when young

men caught sight of a Maserati or a Cowboys cheerleader. "Let's play."

"We're not here to play," I said. "We're here to squash a bug."

"You can squash him with paint," said the guy.

We entered the gates with two vests, two masks, one gun, and one paintball pack between us. I let Todd carry the gun because I didn't like to see him pout.

We entered into a thicket of color-splattered pines. A string of lights cast a ghostly glow on the trees. The vest over my coat didn't help much with the cold and if it hadn't been so chilly, I'd not have risked getting my wool coat splashed. Woodsmoke from a neighbor's chimney mixed with $CO_2$ vapor. Glimpses of players hiding behind trunks had us dodging from tree to tree to keep from getting paint smacked.

"How are we finding Palmetto in this mess?" I said. "If he's even here?"

Todd raised the gun and fired off a round at a man in orange-streaked camo. "We stay alive. Work our way through the grounds. Defeat the enemy."

"Todd, you're forgetting the original purpose of this mission."

In the distance, we could hear the *splat, splat* of an attack. Hoots and screams that could only be made by men or goats erupted from the next quadrant. Todd and I ran from tree to tree until we found the clearing. From a glare of field lights, the new area revealed plywood barriers, rusted-out cars covered in paint, and splattered metal drums. We crept inside, dodging low behind a piece of plywood nailed to a T of two-by-fours.

A group huddled behind a barrier of stacked logs. Glancing over their shoulders, they spotted us and waved for our entry.

Grabbing the gun from Todd, I dashed to the grown delinquents. One motioned to crouch. I ignored his command, shoved a gun into his back, then waved for Todd to join me. "I'm looking for Palmetto. Where is he?"

"You're on our team," complained the guy I held hostage. "We're wearing the same vest color."

A girl pointed at a double-storied plywood shed. "Palmetto's in there."

Looking at Todd, I jerked my thumb toward the shed. We ran. Paint thwacked our heels. I adjusted my straight line into a zigzag, cursing those who dirtied my boots. We jerked to a stop under the shed stairs, throwing ourselves against the barrier. From the scent surrounding the plywood structure, Palmetto and guests were taking a recreational drug break.

"Smell that?" I whispered. "They're not paying attention. Can you cover me while I take a peek upstairs?"

Todd nodded, then crouched beneath the stairs, gun ready.

A deluge of paintballs hammered the front wall. I jumped, but my shivers were more from excitement than nerves. I climbed the rickety ladder and peered through the hole.

Three guys—Jordan and two boys from the corn crib—had sprawled on the plywood floor with their backs against the left wall, passing a joint between them. They toked beneath their masks, allowing the smoke to cloud their goggles. Their attention fixed on the front cutout window, where an occasional paint pellet flew through and slammed into the wall.

Palmetto slumped against the opposite right wall, shooting into the night sky. The wide arcs wouldn't hit a human target, but he seemed content to watch them pummel a low-hanging tree branch and drip to the ground.

I ducked my head below and signaled to Todd, a three-fingered tap against my bicep and point toward the left wall. One tap for the right wall accompanied by a finger waggle to portray the cockroach scuttle.

Todd nodded, handed me the gun, and crouched beneath me. Placing his hands on my waist he boosted me through the opening.

Before I recovered my balance, I'd fired off a round at Palmetto's men, mostly hitting their masks. While they wiped their goggles, I turned my gun on Palmetto.

"I'm back." I smirked behind my mask. "Tell me about Halo House."

Palmetto pulled his trigger.

I collapsed into Todd. We slammed into the wall, thankfully missing the open trap door.

The low hoots from Palmetto's men rang in my ear and I swallowed my pride with a lungful of paint fumes. Getting shot in the chest with a paint pellet stung like I'd been thwacked with a giant rubber band.

The hit made me feel bad for shooting Palmetto's men in their faces. Then remembered what they had done to me at the corn crib. I got over it, kneeled, and shot Palmetto. While he scrubbed at his face mask, Todd jerked the gun from his hand and held it on Palmetto.

"We called 911 again," I yelled through gritted teeth. "I expect Forks County deputies are already searching the arena for y'all. They were sorely disappointed not to snatch you at the corn crib."

Jordan, Tweedlee, and Tweedledum dove through the hole, barreling past Todd.

"Your buddies ditched you, Palmetto."

"You've got nothing," he said. "I don't have anything illegal on me."

"Except what they'll find in your blood tox screen." I lowered my gun from his chest to below his waist. "Hope you're wearing a cup."

His voice rose in panic. "You wouldn't."

I did.

Palmetto doubled over.

I aimed at Palmetto's privates again. "I want to know what y'all are doing at Halo House with those women."

Palmetto lay on the floor, twitching. "If you knew what was good for those grandmas, you'd leave it alone."

"I'm not letting this go. The police know all about your partnership with Parker. He's lawyering up. Guess who's taking the heat? You think Parker's daddy's letting his son go to jail? He's grooming Parker to take over Meemaw's Tea. You're going down, son."

"I don't need a lawyer," he rasped. "My one call will be to my homies to hunt you down and gut you."

"Let me repeat. What's Parker doing at Halo House? He wasn't visiting his meemaw. Why does he know Hazel and Rosie?" My gunsight swung back to aim at his crotch.

Parker responded to my vigilante justice with a couple new cuss words that had yet to enter my repertoire. I fired again. Palmetto curled, then flipped onto his stomach, whimpering.

"Roll him over, Todd."

"No," Palmetto gasped. "Parker buys drugs from the women. That's why he's at Halo House all the time. They get it from their friends or sell their own and he pays them in cash."

"That's disturbing."

"How else do you think they can afford that place? It's not like Medicare covers Halo House."

I didn't know which was more surprising, that Palmetto knew about Medicare or that my elderly friends were selling their drugs. "What's that got to do with Meemaw's Tea?"

"Nothin'."

I marked him with the laser, but Palmetto held up a hand. "I don't know anything about his grandma's company except it gets him into Halo House."

"Parker's going to inherit, idiot. Where does that leave you? Turn him in and you can plea down."

"Parker doesn't do this for the money, dude." Palmetto pushed up and rolled over. "You ain't figured that out by now, you can't figure anything."

Palmetto had to be right. Why enter a life of thuggery when Parker had every opportunity handed to him on a silver platter, including the chance to run a multi-million-dollar company? Why risk it for small-town drug dealing? Belvia had been looking for psychopaths in her company while her daughter had been raising one next door.

But how did I tell the police about the psychopath without revealing his involvement with my friends, who happened to be senior citizens? I had to find a way to separate the murders from the drugs. Prison was no place for elderly spinsters.

"Cancel that 911 call," I said to Todd. "We're letting the bug go." I eyed Palmetto. "For now."

# TWENTY-NINE

Back at 211 Loblolly, I looked around my un-updated kitchen and sighed. The sale of Great Gam's home would mean a certain amount of elbow grease and haggling over materials. That thought made me tired. And sad.

"Dammit," I said for lack of a better phrase.

"Disappointed you didn't turn in Palmetto, baby?" Todd thunked two longnecks onto the battered kitchen table and settled into the chair opposite my slump. "If it makes you feel any better, those paintball hits can bruise and Palmetto's going to have a nasty welt. The thought of it makes me wince."

"Tell me about it." I rested the cold beer against my chest. "And my pea coat is ruined. Although I like that shade of yellow against the green. I may have to Jackson Pollack the back similarly."

Todd's eyebrows creased at my art reference.

"At least I know what Parker's been doing at Halo House. I wish I knew what to do. If I report what I know, Hazel and Rosie could get arrested. And Ada could be charged with aiding and abetting for real. All this to afford a lifestyle of comfort and convenience in their twilight years. What is this world getting to?"

Todd pushed from his seat and left the room. A moment later he returned with a sketchbook and a cup of drawing pencils. "This'll help you think."

"You always know what I need, don't you?" I wondered if Todd did these little things for Shawna, then pushed away that thought. I beamed a smile at him, while feeling a wave of nostalgia and longing similar to the homesickness I had felt at SCAD when separated from my family. I missed Todd already.

"You're easy to read, Cherry. You want to bust this Palmetto and Parker, but you're not a snitch. You're too loyal to your friends."

My head thunked the table at the thought of ratting out the elderly. "At the same time, I can't allow my friends to be drug dealers. Think about those medications out on the street. All those boys taking the little blue pill and not knowing the side effects. The horror of it fills me with dread."

"Little blue pill?"

"That sumbitch Parker Brakeman-Newson. I wonder if his daddy knows his kid is a dealer." I drew a wolf on my sketchpad. "I need to know if this drug thing is related to the Brakeman deaths. Although I don't see how. Parker is the only link. I figured him for a wannabe gangster, not a homicidal maniac."

"Didn't Deputy Harper say drugs made Mrs. Brakeman have a heart attack? And Coralee was poisoned by the same stuff? Maybe Parker wants to take over the company."

"I don't think so. At the board meeting, he sure didn't act like King Sweet Tea. Parker looked bored out of his skull."

"You think his father killed them for Parker? Maybe got the drugs from him?"

"Ron Brakeman-Newson had an alibi for his wife's death. But no alibi for the other deaths. Ron's also involved with Della's ex-assistant." I drew a broken heart, then looked up. "I wonder if Donna Sharp's his alibi. Maybe she knows about Parker's drug dealing too. Now that it's been a few days, I might get her to talk. Luke didn't say anything about not speaking to Donna again."

Todd's brows inched toward his hairline. "You do realize you've been shot and threatened with a knife tonight?"

"Paintball shot. That's a typical Wednesday night for a lot of people my age."

"Isn't it late?"

"Late? It's barely past ten. You got a booty call or something?"

Scarlet-faced, Todd shook his head and searched the ceiling. "I'm supposed to call Shawna..."

I took a deep breath. I'd force myself to get used to this, just like he'd had to swallow that lump of bitterness named Luke Harper.

"Do your Shawna thing. I'm going. If Donna's gone or asleep, I'll leave it alone."

"And if she's awake?"

"Then we're gonna have a PJ party, me and her."

I drove to Donna's, switching my brain from drug deals to Brakeman deaths. Ron and Parker still had much at stake. As did Wally and Pris and possibly the Meemaw's board members. But Parker was the only logical connection between the heart medication and the murders. And he did ride with a posse who threatened ganking. Making him, at the very least, an associate of violent crime thuggery.

So if Ron didn't kill Della, did Parker? Would a thug wannabe kill his own mother? Then grandmother and aunt?

For a whole lotta money, maybe.

My phone sang "I Can't Get No Satisfaction," alerting me to Todd's call. "You know this isn't Shawna, right?"

"Hey, Cherry, you should come back." Todd sounded strangely serious. "I was tossing our bottles in the recycle bin and saw a car drive down the street after you pulled away."

I glanced in my rearview but didn't see any taillights. "What kind of car?"

"A sweet Audi S8, turbo-charged. 605 hp. You should have heard that engine."

"Are you calling me to car talk or do you think I'm being followed?"

"Not sure. But never seen a car like that on our street." Todd's phone beeped. "Gotta go."

"Did you see the driver?" I spoke to a dial tone. "Dammit, Todd. Not helpful."

My feet went cold despite the blast of hot air in the Datsun. My skin crawled, but I made myself pull over to watch for vehicles. After a few minutes, I relaxed and drove on to Donna Sharp's bedroom community. Dark and quiet, her subdivision gave me more heebies. A desolate ghost town would be less creepy. At least the ghosts would know their neighbors.

No vehicles loitered in Donna's drive, but a light flickering in the rear of the house told me she still pretended vacation. I parked on the curb, then crept around the side of the house to look in the window. If Ron played happy homewrecker with Donna, there was no way she would talk to me tonight. Hopefully Ron would have the decency to sleep in his own house. At least until after the funerals.

The back of the house also had curtains, but these were sheer. Someone needed to give Donna better tips on hiding out. She was curled in a blanket on the sofa, again in sweats and a ponytail. With her box of tissues and the TV blasting an LED light show across her face. Probably watching a movie about the other woman and crying about the fate of chatelaines.

I returned to the front door and rang the bell. Considering the circumstances, Donna shouldn't answer. But there was something about late-night callers. I was more likely to answer a ten thirty p.m. door ring than a ten thirty a.m. Bible thumpers didn't tend to come around after dinner.

As I suspected, Donna was like me.

"Hey, Donna," I said at her door crack. "It's Cherry Tucker again. I know it's late, but I want to chat with you about what's going on with the Brakemans. You heard about Coralee?"

Donna sniffled. "I can't talk about it."

"You can't or you won't? It's important. Otherwise, I wouldn't be here this late."

An engine growled as a car pulled onto Donna's street. A jolt of electricity buzzed under my skin. I glanced behind me then twisted forward as the door hit my boot.

"I already spoke to the police." Donna glared at my toe jammed in the doorway.

My boots were going to have a permanent door indentation.

"This isn't about the police," I said. "This is personal. Someone wants to make me look like I was involved with these deaths."

"Why would you have anything to do with the Brakemans'?"

"Exactly. I was trying to help Molly. Miss Belvia had asked me to look out for her."

"Poor Molly."

"Yep, poor Molly is losing folks right and left. You can't help me with Coralee or Belvia's demise, but it all started with Della. Della's death was different than the others. Did anyone visit Della the day she died? One of the board members or family? Parker or Wally?"

"I gave the police the appointments. Della was busy that day. The board members hounded her all the time after Belvia made the public announcement Della would be taking over Meemaw's. Belvia hadn't formally announced it to the board before going to the press. They were pissed."

"Which board members?

"Lisa Russell, especially. She's in charge of Human Resources. She felt she had a right to know before everyone else."

"Lisa Russell wanted to hire leadership from outside the factory. She also wanted to take Meemaw's public."

Donna nodded. "Molly was there when Lisa came in. She can tell you about the fight Della and Lisa had in front of us. It was awful. Molly was real upset. Della had asked her to visit and they barely got to talk because of Lisa."

"Molly saw the fight too? Did you report that to the police?"

"Of course."

Luke had checked into Lisa Russell. If Lisa's testimony didn't verify, he would have brought her in. She must have an alibi. Like Ron. "Anyone else who was there that day? Like Parker? Did he visit his momma much?"

"Sometimes he stopped by. Usually for money. But Parker

would slip in when I wasn't around because he knew I was to keep him out of Della's office."

If Della left the door open for her son, maybe he wouldn't have become a drug dealer. "What about Coralee? Were she and her family in the factory? They were already in town."

"I don't think so. If she visited Della, it wasn't in her office."

"Here's the thing. Parker is buying drugs from Halo House to sell on the streets. I'm concerned it's tied to these deaths."

Donna covered her mouth to hide her gasp. Her bloodshot eyes brimmed with more tears. "Poor Ron. And Della."

It was hard to feel sorry for Ron. Particularly when it seemed Donna would soon dehydrate with all her crying over him. "I guess you didn't know. Do you think Ron and Della were aware of what Parker was doing when he visited his grandmother?"

"How would I know that? Della would never tell me anything so private."

"Maybe not Della." I felt a surge of bitterness toward Donna's protection of Ron. How could she be this blind? My eggshell walk around Donna's secret relationship wasn't working. I was in a hurry for answers. "I know about you and Ron. Ron never mentioned Parker being in trouble?"

"Ron's just been trying to console me," she mumbled.

"Uh-huh." I couldn't help my scornful tone. "Ron hasn't struck me as the consoling type. He's threatened me. Pretty much the opposite of sympathetic."

"You don't know Ron like I do," said Donna. "Della ignored him. He was always nice to me when he'd see me at the factory. We started meeting for coffee. I know better than anyone how demanding Della can be."

"I get the picture. He's misunderstood and lonely." I rolled my eyes. "Usually, you're the guy's secretary in this situation. Not the wife's."

She blanched.

"I don't care about the infidelity. There's something bigger at stake. Could Ron be covering for Parker? Do you think Parker could have killed his family? Even accidentally?" Not that I thought anyone had accidentally killed any Brakemans. Except maybe Coralee. But softening the blow made for an easier confession.

Donna pulled a tissue from her pocket and wiped her nose. "I don't know."

"Donna, if I were you, I'd take that vacation for real. And I'd think about men who let their wives bring home the bacon while they date their wife's assistants. Especially when the wife is murdered."

"Murdered? I thought she was hit by a drunk driver."

Donna not only floated on that river in Egypt, she had parked a houseboat on it.

"All three Brakeman women have been murdered. Donna, you don't want to be a Brakeman woman."

A clattering thump, like a tumbling plastic bin, sounded from near Donna's garage. I slipped from the door to peer around the porch and scanned the drive. The garage's security light didn't reveal any darting shadows or hooded figures.

The door creaked. I spun back to find Donna closing it.

"Just wait," I said. "Whatever you do, don't call Ron and tell him about this conversation. Parker—and Ron too—are dangerous."

She shook her head.

"I mean it, Donna. Go somewhere safe."

The lock bolted.

I stepped off the stoop. I didn't feel safe either.

Donna cut her porch light.

Somehow I didn't think I could get Donna to let me back in the house.

The willies danced along my spine. Someone was out there, I could feel it. I didn't think Palmetto would come after me, but punks like Palmetto had done dumber. I ran from her porch to the security light, opened my satchel, and began searching for my pepper spray.

I'd parked on the street and didn't trust my slow feet. If someone skulked nearby, I wanted to be prepared. I dug through the assortment of pencils, lipstick, and Band-Aids and pulled out a metal tube. The small flashlight I'd needed at the Tea Grove plantation. Mentally cursing, I reached inside the bag again. Heard a quick shuffle of feet behind me. I pivoted.

Too late.

An arm walloped me across my face, knocking me backward. I missed the garage wall. Before I reached the ground, the attacker was on top of me, rolling me onto my back.

Pressing me into the concrete with his body, he slid a bag over my head. I bucked, trying to free my arms from his weight. At the sound of tape ripping, I kicked. A hand reached beneath the bag and slapped the tape over my mouth. He rose a few inches to yank my arms free and gather my wrists. I pressed my palms together as he bound my wrists. A quick jerk to my feet and he hoisted me over his shoulder.

I was tossed in the back of a vehicle and driven off into the night.

# THIRTY

I had one major hope pinned on Donna. Maybe she had been watching from the window, too scared to assist me. Maybe she hadn't shut the door, flipped off the light, and crawled back to her couch to finish watching *The Misunderstood Mistress*. I prayed she'd call the police.

Unless this was Ron. You'd think her thing for Ron would sour if she saw him kidnap me. However, it was possible she'd protect him. Because sometimes women were that stupid.

I forced myself to take an inventory of the situation. My jerking breaths began to slow.

The vehicle moved slowly. Donna's cul-de-sac was located at the far end of the subdivision. The driver still wormed through the neighborhood streets. I had a little time. A fact in my favor. For a minute or two, anyway.

My messenger bag had fallen. Hopefully, my kidnapper hadn't grabbed it and the chartreuse satchel lay in Donna's drive, leaving a clue for my rescue team.

Although my hands were taped behind me, my legs were free. I was in the back of a car. A fairly comfortable car with leather seats. Better than a trunk. Silver lining.

I couldn't speak or see, but I could listen. Mostly to a screaming hate-infused rap. Not my favorite, but at least it wasn't creepy circus music. That would really freak me out.

The music covered the thumping made by my legs as I felt around for people who might be in the back with me. No people. I suspected my attacker wasn't actually a clown-loving serial killer.

As kidnapping went, I could do a lot worse.

The music lowered enough to stop my ears from bleeding. I hollered. With the tape and the bag, a muffled "Mwwww" seemed my best articulation.

"I warned you." Parker's voice shook. "I warned you not to screw with us. Now look what happened."

Considering my bag-over-the-head state, I had to use my imagination to fill in the literal blanks. Parker was anxious and desperate. I didn't know what that meant for Hazel and Rosie. I hoped they had gotten away.

A desperate Parker meant I was in trouble.

Big trouble.

I could rat him out on a number of crimes, but he was now looking at charges of kidnapping and assault. Bigger felonies. And he knew it.

"Palmetto told me to take care of this, so I've gotta. You know he's got mafia connections?"

Palmetto's mafia would be Atlanta gangs. I knew as much from Luke and Uncle Will's tales about local drug rings. This meant Parker was more scared of Palmetto's higher-ups than prison.

This also didn't bode well. Maybe Parker and Palmetto's crew killed his mom, meemaw, and aunt. But poison was tricky and they'd have to know a thing or two about heart medication. I didn't think him smart enough for that kind of murder.

However, I did think him desperate enough for another kind of murder. One that involved snitches.

While Parker told me how I had gotten myself into the situation I now faced, I'd pulled my legs into my chest. With a small amount of pain and a large amount of sweating, I threaded my butt and knees through my taped arms. My shoulders and arms were sore but at least were now in front of me. I grasped the bag and yanked it off my head.

And there he was. Still yabbering on about my extreme stupidity and how I didn't have the sense to leave well enough alone.

Like I was going to allow Hazel to be bullied by Parker and Palmetto's gang into practically stealing pills to sell them to children on playgrounds. Parker did not know me at all. I left nothing alone. So much so that my entire life had been one ginormous donkey-load of trouble. But at least I had a clear conscience.

Except for holding onto information about Shawna's father. I still felt guilty as hell. But that was a different donkey-load of trouble.

The luxury car slowed. I reckoned this was the last stop before we turned onto the highway. Without pausing to think, I smacked the unlock with both hands, grabbed the lever, and flung myself out the open door. I rolled into the street. Then continued to roll and squirm into a yard to avoid Parker's high-performance tires.

The Audi skidded to a stop. The car door swung shut on itself.

I didn't wait to see if Parker had spotted me. With my hands tied before me and my mouth taped shut, I ran toward the first house. Cut across their drive and into the backyard. Continued into the next yard. I couldn't breathe. I paused to rip the tape from my mouth. Bit my tongue to keep from screaming. Ran to the next yard, praising the neighbors for not building fences. Then stopped behind their garage to pant and listen.

Parker's engine raced. The tires bumped into a drive.

He was turning around.

Getting into a house without Parker hearing me would be good. Waking the neighborhood until someone called the police would be better.

I studied my taped wrists then lifted my bound hands above my head. As hard as I could, I yanked down and apart. Took a couple tries, but the tape tore.

Thank the Lord for Uncle Will and his forced self-defense classes. Always press your hands together if someone's taping your wrists. Not that I'd needed that information before.

The Audi revved. Tires squealed.

Why didn't anyone in this neighborhood care about this

vehicle which, to me, sounded like it was driven by the devil himself?

A few lights were on in some homes. I peered around the garage I stood behind. The headlights of a slow-moving vehicle shone on the street in front of me. I jerked my head back to keep my shadow from showing.

If I ran to this house and pounded on the door, would anyone come out before Parker saw me? The house was dark. Like no one was at home. But there was a car in the drive. One of those VW bugs. The new kind with the eyelashes.

I waited for Parker's car to drive down the street, then tore out from behind the garage and pulled on the car doors. An alarm went off. I pelted across the yard to the next house. Their security light flared. I yanked on the door handle of a Toyota Tundra. The alarm whined. The Buick LaSabre next to it wasn't alarmed.

Before Parker could turn around, I dashed across the street and attacked the GMC Jimmy. Three alarms sang. I ran to the back door and hammered on the window. The sticker said the window was also alarmed.

Parker had spun his Audi in the street, bumping over a curb to turn around.

Bringing up my elbow, I made a fist, covered it with my free hand, and slammed my elbow into the window. The window did nothing. However, white-hot lightning shot up my shoulder and into my neck, then down to my fingers.

Parker accelerated toward the house where I danced off the pain.

I gave up on the window and scooted toward the backyard. Except this homeowner with his tough-as-nails windows had also built a fence.

A light blinked on in the second story. And another.

The Audi braked in front of the house.

I ran to the front door and pounded with my good fist. No answer, yet lights were on. Giving up, I darted across the front lawn to the next house.

Parker flung open the Audi door and stepped into the street.

At the next house, I jammed my finger into the doorbell. No lights.

"You're out of luck." Parker pointed at the pistol tucked into his belt. Like he was some kind of gangster from the hood.

If I hadn't been scared for my life, I would have laughed. Or cried. Poor little rich boy.

The front door flew open. "What's going on out here?"

Parker and I stared at the man for a good half-second. He had his own pistol, raised to eye level. The man knew what he was doing. And didn't care he'd answered my ring in nothing but his skivvies and boots.

Parker took the second half of that second to decide to run for it. A moment later, the Audi roared down the street.

"Sir, thank you for helping me." I wanted to hug the man except he still had the handgun ready and aimed. And he was mostly unclothed. It might give the wrong message. "That guy, Parker Brakeman-Newson, tried to kidnap me. He had a gun. He grabbed me from a driveway in the back of your subdivision. Donna Sharp's house. Please call the police and tell them."

"I don't know a Donna Sharp."

"She lives at the end of Magnolia Lane."

He lowered his gun. "Y'all were making a racket. Decent people are trying to sleep. Was that your boyfriend?"

"No, sir. I'm telling you he wanted to kidnap me. Parker Brakeman-Newson. He's in a gang."

"A gang? He don't look like he's in no gang."

"He does dress well, I'll give you that." I pressed my once-taped-together hands into the international sign of prayer. "Please, call 911 and report this."

"I'm gonna call them. Y'all stay right here until I get back."

As soon as the door shut, I hightailed it for Donna's. I hammered and rang, but Donna wouldn't answer her door. Maybe she did leave on vacation. Or had gone to bed. Or *The Misunderstood Mistress II* was on.

I scooped up my bag, still lying in the drive—Parker Brakeman-Newson needed lessons in proper criminal etiquette. Who leaves the victim's bag at the scene of a crime?—and slid into my truck. With the doors locked and the adrenaline fleeing my pores, the shakes set in. I took a couple deep breaths, clutched my shoulders, and thought about a plan.

Would Parker think I'd go to the police? Or would he hunt me down?

Parker might know I'd be reluctant to bring attention to Hazel and Rosie's flight out of Dodge. If they had crossed state lines, they'd be in serious trouble. If I were Parker, I'd watch Cherry Tucker's house just in case she didn't go to the police.

Shinola, I thought. Todd's home. Parker might find Todd. And Parker has a gun.

# THIRTY-ONE

My shakes subsided with a new shot of adrenaline. I needed to get over myself and save Todd. Dialing Todd, I explained the situation and asked him to head to Shawna's. It made my gut hurt, but I knew he'd be safe there.

I had to let him go sometime. Might as well be now.

With a half-tank of gas and ten bucks in my pocket, I had a full night ahead of me. Dodging a gang of country thugs, of all things. I'd maneuvered Todd out of my house to protect him from Parker, but I couldn't return home either. I couldn't go to the farm. That would raise too many questions with Pearl. Grandpa Ed would call the Sheriff if he thought I was in trouble. Uncle Will would gladly have me sleep in a cell. For my own good.

Plus I was in no mood for goats.

My sort-of boyfriend lived at his momma's while he saved money. The momma married to JB Branson. That wouldn't go over at all.

Besides, Luke worked nights. He also might have me arrested. For my own good.

Too bad I couldn't send myself to Shawna's house like I did Todd. Not that I thought she'd let me stay. Or I'd want to stay. I'd rather cut off my nose to spite that ugly face. But I did have unfinished business. And with the whole facing-death scenario I'd done a few times this very night, it felt like a good time to unload my burden to Shawna. If Parker did catch me, I'd hate to have the knowledge of her father's whereabouts on my conscience.

Luke was right. I needed to get it done. Whether it helped Cody or not. Whether she thought it was blackmail or not.

Actually taking it to her on the threat of my death kicked the whole blackmail idea out the door. How could I use the information if I were dead?

With that understanding, I parked in the drive of her apartment building, marched to Shawna's door, and pressed the bell. I was prepared for a full Shawna onslaught. Catty remarks. Nasty looks. An open-handed slap. Or a girly shove.

But not this. Shawna in tiger-striped silk pajamas. Todd in sweats. Answering the door together. With the appropriately shocked looks on their faces upon seeing me.

Matching looks of shock.

Shawna reached for Todd's hand.

My stomach rolled and I fought to calm the hurt welling in my chest. He'd kissed her and he liked it. I'd broken his heart. He was with Shawna.

The Bransons had taken everything from me. Except Luke. But even with him, those gray- and blue-eyed babies kept rearing their adorable heads and scaring me. Maybe in this way, the Bransons had taken Luke too. They had spoiled my relationship with him through my own anxiety-riddled imagination. Based on fear of Bransons.

I shook off the shock, told myself to be happy for Todd, and gave Shawna my best howdy-do.

"What are you doing here?" Shawna pulled her hand from Todd's to cross her arms over her ample chest.

We were back on familiar territory. Good. Hostility kept me from getting mopey.

"I'm not staying long," I said. "I've got a drug dealer after me. Makes me better understand your anger with my brother. I now know how it feels to be kidnapped. Of course you didn't get tied up and have a bag pulled over your head, but still..."

Todd's fingers hammered against his sweatpanted thigh.

"Very funny." Shawna's eyes blazed green fire. "You came here this time of night to badger me about what your brother did to me? Of all the nerve."

"This is not about that, I swear. I was trying to empathize and I guess it didn't work." I shuffled my feet and searched for humility. "So what I meant, in case I don't make it—"

"In case you don't make it?" Shawna snorted. "Are you kidding me? You interrupted us on purpose because you knew Todd came over. You want him back."

"Shawna, Cherry's really been in trouble with local drug dealers. It wasn't an excuse to come over." Todd's shade of Scarlet Lake did not suit him. And his defense needed work. But then Todd was never good with words.

Unless he was spilling his heart about dating my nemesis, that is.

"I know how this looks. I didn't come here to interrupt y'all...doing...sleeping...arrangements." I blew out a long breath. "I give you my blessing."

"You give us your blessing?" She turned to Todd. "Can you believe this? She thinks we have to have her permission. She dumped you on your wedding day."

"It was actually the next day," I said.

"If you want to get technical," said Todd.

"Shut up, Cherry." Shawna turned her laser eyes off me and back to Todd. "Cherry Tucker has treated you like dirt. She led you on while she was sneaking around behind your back with my cousin."

"Step-cousin."

"Shut up, Cherry." Shawna grasped Todd's hands to keep them from drumming a hole through his sweatpants. "She uses you in her asinine capers and almost got you arrested. Drew drug dealers to your door so you can't even stay at your own house. And that was just tonight."

"Sometimes the asinine capers are his idea," I said. "And that house is actually mine. For now."

"Shut it." She whirled back to Todd. "Can't you see? She has rejected you time and again while she makes you dance to her bedbug-crazy tune. All the while, she's making you look foolish to everyone else. But not to me. You are a sweet and caring man. And it's time you get treated as you deserve."

"That's real nice, Shawna, but—"

I'd agree that Todd was sweet and caring. But spite made me interrupt. "He's also got a gambling addiction. That I helped end."

"By using sex as a weapon."

"Have you seen how scrawny I am? How in the hell would I use sex as a weapon? I'm not the one walking around in animal-print lingerie, Cruella."

Shawna's mouth drew into a line so thin I was afraid she'd eaten her lips.

"Cherry," said Todd. "And Shawna. Please."

"Sorry." I had forgotten Shawna's mother also liked to answer the door in animal-print lingerie. Holding tea sweetened with vodka. Very popular with postal workers and milkmen. But that was after Billy had left. Shawna had her own family issues. And that put me back on track.

I reached into my pocket and pulled out the paper Luke had given me. Placed it in Shawna's hand.

Actually, I had to shove it between her hand and Todd's.

"I don't know how you're going to react when you see this. Todd doesn't know anything about it." I shot Todd a look. He had that glazed Bambi-meets-the-hunter thing going on. But he understood to play dumb. Which wasn't hard for Todd. That's how he got so good at poker.

"This is just between you and me, Shawna," I continued. "And I'm not telling anybody anything because it could affect me as much as it does you, believe it or not. This whole deal between us boils down to a problem between our parents. And this paper has information about the parent concerning you. His whereabouts for the past twenty years and his current address." I figured I'd let her read Billy Branson's rap sheet in private.

"Just a cotton pickin'—"

I cut her off. "Maybe they were 'friends.'" I air quoted and mentally kicked myself. I hated air quotes. This was what happened around Shawna. "Maybe not. It doesn't make a difference to me, but it did to Cody. And he acted like an idiot. But he's twenty-one and his brain never thought much past engine parts. A personal revelation like this did him a doozy. But that's neither here nor there. I'm sorry for what Cody did to you. I'm sure it was embarrassing as hell. You don't want people to know about our families' past and you certainly don't want Cody and Casey rubbing your nose in it."

"You have no idea—"

"Take this and do what you want. It's got nothing to do with me. The guilt of knowing such a thing is about too much and I'm sorry I didn't tell you before. I didn't know how you'd react."

"Get out," she snarled.

"I take that back. I figured you'd react something like this." I bowed my head. "Don't worry, I'm getting."

I looked up to meet Todd's cerulean blues. My chest felt like it might cave in on itself. I couldn't leave him like this. "I never meant to hurt you, Todd. I always considered you my best friend. I've been selfish wanting a friendship where you needed more. You grew up and I didn't. The future scares the hell out of me. Probably why Momma left and I'm not much different."

"Just like your momma." Shawna crumpled the paper in her hand. "Stringing men along and driving them to distraction until they can't see what's in front of them."

"Shawna, give us a minute." Todd turned to me. "I understand, Cherry."

I ignored Shawna and kept my eyes steady on Todd. "I guess you were my Peter Pan. But I'm no Wendy. I wish you the best."

At least that was done.


I slept in my truck in the Waffle Hut parking lot, letting my engine run to stay warm. When the manager knocked on my window, I trooped inside and ordered a pecan waffle and a coffee. I used a napkin and a pen borrowed from the waitress to doodle and think.

Likely, Parker would still search for me. He was under orders from Palmetto who was under orders from his Atlanta thug boss who was under orders by his kingpin. Or whatever. I knew there was a strict hierarchy in gangland, but all that bureaucracy was hard to track. Anyway, if Parker found my house empty, there was one other place he'd look. Parker didn't know about Ada's restraining order. But he did know I was friends with Ada. And he did know I worked at Halo House.

"Hells bells," I told the waitress, scrambling from my seat. "They need to be warned."

I left my coffee and the confused waitress for the pay phone.

You'd think an anonymous tip—like "Belvia Brakeman's grandson, Parker Brakeman-Newson, might try to infiltrate Halo House. Consider him armed and dangerous. Any sighting of Parker Brakeman-Newson should be reported to the police."—would be taken more seriously by the Halo House night manager.

Not so much.

Returning to my seat and my cold coffee, I considered the options I had doodled on a handful of napkins.

The smart thing to do would be to call Luke, let them arrest me for my own good, and have them watch Halo House for Parker. They'd have my testimony of Parker's kidnapping and Palmetto's threatened assault.

But they'd never get Palmetto's buddies to testify. The only thing Todd witnessed was me chasing Palmetto to the corn crib and then hunting him again at Splats. Where I shot Palmetto's friends in the face and Palmetto where the sun didn't shine. At point-blank range. Paintball gun was better than real but still wouldn't look good in court.

And even though I had convinced Palmetto that Parker would rat him out, I wasn't sure he would. Parker would have a good lawyer—likely Harry Hunt—who might take on Palmetto just to save Parker's butt.

And I'd get another court-appointed attorney who'd be as good as the wingnut who tried to defend Cody.

If Luke and his deputies could pull together evidence of the Halo House drug smuggling ring to convict Parker and Palmetto, I'd still be selling Rosie and Hazel down the river with the P boys.

Here's the thing. I'd much rather get Parker on murder. I had to stay out of jail-for-my-own-good. After all, I had made a promise to Belvia to figure out who killed her daughter. Daughters. And herself. And by doing that, I could help Luke and Uncle Will. If Uncle Will had a major murder conviction, that'd do him good in the next election. And it'd show everybody his niece wasn't bedbug crazy. Including or excluding the Bransons.

I hoped our deputies could snatch Palmetto in a separate drug raid clear from Halo House. He wasn't just selling little blue pills by the looks of stinky Jordan and associates. But I couldn't implicate my friends.

However, another call from the Waffle Hut payphone, this time to the Forks County "Hot Tips" line, could help the deputies create a separate drug raid. Anonymously, of course. But with distinctive descriptions of Palmetto and his associates.

That done, I headed to my truck.

I was going after Parker. And I'd use myself as bait.

# THIRTY-TWO

At this early hour, visitors didn't yet fill the Halo House parking lot, although a Cobalt Yellow Corvette idled near the front doors. I did a quick scan for Parker and his Audi. I didn't find Parker worthy of rocket-science-type criminal behavior but figured he couldn't be foolish enough to park in plain sight. I'd have to sneak into Halo House to search him out. I hoped to lead him away. Toward a place less public, but with people.

The Forks County Sheriff's Department, for example.

At my pull in, Ron Newson climbed out of the lemon mid-life-crisis mobile and turned a malevolent eye on my truck. Evidently, Ron knew to track me to Halo House too.

I eyed his car. Corvette tire tracks would be easy to trace for Della's hit and run. Luke would have checked Parker's Audi too. I'd place my bets on a Palmetto-type vehicle. Likely stolen. Or borrowed for a joy/murder ride. Thank the Lord they had stolen my Datsun after Della's murder and not before, I thought. I'd hate to be framed for all three deaths.

But why was Ron here? I wondered if Parker sent him. Should I run from Ron, not knowing if my friends inside were safe from his son?

Nope. Couldn't do it.

Shutting off the truck, I considered my options. Dallying with Ron in the parking lot seemed a good way for something bad to happen. I didn't trust the man any more than I trusted his son. But I did want to hear whatever he needed to say to me. Which was urgent enough to wait in the one place he'd knew I'd show. Maybe he could tell me where to find Parker. Or give a good hint to send Forks County's Finest in that direction.

I slipped out of the truck, fisting my keys.

Ron's breath frosted the air as he strode across the parking lot. He had left the Corvette running.

To be safe, I paced toward the entrance, rounding away from Ron.

His faster feet cut off my approach. "Hey," called Ron. "I want to talk to you."

"Save it for the police. Your son accosted and tried to kidnap me last night. He's imploding." I glanced toward the Halo House entrance, hoping for a witness loitering under the covered walkway. Unfortunately, it was too cold for the morning greeters to stand in the vestibule, let alone outside.

"Let me explain." Ron halted before me and waved toward the Corvette. "My car's still running. Get in where it's warm so we can talk."

"No thanks. I don't get into cars with murder suspects." I stepped laterally to move around him.

"You're higher on that list than me." His arm shot out and a strong hand gripped my elbow. "Just for a minute. You've got time. Get in the car."

"Let me tell you something, Ron." I jerked my elbow back and he tightened his grip. "You know my brother 'explained' a woman into his vehicle. You do not want to go there with me. I don't want your explanations. Your kid is a criminal and I will be pressing charges."

"You can't do this to us."

"Your son's not going to be president of Meemaw's Tea. He thinks he's a gangster. Do you know he's carrying a pistol? It matches the tattoo on his neck."

"A gun?" His hand flew off my arm. "You're lying. He wouldn't do that. Della put the stocks in his name. Parker has a future. He just needs to grow up first."

"The way he's going, Parker's future will be behind bars. If he's lucky enough to make it to prison."

"I'll pay you whatever you want." Ron's voice wavered. "He was just trying to scare you. He looks tough, but it's an act."

"I don't want your money. I want to know what happened to your wife and her mother and sister."

Ron's face darkened.

"Did Parker kill them?"

"No," he shouted.

His hands reached again. I sidestepped but he wasn't grabbing for me. Instead, they grappled with an invisible neck. The hands shook, then covered his face. With an anguished moan, Ron crumpled. The polish, reserve, and sneer disappeared as the man wept.

Not knowing what to do, I waited until he pulled himself together.

Red-faced, Ron pulled off a glove and swiped at his eyes with a handkerchief. "I don't know what Parker's capable of anymore. He had everything he could want."

"Except parents who paid attention to him."

Ron's jaw tightened. "I've been there for him. Cleaning up his messes. Della was busy. She didn't tolerate his shenanigans. She'd punish him. I felt sorry for Parker. Della wasn't motherly, but she was an amazing businesswoman, so I dealt with it."

"You mean you paid to deal with his shenanigans. Although I don't think gang activity counts as a shenanigan."

He bowed his head. "He's just a boy."

"Not according to the law. Was Parker at the factory the day Della died?"

"I don't know." Ron blinked at the sky. "I wasn't there."

"Right, you had an alibi. Except Donna Sharp was at the factory. Where were you?"

"Atlanta. At my golf club. This is all just a big misunderstanding," said Ron. "Della was killed, yes. There were...issues between her and Parker. One therapist called it

Abandoned Child Syndrome, blaming Della for being emotionally unavailable. I don't know. Maybe it's defensible. Rehab and counseling, not prison."

I seethed. My mother had abandoned me for real and I hadn't up and joined a gang. "I'm guessing rehab and counseling would leave you in charge of his controlling interest in Meemaw's. Prison wouldn't?"

"Belvia's heart attack is making this look worse than it is."

"Murder tends to do that."

"No." He held up his hands. "Coralee and Belvia had heart attacks. This is your fault. You've been making their deaths look suspicious. It's not murder."

"The police have evidence to the contrary."

"I'm telling you she was already dead." Ron's voice broke. "It's a misunderstanding. He didn't do it."

"Who was already dead?"

"Parker didn't stab Coralee." His eyes squeezed shut. "I stuck the pencil in her neck. I knew it was your pencil. I was afraid for Parker. I meant to have it out with Coralee. But I found her dead. And I was angry. With her. And you. And Parker. And Belvia, for all her machinations that created this mess in the first place. The hell she put us through."

That's a whole lot more than angry, I thought. Who gets mad enough to stab a dead body with a pencil?

I edged toward the sidewalk. "You need to talk to the police, Ron. Tell them about the pencil. You might have seen important clues to her murder."

He stumbled after me. "Didn't you hear me? Coralee wasn't murdered. She had a heart attack like her mother."

"Coralee was poisoned. She and Belvia were given medication that killed them. You need to tell the police what you saw."

"You have to be wrong. Parker wouldn't know how to use medication like that. He couldn't have killed Belvia and Coralee."

Sounded like Ron had thought Parker had killed Della. Ron just didn't think Parker capable of dosing medication for a heart attack. "Is that why you were looking at Belvia's medicine? Trying to see if Parker could have induced her heart attack?"

"No, I was looking to see if Parker had stolen any drugs from Belvia. I didn't want the police to find out he was selling drugs from Halo House." He sighed. "I guess that's the least of his problems now."

But my thoughts had spun back to the digoxin. "There's plenty of heart meds in Halo House if you know where to look. Half the time the residents don't lock their doors."

Ron began to protest again, but I stopped listening. Pris had said Wally self-medicated. My looking under the couch for the pills had made Wally nervous. Wally and Pris were also about to inherit a bundle, unless Belvia had written Coralee out of the will. But that meant Wally or Pris would have also killed Coralee.

The missing will didn't make as much sense in that case.

Before I could explore that idea, I still had a slight problem with Parker wanting to kill me. I interrupted Ron's lamentations. "Do you know where we can find Parker?"

"He didn't come home last night," Ron mumbled. "I've no idea. A friend's house? I banned his friends from the Tea Grove. He was always slinking off and I was forever kicking them out."

I thought of Palmetto's sneak attack at the Tea Grove. "Do you think Parker'd come here? To look for me?"

Ron shrugged.

"Look, Ron. You have to talk to the police. Tell them everything. It'll be better for Parker in the long run."

"What will you do?"

"I need to warn my friend and stay with her until the sheriff's deputies get here. Parker's looking for revenge and to fulfill his gang debt. But please talk to the police. There's a chance your son didn't commit murder."

I ran toward Halo House's front doors, wishing I'd changed my wording to, "A chance your son didn't commit murder *yet.*"

After all, Parker still gunned for me. And I was bedbug crazy enough to return to the first place he'd look.

*   *   *

Before I called Luke to bring the cavalry, I needed to know Ada was safe. Which meant breaking my restraining order.

Which could mean going to jail-for-real-and-not-just-for-my-own-good.

Regardless, my phone was out of juice. I had to enter Halo House. I couldn't risk using the hall phone and getting caught by the staff. Particularly when they suspected me of prank calls about the dangers of a deceased resident's grandson. But Fred would sneak me into his room and let me use his phone. And Fred could tell me how Ada was doing. Maybe she no longer thought me a stool pigeon. Maybe we could return to being friends.

Maybe I was being naive.

Either way, I needed to warn them about Parker.

In the vestibule, I waited for Krenzer to turn her back on the front desk to commune with her coffee maker. I raced past the lobby, bypassing the exposed grand staircase to the rear hall where the elevators stood. Jamming the up button with my thumb, I bounced on my toes and waited for the slow descent. The scent of coffee and bacon drifted from the deli. A passel of folks passed, headed for coffee. I received some cheery "morning"s and one stink eye from a dissatisfied art student. The elevator doors opened. I waited again for Ray Howard to shuffle through with his walker. Before he could tell me once again about the Tokyo peep show he saw back in '52, the doors slid closed.

I shot skyward at a gentle pace that wouldn't upset my balance or digestion. The doors slid open. I eased past Flora Shelley—who had a granddaughter coming today or tomorrow or was that yesterday—and Maria Martinez—who'd won a bingo coupon for a tan at Get A Glo. By then, I worried Parker had enough time to breakfast, drive to Halo House, park, walk up the stairs, and hold Ada hostage while I was stuck between floors two and four.

Suffice it to say, I was more than a little anxious when I reached Fred's apartment.

At my pounding, he opened the door wearing a t-shirt featuring a battleship and a towel around his neck. Fred stepped out, shot a look down the hall, and yanked me inside. "Girl, you know you're not supposed to be here."

I held up my hands. "This is too important. Parker Brakeman-Newson is on the loose. I tussled with him and his gang last night and he's looking for me. He knows I'm friends with Ada and I'm worried all to hell. He's packing heat and crazy stupid."

"You think he'd do something to Ada?" Fred flicked the towel from his shoulders and wrapped it around one fist.

"He's desperate enough to use Ada to get to me. He's buying drugs off Hazel for his dealer to sell. The boys he's running with..." I checked the fear in my voice. "They're connected to an Atlanta gang. And into some serious stuff by the looks of it. Like teaching me a lesson for interfering."

"Where're the police?"

"I need to use your phone to call them. But I thought you could get Ada out of here. Before Parker shows. Take her to Line Creek or something. Until things die down." I bit my lip, hating my choice of words. "Parker's going to find me here. I planned on drawing him away. But I ran into his daddy in the parking lot and came to warn you."

Fred blinked, then caught up. "Use my phone, then you need to get out too. Let the police handle this."

"I will. But I needed to know y'all were safe first. Halo House should be on lockdown, but no one will believe me."

"I'm getting Ada."

"Call her first."

While Fred rang Ada, I wore a path in his living room playing, "If I were Parker, where would I hide?"

Belvia's apartment.

I burned to check it out, but I didn't like the prize if I won that game.

However, if Parker did hide at Belvia's, I knew someone who might have noticed. Molly. I was sure she had a key. She lived a few doors down. And if Parker didn't have a key, he might've asked an unsuspecting Molly for entrance.

Fred returned the phone to its corded cradle. He glanced at me. "Not home. I think Ada's getting coffee. Let me check the canteen and while I'm there, I'll organize a search for Parker. Don't you worry."

"Please, no heroics. If anyone sees Parker, tell them to lock their doors and call the police." I grabbed his phone. "That goes double for Ada. I'm fixing to check on Molly."

Fred nodded and sped out the door.

This phone business didn't help me much. No answer from Molly. Or at Belvia's, although I didn't think Parker would answer if he was hiding there. I dialed Luke, who also didn't answer. I stated something about an armed and dangerous Parker possibly showing at Halo House and sending reinforcements to the residence home. However, Luke still didn't know about my associations with Palmetto or the subsequent stalking and abduction by Parker. He only thought I was on the wrong end of a restraining order due to my prying nature.

As a girlfriend, I'll admit, I was a horrible communicator. And, it seemed, dishonest.

Probably needed to work on that.

As soon as I got those scary Branson babies out of my head and scary Parker off my tail. Bringing me back to "Where In the World Is Parker Brakeman-Newson?" I couldn't lead Parker away from Halo House if he wasn't around to follow. Ada and anybody else associated with me could be in danger.

I headed to Molly's on the second floor. She rarely left her apartment. I had a feeling she purposely didn't answer the phone. But she had a key to Belvia's. There was a good chance Parker had paid her a visit.

# THIRTY-THREE

I sighed in relief when Molly answered the door without an armed Parker beside her. She wore another sweatsuit. Glittery kittens played with a sparkly ball of yarn. Still no pearls and suit. But she no longer appeared anxious and frazzled.

"Molly, let me in. I can't let anyone see me."

She glanced down the hall, then widened the door. "What do you mean?"

"Ada has a restraining order on me. I'm not supposed to be at Halo House."

Molly drew me inside. "I thought Ada was your friend."

"She had me arrested for trying to stop Hazel and Rosie from getting away...Never mind, that story's too long. I need to warn you about Parker."

"Parker?"

"Parker's been buying and selling drugs at Halo House. He's dangerous and I'm afraid he'll try to hurt you."

"Oh, my." Molly sank onto the floral couch.

I sat beside her. "I want you to keep your door locked. If Parker shows, call for help. Don't let him in."

"Do you think Parker's the one who killed poor Coralee?"

"Actually, no."

"But who else would stab her?"

I hesitated, hating to upset her again. Molly seemed calmer. She had a right to know. "The pencil didn't kill her. She was poisoned with the Dixie Delites I gave Belvia."

"The chocolates?" She stilled. "Do you know who poisoned them?"

"Someone who had access to the candy. Considering the slew of Meemaw's folks and Brakeman family who had trooped in and out of that apartment, there's a host of people who had access to the box. They could have easily grabbed and returned it. The poisoning, however, narrows it considerably."

"Oh my stars..." Her words trailed off and her eyes wandered to the picture of the sisters.

"It's okay, Molly." I spoke soothingly, patting her arm. I had misjudged her recovery and opted to veer from murder to a simpler crime of drugs. "I'm concerned Parker could have stolen some of your prescriptions. He sells them to a dealer who is networked in Atlanta."

"Lord have mercy."

So drugs might not make for a better topic than murder. "Just in case, you should check your prescriptions and let the police know if anything's missing. In the meantime, keep your door locked and alert the front desk if Parker stops here."

"I should check my medicine and see if anything's missing now. While you're here." Her voice quivered. "Some of it was Maggie's. I brought everything when I moved here."

I sensed her reluctance to admit she had held on to her sister's medicine. I knew many retirees who stored medications to save money. Except now some were selling the drugs to make cash.

"Go through it and if you think anything's missing, tell Sheriff Will. You should sort them anyway. Anything expired is no good."

"Please wait. I'm so worried about this. It won't take long."

I forced myself to smile and nod. Internally my nerves stewed and popped.

We ambled down the short hall leading to her bedroom. Inside, she stopped at her bathroom door. "This will just take a moment."

While Molly slunk into her bathroom, I watched her bedside clock flip numbers. Knowing this pot would not otherwise boil, I took a stroll and appraised her bedroom art. More Precious Moments and another photo of the sisters. I approached the framed picture hanging on the wall, drawn again to the siblings. I wondered why these photos fascinated me. Because of Coralee and Della? Because of my own sister? Or of Shawna, who might be a sort-of stepsister?

Or something else. The sisters were older in this picture, adults, but in a similar pose to the young girls in the living room. In her expression and apparel, Molly appeared all business, controlled and serious. They shared the same blue eye color, but Maggie's chin was softer, cheeks rounder, nose less beaky than the sharp-faced Molly in this picture. Ironically, age had Molly looking more like her sister. Of course, judging by the hair and clothes, this photo was about twenty years old. Age caused features to wither and sag.

As a portraitist, I always found the sitter's clothing choice an interesting reflection of their personality. This time, there were no bows or matching sailor dresses. Molly wore a suit with the ubiquitous pearls. Her sibling, Maggie, wore a flowered dress. More casual than Molly's suit, but slightly gaudy. Lots of sequins and color.

Kind of like the sweatsuits Molly wore now.

My critical gaze shifted toward Maggie's amusement with the photo session. Maggie had a wide, open smile. My heart twisted. Molly must miss her high-spirited sister. Her hand covered Maggie's, almost clenching it. Clamping down on her sister's hijinks? I rose to my toes and examined Molly's expression. She smiled but without the natural wrinkling around her eyes.

I wondered if Maggie had annoyed her during the photoshoot. Sisters were good for that. Mine did. I gathered Coralee and Della had annoyed each other. I couldn't imagine having Coralee for a sister.

My eyes crept back to the picture. Why did Molly now look like Maggie? Who had really died, Molly or her sister?

Why did I just think that?

"Dear me," Molly called. "I found something."

I spun toward the bathroom door. "What is it? Missing pills?"

"No, there are injections gone from my sister's Lanoxin." She waved a box. "You were right, young lady. We need to call the police and tell them about Parker. He must have stolen them from me."

"I knew it." I narrowed my eyes, thinking of Parker behind bars. "Did Parker visit often?"

"No. But I left my door unlocked if I was seeing Belvia. He would know that. You should tell the police right away about Parker stealing my medicine."

"What's Lanoxin?"

"It's used to force the heart into a normal rhythm."

Sounded like a form of digoxin. My pulse sped up. "Can I see it?"

She handed me the box.

"I thought Parker bought pills." I studied the label, then slipped an ampule into my hand. "Would Parker know what to do with these?"

"I'm sure he could figure it out. You have to break the ampule and use a syringe." She sighed. "Most people would have pills or capsules. Maggie went to nursing school, so she asked the doctor for injection ampules. I have these left over. There was another box and it's empty."

A syringe. Easier to poison the chocolates. Parker wouldn't need to know the dosage. Simple to inject in his grandma's lidocaine patches too. The Lanoxin would seep into her skin with the lidocaine. Plus Coralee had been on Prozac when she ate the chocolates. Murdering Coralee and Belvia wasn't as complicated as it seemed.

I kept my voice calm. "Your sister was a nurse?"

Molly nodded at the photo. "Maggie went to nursing school but had to take care of our grandparents, then our parents. After they passed, she was too old to get a job. I supported her. She earned it after all those years of caring for our family. I owed her for that and for taking care of me and our home." Molly shook her head. "All those years wasted. She deserved an easier life."

"I was looking at that picture. Your personalities really shine through." I pointed toward the photo. "You look like her now."

"We've always looked similar. Anyway, old people look the same to the young."

"That's unfortunately true." However, my eyes remained convinced the photo didn't match the person speaking to me, although a switch made no sense. Krenzer had said Molly didn't have heart issues, but Belvia had told me she did. What was going on? "I notice more than most considering my background."

"As a painter?"

I nodded, feeling strange about Molly's brushoff. "I should take these injections to the sheriff now. He'll be interested in this."

"Why don't you have a cup of tea first? You can call the sheriff from my phone."

"Parker's still out there and I need to know Ada's safe." I backed to the door, feeling confused about what I thought I knew about Molly and what I now perceived. "I'll be back. Keep your door locked and whatever you do, don't let Parker in. Call the police."

"I'd rather you not take the Lanoxin with you. Tell the sheriff to come get it. He may want to look at my other medications and the empty box."

I handed the box back to her. I didn't want Molly to know I suspected her of being someone else.


Molly or Maggie or whoever I'd spoken to warranted a better interview with a trained professional. Was Molly actually Molly or was Maggie pretending to be Molly? But Miss Belvia and every other Meemaw's Tea personnel would have figured it out. What would be the point? Maybe I was dead wrong. But something felt peculiar.

Miss Belvia had told me to "watch out for Molly." She'd been worried about her. Because Molly had grown confused since moving to Halo House? Or something else? Did Belvia suspect she wasn't Molly but her sister?

Molly had the means to kill Coralee and Miss Belvia. Of course, Parker did too. And everyone and their dog had an opportunity. But Molly's motive was doubtful. She had a nice setup at Halo House. Why kill Della and Coralee? She wouldn't inherit Meemaw's Tea. Belvia had said it would stay in the family. The surviving members had a bigger motive, particularly Parker, who had already shown intent to murder.

Unfortunately, that intent was immediately focused on me.

Hell, yes. I had a bigger problem with Parker on the loose than worrying out my Molly suspicions. I needed Fred's phone to try Luke again and to know Ada was safe. I darted through the hall toward the stairs and Fred's apartment. On the staircase, I had gained two steps before I heard my name called from below. I turned and tripped down a flight and into Luke's arms.

"I knew you'd be here," he said, pulling me tight. "Todd called after you showed at Shawna's. Just when were you going to let me know the drug lords of Forks County were gunning for you? And why aren't you answering your phone?"

"Battery's dead. Save your arrest for later. I'll go willingly. We need to talk about missing heart meds."

"Not now." He grasped my elbow and walked me to the second floor. Pulling me into a hallway corner, he eased me against the wall. "I've been looking for Parker since that call. We're going to talk about the very real and present danger of you messing with savvy country boys connected to dangerous city gang activity."

This time, the babies didn't show. Probably scared off by the very real and present dangerous glint to Luke's steely eyes.

"Do you have enough to arrest Palmetto without my testimony?" I still wanted to protect Ada, Hazel, and Rosie as much as possible.

"What the hell kind of question is that?"

I peered at him under my lashes and bit my lower lip. "I'm taking the fifth, Officer."

"Cut that out. After Todd's call, we tracked Parker's vehicle to Palmetto's apartment early this morning. But when my team assembled to make the arrest, Parker took off. I left the team and came here knowing you'd ignore the restraining order on some fool mission—"

"To lead Parker to you."

"Like I said, some fool mission, knowing Parker would look for you here."

"But you haven't found him. Have you?"

The steely glint darkened and his jaw tightened.

I shut my mouth.

"I've got Miss Krenzer checking the camera feed for Parker. But I sure did find you pretty easily, didn't I? Here's what you're doing. Going home. An officer will be there to watch the house."

"But there's something real important you need to know about Belvia and Coralee's—"

The walkie on his shoulder squawked. Luke held up a finger and focused on his earpiece. He spoke a few words into his shoulder walkie. "That's my team. They've arrested Palmetto and some of his boys. We can get them on possession and intent to distribute and traffic, plus there're unregistered firearms and a host of paraphernalia to convince the local judge that this Palmetto is connected to a bigger Atlanta outfit. I've got to go."

"Your hot tip line got a call about that. Will the caller get a reward?"

"That was you?" He paused. "We got another call from someone in Donna Sharp's neighborhood. Did Parker chase you down the street, waving a handgun?"

"I wouldn't call it waving. More like he flashed it to show his serious intent."

"Intent to shoot you." Luke splayed a hand on the wall behind me and leaned forward, resting his forehead against mine. "Sugar, I buy Tums and Sleep-Eze regularly now. I have accepted part of loving you is living with crazy. But I wish you'd quit."

I opened my mouth, caught his look, and shut it.

"You have to help me here. Do you know what happens to gang members if they don't follow the crazy-ass rules handed to them?"

I nodded.

"Then you'll go home to prevent me from adding blood-pressure meds to that list."

"Speaking of meds, Molly's got missing Lanoxin—"

"No, we're done speaking. For now. I've got criminals to indict and a fugitive to find. I shouldn't be here, talking now." His silvery Payne's Gray eyes heated to molten pewter. "Real quick though. Todd also told me you gave Shawna the information about Billy Branson. Thank you, sugar. I know it was hard."

"She didn't seem too happy about it, Luke."

He dropped a kiss on my cheek. "Trust me. Give her a minute to get over the news. Soon there won't be any more issues between an arresting officer and a defendant's sister. We'll be free and clear to be together without worry. And I'm thinking it's time you had a new roommate. Permanently."

I clasped my cheek, feeling my palm heat from the scorch left by his lips. "This is moving awful fast."

"Not really, sugar. That's all in your mind." He strode away, cocking his head to his shoulder and speaking fast into the mic.

I gripped the wall, determined not to let my legs slide out from under me. If Shawna dropped the charges, there'd be no more excuses. I'd have to admit my Branson anxiety and see where it left us. My life felt like goose-greased grass. Everywhere I stepped I was likely to skid and fall on my face. I'd lost Todd to Shawna. I might lose Luke too, if I couldn't get over this hatred of his step-family. How could we move beyond a blood feud other than by leaving our families behind? He couldn't do it to his mother and I couldn't do it to my siblings.

Hell, Luke thought I was crazy, and I was the sanest Tucker I knew. My family needed me.

Speaking of crazy...I glanced up the hall toward Molly's apartment. Or was it Maggie? I'd have to call Uncle Will from home, explain my findings, and leave him to it.

Hopefully, Luke would nab Parker and learn he had stolen the Lanoxin from Molly, poisoned his grandmother and aunt, and literally bumped off his mother. We'd have him for murder, Hazel and Rosie could come home, and Ada would forgive me. And Molly would return to her calm and reserve and seem less nutty.

I had to be mistaken about the weird vibes I detected. Impersonating your sister didn't make sense. Not that any of this mattered. I needed to protect myself from Parker, not worry about Molly's personality disorder.

As I ruminated on that thought, Molly opened her door, glanced into the hallway, and hurried toward Belvia's apartment. Drawing back against the wall, I stilled my movements to watch without her notice. Then jerked my jaw shut with a snap.

Molly was unlocking Belvia's apartment.

I peeled myself off the wall and flew to the stairs. "Luke," I shouted, but I knew he'd gone. He'd taken those stairs at a fast clip while I clung to the wall, reviewing family history and the curious business of Molly.

"No flippin' way," I exclaimed aloud. "What in the hell is she doing? She's going to get herself killed."

A woman peeked from apartment 220. She gave me a sharp look and muttered about noise and blasphemy.

"Call Krenzer at the front desk," I hollered, running toward Miss Belvia's. "Parker Brakeman-Newson is probably in Belvia Brakeman's apartment and Molly Kern just went inside. I don't know what he's going to do."

"I mind my own business and suggest you do the same, young lady. Quietly." She slammed her door.

I skidded to a stop before Belvia's, cracked the door, and slipped inside the empty living room. The overhead light had been turned on. I stole toward the office but stopped at the sound of a cabinet banging in the kitchen. With my heart slamming against my ribs, I edged toward the kitchen entrance, hugging the wall with my back.

"Parker," said Molly. "I know about the drugs."

Another cabinet door slammed. "I don't know what you're talking about."

"Now Parker, I know all about it. But I'm not turning you in. I want you to sell some for me too."

I sucked in my breath. What was Molly doing?

Parker's voice slid into a sneer. "What's the matter? Worried that Grandmother changed the will on you too? I keep telling these women if they can't afford this place they should move out."

"We don't like moving at our age, Parker."

"We can't all live in paradise. But whatever. What do you have? I've got to cut Halo House out of my network now that my cover's blown. This is a one-time deal, you hear?"

My thoughts reeled. I resisted looking in on them but listened to the rustle of movement. I couldn't believe Molly would sell drugs to Parker when she knew the sheriff was expecting them.

"What the hell is this stuff?" said Parker.

He didn't recognize the Lanoxin. What did that mean? I pressed a palm to my forehead and squeezed.

"I can't sell this," said Parker. "What about hydromorphone or oxy? Surely, you got oxy. Everybody does."

If Parker didn't know what the Lanoxin was, he couldn't have poisoned Coralee and Belvia.

"This is all I have," said Molly. "Take it and you can give me the money later."

Molly wanted Parker to have the evidence.

"I told you I can't sell it. Get out of my way."

She was planting it on him. My fists clenched. Was she protecting herself or someone else?

A chair scraped and something thudded. "You didn't see me."

I froze against the wall. Parker emerged from the kitchen, headed toward the opposite side of the living room. I squeezed my eyes shut, opened them, and there was Parker holding a gun on me.

"Isn't that funny," he said. "I was just going to look for you."

# THIRTY-FOUR

Luke was right. Loving me was living with crazy. What kind of idiot knowingly entered an apartment where there was an armed drug dealer wanting to kill her? I had crackers for brains. Likely unsalted.

"Parker," I gasped. "Let Molly leave and then we can talk."

"I knew you'd show up here. You really are stupid."

"Looks that way." I licked my dry lips and squared my shoulders. "But you've got me now. Let Molly go."

His gun hand trembled while he considered my request. His left hand rose to steady his grip.

I sucked in a queasy breath.

Molly stumbled through the kitchen.

Startled, Parker recoiled, then swung the barrel toward her. She cried out and threw her hands in the air.

"Parker, this is between you and me." My hands fluttered, trying to draw his attention away from Molly. "I knew you'd be in here and still came. Doesn't that tell you something?"

"Tells me you got a death wish." He wiped his forehead on his raised arm, then readjusted his grip.

I'd seen circus chimps carrying bang-bang guns with a steadier grip. Thug for real was not as glamorous as thug wannabe. Parker didn't want to shoot me. Although he seemed to like the handgun as an accessory.

"I just might." I spoke as gently and calmly as I could manage.

Gentle and calm were not a normal part of my repertoire, particularly when facing a pistol. "Let Molly go."

"In the kitchen, Miss Molly. Make me some coffee." The barrel swung back to me and he motioned with the gun. "You. In the office. Grandmother had soundproofing stuff put in there so she could concentrate better. Should help kill the noise of gunfire."

I swallowed. He was more serious than I thought. "The deputies got Palmetto. He's been arrested."

"That means I take his place. I really got to do you now." Parker rolled his shoulders and shook out his legs.

"You don't have a chance in hell of getting away with it. Between Palmetto's testimony and my friends as witnesses, everyone will know you shot me in cold blood."

"Palmetto isn't testifying against me. You got a family?"

"Of course. And they want me alive."

"Mine too. And if I go down for murder, they'll know I did it for them. They'll be proud."

"I talked to your dad this morning. He's not proud. He's horrified."

"I'm not talking about Ron. He's never been proud of me. He just wants to use me for Mother's money." Parker strode toward me. "Move."

"Okay, your gang is your family. I get it." I held up my hands, backing into the office. "So you're going to work for your gang in prison. That'll be real nice. Snitching on inmates in return for canteen candy bars. You kill me and you're getting life. You'll never get out. It'll be the death penalty. My boyfriend is a deputy and my uncle is the sheriff. They'll make sure Harry Hunt faces off with the state's best prosecutor. Harry Hunt's not that good of a lawyer."

"You're trying to talk yourself out of getting killed." He raised the gun and staggered toward me. "Get in the office."

I tripped backward through the door while my mind whirred, clicking bits of the puzzle into place. My butt hit the chair where I'd found Coralee. I leaped away, almost colliding with Parker. He pushed me with his free hand and the small of my back hit the desk.

"At this point, you're still a free man. They can't prove you killed your momma yet. But you kill me and they'll pin all the deaths on you. Your mother, Coralee, Miss Belvia, and me."

"I didn't kill my mom. And I don't care who did." The gun shook.

I sucked in the awful scent of the cleanser they used to remove Coralee's blood and gagged.

"Yes, you do. And I'll tell you as soon as you let Molly go." My words came out in gasps. "Even if she wasn't always there for you, she's still your momma. I have a mother like that too. I don't want to see her, but I wouldn't wish her dead. You'll spend your life in prison not knowing what happened."

He narrowed his eyes and ran a hand over his beard. "Tell me now. But I'm not letting Molly go."

I needed to reason with him to survive, but I didn't want Molly killed. Dammit.

"Promise me you won't hurt her," I said.

"I'm not promising you crap, girl. What is it with you?"

"Why do you think Molly wanted you to buy her Lanoxin?"

"I don't know. Because she's worried she's going to get kicked out of this place and needs the money?"

"No. Because she wants to plant the evidence on you."

"What evidence?"

"The police already know you buy drugs from Halo House. So does Molly. It works in her favor if you have the Lanoxin."

"Why?"

"Because Lanoxin was injected into Belvia's pain patches and Coralee's chocolates."

"What are you talking about?" He rubbed his bicep against his forehead and backed into the doorway. "Molly, get in here."

"Wait," I cried. "It's better if Molly is arrested. You shoot her and me and you'll get pinned for all the murders. Maybe your conscience can handle knowing you killed us—"

"I don't have a conscience."

"But now you're also going to prison for our homicides and for the murders of your mother, grandmother, and aunt. Your blood. You know how they'll portray you?" I slitted my eyes and pointed at my head. "Like a serial killer who goes after women. His own women. The male Lizzy Borden."

"What the hell—" He shook his head and stumbled through the door.

"But," I followed him into the living room, "if you help with Molly's arrest, you'll be a hero. The one who saved women. His women."

"Just move."

"Miss Belvia told me to 'watch out for Molly,' not 'watch over Molly.' All that talk about sociopaths who don't seem outwardly crazy. Now I understand. Your grandmother wanted me to intervene before the police arrested Molly. It wasn't just to protect the company."

"Ridiculous," said Molly. "If she thought I killed Della, Belvia would have told the police."

"She didn't want to do it herself. Maybe she didn't want to believe it. Or she was too loyal to Molly. Miss Belvia even sent me to you first, knowing how skeptical I am. Hoping I'd notice something. But I'd been too wrapped up in my own problems to think about you as a suspect."

"She's lying." Molly stood in the kitchen doorway. "She's trying to get you to let her go. By saying I killed your family? An old woman?"

"Wait a minute." Parker looked from Molly to me, lowering his trembling gun arm. "I don't understand."

"That's not even Molly," I said. "It's her sister, Maggie. Molly died six months ago, just after she retired. Or maybe before and Maggie retired her. Molly liked to work."

"What?" He ran a hand over his neck.

"She's trying to confuse you, dear," said Molly/Maggie. "You've known me your whole life."

"You knew Molly," I insisted. "This is her sister, Maggie. Molly took sick and died. For some reason, her sister took her place. I studied their photos and I'm good with details. I'm an artist, remember?"

"That's ridiculous," she said. "You can't tell from a photo. I've aged."

"Parker, look at the sequins," I said, hating the ring of desperation in my rising tone. "Have you ever seen Molly wear a sparkly cat sweatsuit?"

"These are my home clothes." Maggie raised her chin. "A few sequins and kittens doesn't prove anything."

"I bet Molly's home clothes would've been slacks and a sweater set. Maggie's the one who likes the sparkles. Look at your apartment. It's full of tchotchkes. I bet Molly tried to curb your Precious Moments binging just like she tried to curb your silliness during that photo session."

"You don't know me or my sister."

"I know you're not Molly. That's why you were insistent on not doing anything with the company this week. It wasn't that you were retired. You didn't know what to do. You couldn't tell me how to take meeting notes."

My voice strengthened as I became more convinced. "Belvia saw it too. She knew you'd changed. I don't think she wanted to admit to herself that Molly's sister could have hurt Della. That's why she wanted me to figure it out. She hoped she was wrong. And if I found evidence, she planned on taking action against Maggie herself. Privately. Without the police."

"You're saying this woman isn't Molly and she hurt my mom?" Parker's voice shook. "Why would she do this?"

"Della probably figured it out," I said sadly.

"I didn't do anything," said Maggie. "She's fabricating this whole story to confuse you, Parker."

"Maggie," I said. "What would Molly say if she knew you were doing this? She'd want to you to do the right thing, wouldn't she? To give this up. It's over."

"Nobody's going anywhere." Parker looked between us, then centered the gun on Maggie's chest. "Talk."

# THIRTY-FIVE

Sam Hill, we had a flippin' hostage situation. Sweat beaded my neck despite the ice flowing through my veins. I clamped my lips shut to force my breathing to slow and tried to focus.

"Talk, old woman," repeated Parker. The gun shook and he tightened his grip. "Or I'll kill you first."

As Maggie stared at Parker, the calm veneer crumbled. Her neck flushed and the powdered cheeks darkened.

"Molly would want me to have what I deserve." Maggie's nostrils flared and her lips pulled back. "I took care of her all her life. First our grandparents. Then our parents. Then Molly. I was the one who made sure she had hot food on the table when she came home late from all those meetings. I got her suits dry-cleaned and ironed her stuffy blouses. She was too busy to have her own family, working for Belvia like she did, but she didn't care because she had me. She promised to take care of me. Like Belvia promised to always take care of her."

"Then why..." My voice squeaked. I took a deep breath. "Why would you kill them?"

"Della was trying to cheat me out of what Molly deserved. We were going to live comfortably. Have this apartment near Belvia and be taken care of in our old age. Della had the audacity to accuse me of taking advantage of Belvia because Belvia was blind. But that was Belvia's business wasn't it?"

"But that was promised to Molly, not you," I said. "Della was trying to protect her mother."

"I did Belvia a favor. She loved Molly. Pretending I was Molly made it easier for her. Della should have understood. She only cared about the company, not about the people."

Parker's head jerked to the side like he'd been slapped. Recovering, he adjusted his stance and motioned with the gun. "Keep going, old woman."

Maggie's eyes flashed. "When Molly died, Belvia was the first person I called. Even before the ambulance. When she heard my voice, Belvia had thought I was Molly. We sound the same. How could I contradict Belvia? No one contradicts Belvia."

"She could have handled the truth," I said.

"No, I knew she wanted me to be Molly. And it was easy. Even for the death certificate, it was easy. We were at home. What's one more old woman? Nobody notices us after a certain age." Her lip curled. "I dressed like Molly and acted like Molly. I wore Molly's scent. I was a comfort in Belvia's old age, having her friend nearby. It would have worked out fine if it wasn't for Della."

"Maggie, it was all a lie." I shook my head. "That's fraud."

"Molly had planned on retiring anyway. All I had to do was live down the hall and spend time with Belvia. I deserve everything Molly was promised." Maggie shook her finger at Parker. "I was doing a good thing for your grandmother. Always at her beck and call by that pager. Your mother shouldn't have interfered. What harm could come of it? I would have been destitute."

If Maggie hadn't used murder to solve her problems, I would've felt sorry for her. "I'm sure Molly had left something for you. You wouldn't have been destitute."

"I was doing it for Belvia."

"You had a golden egg, but Della threatened to kill the goose."

"What goose? Did she kill my mother or not?"

We looked at Parker. His face had drawn tight and pale, his eyes red with unshed tears.

"I didn't mean to kill her," Maggie told him. "It was an accident."

My fear dissipated as anger took its place. "You turned the car around to hit Della. I saw the tracks myself. Donna said Della had called you in for a meeting that day, but it was interrupted by the Meemaw's Tea infighting. I bet Della had called that meeting to end your masquerade. When you left the factory and saw Della jogging, you turned the car around and ran her over."

I couldn't keep the snarl out of my voice. Parker might be a drug dealer and criminal lowlife, but this woman had murdered his mother. "And you deliberately killed Belvia. With Molly's heart medicine. How could you do that to Molly?"

"I didn't plan on it," she cried. "But after Della died—"

"You mean, after you murdered Della."

She glared at me. "After Della died, Belvia said she would change her will. You were there when she signed it. Maybe Belvia had listened to Della and was going to cut out Molly's retirement. What else could I do? I didn't know what was in that will."

"What else could you do? You stole it, didn't you? Wasn't that enough?"

"I just didn't have time to read the full will when Belvia caught me. I still have the will. It's not really stolen. I couldn't replace it because she died so quickly. And then you got the police involved, so I couldn't put it back now could I?"

"You pumped her full of Lanoxin and then she found you stealing the will? No wonder her heart went. That's identity theft, robbery, and murder." I pulled in a breath. "I think Molly kept you at home as a community service."

"I don't know what you mean." Maggie steepled her hands together and turned a tearful gaze toward Parker. "Your grandmother was ninety and blind. She was miserable over the death of Della. It was a natural way to go. And she went quickly."

"Seeping a Lidocaine patch in Lanoxin to force a heart attack is not a natural way to go, Maggie."

"I only did that because Belvia didn't eat the chocolates. But I'm not sorry that Coralee ate them. And someone else had the same idea. I saw that pencil. Coralee was greedy and mean. You don't get a pencil stuck in your neck for being nice."

"Lord Almighty. You are crazier than a sack of wet cats. Now I'm wondering if Molly's death at home was natural."

"I. Am. Not. Crazy. Molly had pneumonia and died," Maggie screamed. "Molly wanted me taken care of."

"Maybe in an institution," I muttered. "Maybe that's why you didn't want to rely on Molly's will."

"Y'all shut up." Parker raised his gun and pointed it between us. "I can't take this anymore."

"Calm yourself, Parker," I said. "It'll be okay. Put the gun down."

"Shut up. I need to talk to my boys." He drew a phone from his pocket, pressed on the surface, and tucked it under his chin. Steadying his gun with his left hand, he spoke with his eyes on us. "Palmetto, that you?"

He listened for a moment, his bloodshot eyes growing wide. His chin jerked and the phone thudded on the carpet. He stared at it for a moment before slamming his boot onto the screen.

I flinched. "I guess a deputy answered Palmetto's phone. I told you he'd been arrested."

Parker lurched and the pistol jostled in his grip. "You ratted us out."

"I didn't, I swear. It would have implicated my friends." My heart hammered and my hands flew into the air. "It's not too late for you. You can reduce your sentence by testifying against Palmetto."

"I don't squeal. This is because of you." He swore. The barrel veered toward Maggie. "And you. You killed my mom."

"Parker, honey." Maggie held her hands out. The maniacal rage had ebbed. "Why don't I make you some tea?"

"No tea, Parker," I hollered. "She'll poison you."

"Just stop," he screamed. Parker pitched forward and the gun swayed, careening between Maggie and me. "I can't take this. I need to think."

A knock sounded on the door. We spun simultaneously toward the sound.

"Don't move." Parker staggered toward the door.

"He's got a gun," I shrieked. "Parker's coming to the door with a gun."

Parker whipped around to face me. "I told you to shut up."

The gun fired, cutting off my scream.

# THIRTY-SIX

Behind me, the wall splintered into a cloud of paint and plaster. I lunged at Maggie, pulling us to the ground. She fell, clutching me and panting erratically. I dragged her toward one of Belvia's living room chairs, wedging us behind it.

Parker's accompanying howl sounded inhuman. Fury and anguish fought for control, ripping him in two.

"Parker," I said. "I know you don't want to shoot us. It'll be all right."

Someone hammered on the door.

"Go away," screamed Parker.

The hammering continued.

Parker paced before the door, muttering curses.

"Parker, we're taking care of this," I called. "We're turning Maggie over to the police."

Maggie lay beneath me, still panting. Her eyes had gone wide, staring at the dust motes from the exploded plaster flying around us.

"But first you need to set the gun down," I said. "Can't get Maggie to the authorities until you disarm."

"She killed my mom," he howled.

"I know, Parker. We're going to handle this. Put down the gun."

A key scraped in the lock.

"I've got a gun," screamed Parker. "Don't come in here."

The door cracked and swung open.

Shitfire, I thought. I was not the only one with a death wish.

"Armed man," I hollered and peered out from behind the chair. "Don't come in here."

"Sheriff's deputy. Stand down. Put down your weapon." Luke's voice carried through the doorway, his raised handgun visible at the edge of the frame. "Cherry, you in there? Who else? Anybody hurt?"

"No one's hurt. It's just Maggie, Parker, and me. Maggie and I are on the floor, behind a chair. Parker's against your wall. He's sweating something fierce. Listen, he doesn't really want to shoot anybody. He just needs to calm down."

"I heard a gunshot."

"He did shoot the wall, but he's all upset because Maggie killed his momma."

"Shut up." Parker wiped his forehead with his gun arm. "I will shoot you. You come in here, cop, and I'll shoot them both. And you."

"You don't want to shoot me," I said to Parker. "And you really don't want to shoot a deputy. That's about the quickest trip to hell. Luke will blow a hole in you so wide, they'll never get the blood out of the carpet."

"This Maggie is a resident?" Luke called.

"Sort of. Long story." I looked at Maggie. "You okay, Maggie?"

"Can't breathe." Her hands scrabbled beneath her.

I eased up and rolled away to give her some space. "It'll all be fine. Parker's going to lay down his gun—"

"Shut up."

"—and Maggie's going to confess to three murders. And a burglary. Isn't that right?"

"Glad it's all under control in there," said Luke. "Let's deal with Parker for now. Parker, lay your weapon down. I'm coming in, but if I see it in your hand, I'll shoot you."

He barked a barely coherent suggestion.

"Parker," I said. "You're not winning any favors with talk like that. Just lay down the pistol."

Beside me, Maggie hunched into a tighter ball and shoved her hands into her sweatsuit pockets.

"Don't worry, Maggie." I inched away to get a better eyeball on Parker. "Luke won't let anything happen to us. I'm good at keeping a cool head."

"You stay behind that chair, Cherry. Don't try anything," yelled Luke. "Parker, put down your weapon now."

"You got no choice, Parker, and you know it," I said. "You don't want to die."

Parker's shoulders shook. He swiped at the tears dripping from his face with the back of his arm. "I can't think."

"You don't need to think, son." Luke's deep voice floated through the doorway. "Listen to me. Slide your body down the wall."

Parker's knees bent, his legs shook, and his body slammed onto the carpet.

"He's down," I said.

"That's good," said Luke. "Real good. Now, Parker, put your gun on the floor."

Maggie's breathing accelerated and she moaned again.

I glanced from Parker and saw her fumbling with a syringe. "What is that? Are you having a spell or something?"

"What's going on?" said Luke.

"Maggie's not well." I eyed Parker. "He's got the gun on the floor. You need to let go of it now, Parker."

"That's right," said Luke. "Son, take your hand off the weapon and stand back up."

Hunched and shaking, Parker stared at the gun in his hand.

I held my breath. Beside me, Maggie struggled into sitting. A tiny clink, like the tapping of a nail polish bottle, caught my ear. I glanced at my feet where a broken ampule had hit my boot.

"What's that?" I spotted another broken bottle next to it. A third had rolled under the chair. "What's the matter? Is it your heart, Maggie?"

"Everything okay?" called Luke.

"Maggie might be having a heart—"

At Maggie's lunge, I screamed and kicked away. The glass bottles rolled, tinkling as they hit the wall.

"Parker, drop that gun now," Luke continued. "I'm counting to three, then I'm coming in. Remember what I said. If you're holding that gun, you'll give me no choice. I'll have to shoot you."

Parker cursed and hammered his fist on the carpet. "Leave me alone."

Maggie's arm slammed into my throat, pressing on my windpipe and knocking me back. I wheezed and pushed at her surprisingly solid arm. The scent of chamomile and lavender filled my nostrils as I fought to breathe.

"Parker," called Luke. "One."

Her body collapsed on top of mine, slamming into my legs and pinning me. One heavy arm thrust against my neck, crushing my windpipe. A vein beat in her forehead. Her raspy breath rushed from her throat, pulsing hot against my skin.

I gasped and choked.

She lifted slightly. I took a ragged breath and saw her hand draw up, fisting the syringe. Her other arm pushed against my throat, cutting off my breath. I clawed at her arm, whimpering.

"Two," called Luke. "Don't make me do this, Parker."

The needle buried deep into my thigh. I slapped and kicked. She held tight to my neck, fighting to steady the injection. Damn, she was strong for a senior. I clawed at her soft hands and pushed at her bony shoulders. Jerked my head, trying to jostle her heavy arm. Her body felt as fragile as a bundle of dry twigs and heavy as a load of bricks.

With an eerie deliberateness, Maggie ignored my frantic twitching and bucking. She gripped the syringe, struggling to get a thumb on the plunger. I heaved my body side to side, rolling Maggie with me. The needle dug into my leg. Maggie grappled to hold on. Her arm slipped from my throat.

Pulling in a deep breath, I thrust my head and shoulders forward. Strained to sit up.

"Three," called Luke.

She adjusted to get her free hand on the plunger, and I wiggled backward.

Squirming and rolling, I hit the wall. Used the leverage to pull my hips up. I shoved at Maggie, wriggling up the wall. Maggie's dead weight slid off my legs and face-planted into the carpet.

I popped up with the syringe still stuck in my leg. Yanking out the syringe, I glanced across the room.

From the floor, Parker gaped at me. Still holding the gun.

"Parker," I rasped. "Let go of that gun."

Luke burst through the door. "Get down," he yelled.

My heart pounded and my skin crawled, urging me to flee from Maggie. But the sight of Luke swinging through the door and Parker armed sent another tremor through me. I hurled my body behind the chair. Maggie had pulled herself into a semi-squat. I tossed the syringe and threw myself on top of her. Her breath whooshed from her body. I tightened my arms around her. She shuddered but didn't try to buck me off.

I squeezed my eyes shut and clutched her.

While time oozed like pine sap, tension coiled and threatened to explode within me. The erratic pounding of Maggie's heart thudded through her back. Her breathing whistled. Luke's police belt jangled and the hissing from his earpiece sounded deafening.

"Get your hand off the weapon," shouted Luke. "Now."

I held my breath. A cold dampness inched across my neck and my stomach unknotted and opened into a pit of churning nausea. Luke was completely exposed. Standing in front of an armed man crazed with confusion, fear, and grief.

I'd never felt so scared in my life.

Beneath me, Maggie wriggled out of my clutch. I drew my arms around myself as the heat from her body escaped. I couldn't break myself from that rigid crouch. Nor open my eyes.

A metallic click and a howl accompanied the sound of a body slamming into the floor.

Outside the door, people shouted and a set of heavy footsteps thudded into the room. Whispered murmurs rose to a fevered pitch of voices. Someone was panting. Hard.

And then I heard the chair shoved away. Arms went around me and his voice, sure and strong, said, "Cherry?"

I hadn't heard a gunshot. My eyes popped open.

Luke crouched before me, the lines in his face drawn tight, his jaw rigid. "Sugar, are you okay?"

I propelled myself into his chest. "Never do that to me again."

He yanked me back to look me in the eyes. "You're lecturing me on dangerous situations? When I found you holed up with an armed drug dealer?"

"I was fine. You're the one who busted into the room to face him."

"It's part of my job. I'm trained, for cripes' sake. Lord Almighty, you're the one always reacting on instinct." His hand cupped my cheek and he traced a tear with his thumb. "You're crying over me, baby?"

"No." I sniffed and scrubbed my cheek with the back of my hand. "You know I don't cry."

"Right." He kissed my cheek. "Listen, if I can live with you pulling these crazy stunts, you'll have to do the same for me."

"Did you shoot him? I didn't hear the gunshot."

"Tased. Last minute, I decided to holster and switch to the taser." He squeezed my shoulder, then stood. "Parker's cuffed and Deputy Johnson's taking him out. Where's this Maggie?"

I stared at him. "You didn't arrest Maggie?"

"I thought she was a hostage. I was focused on disarming Parker. Who's Maggie?"

"Oh no." I jumped to my feet and ran toward the back of the apartment. Pushed open the door to the bedroom suite.

A hand captured my shoulder and yanked me back. "Let me do my job, Cherry. Get out in the hall with everyone else."

"We're too late." I turned, burying my head in his shoulder, but I couldn't get the image of Maggie's body lying on the bed with a syringe stuck in her neck out of my head.

"There's your culprit in the Brakeman murders," I cried. "I couldn't save her. I couldn't save any of them."

Outside Belvia's apartment, a large crowd had assembled. Nearly all of Halo House's population—who didn't have appointments or tee times—had gathered, despite the lockdown procedures Krenzer had tried to enforce. I wandered into the hall wrapped in another victim's blanket. Behind me, ENTs loaded Maggie on a crash cart under the supervision of Deputy Luke Harper. Parker was already in custody.

My adrenaline rush had run its course. Exhausted, I wandered through the crowd, saving my witness testimony for the officials despite the call for news from the residents. Next to the elevator, I found Fred, craning his neck to see through the mob, and thanked him for his help.

"I found Ada in the deli and got her to her room," said Fred. "I don't know how Parker had snuck into the building without us seeing him though."

"He had a key to the building." Ada wiggled around a walker to stand beside us. "Hazel told me. He could slip in and out on his drug-purchasing rounds. Occasionally, he'd officially check in to see Belvia, in case residents reported seeing him."

"Nice to know that now," I spoke stiffly.

Ada flushed. "I'm sorry, Cherry. I only did the restraining order to get you off my back about Hazel."

My chin rose a notch and my voice remained frosty. "And how are Hazel and Rosie? Did they pick up a young Brad Pitt yet?"

"On their way home to turn themselves in, I believe." Ada narrowed her eyes. "Particularly as I told them Parker and his gang wouldn't be around to harass them."

"Thanks to me."

Ada squished her lips to the side but gave me a grudging nod.

"Y'all quit." Fred pushed us into a hug. "Neither of you really want to fight."

"I'm sorry, Cherry."

"I miss you, Ada." I tightened our embrace. "I hated that our friendship would put you in danger."

She released me and winked. "I live for danger. Don't you know that by now?"

"Listen to me, Ada." Fred put a hand on her shoulder. "I know you were worried about what Parker would do if he thought Hazel had ratted on him. However, you abetted a crime. You should have gone to the police. Instead, you protected two fugitives."

"I was watching out for my friends."

"I won't stand for this sort of thing, Ada."

"Are you breaking up with me?"

I drew in a startled breath. I hadn't even known they were dating.

Around us, the crowd shifted. A murmured rumble spread, winding through the residents like a senior version of telephone.

"Hey, Fred, why don't you come over for sweet rolls and coffee," called a woman. "I keep my rolls hot."

"Fred, I have all the seasons of *Columbo* on DVD. And *Antiques Roadshow* on the DVR."

Ada spun, darting angry looks at the women around her. "What is this? A feeding frenzy? Back off, girls. I'm not letting go that easy."

I glanced at Fred, expecting a look of triumph. Instead, his rheumy eyes spoke of a more serious intention. A similar look I'd seen in Luke's recently.

"Ada, I know you're a pistol, but I'm getting too old for these games," he said. "I love you, but when Parker went after you, I thought I might have a stroke. For real. I can't do this anymore if this is how you'll behave."

"Just what are you saying, Fred?" she said. "I know I have friends in low places, but—"

"No more of this monkey business. I can't take it. Leave the monkeys to Cherry."

Ada bowed her head. I knew how she felt, but Fred was right.

His color didn't look good. She needed to protect his health as much as she wanted to protect her friends.

Ada's eyes didn't leave the floor. "I can't take you telling me what to do."

My hands flew to cover my mouth. Todd and Luke were right. Ada sounded just like me.

"I'm not telling you, Ada," said Fred gently. "I'm asking you. To marry me."

Ada's head jerked up.

I blinked away tears and bit my lip, waiting for Ada's response. Around me, hearing aids whined as the residents pumped up the volume. The crowd leaned in.

"If you're asking, then I'll say yes. I promise not to involve myself with any more murderers, thieves, or drug dealers. However, when it comes to monkey business?" Ada shrugged. "I've always had trouble understanding that definition. I can't help it that odd things just sort of happen around me."

"Good enough." Fred opened his arms and Ada collapsed against him.

I was happy to see that post-seventy, kisses could still sizzle.

Fred came up for air and smacked the elevator's up button. "Champagne on my account. Meet us at Last Call. We'll be down in a few."

He and Ada shuffled into the elevator. Thumbing his floor button, he glanced through the doors at me. "You'll be our maid of honor, Cherry. Try not to get shot or arrested before then."

Ada winked. "Give me a call if you do—"

"Ada," said Fred.

"And I'll report you to Deputy Harper." She waggled her eyebrows. "You might enjoy a house arrest with that one."

# THIRTY-SEVEN

The next day, my class was reinstated through popular demand. Not exactly an art appreciation moment though. Halo House's curiosity seekers suddenly found hot yoga boring compared to the artist who had survived the fall of the Brakeman empire.

Charges weren't brought against Rosie and Hazel, although Krenzer gave them a slap on the wrist along with permission to room together in Ada's apartment once she became Mrs. Fred. They'd save money by subleasing their own apartments now that Halo House had become an even more popular senior destination due to its infamy in the Brakeman case. According to Krenzer, the reservation line had been ringing off the hook.

The sheriff's department had recovered the missing will from Maggie/Molly's apartment. With Miss Belvia's will intact, her remaining Meemaw's Tea shares and CEO successorship went to Coralee's daughter, Pris. Belvia had changed her will after speaking to Pris and finding in her estranged granddaughter the family member who most followed in her footsteps. Pris's earlier remorse had been letting her mother keep her from her family, not from covering secrets.

Pris had confided in me at the Forks County Sheriff's Office following Parker's arrest for aggravated assault, possession of a firearm in the commission of a felony, and disorderly conduct. We still waited on the charge of distribution of controlled substances.

"I'll do what I can to help Parker and Ron, plus keep my dad nearby," Pris had said. "Wally's not able to deal with the 'reality of

Coralee's departure.' I'm putting him in rehab. It's time the company made good on its marketing slogans and really focused on family."

"'Meemaw's puts the Tea in tradition,'" I'd quoted. "You'll make a good sweet tea queen. Even if you weren't raised Southern."

However, when it came to my art class, I had to push my art style past my traditionalist taste and into the twenty-first century. My students lived for the moment and my notoriety with the Brakeman murder case wouldn't last. They'd be back to yoga in a hot minute. The female Halo House artists were pleased with my decision. For every nine women, there was now one man. Better than average for most Halo House activities.

"All right, students." I looked around the room of easels. "Remember, this is about capturing personality as much as it is capturing line, shape, and depth. I want to see all the things I've taught you this semester. Form through the use of tones and shading. Perspective through foreshortening. Watch your use of light and shadow."

I turned as Todd and Fred entered, hauling a velvet chaise lounge between them.

"Hey, baby, where do you want this?" called Todd.

"Good timing," I said. "Right in the center of the room."

Todd and Fred heaved the sofa to chest height and backed through the easels.

The bathroom door banged open and Rosie sauntered out. Walking to the chaise, she winked at Todd, dropped her robe, and stretched on the sofa in true odalisque fashion.

Todd picked up his jaw and fled the room.

Charcoal scratched on paper without grumbles. I left the students to it and followed Todd. Behind me, Ada dragged Fred from the room, lecturing him on the necessity of abandoning his art career for married life.

"Sorry about that," I said to Todd. "I should've warned you."

He shuddered but recovered with an easy smile. "Hey, Shawna's going to meet with her father. It's good she knows the truth. Thanks for telling her. Too bad she's still angry with y'all. She said your mother was likely the reason Billy went to prison in the first place."

A nerve hammered near my eye. "Christy Tucker may have been loosely moraled, but I doubt the Georgia penal system would allow her to lock a man up without their consent."

Todd's hands rose. "I'm sure it'll work itself out. Shawna's not dealing so good with her dad's prison record."

"I could care two hoots how Shawna feels. But at least Cody benefits." I folded my arms. "Miss Belvia had foreseen me agreeing to her crazy scheme. Her will had all these codicils, including one bequeathal to Cody Tucker's legal defense fund, stating if the charges were dropped against him, the funds would then go to a new wing of Line Creek Hospital called 'The Branson Annex.' A carrot and a stick. Her favorite way to do business."

"JB's got a big enough ego that he'd want that wing. That's great for Cody."

"Yeah, I found Della's killer and the Bransons will still look like heroes. But I can take the hit if it means freeing Cody."

"You did good, baby."

"Hey, y'all." Fred slung an arm around my shoulder. "Ada and I were just talking about having a Vegas wedding. How about a road trip?"

"Vegas." Todd's eyes glowed. Like big blue poker chips.

I chewed my lip. Our last visit to Vegas had ended in an annulled wedding. Vegas and I had a poor history.

"Halo House has gotten too toxic for our tastes." Ada grinned. "We want a proper wedding. Vegas would be less vice-ridden."

"You do have a point," I said. "As your maid of honor, I'd be happy to go. And your vows will stick, unlike mine."

A road trip with my buddies. Like in college after final projects were due and we needed to blow off steam. I threw myself into a group hug but pulled away at my phone's ring. I crossed to the doorway where I could keep an eye on my students and speak privately.

"Your cousin is something else," I said. "She still blames us and my mother, like I told you she would."

"Step-cousin. I heard. I called her. I told her I dug up that information, not you, and said we'd use it in court if she didn't drop the charges."

"What about your job? Won't you get in trouble?"

"I put it this way: 'Shawna, I'll have to testify about how I had to investigate your father's relationship with the defendant's mother in order to better understand the case. Thereby revealing information about Billy Branson to a packed courtroom of Halo's curiosity seekers. And I'll also have to testify that I love the defendant's sister and plan to marry her. In fairness to the court.'"

I picked up my phone from where I dropped it on the floor.

"Sugar, you still there?"

"That's blackmail. You said it wouldn't be blackmail. And you didn't even need to do it. JB'll make her drop the charges because of Miss Belvia's will." I glanced over my shoulder to where Todd, Fred, and Ada watched me, then swiveled my gaze to the class, now sketching Rosie's newest pose. "But you're willing to jeopardize your career for me? In a court of law?"

"Did you get the last part of what I said?"

I closed my eyes. The babies crawled forward, holding their arms out to me. "Have you thought about what it'll be like for our children to have relatives who hate each other? Making snide remarks about their parents? Using holidays as a bargaining chip? I have these fears—"

"What fears?"

"Stupid fears."

"Tell me anyway."

"We'd have beautiful children, Luke."

"Of course we will."

"Your momma would fall in love with them."

"Of course she will."

"JB too. They're just too adorable. One with blue eyes and one with gray—"

"Sugar, you've got me in a state here. Your fear is our children will be too adorable?"

I shook my head. "My fear is JB hates me and my family so much, he'll take those babies from me somehow. Call me an unfit mother or something. Based on my past. That's how Grandma Jo and Grandpa Ed legally took possession of us."

"They had to declare your mother unfit."

"Yes."

"Listen to me. I will never let that happen to you."

My eyes flew open. "How could you prevent it?"

"My family comes first."

My heart sank. "Of course. Wanda is good people, but JB—"

"Cherry, you and our imaginary children are my family."

I picked my phone off the floor again. In the classroom, Rosie stood on the chaise, one foot on the armrest and twirled her robe above her head. I looked away. Unfortunately, too late.

"You're willing to put your career and your family on the line?" I took a deep breath. "For the person who causes you to buy heartburn and sleep medication?"

"Yes. Although I probably do need to add blood-pressure meds to that list."

My heart swelled. And not at the thought of blood-pressure medicine. "Are you asking me to give up any monkey business?"

"I had no idea you were into monkeys."

"I'm trying to keep them out of my circus tent. I tried hard with Belvia Brakeman, but like Ada said, I can't help it that odd things tend to happen around me."

"Sugar, I'm not asking you to give up anything. Except Todd McIntosh as a roommate. Although leaving drug traffickers alone would be a plus."

"I love you."

He paused, letting the words sink in. "So are we going to make this real? You'll take me to Sunday dinner at the farm and break the news to your family?"

"Actually, I may not be available Sunday." I glanced at my

friends. "What do you think about a road trip to Vegas? To celebrate a wedding."

"Whose wedding?"

"Just bring your best duds." I grinned. "We'll see."

# LARISSA REINHART

A 2015 Georgia Author of the Year Best Mystery finalist, Larissa writes the Cherry Tucker Mystery series. Her family and Cairn Terrier, Biscuit, now live in Nagoya, Japan, but still call Georgia home. Visit her website, LarissaReinhart.com, find her chatting on Facebook, Twitter, and Goodreads, or join her Facebook street team, The Mystery Minions.

**The Cherry Tucker Mystery Series**
**by Larissa Reinhart**

<u>Novels</u>

PORTRAIT OF A DEAD GUY (#1)
STILL LIFE IN BRUNSWICK STEW (#2)
HIJACK IN ABSTRACT (#3)
DEATH IN PERSPECTIVE (#4)
THE BODY IN THE LANDSCAPE (#5)
A COMPOSITION IN MURDER (#6)

<u>Novellas</u>

QUICK SKETCH (prequel to PORTRAIT)
(in HEARTACHE MOTEL)

Available at booksellers nationwide and online

Visit www.henerypress.com for details

## Henery Press Mystery Books

And finally, before you go...
Here are a few other mysteries
you might enjoy:

# MURDER ON A SILVER PLATTER

Shawn Reilly Simmons

## A Red Carpet Catering Mystery (#1)

Penelope Sutherland and her Red Carpet Catering company just got their big break as the on-set caterer for an upcoming blockbuster. But when she discovers a dead body outside her house, Penelope finds herself in hot water. Things start to boil over when serious accidents threaten the lives of the cast and crew. And when the film's star, who happens to be Penelope's best friend, is poisoned, the entire production is nearly shut down.

Threats and accusations send Penelope out of the frying pan and into the fire as she struggles to keep her company afloat. Before Penelope can dish up dessert, she must find the killer or she'll be the one served up on a silver platter.

Available at booksellers nationwide and online

Visit www.henerypress.com for details

# MACDEATH

Cindy Brown

## An Ivy Meadows Mystery (#1)

Like every actor, Ivy Meadows knows that *Macbeth* is cursed. But she's finally scored her big break, cast as an acrobatic witch in a circus-themed production of *Macbeth* in Phoenix, Arizona. And though it may not be Broadway, nothing can dampen her enthusiasm—not her flying cauldron, too-tight leotard, or carrot-wielding dictator of a director.

But when one of the cast dies on opening night, Ivy is sure the seeming accident is "murder most foul" and that she's the perfect person to solve the crime (after all, she does work part-time in her uncle's detective agency). Undeterred by a poisoned Big Gulp, the threat of being blackballed, and the suddenly too-real curse, Ivy pursues the truth at the risk of her hard-won career—and her life.

Available at booksellers nationwide and online

Visit www.henerypress.com for details

# THE AMBITIOUS CARD

John Gaspard

## An Eli Marks Mystery (#1)

The life of a magician isn't all kiddie shows and card tricks. Sometimes it's murder. Especially when magician Eli Marks very publicly debunks a famed psychic, and said psychic ends up dead. The evidence, including a bloody King of Diamonds playing card (one from Eli's own Ambitious Card routine), directs the police right to Eli.

As more psychics are slain, and more King cards rise to the top, Eli can't escape suspicion. Things get really complicated when romance blooms with a beautiful psychic, and Eli discovers she's the next target for murder, and he's scheduled to die with her. Now Eli must use every trick he knows to keep them both alive and reveal the true killer.

Available at booksellers nationwide and online

Visit www.henerypress.com for details

CPSIA information can be obtained
at www.ICGtesting.com
Printed in the USA
LVOW13s1014151116

513032LV00010B/204/P